C000163391

This is the first book in the Rupert Brett Deal series.
The current titles are listed below in chronological order:

By Simon Fairfax

No Deals Done, *'til it's done.*

A Deal Too Far.

A Deal with the Devil.

A Deal on Ice.

SIMON FAIRFAX
NO DEAL'S DONE
'TIL IT'S DONE

To Elinor, the wind beneath my wings, for all the love, encouragement and badgering. Without whom.....

ACKNOWLEDGEMENTS:

First of all thanks to my editor Natasha Orme for all her work in getting me into line. A splendid job.

So many people helped me on my journey for my first book either directly or indirectly, providing information, technical help and encouragement these include:

Nigel Beaumont (Purdey & Sons), Frances Campbell, Terence Cox, Michael Ford, Netta Jordan, Andrew Klein, Scott Murdoch, James Petit, Patricia Salter, Jamie Salter, JohnP Smail, Vittorio Scappini, Dave Taylor, Paul Vockins and 'AJ' Webster.

CONTENTS

CHAPTER 1

BRISTOL, February 1986

The wind howled through the stanchions of the bridge creating a banshee of whistles and shrieks, adding to the eeriness of the puddled lights seeping around the base of the bridge pillars. The darkness enveloped the couple who had left the warmth of the George Hotel after a meal and large amount of wine and cognac, to walk off the supper and clear their heads. Due to the conditions and low visibility, no one else appeared to venture out on to the bridge as most fellow diners had left the hotel or retired to their rooms.

A number of cars purred past, drivers concentrating in the gloom: no one wanted to drive off and fall into the deep gorge below. They were moving slowly together, almost staggering and to the interested observer, the woman seemed to be keeping the man upright as though he were either very drunk or semi-comatose. His state worsened as they approached the middle of the bridge away from the main lights of the towers. A strong arm supported him around his waist, another holding his left arm firmly to his side. The man faltered, stumbling just before he leant against the outer railings of the bridge, seeming to gain support and balance from the cold steel, leaning into the tensile strength of the woman. She whispered up into his ear in a seemingly endearing fashion as she looked around furtively, the wind pulling at her hair, throwing wisps across her eyes and face. Vision was limited, due to weather conditions, but having looked in both directions she seemed to relax slightly, cast another glance at her companion and heaved. The man experienced three emotions in quick succession: surprise, shock and fear. From standing on the edge of the bridge, he began a quick cartwheeling flight, his howl of fear lost in the wind and ending with a subdued smack as he hit the water far below. The woman turned, and walked quickly, but precisely, back towards the end of the bridge and the hotel car park. The hazard lights of the Porsche glowed twice as she flicked the key fob, opened the door, removed an envelope from the inside of her coat and left it on the dashboard. Re-locking the Porsche, she moved away to her own car; an innocuous black Ford XR3i.

Driving quietly out of the car park, she travelled to a secluded lay-by north of the bridge. Here she removed the covering number plates from her car. Next her appearance changed: despite the cold she quickly stripped down to her underwear, kicked off the very high heels, and donned jeans, and jumper. Next went the hair extensions, heavy jewellery, makeup and other subtle appearance changing additions, including the removal of a ceramic cap to her front tooth. It had been cracked and chipped since she was a teenager and she had never had it formally repaired. All this went into a plastic bin liner and was thrown in the boot of her car. The tall, busty, sexy, well-made-up woman who had dined at the hotel bore very little resemblance to the slim 5'2" plain looking brunette who now drove the Ford. She had always been blessed with chameleon looks, almost reminiscent of supermodels who took to make up and clothes like muses.

At the same time a 999 call was being placed by a woman walking her dog on the other side of the bridge. The light had been dim and the conditions difficult, but as she made the call from the phone box, she swore that she had seen two figures up on the bridge prior to the fall.

The woman in the Ford stopped her car at a service station in Swindon just off the M4. She was careful, calls could be traced and searched, especially from motorway services. She dialled a London number. It was answered by a man's voice within three rings and she gave an ambiguous description of the events that had occurred.

"Just to say that it went off alright and everything has *fallen* into place." A wry grin breaking across her face at her own dark humour.

The recipient answered with a thank you and confirmed that the usual arrangements for the cost of 'delivery' would be met by return.

As he replaced the receiver his chunky, gold identity bracelet caught the plastic with a clunk. Moments later, he dialled another number.

"Simions? It's me, yes, all done. Where? Bristol as planned; suicide note in the car and apparently he fell for her charms - literally." he chuckled at his own witticism before continuing.

"Yes, a cold hearted bitch; I wouldn't want to get on the wrong side of her: you would never see the knife coming."

"Mmmh, good." Simions responded ignoring the poor joke, "Now our partnership is dissolved I can get on with placing the agency where and how I want. Never could stand his damned morality" he finished, before replacing the receiver.

CHAPTER 2

LONDON, October 1986

The streets of the West End were busy; a hum and vibrance were palpably apparent, as only they can be in London when the economy is booming and everyone is optimistic.

The last vestiges of summer sun created a balmy atmosphere, reflecting off the shop fronts and warming the back of Rupert Brett, who, after 3 years of heavy drinking, wenching and enjoying university life, was now newly qualified with a degree in Estate Management. With the brash confidence of youth, Brett thought he knew everything and was ready to face the world of commercial property.

Passing down South Molton Street was a real pleasure in the early mornings, he thought; letching appreciatively at the passing flow of West End 'flora and fauna'; all gorgeously presented; heavy 80's makeup, big hair and heads tilted at just the right arrogant angle to attract, but not dissuade. As he crossed Davis Street, the aroma of fresh coffee wafted across the air, together with the beat of Pet Shop Boys' new anthem blaring out "West End Girls": soon to be adopted by every West End wannabe. He hummed a few lines, finding it hard not to, and made his way to Grosvenor Street, and the reception of Cowl Rubens & Co.

The building was typical of the street; stuccoed lower elevations, large Georgian windows and dirty London brick on the many upper floors. Steps led up to the impressive porticoed entrance; wooden, panelled, double doors swung smoothly inwards. The interior conveyed both an atmosphere of a gentleman's club and the sharp, cutting edge of one of the major players in the property market.

The reception was heavily carpeted, cream walls, wooden panelling to dado height, and contemporary up-lighters balanced with the recessed lighting. The walls were dressed with a mixture of modern art in various guises. Heavy chesterfields in dark, red leather were strategically placed in the centre whilst faux antique coffee tables and brass table lamps completed the look. In short, it was an entrance to impress those who were confident, or powerful, and intimidate those who were not.

Rupert recalled with trepidation, his first meeting here 3 months ago for his initial interview on the merry-go-round of graduate intakes. The brash confidence of youth had taken its first beating then; when faced with a panel of partners who, he was painfully aware, were as eager to see the many other graduates competing for places as they were him. Cowl Rubens may not be the largest firm in the West End with around only 200 staff but since being founded in 1957 by its two enigmatic partners, it had grown from strength to strength. Its reputation as a tough breeding ground for "baby surveyors" who went on to greater things, was well justified. Many of both the fledgling and well established practices were products of training and attitude imbued by the firm.

Some, he had heard, decried its methods, saying they were "wide boys" and very sharp but they always stayed the right side of ethical and the rest Rupert attributed to jealousy. However, the bottom line was that the world of commercial property was not for choir boys and it was kill or be killed. He went to the reception desk and before him sat a very pretty, dark haired girl, with heavy eye make, bright lipstick and chunky jewellery. She had a rather world weary smile, which he felt, could be turned to various levels of wattage according to how smart, important or attractive the recipient was.

He received, he felt, the grade 2: "yes, your quite cute, poor bugger, first day, I won't be too hard on you, but don't get any ideas" level.

"Good morning, may I help you?"

The accent was smart east London, the slight nearly ironed out estuary vowel sounds giving the game away. Still, pretty face he thought and great cleavage when she leaned forward, just slightly.

"Good morning, yes, I have an appointment with Andrew Sheen at 9.30" he said, his well-rounded public school vowels a contrast to hers.

"I'm starting work here today," he added rather proudly; then instantly regretted it, feeling rather foolish and exposed like a puppy trying desperately to impress. *Did I really just say that?* he asked himself. Vowing not to make the same mistake again.

She smiled, compressing mockery, pity and superficial politeness in that one gesture.

"Name please"

"Rupert Brett"

She called an extension.

"Fine, will do." She replaced the receiver. "Take a seat please, Mr. Sheen's secretary will be down shortly."

Walking over to the sofas, Rupert admired himself in the wall mirror in an effort to recoup his position. He saw a 22-year-old young man of just over 6ft with dark brown hair fashionably cut, quite striking blue eyes, a full mouth and a general eager expression with an assurance that anything was possible.

He gazed from his new, double vented, pinstripe suit, pale blue shirt and de rigueur paisley tie, down to his highly polished brogues. Confidence rising, he shot his cuffs, reached for a newspaper and sat down. The entrance hall had two staircases and over the next five minutes he people watched: a steady procession of "suits and secretaries" passed through on various missions, with snatched pieces of conversation which he eagerly absorbed, wanting to pick up on all the jargon as soon as possible.

Just then the doors opened to admit two more graduates, whom he knew from his university days; Mike Ringham and Claire Sewell- as ever making an entrance together, although as a surprise to many, not an item, just intrinsically linked by manner and manners. The former, patrician to a tee, from his great height of 6ft 3, capped with wavy hair, already gelled and slicked, keen grey eyes, long aquiline nose, and lean frame. His carefully etched features creased into a tight smile.

"Rupes, always on time y' bugger." As always, his lazy, upper class drawl warmly embracing all those he met.

"Ringo!" he retorted. Rising, he took Mike's hand and shook it warmly. He turned his attention to Claire Sewell, a much more attractive proposition. She was a tall, willowy girl with strawberry blond, heavy layered hair, kept neatly in place by a single velvet scrunch band. Her framed oval face, which while not beautiful, was striking featuring a pair of lovely, green-hazel eyes that engaged his own. High cheek bones and a cheeky smile completed the picture-perfect female as far as Rupert was concerned. She was tailored in an elegantly cut, dark navy suit, with a long skirt slit to the knee. She glided towards him, proffering a cheek which he duly kissed and was immersed for a moment in a heady cloud of "Poison".   After a long friendship and one rather glorious one night stand, they had nearly become an item at university, but it was not to be and they had fortunately managed to return to the status quo without too much damage to either party. There was never a shortage of suitors but none lasted more than a few months.

"Hi sweety, how are you?"

"Fine, on good form actually. You?"

"Oh, first day blues, you know," she said airily, "but apart from that, pretty good".

Mike moved across the room to the reception desk, introducing both himself and Claire, and was awarded a grade 4 smile. *Typical, and as smooth as ever,* Rupert thought.

After another five minutes of small talk, Dawn Harris Andrew Sheen's secretary, appeared to take them up to his offices. A smart woman in her mid 40s, she had Career Secretary stamped all over her. She led them to the lift and they were taken to the 4th floor. Like most of these Georgian converted offices it was a rabbit warren, with a poor net to gross. Dawn led the way through what must have once been 3 or 4 separate buildings; with all three thinking that they would never find their way out.

They were shown into Sheen's office; a brightly lit room, with cream coloured walls, cornices, a central chandelier, deep carpet and up-lighters emanating a warm glow throughout. Comfortable reproduction period furniture completed the picture of cosy formality, with two book cases lining the walls, adding a more studious balance.

Andrew Sheen rose from behind his desk and came forward to shake hands. A short, slightly chubby individual with light, almost opaque eyes and glasses perched on the bridge of his nose. He had an air of jovial insouciance about him which had fooled more than one opposing surveyor until, too late, they had realised the razor sharp mind behind the façade.

"Morning," he said "welcome on board, now its Mike...,
Rupert and.. Claire..?"

Feigning vagueness was one of his traits, while the individuals
concerned felt, ridiculously pleased at being both remembered
and treated informally.

"Have a seat, please." He gestured magnanimously. "Coffee
anyone?"

They all nodded, proffered their acceptance and sat down.

"Four coffees please Dawn and biscuits, don't forget the
biscuits." He turned; focusing on them conspiratorially, auto-
matically bringing them in, making them feel wanted, as though
part of some private joke or intimate club. "Very important to
start the day off properly and cream biscuits are just the thing."

They were warming to him, it was hard not to. It was all part
of the technique and the charm; very professional, hard to resist
and most of all effective.

"Now, after we've had coffee I will take you on a guided tour
of the various departments. Don't worry, you won't remember
anyone's name. It will all be terribly confusing, but at least it
will give you some idea of who's who and what they all do. The
most confusing thing for anyone coming here, is to navigate the
building itself." He smiled. "We have seven floors! Quite a little
maze. "It will all come together though, I guarantee it".

He smiled, winningly. His thoughts were however, much
more incisive. He was assessing their reactions and judging
character traits. *Typically they thought they knew it all*, he thought
to himself, *degree, probably one year out on training mid-course,
yeah, yeah*. Whereas in reality he considered they knew only two
things: how to put the suit on and how to shave.

Once the coffee had been consumed, there proceeded a
whistle stop tour of the various individual departments com-
prising the firm. In Sheen's eyes they rated (in reverse order)
from Management, through Rating, PSD (Professional Services

Department), Agency (retail offices and industrial) Development and Investment. Investment was the most arrogant and beneficial to the firm; it made far more money in fees than any other department on a pro rata basis.

"On graduate rotation, as I think we explained at your second interviews, you will be seconded to different departments, for between 3 to 6 months. This will be dependent on aptitude and the specific preferred career path chosen by yourselves on your application forms. There are really eight different departments; which include specialist areas of agency, professional etc. All of them with different roles to play, fitting into the bigger picture and endeavouring to provide our clients with a "one stop shop".

"Like a supermarket" Rupert offered.

"Absolutely," he re-joined.

Energy fizzing out of him, Sheen led the way to an intermediatory landing and the lift.

"Right, we'll start at the top and work down," Sheen declared.

They all squeezed into the lift and flew to the top floor.

They were introduced to the various team members of the Building Services Department and moved on. No one was really interested in this department, rather dull and not cutting edge enough for any of the three.

Next was the Professional Services Department, a single corridor ran through the floor with a number of rooms running off on either side..

"Whatever the more glory-orientated individuals and departments may tell you; even they have to be able to read and interpret a lease or get us to do it for them," he crowed.

The others picked up that there was more than a little rivalry involved here.

At PSD, the overview was something that was to have a bearing upon all their lives in the future; much more than they could have foreseen. "Leases and their main clauses, are very important to us, as you know. The strength of the lease can determine many things, including value. We are here to get performance and value for our clients. Property is another asset class like stocks and shares etc.

"You will not get knowledge of all this from an accountant's balance sheet or lawyer's view. You must understand all the foibles and how they affect value.

No, you have to be in the market, understand all aspects of the whole and be part of the other parts of a team, utilising that knowledge. OK. pep talk over," he joked.

But the smooth delivery and passion behind the speech had hit its mark and all three were impressed. They knew that they would all need to do a turn in PSD to gain at least some idea of how to read and analyse a lease.

"We have various sub divisions in this department, split geographically by area with senior staff overseeing each area. This is Chris Hughes," he said, introducing a particularly tall surveyor whose large shoulders earned him the sobriquet of 'The Honey Monster'. Chris blinked through a haze of smoke caused by a cigarette dangling from his fingers

"Hi," he said, speaking with a strangely soft voice, but shaking hands with appropriate vigour and giving Claire the practised once over, his eyes resting appreciably on her legs.

"Which one of you poor sods is first into the PSD mangle then?"

All three looked back towards Sheen who in turn grinned wolfishly.

"We haven't decided yet Chris, but you'll be the first to know"

"Always room, always room," he gestured expansively. "Now, if you'll excuse me I've a fag to finish and a lease to read before lunch - in that order."

"Come on," Sheen said. "We don't want to upset the Honey Monster."

They all grinned at the comparison before leaving. The others in the department were rather less interesting, except to Mike who muttered afterwards that he rather fancied one of the secretaries. *He always went for the short dark ones,* Rupert thought.

The rest of the floor led through to the Management Department. Each of the rooms leading off opened to groups of small teams surrounded by piles of files and an overriding Dickensian feel of Euriah Heap and Bob Cratchit. One half expected to hear the scratch of quill pens on parchment.

There was no drama here from Andrew Sheen. No flourish. In fact, almost an apology.

Nods of acknowledgment were made in each room with wan smiles. The overriding impression was a sea of brown and grey polyester suits.

The next floor held a different breed of individual. Down on this floor was where the various retail departments were housed. The corridor opened out to four main large rooms which had been created by knocking through the walls of the original rooms.

The result was a cacophony of noise and frenetic activity not present in the other departments. Everywhere one looked were piles of brochures surrounding three or four desks set in a series of U-shapes, headed up by either a main desk of the head of the team or a door to his office.

The individuals looked different too; none of them appeared over twenty five. They were sharper, the ties brighter or more garish, the haircuts smarter. The overall impression to the three graduates was that they were all very streetwise. In short, they were wide boys to a tee and very clued up.

Every voice could be heard or overheard, a myriad of conversations occurring at any one time. Everyone appeared to be shouting or talking in loud tones, quick exchanges of information bouncing back and forth.

"Well, here we are, the heart of CR's activity; Retail Agency," announced Sheen over the noise. "The country is effectively divided into four areas: North East, North West, South West, and the South East with a specialist London team for inside the M25. Each large room is responsible for a given area and headed by a partner or associate, who in turn reports to an Equity partner." He proceeded to introduce them.

"Boys, this is Claire, Mike and Rupert they will be joining you at some time in the next 12 months."

"Hi."

"How do?"

"Morning!"

They all shouted simultaneously and continued straight on with their conversations without pausing for breath or thought.

"No way," the fourth person shouted into the receiver cradled between is face and is shoulder. "The rent sounds full, and it makes no difference until I know the Zone A! You do know what a zone A is at Michaelmans don't you?" he finished sarcastically.

"Oh, not you lot. Welcome aboard an' all that!" he waved across, grinning and clearly enjoying himself.

"Hah, I've got some graduates here," he continued down the phone. "If I send them over perhaps they can help you analyse the rent. 25 quid! It's St Albans not Berkhamstead you know, it won't buy you a square inch in St Albans. Call me when you can tell me the answer, cheers."

He put the phone down quickly and retorted; "The guy's an idiot. Wouldn't know a zone A from a premium. Sorry about that," he scolded, getting up to shake hands.   He was a tall, solidly built man, with slightly rounded shoulders and wavy, dark, almost red hair. Extremely good looking in a very roguish way, he had an oval face, blue eyes and a winning smile. A bright blue, striped shirt, encased the extended arm. He shook hands with all three graduates, his eyes taking in all Claire's attributes in one sweeping glance.

"Angus Stewart, how do?" His voice had a very slight, soft, Scottish burr, which he inflected further in Claire's direction. *He's lingering just slightly longer with her handshake,* Rupert thought, feeling rather protective towards her in front of this obviously predatory male. She returned the grin knowingly, well aware of the impact she could have and the impression Angus was making.

"A small problem, Angus?" Sheen asked mischievously, a grin playing on his lips.

"Ha. Gus, over at Michaelmans has got the fag end of a lease for sale; originally 25 with 5's, wants an assignment for 45K; which in effect is just key money as the premium won't stack unless the Zone A is well below Open Market Value. I can buy three positions at OMV without the hassle of an impending lease renewal." He snorted.

"Did you get all that?" Sheen asked the three.

They were learning quickly that the jargon of the real world left behind the basics of student academia. Explaining the intricacies to the three, Sheen finished with two very important points: that knowledge of the market was key and that serving of legal notices on time was of paramount importance otherwise heads rolled if the correct notices were not served, as it severely damaged the value of the interest concerned.

All these factors had to be taken into consideration and it all fell down to one thing: market information. Knowledge was king. It was the chief commodity and the only way to get it was being in the market day and night, listening, gleaning information, being in the bars, pubs and all the time talking to the right people.

Claire beamed in admiration, impressed by the staccato response and energy. "I hadn't realised it was so…alive and exciting. One imagines a sort of sedate, rather regulated atmosphere, not this," she gesticulated around the room.

"If you tell someone that you're going to be a Chartered Surveyor, most people put you one above accountants on the 'Boring Scale,'" she finished vehemently. "But this, this is so much more...sparky."

The final word finished with a long and rather challenging look at Angus which left the onlookers in no doubt that it was not just the department that appealed to her.

"Sign her up Andrew, sign her up," Angus cried.

"Easy tiger, easy. It's called a rotation. Not because their heads spin but so they get a broad base of knowledge. No good throwing them in at the deep end yet."

"I'll look after her," Angus repined, smiling through half closed eyes.

"I'm sure you will, Angus," Sheen replied meaningfully. "Come on let's away before Angus tries to close another deal."

They nodded their replies but Rupert caught the chemistry between Angus and Claire and was put in mind of one of his favourite quotes: "Beauty provoketh fools sooner than gold."

They left the room and entered the next corridor. Claire looked briefly over her shoulder, eyes meeting with Angus. He smiled, put his head down and thought, *I knew it, I knew it, knew she'd look back. Gotcha!* He returned to his desk picking up the phone for the next deal.

They entered the next dealing room which was empty, except for a secretary with her back to the door, hands flying away on a word processor, ear phones plugged in, her foot on the pedal of a transcriber for the tape to which she was listening. All they could see of her was dark thick hair, a white blouse, surprisingly broad shoulders, lightly tanned arms and Russian wedding ring style bangles in three different types of gold clicking occasionally against the keyboard. In profile it could be seen that she was wearing dark, heavy "Nanamouscori" style glasses. She must have caught a movement out of the corner of her eye as she half -turned in concentration.

"They're all out at a promotional bash," she said in cultured tones, pronouncing the third word as I't.

"They'll be back this afternoon sometime. Can't help I'm afraid; just temping for the week." She shrugged dismissively and returned her full concentration to the screen.

Typical, thought Sheen cynically, *some empty headed Sloane doing the temping rounds to pay for the perma-tan, looking for the right man.* Aloud he said; "They might be back this afternoon but won't be sober."

A grin creasing his face and again bringing them into the conspiracy, likening it to bunking off school and hoping the staff would turn a blind eye, providing the results were good. "As long as they get the deals done, we don't care and some of their best work is done in the pub. This is the North West team," he added, waving at the virtually empty room with the same layout and decor as before.

They moved on through the Development, Industrial Agency and then Office Agency departments, meeting other graduates and staff, including Tina; a dark curly-haired, bubbly girl in her early twenties with flirty eyes.

In the next corridor, they stopped briefly to chat with Howard Bruman, who was bemoaning to Sheen about the lack of action on a new development.

"Oh, any time now, as soon as the Building Department get their act together. I think they must have an Italian project manager though," Howard drawled sarcastically in a rather refined voice

"Italian?" Rupert queried, looking puzzled.

"*Si, e domani, e domani.....!*" he retorted, pleased that someone had bitten.

"Too much Tuscan sun for Howard I feel. We're lucky to have

him here really," Sheen continued. "Usually to be found at this time of year enjoying the end of the season at his villa in Italy. Aren't you Howard ?!"

"Oh, a man's got to eat, a man's got to eat," he said lazily, not at all perturbed. Waving airily, he went back to his desk, his jowls creasing as he sat. The others laughed.

"Come on, let's go." Sheen turned in Howard's direction for a final niggle.

"What is it Howard?"

"*Andiamo,* dear boy, *andiamo,*" Howard responded lazily. They all grinned and followed Sheen.

Down, finally, to the ground floor, through the back staircase and further disorientation.

"Just in case you have lost all sense of direction and level, we are now on the Ground floor, with Reception, meeting rooms and that entire end of the floor is given over to the Investment department, with Auctions off in another area." Sheen explained, waving his hand in the air.

The door opened to one large room, about twice the size of any two of the retail rooms above. Desks were set out primarily in a vague state of order around the periphery of the room, leaving free access to separate smaller offices.

The room was unlike any other they had encountered; the atmosphere was of studied seriousness. They were all surveyors sure enough but more sombre than one would expect of their agency cousins. There were more pinstripes here than anywhere else. Despite a proliferation of ostensibly young surveyors, it was more hushed and concentrated than frenetic. Despite this, there was a hurried intensity, that bespoke money, power and a sense of purpose.

"Finally, the Investment Department. Whatever we create through lettings, rent reviews, developments et al, it all comes down to the bottom line of the sale of the freehold investment.

"Don't tell them, but they are all really failed City merchant bankers and traders trying to eke out a living here."

There were howls of derision at this from those who heard and the sombre atmosphere disappeared for a moment as various agents threw caustic comments:

"Go and read your bloody leases, leave the real deals to us."

"Rent review surveyors? Theorists to a tee, wouldn't know a deal if it hit them on the head."

The cries continued and, once again, Sheen proved to be the perfect antidote to the situation, encouraging repartee and dispelling sobriety whilst bringing everyone into the fold, making them feel part of the whole.

"I won't bother introducing everyone individually," he continued gesticulating at ten or so of the team. "Suffice to say, you'll know them if you need them for a spot yield or comps for open market value."

The Investment surveyors were closely linked to the City, in that they had to be aware of what was going on with money rates on a 5 & 10 year basis; understand the market mores of what was fashionable and for what reason etc. In short, they were almost a jack of all trades and masters of none.

"This man you must meet though," he said indicating a sartorial treat of a man, seated in one of the offices to the side.

"This is Hugo Curtiss, senior partner of the investment team and what he doesn't know about funding isn't worth knowing."

High praise indeed, considering his earlier acerbic comments on other departments and other surveyors, Rupert thought.

Hugo Curtiss stood up and came from around the other side of his desk. He was a tall, imposing figure, of late thirties-early forties with dark, almost black hair parted to the side and expensively cut. He had dark brown eyes and straight regular features with a square chin that gave his face strong good looks and prevented him from being dandified. Although giving the impression that he was still strong and fit, his large frame was beginning to give up the fight against business lunches and too much Chardonnay, but the extra padding suited him, lending an air of gravitas and authority. He proffered a well-tanned hand which proved to have a crushing grip.

"Dear me, after an introduction like that I don't know whether to beam or be abashed, but I am pleased to meet you." His voice when he spoke, was of rich brown tones, resonating perfectly and causing one to listen almost by command.

"So the final stop of the tour I presume, how do you like it?"

"Fascinating really," Mike responded carefully, "so much activity unified to produce a complete result-service!"

Curtiss considered him carefully and he felt that the layers of confidence were being peeled away.

"Hmm and what about the Investment Department? What are your impressions? Do any of you fancy a position here after the initial circulation?" he asked provocatively.

"Well, as a matter of fact, yes I do, rather. Slightly more refined than retail agency, dare I say it; but still with opportunity to deal and trade," Mike finished smoothly.

"Interesting observation, we'll see how you do. What about you two?" he continued looking at Rupert and Claire " Any preferences yet?"

"I'll see after rotation when I can assess the departments more accurately," she answered sensibly.

"What, you mean you're not going to take Andrew's word for it" he chided " You must be losing your touch Sheen."

Andrew responded with a smile.

"Well Rupert, what about you?" Sheen asked.

"Like Claire, I think I'll keep my powder dry. I do have a hankering for the Development Department, but we'll see."

Curtiss and Sheen exchanged knowing glances "Development

eh. That will be interesting, you haven't met Mr. Threephones yet, have you? Hope you can swim," Sheen finished cryptically.

They were introduced to various other team members and left the department for the basement and the WP section, storage rooms, shower room for the directors and sick room.

"Right, lunch!" Sheen commanded. The others looked at their watches it was 12.30; the morning had flown by.

They went to a local on the corner of Davis Street and South Molton Street. The pub was already starting to fill up with custom, the atmosphere smokey, the clientele shouting the odds above pints, spritzers and white wine. Across the small bar fake Dickensian glass panels gave just enough light to see. Rupert spotted one or two faces from the mornings excursion in and amongst the crowd.

Some of the Retail boys were already onto their second pints. *Mixing with more agents,* he assumed, *from other firms;* getting the gossip, the tips and deals which would precipitate another afternoon of frenetic activity. *How did they do it?* he asked himself. *Drink all lunchtime then go back and do an afternoons work whilst still acting sober and remembering what had been said.* Lunchtime drinking at University had meant skipping lectures in the afternoon or at worst, dozing at the back of the class unobtrusively.

"Right." said Sheen after the third round when all the barriers and inhibitions of the three were starting to evaporate.

He had been continuing the assessment of their abilities, strengths, weaknesses and personalities until the final hour; the pub being the last test. He knew that how they handled themselves in such a scenario would ultimately decide the issue.

"This afternoon I will settle you in to your new homes."

CHAPTER 3

For the next few days, working life became a very steep learning curve for the three new graduates; coming to terms with the long hours, commuting and not least of which, the new jargon and working practices.

At this moment however, Mike Ringham was enclosed in the depths of the Management Department and not a happy surveyor.

" ....and" he continued in hushed, but exasperated tones " ..and…just to make my life really interesting they sent me off to the Siberian salt mines of surveying the Management Department. Can you credit it? I was told that it would be "good experience" for my future career as a hot shot investment surveyor."

"Well, it could be worse," said a voice down the phone, "you could be doing rating. Think of that, all those lovely Local Authority workers in their scruffy, sports jackets, with red hammer and sickle ties, calling you comrade and not permitting you ask for black coffee in case it offended someone." The voice chuckled. "Oh, don't. I'm surrounded by "polyester man" at the moment. If I see another nylon shirt, I think I'll vote Labour and be done with it. However," the voice grew more conspiratorial "there is rather a nice vision on the horizon in the shape of-"

"No, let me guess," the voice interrupted, "petite, dark hair, wide set eyes with great tits. When are you going to stop chasing secretaries? It will be the death of you."

"Hah," Mike responded. "Hark whose talking. Anyway, your only eighty percent right; she's a surveyor and has long legs"

"What, a change from type? Careful, you'll be dating an intellectual equal if you're not careful."

"But I talk to you," he replied. "See you at the Guinea after work? It is Friday, after all."

"Definitely, just one thing though, do they let management surveyors in there?"

"Piss off!" he retorted and slammed the phone down, grinning in wry amusement.

Mike had been good friends with Julian Charteris through school and University. Julian now worked for Halbern and Beams across the way in Grosvenor Street. A well-established firm and one of the "Big Five", it was about three times the size of CR with a proportionately inflated opinion of itself. This manifested through to many of its employees, who considered themselves a cut above.

On the other side of the floor in PSD, Claire Sewell was carefully reading through a lease, analysing it as she went. She looked up with a puzzled expression on her face.

"When is *time of the essence* and what exactly does it mean?" she queried. Chris Hughes looked up from what he was a doing and across to where Claire was sitting. "Time is of the essence when, the lease specifically states so in the wording; for example when a notice or counter notice has to be served within a certain timescale. It is particularly important when triggering a Rent Review Notice on the usual five yearly review period, or and much more dangerously, when a counter notice needs to be served at the end of a lease. The landlord can easily get possession if the tenant does not object in writing on time. The landlord and tenant have both got to respond in the timescale if the lease says so. In simple terms they are screwed if they don't comply.

"The number of rent reviews and lease renewals that have, in the past, been messed up by failing to comply with timescales beggars belief. Although, in recent years, tenant's surveyors have objected to the clause and only a few modern leases include such an onerous provision," he continued conspiratorially. "I'll tell you, I nearly got caught on it once when I was baby surveyor and dear old Sheeny saved my bacon."   "Sheeny? He's good isn't he?"   "He is technically; but a bastard to work for. You wait till you've been "Sheened". Usually happens about 5.30pm. But tell me," he queried. "Have you found a lease with a *time of the essence* clause there?"

"I'm not sure, take a look and see what you think," she offered. Chris took the offered lease and studied the potentially offending clause.

"I can see why you thought so but not in this case, no." He proceeded to explain the legal reasons why it was not so and was impressed by her quick grasp of the facts and reasoning behind his view.

Chris felt that Claire was settling in well and hoped that, not the least because of her physical attributes, that she would decide to go full time into PSD when she finished rotation. He looked at his watch.

"Come on," he said. "Let's piss off before we get Sheened. Its five thirty 'my life already'," doing a mock Jewish accent. "Boswells beckons and its Friday."

They both slipped their jackets on from behind their chairs and hurriedly left the office; picking up four more of the PSD staff along the way to be joined by two more waiting for the lift before Sheen appeared .

Boswells was a smart pub just off Manchester Square not usually frequented by the agency boys. Subdued lighting and a series of green leather upholstered bench seats created a cosy atmosphere. They had just ordered another round of drinks when Rupert hurried in looking exasperated and stressed out.

"I don't believe it," he said. "Five thirty he calls me in to discuss a clause in the lease, sits me down picks up the phone and makes a call, then-"

"Don't tell me," Chris interrupted. "He then puts the phone down, takes off his cufflinks, calls Dawn for a cup of tea, checks on other papers and all the while ignoring you. Finally he looks at the lease and goes on for half an hour being really pedantic. Am I right?"

"How did you know? Except it was an hour not half!"

"You've been Sheened," they all chorused.

"What exactly is time of the essence anyway?" he asked.

Claire and Chris laughed, while he explained patiently the facts again to Rupert who subsequently ordered a round and whilst waiting, cast his eyes around the pub. In one of the booth-like settings was a vaguely familiar profile. Frustratingly he could not quite remember where he'd seen her. She moved, showing her arm as she sipped her wine, showing three golden bangles on her arm. Of course, he thought; the rude temp from agency. *But who was with her?* he wondered. All he could see was a shock of steel grey hair, suntanned neck and well tailored shoulders; turned almost fully with his back to him and completely unrecognisable.

They were having a deep conversation and she seemed to be reading something to him from a book. *Probably planning their next holiday together,* he thought, *no prizes for guessing where she got her tan.* His round arrived and he made the two journeys necessary to transport it to the table. When he looked again they had gone. *Oh well, another mystery,* he resigned to himself.

After three rounds the group broke up, with Claire and Rupert walking down to Bruton Place to meet Mike at the Guinea. When they arrived at the tiny pub it was packed, seemingly full with agents; all half cut and having a thoroughly good time. Mike, by virtue of his great height was to be seen halfway down in the first half of the bar with, of all people, Angus Stewart and a few others, including Julian Charteris. Not quite as tall as Mike, he had dark brown hair, parted off centre, a square determined face, deep set eyes and a straight nose. They saw each other and amid mutual shouts of acknowledgement above the din, shook hands whilst Claire received two kisses on her cheeks and a wink from Julian as he slyly indicated the girl on Mike's right hand side.

"This is Jemma Smythe," Mike introduced her. "Works in Management, but don't tell anybody or they might throw her out," he shouted above the din.

"Pig!" she said poking her tongue out and giving him a withering smile which was anything but humorous.

"Anyway, look who's talking, how many loo roles did you order today?" she finished sarcastically, rising to the challenge.

"Ok, Ok," he protested holding up his hands in mock surrender. He smiled down at her thinking, not for the first time, that she was everything he had described to Julian earlier and looking at the swelling under her white blouse, had great tits too.

Angus proceeded to engage Claire in conversation while Mike and Julian wanted to know why the group was so late.

"Oh, we went to Boswells for a couple of sharpeners first with PSD, but I got caught before that by Sheen," Rupert groaned and they all laughed.

Overhearing the conversation, Angus chimed in; "He's famous for it. Friday nights especially! You were lucky to get away so early."

They all laughed while Angus told more stories. Rupert thought, *this is what it's all about, being in the market.* He scanned the pub, looking at all the agents there and feeling part of it.

"Come on," said Angus, when he had finished telling another improbable, but very amusing story of one of his exploits in CR.

"We're off to Smollenskys."

"Smollenskys?"

"It is the only place to go, has to be done. Smollensky's Balloon, just around the corner."

They all piled out, Angus picking up some more mates on the way out. They walked around the corner to Smollenksy's Balloon; a newly opened drinking bar/restaurant just short of a night club. It was bright, with all kinds of lighting, huge glass frontage, different levels and music playing loudly.

The film, Top Gun, had recently been released in the West End and was proving hugely popular, the sound track of which was playing at the moment. Angus as ever the party animal started dancing, leading the way and by this time he was starting to fly, leading the pack. After about an hour he and another retail agent were having an animated conversation about a girl at the bar. The object of their discussion was late twenties, curly blond hair, heavily made up almond shaped eyes and bright red lipstick. She was wearing a suit with padded shoulders, that nipped in around waist, a short skirt and long, black stocking clad legs crossed, while perching on a bar stool talking to her friend. She was sexy and knew it.

"You've got no chance Angus," his friend challenged. "She's out of your league."

"Dirty though, has to be done; just look at those legs. I swear I saw a stocking top when she crossed them just now."

"Tenner, says you can't."

"Done!" he shouted.

With that Angus turned and sauntered towards the crowded bar. He had a distinctive walk; it was almost a shuffle with his upper body, as though he was conscious of his height. He partly rounded his shoulders accordingly, in an almost humble, Euriah Heap fashion. Women found this nonthreatening and consequently appealing. This coupled with his natural good looks was fatally attractive.

He approached the two women at the bar, the blonde target of his appreciation facing him. He smiled his most winning smile; a victor of many similar conquests.

"I couldn't help noticing you from across there," he opened, inflecting his Scottish burr a little more, as he did on all such occasions and at the same time gesturing his hand in the direction to where he'd just been standing. The girl at the bar turned slightly as if noticing him for the first time, swept him with a glance and replied slowly in measured tones.

"So, you've noticed me,…what now?"

For a moment Angus was thrown. He usually received an embarrassed giggle, shy looks at a friend or a "phewah come on", look of encouragement. This cool, detached challenge, while not quite a rebuff, was definitely a put down and threw him off balance.

"Lovely," he said trying a new tack.

"Mmmm…." she left the murmur, hanging in the air, whilst engaging direct eye contact, not helping him with a response at all.

"Angus," he said extending his hand. "May I buy you both a drink?"

Ignoring the offer of introduction she replied.

"As you can see we both have full glasses, so no thank you."

"This is getting tricky," he stated, appealing now for the sympathy vote. "Aren't you going to help me out, even a little?"

"No," she answered, a small smile on the edge of her lips.

With that he opened his arms magnanimously, made a mock bow and turned away. Her friend commented that she was rather hard on him.

"Oh no, he'll be back. His ego's writing cheques his mind has got to cash. You'll see," she predicted.

Angus continued to walk back across towards his friends, the sound track changed to the Righteous Brothers' "You've lost that loving feeling", then an idea occurred to him. He grabbed a slim, black cocktail shaker from the bar and holding it like a microphone turned back towards the girl, motioning to his friends, including Matt who had bet him, to follow. He approached the girl as his curious friends arrived behind him in a loose semi-circle. Miming the actions of Maverick, in Top Gun, he began to sing in time.

She started to look embarrassed as everyone stared, smiling, encouraging Angus as he got to the chorus, hamming it up outrageously, on bent knees. She relented, burst out laughing and shouted over the music, "Ok, Ok, anyone with that much nerve deserves the reward. Sit down" she ordered indicating a bar stool.

Everyone clapped, Angus pulled up a stool and turned around to wink at Matt, who raised his eyes upwards in disbelief. Claire and Jemma exchanged knowing glances, shaking their heads, both girls' faces a play of emotions.

She introduced herself as Susannah and her friend as Carole. Angus began to flirt outrageously with both of them, to the extent that they both wondered who he was making up to.

The others broke into groups, with Matt taking up where Angus had left off with Claire. At about midnight, the evening broke up with Susannah firmly attached to Angus' arm, and everyone heading outside to hunt for a taxi, much the worse for wear.

CHAPTER 4

They caught a taxi just outside Smollenskys, in Berkekly Square. Susannah gave an address in Islington and the cab sped off. She turned to Angus, reached for his face in both hands and kissed him hard on the mouth. He returned the kiss in kind, holding her tightly, his tongue probing her open mouth. She responded eagerly. Turning onto her back in Angus' arms, she linked her arms behind his neck. His hands explored her body. Settling over her left breast he gently kneaded her nipple, which was already becoming hard through the thin material of her blouse.

He was becoming hard beneath her thigh and, feeling this, she moved her hand down to rub gently between his legs. He moaned encouragingly and she smiled between kisses.

The taxi slid past Upper Street into one of the nearby small, Victorian squares.

The cabbie pulled to a halt outside the address given and turned on the interior light.

Looking at the meter, he said; "That'll be seven fifty, please guv."

They both hastily rearranged themselves; Susannah pulling

her coat together over her open blouse, while Angus moved with awkward movements and stepped out of the cab.

"Here's a tenner, keep the change." He leaned inside through the window of the cab grinning.

"Thank you," the cabbie replied. "Good luck! Not that you'll need it."

Angus waved conspiratorially and turned to follow Susannah up a short flight of steps to her front door. The flat was typical of the latest gentrification of the north London boroughs occurring at that time; a conversion of a terraced town house into three flats, of which she had the top floor.

They staggered drunkenly through the inner door to her flat, which opened onto a small landing. She disentangled herself from Angus and headed for one of the doors leading off.

"The kitchen is through there," she indicated. "Put the kettle on."

As the door was closing, Angus had a view of a bright blue bathroom, cork tiles and brightly coloured pictures on the walls. He found the kitchen and filled the kettle, fetching two mugs off the wooden tree. She re-appeared silently on stockinged feet behind him. He planted a kiss and headed for the bathroom. When he returned a few moments later, she had her back to him and was making coffee.

He came up behind her, slipping is hands around her, onto her breasts and was pleased to find that the buttons of her blouse were still undone from his exertions in the taxi.

"Mmmmmh," she murmured throatily, resting her head back and pushing her bottom against his body. He kissed her and slipped his hand into her open blouse, cupping her breast, his other hand undoing the final two buttons with well practiced ease.

She moved in his arms to face him again, hands moving over

his body, while he pulled apart her blouse, exposing a lacy bra, which he undid and slipped down exposing heavy, large-nippled breasts. He brought his mouth down to suck them while she brought one hand behind his neck in encouragement. With the other she undid his trousers and slid her hand in to stroke the hardness she found there.

Both aroused, their actions became wilder; she pulled his boxers down and gently raked his balls with her nails. He moaned in ecstasy.

"I want you," she said huskily.

She pulled her short skirt up above her waist and pushed herself up onto the working surface with her legs apart. Angus looked down and saw that above the stocking tops, her bare, lightly-tanned skin led to a pale bikini triangle between her legs, from which there emerged a thin line of dark pubic hair. Unable to resist any longer he entered her with one, swift movement. Her legs clasped behind his back and her pelvis ground against him in time with his short, rhythmic, thrusts.

She began to cry out in and then shouted; "Now, now aaaaaah!" she screamed.

She dug her hands into his hair and arched her hips forward. Angus shuddered as he climaxed, throwing himself forward one last time before his legs gave way and he fell towards her. They sagged together, totally spent.

"Take me to the bedroom," she whispered.

Angus took her surprisingly, light weight and moved towards the door indicated, pushing it open with his back. They collapsed onto the bed discarding the final pieces of their clothing. Falling naturally into a lovers embrace, sleep overtook them.

On the other side of London, Rupert, Claire, Mike and Jemma shared a taxi to Mike's Kensington flat, where coffee was made and drunk by the four, who were reminiscing about the evening's events.

"You have to hand it to the guy, he's got balls. I couldn't have done that and got away with it and more importantly, got the girl," Rupert said, extolling the virtues of Angus' antics.

"Well, I suppose that's one way of looking at it," Jemma commented. "He's had nearly every secretary and surveyor in the firm; and probably the west end come to that," she finished tartly.

The others looked at her with various emotions on their faces.

"Don't look at me like that," she cried. "No, I haven't succumbed, although I was approached," she said, grinning wickedly in Mikes' direction.

"Wo ho, Ringo, sounds like you've got competition, old chap," Rupert chided, grinning from ear to ear.

"I don't know what you mean," he said, in his best patrician tones and denouncing any suggestion of attachment between him and Jemma.

Claire glanced at her watch and yawned affectedly.

"Ya, well, some of us need our beauty sleep if we are to catch up with Mr. Stewart."

"Me too," said Rupert finishing his coffee. "I'll walk you home."

They both lived a short walk away, just into the borders of Chelsea, so made their goodbyes and left. The door closed on them and Jemma looked slightly ill at ease.

"Well, I suppose I had better make a move too," she said.

"No, don't go yet. Haven't you time for one more cup of coffee or a night cap?" he drawled gently. "I've hardly spoken to you all evening. Stay and chew the cud."

"Stay and chew the cud?" she mocked.

He grinned, sheepishly.

"A single malt? I've some fine Oban Reserve." Mike offered.

"Done. Better than grass." She repartieed

He proceeded to pour two drinks from the corner cupboard, whilst she inspected the flat more closely. It was furnished in exquisite taste; a mixture of dark greens and blues, with light champagne coloured carpet throughout. The walls were adorned with various prints of hunts, shoots and portraits, blending with the antique furniture. He followed her gaze.

"I know what you're thinking."

"Now, how could you possibly know that? You're a man," she teased.

"Well, I'll open myself up to ridicule. I know it looks as though I'm a young old fogey, but this happens to be my parent's place in Town and I'm here by default. It is free after all."

"Well, I could think of worse poor houses," she mocked. "Seriously, I like it very much. It has great style. Ok, not contemporary, but timeless. A bit like you really," she ventured bravely, her blue eyes twinkling.

He blushed, handed her the glass and joined her on the sofa.

"I never know which way you'll turn next you know, you constantly surprise me."

"Good," she said smiling.

They sipped their drinks and he kissed her gently on the lips, sliding his arm around her shoulders. They slipped into companionable silence as if by mutual consent, then started talking easily on subjects of mutual interest, until at around 2.30, Jemma looked at her watch and said she had to go.

He ordered a taxi and walked her to the door when it arrived.

"I enjoyed tonight, thank you."

"Me too. Can I, uh, can I see you for supper tomorrow? Sorry, that sounds so keen, I meant some time."

"Don't be sorry. I hate playing games." She smiled "Yes, I'd love supper. Call me."

She scribbled her number on a piece of paper, kissed him lightly on the lips and left in a haze of Anais Anais. Turning for one last look over her shoulder, she passed through the door of his flat down to the waiting taxi.

Mike closed the door gently. Deep in pensive thought, his mind was a mix of emotions. He shook his head slowly from side to side and smiled to himself.

CHAPTER 5

The morning light was breaking through the skylights, bathing the office in warm sunlight. Simions was relaxed, smiling like the cat that had got the cream. Sat at the desk, he reclined backwards with the phone pressed to his ear. It had been a profitable meeting and he now had all the information he needed to break the deal.

"Shingler? It's me, how are you on this fine morning? Good, good. Listen, I got all the information from her last night. Yes, the whole lot; placed with the agency, rents, breakdown of Zone A's, everything. I will send it over by courier today. No, I don't trust the fax. This information has only one source and if my number is on the fax it all leads back to me.

"I think that we should broker it out. Let's leak it through Ricky Barstow. That way I get half an agency fee and we get to manipulate the deal.

"Perfect. Get it done and we can then push the proceeds off shore, cleaned and free."

They discussed in more detail the transaction and how it would be processed before ending the call. He then called one of his secretaries to order a motorcycle messenger for Mid-Town later that morning. Humming to himself, he felt pleased as he knew all hell would break loose in the market once this information started circulating.

The same Monday morning at CR, saw Angus standing to one side of his desk holding court, surrounded by the other members of the department. He was looking more than a little shabby for Monday morning, with a lived-in look to his suit, skin drawn tight across his cheeks and bleary eyed.

"So boys, there we were in the flat, after Smollenskys, she leaned over the work top thrusting her arse at me begging for it. One hand for balance," at which point he placed his hand horizontally six inches in front of him palm down, with the thumb pointing to the floor at the same time making pelvic thrusts with his hips, "many thanks, had to be done!"

He repeated the actions, while the team fell about laughing, shaking their heads in despair and admiration. At this point Claire entered the office quietly, through the doorway behind him. The others looked rather embarrassed like a group of school boys caught reading Penthouse.

"Morning Claire," one responded alerting Angus to her presence.

Claire continued walking in, serenely, managing to achieve an air of insouciance and giving Angus her most pitying smile, patted him on the shoulder patronisingly saying.

"I think we need to work on the technique a little more, dear."

They all creased up, wolf whistling and bating Angus.

"So what brings a pretty girl like you to this den of iniquity?" called a mocking voice from the end of the room, just inside the partners' office.

The voice belonged to Tom Lovich; a large, craggy man in his late thirties with slightly prematurely grey hair, clear blue eyes and a likeable, lived-in face that endeared him to many. In fact, despite being one of the most successful retail agents in CR, and probably the West End in his own right, he was very popular both within the firm and outside. He could always be relied upon to provide a balanced view to any situation and tended to transact his deals with charm and good will, rather than latent aggression, which appealed to clients and competitors alike.

Claire turned her back on Angus and walked forward to introduce herself.

"Claire Sewell, how do you do? I've just joined on the grad recruitment and needed to get some information from your town files on Watford rents.

"Well, that's a lucky escape. Watford isn't one of the mad Scotsmans'

towns so you won't have him letching after you all the time."

"Oh, don't worry," she replied. "I've seen the "Great Scot" in action already. Very impressive you know."

"Oh come on," Angus replied turning on the little-boy-lost charm and smiling pathetically. "I'm not that bad, just misunderstood."

"Come on, I'll show you where the files are before he ends up in tears."

Angus made lewd actions to their departing backs as they entered the filing room.

"What is it you wanted?"

"We have a review on High Street, acting for the landlord, and we think we can see a 20% increase in rent, which, if true and provable should be of interest to you lot as well."

"Coincidentally, we're working on two acquisitions at the moment. If we can put them together and prove a strong rental growth, without going to the market, it will be to our advantage."

They poured over the town files and other associated special files for the next half an hour and came up with conclusive proof for the rental increase.

"Right, we had better close this *before*, the tenant's agents get to this info. I'll speak to Sheen, get you rolled in on the meeting with the client. Nothing like a PSD surveyor to convince them that it all rings true. We will then hopefully get a better offer from the client to buy the freehold and back to back it before the market gets wise."

"Back to back it?" she queried.

"Yea, when you have the opportunity to take a lease from a tenant or buy a shop with vacant possession – sometimes just called VP - and at the same time have a new tenant waiting in the wings to take a new lease on the unit at a much higher rent. Simple in theory, but, if you can pull it off it can make millions for the client. Mega fees for us and if you are really clever, you can buy two or three other units in the same town before the good news hits the streets."

Tom made some calls arranging for a meeting the next day and cleared it with Sheen who was more than happy for Claire to be brought to the front line.

The next day saw Tom and Claire heading for the City by tube. They got out at St Pauls and took two side streets to the client's offices. The client in this case was a major insurance company, Capital Assurance, with a few smaller funds held under the same umbrella.

"So we have to give them a cast iron case that we are right. That's where you come in, as you are on the *professional side,* so no pressure, ok?" Tom explained.

"Oh absolutely, just call me Marie Antoinette. But what do I say for God's sake?" she exclaimed.

"Just tell him the truth, exactly as you told me, without any embellishment. If a retail agent told the same story he'd gild the Lily so much the colours would run. The thing about fund managers is this: they have, with a few exceptions, no imagination. Give them colour and they want black and white; give them black and white and they want monochrome. Oh and flirt with your eyes the way you do, they may be fund managers but red blood still flows through their veins."

With this final comment he shot her a winsome grin, as they entered the building. The Capital Assurance building was of a classic, ugly and boring 1970's construction.

They proceeded to the fourth floor where they were met by a secretary at the lift doors who escorted them to the end of the corridor and a waiting area with brown padded chairs, a small coffee table hosting the day's newspapers and a copy of the Estates Gazette: the bible for all surveyors.

Claire, despite her outward confidence, was becoming more nervous as the enormity of what was expected truly began to dawn upon her. The whole deal hinged upon her ability to sell not only the position, but also her onward skill of being able to deliver the evidence necessary to make the deal tick. The one point in her favour was the totally relaxed attitude of Tom Lovich, who was taking it all in his stride as though a minimum of £100,000 of fees riding on the next meeting didn't matter. Again, she was struck by just how confident not only they were, but the whole CR team was when dealing in millions of pounds worth of property as though it were Monopoly money. Tom picked up on her nerves.

"Relax. Just think; property is normally ten percent knowledge and ninety percent bullshit. You've got it in inverse proportions, how can you fail?"

She laughed at this and began to relax.

They were shown into the fund manager's office; Kevin Marsh was about forty years old, round with a slightly jowled face that was getting fat from too many lunches. His hair was receding, giving him an air of maturity beyond his years and his forehead was lined above a pair of small, close set, shrewd eyes.

"Tom, good to see you," he said with a smile, extending his hand.

"And you, Kevin. ," he said, waving an arm as introduction, "and this is Claire Sewell from our PSD team, who is running the rent reviews in Watford."

Running the rent reviews in Watford? Claire thought, *talk about in at the deep end. Fuck it! Why not say I'm running the company as well!* Outwardly she smiled confidently, remembering to flirt discreetly with her eyes.

"How do you do?" she said.

"Excellent," he said shaking hands. "Good to have a professional touch on the team. Nothing like hard facts to back up hunches. Sit down, please. Coffee? Good."

He ordered coffee from his secretary.

"Did you see Arsenal at the weekend?" Tom opened.

"Don't, I nearly wept. What about that missed goal in the second half?"

The conversation carried on in this vein for a few minutes as he was obviously a great fan. He switched suddenly, to take Claire into the conversation as the coffee arrived.

"Do you follow football Claire?"

"I'm afraid not, it's all a bit beyond me."

"What sport are you into then, tennis?" he questioned, rather patronisingly.

"Well a bit, but I love riding," she offered, then instantly regretted it in the ensuing moments silence.

"Ah yes," he responded. "My wife's into horses, likes dressage. Every Saturday morning, out at the stables. Can't see it myself but there we are."

"Oh yes, great fun," she answered enthusiastically, whilst privately thinking that short of paint drying or football, nothing could be more boring than dressage. *Stick to the eyes and cleavage,* she thought, *eyes and cleavage.*

"Right, let's get down to it what have you got for me?"

"Well, you remember the two units we're trying to buy for you at the moment in Watford?" Marsh nodded in acquiescence and Tom continued, "Offers have gone in and we're at around the £2m mark for each unit. The rents equate to a Zone A rent of around £65 per foot unit. It shows you a good return in today's market of about 5%," he paused for effect.

"Well, we have good reason to believe that the lid is about to blow off these rents to the tune of £79 ZA. That, as I don't need to tell you, is a hike of just over 20%."

Marsh nodded as he listened to Tom continuing to outline the basis of evidence and the effect it would have upon the proposed purchase. It sounded like a good opportunity and, as always, Tom knew what he was talking about. "So, if we can just tweak our figures to reflect a small proportion of the increase to say £2.1m we can see a clear profit of about £300,000 per unit in a matter of months, once the fund's valuers do the revalue. All that profit, just for being aware of the market," he added enthusiastically.

"Yes, I see what you mean," Marsh said slowly. "It would be excellent for the capital growth of such a small fund but, let us look at the facts, all this hinges upon the rental growth coming through at the rate you're predicting. Correct?"

Tom nodded, deliberately staying quiet and knew what was to come next.

"So how did you come by the information? Is it reliable? And what are the chances of theory becoming reality? Because if it is just some agents' bar talk, I'll not bid a penny more than we have already. Even if the deal is not on the open market." Dogmatic to a fault.

"I'll hand you over to Claire." Tom interceded suavely. "It is she who has unearthed the evidence and came to me with the info, to try and put a deal together."

Claire's mouth went dry, as she marshalled her thoughts for the thousandth time that day. She proceeded in clear and concise tones to explain exactly what she'd found, emphasising where necessary and smiling appropriately with her eyes. She finished by passing a schedule of evidence to Marsh. He regarded her carefully.

"It all makes sense. In fact, do you know why I believe it's kosher? Because the information came from Michaelman's PSD and they, like me, would never credit that one department would talk to another agency team, even within their own firm., he said, cynically.

"Alright. Tom, put a report together. I'll get board approval to increase our bid based on these figures," he waved a hand toward to Claire's documents now on his desk. "Hopefully, we will be able to construct a suitably advantageous offer to secure our position and capitalise on this information."

Tom was pleased with the result but kept his response to a nod with a dry smile.

They discussed other potential deals on the back of this but Marsh was clearly not interested.

"I've some tickets for the Arsenal-Liverpool match in November, thought you might be interested?"

"Now that is a result. What date?" he was more animated than Claire had seen him all through the meeting.

"The 25th."

Tom consulted his diary.

"You're on. I look forward to it."

Marsh turned back to Claire, shook hands and showed them to the lift.

"I look forward to the report, Tom. Good work, Claire. How long have you been at Cowell Rubens for?"

Tom quickly gained eye contact with her and cut into her proposed reply.

"About a year now isn't it Claire? I think we may try and poach her for our department in the future."

She nodded and smiled, continuing the subterfuge for Marsh's benefit.

"Well, about time you had a professional on your team, Tom," he joked, immensely pleased at his own humour. They all laughed dutifully and entered the lift, waving goodbye. The doors closed and Claire let out a dramatic breath. Tom grinned, enjoying the moment.

"Good fun isn't it? Well done, you played the straight guy well to our over-zealous agency boys role. Sorry about the time zone change. But if he knew you were a graduate who'd been with us for only one week, it would all have fallen down like a house of cards."

"I guessed that might be the case, so I did what you said; smiled and looked dumb."

"No, dumb is not a word I'd use to describe you; you caught on fast and did well. Just don't get him on football; he bores for England given half a chance."

"I guessed," she said "it's incredible. We put a deal in his lap for a massive profit virtually by return and he hardly blinks, other than to try and find a hole in the argument. Then mention football and he gets all excited like a little boy in a sweet shop."

"That's fund managers for you. You never know what's going to wind their crank."

The doors to the lift opened, depositing them on the ground floor where they made their way out of the building and back into the busy hustle and bustle of London's streets.

"What affect do the Independent valuers have on the fund and why the urgency?" she queried.

"Well, the independent valuers re-value the fund every

quarter and if we can provide new evidence for the revaluation, it improves not only the value of these two units but the fund as a whole."

"Which in turn makes dear old Kevin's "brucey bonus" look good for the end of the year. Not that he has any ulterior motive of course," Tom finished cynically.

"I see," Claire said. "So it really is in his interests to push it through."

"Very much so. Which reminds me, we have to find a home for those other two shop investments that Kevin's not interested in," Tom mused. Maybe MAS Investments" he thought out loud.

"But isn't that really investment work?" Claire asked.

"What they don't know won't hurt them and I'm not about to hand them a deal like that on plate for only half the fee," Tom said firmly.

Claire was beginning to grasp the rivalry, even within the firm, which was always resentful where fees were concerned. She was also reminded, not for the first time, about how information was key.

They caught the tube back to the office and Claire went back to her department to start preparing her side of the report for Tom. She entered the room she shared with Chris Hughes on a high, excited at the turn of events and the buzz it gave her.

"How did you get on?" Hughes asked, noticing the look of elation on her face.

"Amazing. My God I was so bloody nervous. Straight in at the deep end but Tom looked after me at the dodgy bits."

She proceeded to tell him all that had happened, recounting the events enthusiastically.

"Oh dear. We've lost you to the death or glory boys," he commented nonchalantly, head on one side, squinting through the ever present haze of smoke. "I knew it would happen, it was just a question of when. You like the kill, it's written all over you, even if you didn't know it."

She smiled beautifully, knowing exactly to what he was alluding. "Just remember though," he continued, "the glory is great, but no deal's done 'till it's done!"

"What do you mean?"

"Well, there are an awful lot of pitfalls to pass by yet, and fund managers are some of the most capricious animals on God's planet."

Claire felt as though some of the wind had been taken out of her sails.

CHAPTER 6

The week was spent putting the report together, verifying the evidence and compiling schedules. Once completed the report was sent across to Kevin Marsh's office for final board approval. The board met every Tuesday morning to discuss business, review purchases, approve (or not) new acquisitions and consider strategy. The report arrived in time for the weekly meeting and following this, Marsh called Tom Lovich.

"Tom, morning. Kevin here. How are you?"

"Not bad considering it's Tuesday. What gives, did we get board approval?"

"Well, yes and no. I approved it as you know, but the other two members wanted more information and further projection of cash flow figures to substantiate the growth projections," he finished rather evasively.

"I don't believe it," he said aghast. "We hand them a stunning deal on a plate which you could sell on for a profit in a thrice and they quibble."

"I know you're frustrated. Anyway, we can't sell on before one year after purchase, our mandate won't allow it. Look, get me some more figures, they shouldn't be difficult to formulate. The following are the variable criteria they want the spread assessed on-" he read out a set of yields and rental figures for analysis. Tom noted them down.

Almost as an afterthought, Marsh said, "Why don't you get someone to bring them over? Maybe that Claire, might just swing it. I want this deal to go through as much as you it is just … shall we say, politics."

"Ok fine, will do, when do you want this set up for?" Tom said resignedly.

"Say, Thursday? We have a mini meeting on Friday for over-flow business. Shall we say 2.30pm?"

"Consider it confirmed. If there are any problems, I'll call you." Tom slammed the phone down as hard as he could without breaking it. "Fucking arseholes! They couldn't organise a bun fight in Mr. Kiplings." The boys in the office looked at Tom in surprise; it was rare for him to lose his temper. "I'll tell you in a minute," he said, waving a hand in the air as he picked the phone up to dial internally.

"Claire. It's Tom. Can you come down please, great, bye."

Claire arrived five minutes later looking pensive.

"Right. Kevin Marsh just called, it failed at board; vetoed by the other two members. If I'm reading the situation correctly, it's because their jealous and they want Kevin to go through some more hoops.

"But we've been thrown a life line, some more projections and we can still swing it." The office groaned at the asinine stupidity of the board.

"What exactly do they want?" Claire asked pragmatically.

Tom gave her a rundown based on what Marsh had said on the phone. Claire nodded in understanding and turned as if to go.

"Oh and one final, small, detail. They want you to do a pre-sentation to the board."

"What? You are joking. Why me?"

"Well, Marsh was impressed and I think Wilson who is a lecherous little weasel, will greatly appreciate your other assets. Marsh thinks that might just win the day."

Claire was incredulous.

"You are not being serious are you? You think just because I go up there, smile nicely and flash my cleavage, it's going to make a difference. I don't believe it."

"I am telling you it will. Look, they're boring old farts, and like most men, rather stupid where a pretty women is concerned. Use your assets, work it to your advantage. I'm not asking you to sleep with them, just woo them."

Claire grinned shaking her head.

"Welcome to the world of surveying," she muttered, rolling her eyes upwards.

Leaving the office, Claire went away to formulate new numbers on the computer within the parameters defined by Kevin Marsh. The next few days were spent reworking the report and rehearsing her presentation to the board, with Tom playing question and answer sessions, giving her the third degree until she was word perfect and completely confident with every possible scenario that could be thrown at her.

Thursday morning arrived and she was walking nervously to and fro along the corridor of her floor and overheard a conversation, thanks to the strange acoustics of the building.

She saw Rupert, who had just finished a conversation with another agent, walking further along the corridor to an enlarged area that would formerly have been an ante room and now housed a photocopier for the department on that floor.

"Hi," she called to him.

They caught up on other gossip as they hadn't seen each other for over a week due to circumstances. Rupert backed up Tom;

his confidence had risen too in the short time he had been there; it was as infectious as measles in the place. He felt the power of the market; imbuing him with a will to win. Claire took it on board, inspired by his fabulous confidence. She was ready to take on "Wilson the weasel"- as she now thought of him; and his colleagues.

Rupert wished her luck and Claire left to go down to the the Retail Department. She looked good in a beautifully cut suit of steel grey with a silk blouse. Her newly cut hair had been fashioned into a layered style which complimented the shape of her face. Her makeup was immaculate; heavy, smokey, grey eye shadow, strong lipstick, subtle pearl earrings and a showy necklace which drew the eye. Angus blew a mock wolf whistle, which caused her to sashay even more as she entered Tom's office.

"Wow!" he said in admiration and thinking, not for the first time that she looked like Rene Russo.

Pleased at the result, she smiled, and asked, "When do we leave?"

"*We* don't leave at all. *You*, leave in five minutes to give you enough time to get there and prepare for the meeting. If I go with you," he continued, shouting down her protests, "your case will be diluted and it will lack credibility. The best chance we have is you on your own. Trust me. Oh, and undo another button, it will work wonders."

"You shit!" she said, before she realised what she was saying and to whom.

"A little harsh, but true," he mocked. "Now go to the meeting, and good luck."

She left, her head high, tossing her hair in mock fury.

She crossed the city to the Capital Assurance offices, spoke to reception, collected her pass and entered the lift. As the lift moved smoothly upwards, she gave her appearance one final appraisal in the mirror, smiled resignedly and undid one more button of her blouse.

Two hours later Claire returned to CR, utterly drained and with no feeling either way as to how she had performed, despite having been able to answer all their questions. She made her way up to the retail department.

"Well, how did you do?" asked Tom when she entered his office.

"Oh don't. What a ghastly, little weasel. You were right, he spent the whole time looking at my tits! Anyone would think it was them that were talking."

"I told you," he said. "But I see you took my advice."

"What?"

"Your other button, you undid it," he remarked indicating her blouse. She grinned knowingly.

"Well, any feedback yet?"

"Oh yes, Kevin did call about ten minutes ago. He was impressed."

"And..?"

"We've got board approval."

"YES!" She drove her clenched fist up into the air, a look of glee on her face.

"What now?"

"We put in the revised offer formally. I've already got reassurances from Michaelmans that £4.2m is acceptable and then we instruct lawyers. Well done Claire, you did well. I'll let Sheen know and, if you want, there's a place for you on the team when you're ready."

"I'd like that very much," she said and floated out of his office on a high.

Claire took the stairs up to the office she shared with Chris, using the exercise to work off the excess adrenalin. Claire knew information was key. She knew information was power. She knew information equalled fees and therefore money. Yes, it needed guile, charm and - in her case - sex appeal but the sheer delight at getting her first deal done rammed it home to her.

She entered the office grinning from ear to ear, taking off her jacket to hang it up and at that moment Chris looked up from his desk.

"Well, no need to ask how it went. Is that just your gut feeling or have you been told officially?"

"Kevin Marsh phoned about ten minutes before I arrived to confirm that we had board approval. I had to face all three, including "Wilson the weasel" by myself. Tom didn't even come with me, can you believe it?"

"Good tactician Tom, always reads his man well. In his position I'd probably have done the same," he said sagaciously and as she was leaning over her desk exposing an ample view of her cleavage, finished by saying, "Nice blouse though."

She looked down and grinned embarrassedly, doing up the extra button

"Mmmh, Tom's idea. Wilson spent all his time with his eyes glued to my tits," she exclaimed.

"Wilson's just gone up in my estimation," Chris retorted, winking.

"Chauvinist pig!" she cried.

"Speaking."

She burst out laughing at his riposte.

"Now it's just down to instructing lawyers and getting a contract," he said.

"I know, I know; no deals done 'till it's done!"

CHAPTER 7

The next two months raced away for Claire. It was a race against time to get the deal completed prior to the fiscal and calendar year end for Capital Assurance. However Capital were not the only ones leaping forward into unknown territory. The UK economy was experiencing previously unknown financial growth for the first time since Harold Macmillan's prophetic statement of "You've never had it so good" in the 60's. The prime minister, Margaret Thatcher, was being accused of selling the family silver as she negotiated the public floatation of such state luminaries as British Telecom and British Gas.

There was talk in the City of the Big Bang, which would affect share dealing as never before when the new rules were implemented and allowed transactions to be completed outside the arena of the City and, more importantly, by computer.

As a consequence City bonuses were going through the roof and the Age of the YUPPY had been born. This, combined with the low cost of borrowing at around 6%, was causing a housing market boom the like of which had never been known before. New areas were being "gentrified", like a pebble hitting the waters of a pond and spreading inexorably further outwards in the never ending quest for a good deal, as previously affordable areas became caught up in the vortex of greed and hyperbole.

The other driving force was that of tax relief on mortgages. If two people, married, or otherwise, obtained a mortgage on a property, they were entitled to dual tax relief, giving a massive incentive for friends to club together and get their feet on the bottom rung of the housing ladder.

Consequently, the Christmas period of that year was one of considerable euphoria, with everyone buoyant and harbouring optimistic feelings for the year ahead. Heady days and nights created a party atmosphere, which was exacerbated by the onset of the festive period.

The Christmas party for Cowell Ruben & Co. was scheduled to be held at Claridges on Brook Street, with no expense spared and all rooms to be had at a discount for any of the employees. It was an invitation to disaster which was frequently accepted and regretted in equal measures the following day when recriminations set in.

For the graduates, it was the end of their probationary period, a confirmation of a new position in the world and a taste of things to come. The three were looking forward to it immensely; a chance to let their hair down, meet others on a less formal basis and play the age old games of politics and romance as the mood took them.

The whole of the staff from CR were there, as it was a three line whip to attend with no exceptions short of a deathbed excuse, even holidays taken at this time of year were frowned upon. The staff started to arrive at around 7.o'clock filing through to the bar prior to being seated in one of the main banqueting halls for the formal dinner.

Everyone was dressed in their finery with the girls in cocktail dresses, the men in black tie, and the Scottish contingent led by Angus, dressed in the traditional regalia including the kilt.

"So tell me Angus," Claire taunted, coming upon Angus as he entered the main hall." What DO you boys wear under the kilt?"

Angus turned. *She looked stunning,* he thought. And Claire was definitely turning heads. She was dressed in a black, lace covered silk dress, which by virtue of the lace, looked almost completely diaphanous and very sexy with her hair piled up on her head. A shot silk wrap encased her shoulders and she wore long back evening gloves, black stockings and delicate high heels.

"If you're lucky you might find out later," he replied, exaggerating his accent to its full homeland level, clearly intoxicated by the sight of her.

"Dream on, baby!" she retorted and turned on her heel to sashay away. Over the past three months Angus had been pursuing Claire relentlessly, both inside and outside office hours, with mutual watering holes being frequented by both of them. The result was that that they had spent much time in each other's company, albeit as part of a group. To date, Claire had resisted all attempts to go on a dedicated date with Angus, although she had to admit that he was great company. But she did not fancy being thought of a one of his "squeezes" as she explained to Jemma and Mike, who had now become the worst kept secret at CR.

"It's a wee nip I'll be bound," exclaimed Rupert arriving on the scene in time to join in the fun and doing an appalling mock, Scottish accent. Even Angus laughed at the quip but his eyes still followed Claire across the floor.

They were soon seated at their tables and dinner began in earnest with speeches afterwards by the two senior partners, one of whom had retired and only acted as a consultant. Paul Ruben's speech was, as ever, charismatic and inspiring, encouraging the "team at CR" to continue to strive for excellence in an increasingly exciting market and prophesising great and better things to come for the new year.

After dinner, the dancing started and Rupert who had been making up to a particularly attractive blond secretary from Investment, called Kate, was first onto the dance floor. He'd had his eye on her for two or three weeks and was not surprised to learn that the investment team had odds of five to one against anyone succeeding, as Angus and three others had tried with no success.

Although he could not help feeling a mixture of surprise and jealousy as he saw that Angus appeared to be finally making head way with Claire, he knew he had no right to feel jealous or proprietorial. But he could not help it, particularly with a person of Angus' reputation. He therefore swung himself even more into the task of seducing Kate.

As the party broke up, they were one of the last couples to leave and it transpired that Kate had pre-booked a room as she lived a long way out in North London. Giggling on the way to the lift, Rupert's eyes met briefly with Claire's, who was arm in arm with Angus on their way to get a cab. Was that a shrug of regret he saw in her eyes, or triumph or pain? The expression flitted across her face too briefly to catch and was replaced very quickly by a knowing smile and a hearty wave goodnight in his direction.

They got a cab from the hotel and headed for Claire's flat in Chelsea. Angus put a tentative arm around Claire's shoulders and found to his delight that it was not rebuffed. *Not a quick grope this time*, he thought, thinking out his strategy in advance and delighted that after weeks of pursuit, he finally had his quarry snared. The cab arrived at her flat and she alighted out of the door first.

"I'm paying for this Angus. Give the driver your address, it's on me."

"What do you mean, no night cap?" he said furiously, amazed and frustrated that he was so close.

"I'm too pissed Angus, it's not right. We'd just regret it later. Sorry but no. Goodnight sweetie." She blew him a kiss and swiftly closed the cab door, leaving Angus with only the intoxicating smell of her perfume to take away.

The cab journey home was a long one and Angus fumed the whole way. It was too late, he decided, to call Susannah. Claire always seemed in control he reflected, no matter which way he turned or what tactic he tried. He cursed to himself and vowed to get a date with her in the New Year.

CHAPTER 8

I t had been nearly a year since Simions' partner had been pushed into the gorge in Bristol. Simions reflected how the man's death had changed the dynamic of his business; no longer was he restrained to work within legal parameters. He could, and had, engaged in a very sophisticated corporate espionage scheme that had proved, so far, very fruitful to him. His company, MAS Investments, had tripled their profit on the previous year and it was only the start. Greater things were around the corner.

Whilst the employees of CR recovered from the previous nights' celebrations, he and David Shingler meet up for their own end of year celebratory lunch. Shingler, a sleeping partner to his firm and an agent in his own right, had been the perfect foil to his temperance. Simions wanted order and calm, but sometimes it had been necessary to step to the other side of the fence and Shingler had been the man to facilitate this.

They met at his Manchester Square offices and proceeded to his club for lunch. The Carlton was discreet, served excellent food and there was always a quiet corner where they would not be overheard.

After the waiter took the first course, they were able to speak freely.

"It's been a great year, Paul. But we need cash flow. We'll need another sale of property to fund everything," he finished vaguely knowing that even here they could be overheard.

"Agreed. It's been a long pull, but no one suspects and we have the market tied up. Virtually nothing moves without us knowing about it. We can divert the money as we wish."

"I know we've discussed this before but I want to consider a move into more recreational areas. Especially through our clubs."

"You know I don't like that. It's still too close to home. Look we've got great legitimate transactions; the market cornered and an untraceable way to create cash. Why risk screwing it up?" he exclaimed.

Shingler held up a placatory hand, never happy to be the junior partner in the relationship. But it had always been Simions' money and therefore his final decision.

"Fine, just a thought, just a thought."

Simions looked away, pleased and yet disturbed that his erstwhile partner still wanted to progress into murkier and more risky waters. He did not know that Shingler had already put into place the distribution within the clubs.

Deliberately changing the subject to avoid any further discussion on these lines Shingler asked: "How are all your placements going?"

"Yes, very well. One in particular was an excellent find, Miss Carmichael. Just proved very valuable to me in our last project," he said.

"Yes, I've heard good reports from Pauline on her. As you say;

a good find. Maybe I could use her for some agency work in due course."

"Possibly. But you know I prefer to keep the two areas separate. Safer that way."

Shingler shrugged in acquiescence and proceeded to start his main course that had just arrived.

Now six months in, each of the graduates was allocated to their final department of choice. Claire, as promised, was to move to Retail under Tom Lovich, Rupert to the Industrial Department under Martin Head and Mike was to go into Investment, where he really wanted to eventually settle.

"No more bog roles and moaning tenants," he read the internal memo and cheered, despite a massive hangover from the night before. He had returned discreetly to his apartment with Jemma to polish off one more glass of brandy. Over the last months, their romance had blossomed into becoming secret lovers and trying, for the most part successfully, to keep their romance a secret at CR. *Now it would be easier*, he thought, as they would be in separate departments and whilst they both enjoyed each other's company, the relationship was taking on an alarming intensity. They both felt it would benefit from a little breathing space.

"Hah, you'll miss all this when you're gone. It's all "Yah merchants" and smoothies down there, you'll come crawling back for a taste of real life," she taunted.

"Oh yah, absolutely. I think all moaning tenants should be put against a wall and shot," he replied.

"Something tells me you're going to do very well in Investment," she said sarcastically. From Jemma's view point, it was perfect timing. She was surprised at how well they had got on right from the beginning and although it had begun slowly, the sex was fantastic. She thought back to last night and blushed slightly thinking of their loving making until the early hours.

Jemma had, she reflected, never found a lover who understood her body the way "Ringo" did. She delighted in the pleasure that caused her to act with unrestrained passion and imagination which consumed them both.

Rupert for his part, was also pleased, as Industrial was one step closer to retail warehousing, the new sector in which to become involved; Simion's sector.

CHAPTER 9

LONDON, November 1988

She slammed closed the door to her flat, with a crash that made her feel slightly better; furious at the departing figure for the betrayal and insults. She went up the short flight of stairs to the internal landing, stamping her feet in frustration and anger at him. *I still cannot believe it,* she thought to herself, *the arrogance and moral superiority was incredible.*

She shook her head as if to shake off the assault, as a dog shakes water from its coat. Words unsaid buzzed in her head, she wanted to vent her spleen on something or someone. There was nothing to hand. Instead, she opened the door to the drinks cupboard took down the bottle; picked up the nearly empty tumbler and poured herself another stiff whisky. She felt the amber liquid pass down her throat, burning as it went, shooting straight into her bloodstream; the effect was almost instantaneous. After a minute, her muscles started to relax as the alcohol entered her system. She brought the cool glass up to her forehead and rolled it backwards and forwards, closing her eyes.

The anger gone, her shoulders slumped; she started to cry quietly, gentle tears ran down her face, sobs racked her body. Why now, she *thought, when things were just going right? She poured a second whisky and took a large gulp. The doorbell went again, its sharp note buffeting its way into her consciousness with a jolt. Well, she thought, if he thinks that he could just come back and all would be forgiven, he had another think coming.*

She was about to run down to the door and then hesitated, make him wait, one more buzz. The doorbell went again; it had to be him as it was the internal bell, inside the building. Persistently it went a third time; keen, I'll give him that, she thought. Oh well, she mused, I never liked it much anyway flicking the pieces of the broken vase away from the door with her foot, so that it would open wider. Running perfunctory fingers through her hair she turned the locks and opened the door.

"Well!" she said as she looked up "I suppose you've come to-"

She stopped dead. It was a woman, a stranger; well dressed, in a smart two piece suit, early thirties, with a clipboard and a handbag, which she juggled rather awkwardly, trying to free a gloved hand. She smiled, disarmingly, showing a slightly chipped front tooth and a small scar on her left cheek.

"Good evening" she said "Have I come at a bad time?"

"Well no, that is yes, but... sorry, I was expecting someone else. How can I help you?"

"I'm Tina Bright, from Turner and Ewell estate agents," she offered a gloved hand to be shook. "I have an appointment for 7.30pm. It is flat 6 isn't it, Miss Gardner?"

"Flat 6, yes, but not Miss Gardner. You must have something wrong."

The woman's face dropped in dismay.

"Oh no, this is my first time, could you just wait while I phone my office?"

"Yah, of course, no problem." The ludicrous situation appealed to her sense of humour, here she was on the brink of a nervous breakdown and this poor woman seemed in worse straits. The agent struggled

with her hand bag to pull out a large, bulky, mobile phone.

"Oh don't bother with that, they never work here anyway; the signal is bad, the walls are too thick. Come on in and use my phone."

"That's terribly kind" she uttered. "I feel so foolish, I must have the wrong flat."

"Oh, no problem." she said waving her hand nonchalantly.

Miss Bright began to follow her up the inner stairs of the flat. As she reached the main landing, she removed her gloved hand from her jacket pocket, took a swift stride and reached her hand around in front of the other woman's face, clamping the white pad soaked in a highly diluted etorphine solution over her mouth and nose. Her other arm dropped the handbag and clipboard, before trapping the woman's arms: her victim struggled for only a matter of seconds, then slumped into unconsciousness.

The woman calling herself Miss Bright, caught the recumbent form carefully, slipping her arm under her legs to support the unconscious woman. She picked her up and carried her to the bedroom, laying her gently onto the bed, leaving no friction or scuff marks on the carpet.

Miss Bright went out of the bedroom, into the kitchen and seeing the whisky bottle she smiled to herself. Carefully she picked it up in her gloved hand and returned to the bedroom. She gently lifted the sleeping woman into a semi elevated position and poured the remaining contents of the bottle bit, by bit, down her throat. The unconscious figure began to stir gently, then dropped back into a fitful slumber. Miss Bright looked at her watch; five minutes so far; another ten to ensure that the original knockout chemical was out of her system.

While the minutes ticked by, she removed the other women's outer clothes; leaving her just in her underwear, pulled back the bed clothes and lay her carefully length ways down the bed. She turned on the side lights, and looking through the record collection, selected a mournful ballad, placing it on the turntable.

She retrieved her hand bag from the hall and took a small bottle, syringe and cellophane packets from it. She carefully wrapped the hand of the sleeping women's hand around the bottle, using the other to encase the syringe, filling it with the solution. She glanced at her watch one final time and injected the contents between the toes of the comatose figure. As the needle pricked the comatose woman twitched; her eyes opened briefly in uncomprehending pain, then slumped back again, she twitched in spasm one final time and then was still.

Quickly, Miss Bright switched off the top light, placed the cellophane packages in an open packet of sugar in the kitchen cupboard, collected her belongings and went down the stairs closing the door behind her.

CHAPTER 10

LONDON, June 1987

The summer of '87 was progressing well for Rupert; he had his first deal in the lawyer's hands. Bought on the open market, in competition with others, it was for a small development company specialising in the conversion of large industrial units into small, nursery units. Rupert had been thrilled, especially as it was the result of one of his old university friends giving him "an early" tip off, which allowed him to place it with his preferred "runner" who proved to be successful in their bid.

He felt that despite his successful acquisition of the site, he was not interested in the aftermath of dealing with tenants and getting down to the nitty gritty of letting the units. Like Mike Ringer, he had unknowingly succumbed to a disease of the 80's: he had become a deal junkie. He was only interested in the kill and the glory of doing deals almost for their own sake, despite the fees generated. In this his confidence rose, his character became more aggressive and his reputation in the market increased.

To this end he was canvassing specific areas in search of suitable sites for development. A time consuming task but one that he enjoyed. Once he identified a potential site and established the names of the freeholders Rupert was then approaching and following up clients with the potential interest to buy the site.

The work was incredibly speculative, where one fell or rose by one's own ability. It was the ethos of CR in a nutshell and Rupert had embraced it with glee.

After his last foray, he had found a potential gem of a site in the "Golden Triangle" area of Watford, St Albans and Hemel Hempstead. The problem was he needed a client to purchase the huge 10 acre site. So for the moment, he stalled in attempt to come up with an answer, knowing that if he asked for help, he would lose control of the deal.

Sat in Boswells after another hard day trying to find an answer, Rupert felt spent. He had arranged to meet Claire for a drink in an attempt to broach the subject to see if she had any bright ideas to his ongoing dilemma.

Claire's career in retail was flying. Perhaps not on the same scale as Rupert's but she was making amazing contacts on the client side and information was everything. She really was making it in a man's world; learning under Tom's tutelage how to manipulate and use her obvious attractions to her advantage and show off her innate ability.

"Well, funnily enough I do actually," she answered. "Do you remember that deal I did last year in Watford? We had those two other units that were going begging because Capital didn't want any more exposure in the town?"

"Yes."

"Well, Tom suggested that we put them to MAS Investments. Now, in the normal course of things they would not be looking at such a small lot size, it was only £3.5m. However, the owner Paul Simions, has his own private pension fund and a special requirement for small lot sizes.

"So, I still don't really see how that helps me."

"I think it does, you see, because I met Simions with Tom, just for an initial meeting almost for the experience alone. Anyway he stated that he was looking for larger projects where he could add value by developing, rather than just pure investment. Now we know he likes Hertfordshire, he has an appetite for development and is prepared to take on planning battles. What more do you want?"

"Claire, my dear, you're a star," he complimented her.

"Well, it will cost you. Mine's a G & T."

"Just one thing, is this Tom's exclusive client, do I have to go through him?"

"I would anyway, it will give you cover. I guarantee he won't steal your deal and he will give you good tactical advice."

"What like how many buttons to undo?" He grinned at his rejoinder.

"You don't have the figure for it darling, trust me," she replied tartly raising her glass. And the price has just gone up to dinner."

"My pleasure. But I thought that was Angus' province?"

"Oh, not you as well. Yes, well there is some smoke and fire, without wishing to mix my metaphors but I'm still not sure and no, it hasn't been consummated yet. Apart from that, no comment."

"Ok, Ok only joking," he said holding up his hands in mock surrender.

"Sorry, I just hate being known as another of Angus' conquests. Let's drop the subject and have a good evening without mentioning the Scottish hooligan again."

"Done."

They moved on to an Italian restaurant around the corner in Dover Street and not for the first time they both thought about what might have been if the relationship had developed further at university. At the end of the meal and the evening, they walked arm in arm to get a cab on Piccadilly. Claire spotted one and whistled with two fingers in her mouth. Rupert grinned and did his best George Peppard impersonation

"*I never have, been able to do that.*"

"*Oh it's easy. You just put your fingers together and blow,*" she replied copying Audrey Hepburn's inimitable, mellifluous tones.

They both grinned at the old joke between them; fitting easily into the compatible, easy, platonic relationship. They arrived at their destination, paid for the cab and stood opposite each other to say goodnight. Rupert politely refused an invitation for a nightcap, sensing for a brief moment a hint of tension between them. He kissed her lightly goodnight and turned to walk the short distance home without turning around, although he could feel her eyes on his back.

He sighed to himself as he heard her door click closed. He still had Kate, and Claire, well, she had Angus; or would one day, he mused.

The next day at the office he went up to see Tom Lovich and explained the situation, together with his problem of who to run the deal with. Tom, as Claire had predicted was enthusiastic and encouraging. He also thought, not for the first time, that Claire had a good agents' head on her shoulders.

"Ok, here's what we'll do. I'll set up a meeting with Paul Simions at MAS, on another subject entirely, which I have to do anyway. That way we'll get our foot in the door, see the main man and not one of his minions, who would probably pooh pooh it anyway. Also, by seeing him face to face, it will have a lot better chance of succeeding and stop us being shafted on the introduction."

"Why would that happen? We are going to introduce it exclusively to him off the market," Rupert asked rather puzzled.

"Paul Simions, although a good operator, always brings in a firm of agents called Shingler Cariss to advise on his bigger projects, especially where there is a possibility of retail in the future. No one has ever got to the bottom of the relationship, but it is very strong and while he always pays full fees, he'll wriggle any way he can, given half a chance.

The joint senior partner is one David Shingler, who is a smarmy, arrogant, little shit and I wouldn't trust him as far as I could kick him. If anyone would try and steal the deal it would be him. Also, this scheme, if it goes ahead, will want funding. MAS never bank role their own developments and try to get everything off balance sheet as soon as they can. So we will roll in the undeniable talents of Hugo Curtiss. You know Hugo, right?"

"Head of investment?"

Tom nodded. "That way, we'll ensure that CR get a share of all of the pie. It will be a complicated deal and Shingler doesn't have the same expertise as Hugo."

"I see, it all sounds rather Machiavellian. Would we be better going somewhere else?" Rupert questioned rather naively.

"No, MAS is a good call and there is no one more tenacious. Once Simions gets his teeth into something he never lets go until he gets what he wants. We'll run it with him and see how we go."

Rupert felt that he was already out of his depth and was pleased to have Tom holding his hand. On the plus side, he was still very excited and his learning curve was going through the roof.

The meeting was set up for Friday morning at MAS's offices in Manchester Square. Tom and Rupert arrived by cab in the square. It had classic Georgian architecture of white stuccoed buildings of elegant proportions, surrounding a small wrought iron fenced park in the centre. To the north side was the famous Wallace Collection art gallery. A short flight of stone steps led up to the black painted front door.

"Oh, I know where we are now," Rupert exclaimed. "Boswells is just around the corner.

"That's what I like; the mark of a true agent, knows his way around West End by the bars," Tom commented.

They buzzed the intercom, announced themselves and entered through the main door. The reception area was completely different to that of Capital Assurance. It was heavily carpeted, beautifully, yet discreetly lit, with classically upholstered sofas facing each other across a coffee table laid out with newspapers and magazines together with a press cutting book relating to MAS Investments.

Tom walked up to the lovely blond receptionist, who smiled in recognition, and confirmed the meeting.

They both sat down, whilst Rupert began to flick through the press cuttings. Tom had explained, on the way over, a little about MAS, including the rather unfortunate incident with Paul Simions' partner, who had committed suicide by jumping off the Clifton Suspension bridge some three years ago, with an odd note left behind and a total mystery as to motive.

"So don't mention suicides," he had chided

There was of course, no mention of this in the press cuttings, just slick reporting chronicling the meteoric growth of the company which seemed to go from strength to strength.

After five minutes, a smoothly groomed secretary (another long legged blond) appeared who escorted them up to the top floor of the building. Upon leaving the lift they were faced with the same immaculate décor: deep carpet and light airy space, all exquisitely created. The door opened into an office which could only be described as beautiful. Natural light entering from roof lights created a feeling of extra space. Original cornice work and contrastingly modern furniture, of impeccable taste, which could so easily have clashed with the room, was perfectly matched and gave the office a mature, professional touch.

The principal desk dominated the room; reflecting the personality of the figure who sat behind it; almost in profile due to the harshness of the sunlight. He seemed vaguely familiar to Rupert, who racked his memory trying to remember where he had seen him before. He put it down to the publicity photos he had seen downstairs.

Paul Simions replaced the telephone receiver precisely, almost delicately, as he did most things in his life. He stood up and walked around his desk in a measured way. He was a man of medium height and build with steel grey hair, gaunt, almost hollow cheek bones, startling grey blue eyes and a smile which did not reach them. He was still lightly tanned after a recent foreign holiday which was set off to good effect by his navy suit of immaculate tailoring.

As he extended his hand he commented; "Good of you to come over Tom, I hope you have some good news for me."

There was no direct menace as such, just a hint of arrogance and the feeling that he always expected people to obey him. He was introduced to Rupert, who felt that his soul was being read and analysed before his very eyes.

"Good morning," he said and immediately turned his attention back to Tom in a curt dismissive manner before Rupert could even utter a polite reply.

"What, no Claire today? I am disappointed, she rather brightened up my day when she was last here," he said smoothly.

"Ah, sorry we keep her for special occasions only; weddings, bar mitzvahs, that sort of thing," Tom joked.

They all sat down, coffee was brought in by one of the lovely secretaries, who left discreetly, leaving only a trail of perfume behind. The discussion centred around the business that Tom had come to discuss. Rupert perceived Simions to be arrogant, precise and rude beyond belief. He jumped off at tangents, cutting in on a course of reason, overriding arguments with a deprecatory wave of his hand. He was a prize A1 bastard, Rupert decided.

"Right is that it?" he said as things came to an end. "I've another meeting in 10 minutes."

"Actually no," Tom responded, "we have another proposition for you, care of Rupert here. It is good and I am sure you won't be disappointed," he finished strongly.

Simions raised his flinty eyes in the direction of Rupert, lifted his arm to look at his gold Rolex and stared straight ahead.

"Ten minutes. What have you got?"

Rupert had rehearsed this in his head for days; Tom had warned him what it would be like.

"I have found a site in Hertfordshire, within the "Golden Triangle" area annexed by two major roads, one of which is soon to be upgraded to a dual carriage way leading straight to the motorway," he put a copy of the road atlas on the table before them.

"It is-"

"When you say "found a site"; what do you mean? Who's on it? What is it used for?"

"Let me explain," Rupert continued, keeping his temper and refraining from being too aggressive. "I canvassed the current owners, who are in occupation as an engineering company, Cauldron Domestics, who not only distribute but also have a small wholesale operation on part of the site. They make stainless steel cook ware. They trade as Stainless Cook, you may have heard of-"

"How big's the site?"

"10 acres from the ordnance survey sheet. But it's all flat, usable land, with good access and large frontage to the road. I have checked with the Highway Authority and provisions have been made in the new road documents to allow a traffic light, governed slip road. It will give perfect access."

"Will the owner sell and at what price?"

"Yes, he will. Or so I've been told by-"

"By whom?"

"The MD. I have a letter and have made numerous telephone calls but he won't release any more information until I name my client, hence the meeting today with you."

"Why does he want to sell?"

"He has been canvassed before; but now the road is going in he sees pound signs, and does not really need to be in such a high profile spot."

"Have you taken this to anyone else?" Simions asked, his eyes boring in to Rupert.

"No, I went to Tom with it," he said nodding in Tom's direction, "and we decided to come to you first".

Simions eyed Rupert again, as if reassessing him.

"Do you know what Retail Warehousing is?" he asked.

"Industrial sheds with planning consent?" he offered, thanking God he had spent so much time around the industrial boys.

"Exactly, just sheds with planning consent for retail sales and some fancy paintwork! The key to this site is planning."

They went over some more details with him, his next meeting forgotten. The more they talked, the more animated he became and some small degree of emotion apparent in his manner.

"Right," he finally said, "you tee up the meeting with the MD. I'll get my people on to it." Simions, got up and shook hands, first with Rupert and then with Tom.

"Oh," he said, almost as an afterthought, manner vague as though it had only just occurred to him. "We'll have to bring in Shingler Cariss for the Retail Warehouse input, alongside yourselves of course," he finished smoothly.

"Of course, we'll send our letter of confirmation across tomorrow confirming terms of engagement and our fees, just to keep it all straight. Usual terms of introduction, especially as we brought it to you off the market?" Tom finished.

The two expert fencers, fought their position; smiling all the time yet, understanding the subtle nuances that were being made and sought throughout the game.

"Of course, you know we always pay our fees to good agents like yourselves."

Then to Rupert. "Thank you for this I look forward to meeting you at their offices."

Rupert grinned. "Indeed. I'll be back to you today, hopefully."

They were shown down stairs by one of the blonds, smiling falsely to them as she showed them out. Once outside and down the steps, Rupert let out a long sigh.

"What a bastard!" he said.

Tom grinned.

"You should see him when something goes wrong. All the toys come out of the pram. Well done, you handled him well. He always interrupts and baits people to get a reaction of some sort."

"You called it right over the Shingler Cariss issue. Why does he always bring them in, I wonder?"

"We'll probably never know, some dodgy deal or other. OK, we, or rather you, have work to do now. Draft out a letter of confirmation setting out all the information you've provided and we'll kick it into shape and get it off to him asap."

As they made their way back to office, they cut through St. Christopher's Place, a new development between Barrett Street, leading to Oxford Street. The open-plan piazza was bathed in sunlight and the various bars and cafe's had tables and chairs out on the pedestrianised area. They decided to stop for a beer to celebrate and to watch the parade of girls pass by in low tops and short skirts.

"I'll say one thing for him though, he certainly has some great looking women working there," Rupert commented as their first beer arrived.

"Mmm, he certainly likes pretty things around him. Typical "boy done good", straight from the Little Italy slums, through elocution lessons up to the West End." Tom added cynically.

"Really? Not that it surprises me that much; he tries too hard with the accent and the manner, too precise, too controlled. What did his name used to be then, Paulo Simione?"

"Yes. How did you guess?" Tom looked hard again at Rupert, considering him in a new light.

Rupert shrugged.

"Yea, he's done well but I wouldn't want to cross him or I might end up jumping off a bridge. Come on Rupert, enough maudlin talk, get another round in," he chided.

Just as Rupert stood up to do as he was told, he spotted a familiar figure on the other side of the road walking down James Street from the direction of Manchester Square. It was the temp with the gold bangles.

"Talking of girls; look there's that temp who worked in retail."

They both stared across.

"Oh yes, Nana Mouskouri. Now you listen to Uncle Tom and stick with Kate."

"Is that her name?" he asked, ignoring Tom's advice.

"No idea, that's just what we called her. Don't change the subject, how is Kate?"

"Oh on and off you know, on and off," he said vaguely. *To tell the truth*, he thought, *more off than on at the moment*. He knew it was his fault but he had other things on his mind and could not give her the commitment she craved. It would probably finish like all his other relationships and just fade away through lack of interest.

After they had left, Simions drove across the West End with his chauffer at the wheel, gliding through the traffic. He picked up the car phone in the centre console and dialled a number. When it was answered, he made no preamble just went straight in. "David, it's me. I have just had a very interesting discussion with some people from CR. Lovich and a new boy. He has found a very interesting site. Up in the Golden Triangle. Yes I know, just what we are looking for. Why didn't your people find it?" he chided. "Well, that may be but I have reserved your position and will get the boy...Brett - no his surname - to meet with you. But I want a girl ready to get into them through the agency, ok? Say for 2 or 3 weeks time should do it. Get hold of Pauline. Start setting up now and maybe," he mused, "in Claire Sewell's team as well. I will confirm as soon as we know more. Good."

He cut off the call and smiled to himself. They'd sold three properties in Italy in the last 6 months, netting them half a million pounds worth of Lira. It would be eaten up quickly enough with this new venture he knew: bribes had to be met, secretaries paid off and of course Pauline at the agency. But it was worth it now that the deals were rolling in.

The beauty of it was; he was divorced from it all. It was always done through Shingler and he never spoke directly to Pauline, the figurehead of Secs in the City. Nothing could be traced back to him, even though he was a shareholder through an off shore company. That was the benefit of corporate espionage, it was all so distanced.

When Rupert returned to the office, he contacted the MD of Cauldron Domestics and agreed to a meeting on Wednesday of the next week at his offices. He would, in Tom's words, rise or fall on his own merit and no one else could be blamed or praised.

"Just one thing," Tom offered, "a word of warning if Shingler goes and plans a meeting. Try to avoid at all costs, having the meeting at his offices."

"Why?"

"Just trust me. You will be disadvantaged, undermined and taken for a ride. He has some very clever techniques, which all seem to work well on his own territory."

CHAPTER 11

The following Wednesday, Rupert went directly to MAS's offices to go through matters prior to meeting Cauldron and then accepted a lift to Cauldron with Simions in his Jaguar, a chauffeur at the wheel.

On the way they discussed tactics and went over plans for redevelopment. Simions had already got one of his regular architectural practices to draw up schemes. It showed the redevelopment potential for the site, both for its existing use and for retail warehousing. He had run some figures on his own system and these compared favourably with Rupert's own but slightly sharper figures which produced a higher capital value per acre for the site.

The final set of figures and drawings related to a retail warehouse park, with big crinkly tin sheds and, much more importantly, higher rental levels.

"One point still gives me cause for concern, " Rupert said. "The level that we think we need to pay will only justify retail warehouse rents, which in turn means that we need planning permission for retail use.

"The Structure Plan is nearly completed for this area and it only details employment use. How do we get around that? We do not want it to be called in by the Secretary of State, they will bury it for months."

"Just leave that part to me," Simions replied cryptically. "By the way, do I recall correctly that you mentioned that home was rural Warwickshire?"

"Yes, our home is just outside a small village about 15 miles from Solihull."

"Do you shoot?"

"Yes, actually, Father's got half a gun on the local Estate. I was up there at Christmas. But, best of all, we got some rough shooting in over the New Year in Scotland on the Macpherson Estate."

"Good." he replied "I'm arranging a clay shoot not far from here on the Hoo estate in Hertfordshire. I'll get you an invitation. It's in two weeks' time, keep it free."

The answer was abrupt and gave no recourse to continue as they entered the factory complex.

They parked the car and entered the offices at the front of the factory. They were shown up to meet Graham Carpenter, the MD, and the Finance Director, Christopher Wall. Rupert smiled inwardly at how different the two men were; the MD who was short, hard and compact with an innate toughness, honed by many a boardroom battle he had a pugnacious chin that jutted forward below a strong face with small close together eyes. Wall, by contrast, was tall, lean with prematurely receding blond hair. Wire glasses perched on the bridge of his nose, reflecting in front of his clear eyes. They made a very shrewd pair and would not, Rupert supposed, be easy to negotiate with.

"Sit down, sit down please." Carpenter gestured to the chairs. "Kind of you to come in and see us."

Simions introduced MAS Investments and gave a brief, potted history of the company and its objectives; together with a smooth glossy brochure. It all sounded very plausible and placid, with no hint as to the avaricious aggression that lay behind the driving force of the company. When he finished, Rupert, as they had agreed proceeded to give an outline of the events to date and their proposals as they saw them subject - of course - to looking over the factory and land.

"It seems to me," Carpenter interjected smoothly, "that this would be a perfect opportunity to break and show you around the factory in order to give you a better idea of what you are looking at."

On the way around, they discussed the layout of the existing works and the site ratio which represented the amount of land covered by the buildings in relation to the site as a whole.

"High site ratio isn't it Mr. Carpenter? What, nearly 60%? Any redevelopment would only be allowed at 45% which will play havoc with our figures."

"With respect, Mr Brett, that is your problem. Do not forget it was you who approached me, not the other way around."

"True," he said ignoring the rebuff, "but we, of course, wish to offer realistic terms and I only wanted to point out the fact in order to give credence to any offer we should make."

At that moment, Simions cut across.

"Would you accept a subject to planning deal, for say, 6 months? Non-returnable deposit if we fail to get planning."

The change in direction threw both the men for a few seconds, they looked and conferred without actually speaking.

"No. We could not agree to any such terms, even if the resultant figure were higher than those proposed on a speculative basis. We are not gamblers, Mr Simions. In basic terms; we make pots and pans, that is our business. Therefore any offer would have to be without condition."

"You are making it very hard for us to give you the best price."

"I reiterate, it was you who came to us. We are just simple manufacturers, not developers."

There was silence as they continued the tour. Upon returning to the offices they went through ancillary matters as to timing for possible vacation of the site. As the meeting ended, Simions added; "Would you be prepared to do one small thing for us?"

"It depends," Carpenter answered predictably.

"Well, it is only a small thing. But, would you write a letter confirming that you will be relocating in this area and continuing with production? It would just help with, what I perceive to be, a difficult planning battle."

"One which you wish us to be a part of," said Carpenter grinning. "I do not think that will be a problem."

"Good. Thank you gentlemen for your time, it has been most interesting," Simions finished noncommittally.

They shook hands and left the building heading to the waiting car. Once inside the car it moved smoothly forward, through the factory gates and only then, did they permit themselves any sign of emotion.

"Well done," he said softly, "You played the injured innocent just right. I knew they wouldn't go for a subject to planning deal. What they don't realise is that they are sitting on a gold mine, because the value is all in the planning and we're going to get it."

"I can't believe how well it worked just as you said it would," Rupert enthused, caught up in the moment. "But, we are still taking a massive risk on the planning issue and the Structure Plan for the area does not seem to give us any joy either."

The Structure Plan covered the county as a whole and was produced by every Local Authority throughout the country every five to ten years and effectively cast in stone the planning designation for any area of the county. It had for this area given the designation of Employment Uses, which effectively meant manufacturing and distribution warehousing, not retail warehousing, which the planners declared would impact disastrously on a town centre.

Once the plan had been adopted after review it was always an uphill battle to fight it, which would necessitate a costly planning appeal, with limited hope of success. The current plan was near to being adopted and through most of the consultation process, it would only be a matter of weeks before it was passed at Committee.

"Leave the planning problems to me. I have my consultants working on it at the moment," he finished curtly.

The rest of the journey was taken up with discussing timetables and plans for the proposed scheme, together with the numbers that Rupert would run on the computer in order to put forward an offer. They were going to adopt two or three scenarios, none of which would make any reference to retail warehousing.

When he finally returned to the office he spoke to Tom who called an impromptu meeting with Hugo Curtiss from Investment, Martin Head from Industrial and Claire who was starting to concentrate more on the Out-of-Town market that was retail warehousing; it also took her further away from Angus' orbit.

Rupert relayed the details of the meeting to the others who were excited at the prospect of a new development and funding but, also like Rupert, sceptical as to the planning.

"I wonder how he's going to pull this off?" Tom mused.

"Yes, he appears far too confident to be going on a wing and a prayer. Some nefarious practice no doubt." Hugo finished. He had no illusions as to the morality of Paul Simions or his methods for achieving his ends.

"OK," Curtiss continued, "I will speak very carefully to a couple of funds. See what they are looking to fund this at; probably around 7% I should think. Simions certainly won't want it on his balance sheet so they will have to give interim finance as well," he mused almost to himself.

"Interim Finance?" Rupert queried.

"Yes, in simple terms when a developer goes to a fund he can either ask them to buy him out at the end of the deal, he bears all the risk and they pay him a sharper yield, which means more money, or, he can ask to borrow the money from them from day one as the project progresses. This costs the fund more and they have more exposure to the risks of development, but the extra risk means they won't pay such a sharp yield and it will cost them less."

"I see, but why do you have to tread carefully now, wouldn't it be better to get it secured and signed up ready before anyone like David Shingler starts wanging around the market."

"If we give a fund the exact location, one of Ricky Barston's moles will hear about it and it will be, as you so delicately put it, *"wanged around the market"*."

Ricky Barston, Rupert thought, even he had heard of him. The man was incredible. He had come from a corporate background and changed to agency, specialising in development sites. But unlike others, he was not in it for the long haul process of development, just the buying and selling of sites for clients, like a stock broker or City trader. He offered the deals around, non-retained, picking up a fee on the introduction alone, sometimes taking a half or quarter percent, just to get maximum exposure to the market. Some rumour started that he even had a fee on a sixteenth!

His network of contacts was amazing and no one could pin down where he got his information from, although there were a few astute guesses as to corrupt fund managers and agents who sold information for a fee. It was rumoured that he and his side kick, Steve Reid, were making £750,000 a year each on non-retained work just by broking.

Tom broke into his thoughts.

"Right, we'll all work on the various angles. Main thrust down to you Rupert; run the numbers after Simon's input and let's see what you come up with."

They all got up to leave the room, the meeting finished.

"Are you coming out tonight?" Claire asked as they walked along the corridor. "We are all meeting up at Smollensky's and on to a restaurant afterwards, you remembered it's my birthday?"

"Oh shit, Claire! I'm sorry, it had gone right out of my head, but I'll be there don't worry," he promised. "I just have to go over some lease stuff with Martin Sheen.

She shook her head in despair. "You'd better be," she threatened.

CHAPTER 12

That night Claire was out to howl. All her friends were there and Smollenskys was heaving with people; even Rupert managed to put in an appearance after leaving late, but he came with a card and a present which he gave to Claire at the start of the evening whilst she was still sober.

"I know, I know," he held up his hands in mock surrender. "I was '*Sheened*' again. You would of thought I had grown out of it by now," he groaned.

She accepted the present gratefully with a hug and a kiss on the cheek, promising to open it later. The party got into full swing and they proceeded to leave Smollenskys for the Italian restaurant in Chelsea near Claire's home. Then an odd thing happened; Angus bailed out and decided that he was not going on to the restaurant. He gave some feeble excuse which did not seem to wash with Claire.

"Come on Angus, if I have to be up early in the morning so can you. I'm booked in to ride tomorrow at 7.00!"

"Ride?" he queried.

"Oh ya, I've been riding out in Hyde Park every morning for two weeks now before work."

"I knew there was something about your perfume." he chided

She bit: "Ha ha, I use the executive shower in the basement, so stuff you. She changed tack, "Sure you won't stay on?"

"No thanks I must be off."

He kissed her perfunctorily and moved off. Ever the predatory animal, to his mind a birthday party was no place to try and seduce the object of everyone's attention. It just never worked out; the birthday girl was always everyone else's property. He had played the game so far and it was coming to a head and tonight was not the night.

The evening carouselled onwards and to her credit, although very drunk, Claire did not disgrace herself but ended up alone in her flat. *Soon*, she thought, *on my terms, soon.*

She woke with a massive hangover and after two aspirin, and a glass of water, she dressed and set off for Hyde Park stables. The morning air was wonderful; even for London and after an hour on horseback; cantering through the park in the early morning, before the traffic started, she felt revived and refreshed. *A shower at work and she would be ready to face the day*, she thought. She had one final long canter down the sand track with her hat held by the chin strap in her hand and the air blowing through her hair. *Should be ready for polo in two weeks' time*, she thought.

She handed back the horse, a lovely bay thoroughbred, paid and caught a cab to the office.

The basement arrangement was perfect; it had a rear entrance of Seymour Mews that went straight to the shower room; which doubled as a sick room with a daybed. She had a scolding shower, dried her hair and had just finished applying her make up in front of the mirror when a gentle knock sounded at the door. She was dressed in only her knickers, so grabbed a towel to cover her upper body.

"Who is it?"

"It's me." The door inched open to reveal Angus, grinning. "I thought I'd come and scrub your back," he joked.

"How did you get in? I thought I'd locked it."

"Apparently not," he said, half turned to check the door and closed the distance between them deliberately. They were now only two feet apart and Angus could smell *"Poison"* embracing him.

"Angus, this is not a good idea," she said, but her body language was at odds with the words.

He moved closer and kissed her gently on the lips. She responded, forcefully with pent up passion and the realisation that the chase was over, just as she had planned. The towel slid to the floor to reveal, high heavy breasts, with large nipples contracting with arousal. Angus gazed down, admiring the flat stomach, stocking clad legs and skin glowing from exercise. He gripped her harder, crushing her lips with his kiss, as his tongue joined with hers, both of them murmuring together. She slid her hand inside his partly undone shirt and wrenched downwards in a sharp motion, causing the buttons to pop off, and pulled at the belt buckle of his trousers undoing them so they fell to the floor. She put her hand inside and gripped him lightly and began a gentle stroking up and down; feeling him swell to her touch.

He stopped kissing her and moved his lips across her face, down onto her neck and shoulders, cupping her breasts in his hands. She leant back against the daybed on her elbows, thrusting her body forward. Angus took first one breast, then the other in his mouth, sucking the nipples hard, causing her to moan in ecstasy with her head thrown backwards. He gripped one of her breasts and gently cupped it, whilst his mouth moved slowly down her body, over her taught stomach, lower between her spread legs, where he kissed her hard and with one flick of his teeth, removed her flimsy panties.

He probed her deeply with his mouth and tongue; biting gently, sucking, she screamed in lust, bringing up her knees, gripping his hair and pushing him deeper, riding her groin against his mouth, wanting more. Then he stopped; he wanted her now, he moved up over her body, gently spread her legs and just as he was about to enter her she whispered; "No, this way."

Turning, rubbing her bottom against him and looking over her shoulder, eyes half shut with passion; hollowing her back, emphasising her rounded bottom. He entered her from behind and she squirmed against him, gripping him tightly inside. It was like nothing he had experienced before. Her internal muscles gripped and released him like a hand. The climax grew quickly within him, until he could hold on no longer; thrusting for the last time against her. She continued to move, pleasuring herself, he cried in agony and ecstasy, until she finally succumbed, arching her back for the last time, crying out.

They both sagged forward, panting hard, gently perspiring where they touched each other's bodies.

"Wow," he exclaimed "that, was the best," as he hugged her, gently stroking her body.

"Mmmm," she murmured turning to face him "Shit! The door's still open, close it and get some clothes on quickly."

He burst out laughing, realising how embarrassing it could have been. He closed the door quickly and said with more bravado than he felt; "Just adds to the zing."

"Oh, right," then looking over her shoulder with a suddenly shocked expression on her face.

"Oh Tom, morning."

Angus spun around to see an empty room.

"You cow, you really had me going."

She burst out laughing.

"And going you had better, you've got to buy a new shirt before work."

"What?" he exclaimed, looking down. "From where at this time in the morning?"

"Selfridges opens in ten minutes, you'd better get going. Oh and one other thing, if I hear one word of a boast about this in the office, I'll come after these," she said, holding his balls gently, "with a blunt, rusty, knife, *Capito*?"

"OK, I promise," he said. "But how about dinner tonight and we can do this all over again."

"Lovely idea." A lascivious look on her face. "Call me later, and thank goodness I'm no longer in your room."

Claire had been promoted to Senior Surveyor from this week and moved up to the newly formed Development Department.

Angus ran up the stairs from the basement with a huge grin on his face, looking down at the battle honours of his shirt. *Wow, what a fuck*, he thought. Then he stopped. He still felt in his own mind that somehow she had contrived to stay in control as though she had planned both the act and the actions and that she had taken him, not the other way around. *Well, tonight would be different*, he thought, *after dinner- yes. Many thanks!*

Claire for her part was grinning to herself, smiling in deep satisfaction. It had been good and she felt totally in control. It might be different tonight, but for now it was a great feeling of sexual emancipation.

Rupert had been at his desk bright and early, if rather bleary eyed and struggling with the alterations to figures, which he had already faxed across last night, to find a reply by return waiting on his desk this morning. The second set was sent off minutes later and he received a call after about twenty minutes.

"Rupert Brett."

"Simions. The figures are fine, we just need to put it into presentation format, then send off the letter with the lower figures to Carpenter. He'll always expect a bit in it, we'll have to go higher, but protest strongly to convince him it's our best shot, ok?"

"Fine, I still think it's a cracking figure anyway and that he'll be surprised."

"Maybe, we'll see. Oh and one other thing, with regard to the shoot. You have received the licence I sent you for Gavin Knott, the chief planning officer for the council?"

"Yes."

"I want you to take it down to Purdeys in South Audley Street and collect a gun for me. It is to go on my account, but with that licence, not yours or mine, ok? Understood?"

"Yes, but if it is a new registration, I don't think they will allow it out of the shop unless the licence holder is present, will they? But I'll try."

"Do. If there is a problem, call me on my mobile number. I'm having lunch with Knott today in the west end. Speak to you later, good bye."

The call cut off. *And a jolly good morning to you too*, Rupert thought to himself. Now why would he need a gun put onto Knott's licence? No, it couldn't be. Surely this was not the means by which planning would be obtained? Oh but it had to be; hence the certainty of getting consent. It was very clever in a corrupt sort of way. Untraceable, easily deniable, *providing* Simions and evidence for the future to blackmail him if necessary. Simple but clever; no cash just a very expensive present. *What did a Purdey cost these days?* he wondered, £15-16,000? *Plus all the bits. Knott must love his shooting.*

He got a cab down to South Audley Street which pulled up outside Messers. Purdey, situated on the corner and entered the time honoured portals of what he considered to be the greatest gun maker in England, if not the world. The smell of gun oil assailed his nostrils, along with an unhurried aura of class and tranquillity; a haven in the centre of mad London. *His Tiffany's,* he thought to himself with a smile. The wooden floors echoed as he walked across the shop and down the few steps to the gunroom, which was lined with glass cases holding shotguns of various shapes and sizes. He turned to the counter and addressed a bespectacled man wearing a black full length apron over his shirtsleeves.

"Morning, I've come to pick up a shotgun for Paul Simions of MAS investments. I believe you are expecting me."

"Good morning, sir. Yes, Mr. Simions telephoned telling us to expect you. Now, here we are," he said, moving over to a glass case, unlocking it, removing a shotgun and placing it on the viewing table with a padded top located in the centre of the room. "Side by side, single trigger. I will just get the form, sir, to check that everything is in order."

He returned with a standard green Purdey order book and flicked back through the pages to the appropriate place.

"Ah, here we are, sir. Rather unusual this, as we didn't actually measure the gentleman himself. We took the measurements off a rather inferior gun, if I may say so, not at all good practice," he finished, frowning in frustration and semi horror at such a breach of protocol.

Rupert kept a straight face and nodded in agreement, saying nothing.

The man then proceeded to go through the list of specifications: chokes, engraving to the side plates, safe automatic, each item lovingly described and demonstrated. Finally, he handed the gun over to Rupert, who took it feeling the beautiful balance and weight. At only just under 7lbs, it felt incredible. He broke the gun, even though he knew it would be empty, looked down the barrels and closed the breach. He raised it to his shoulder. The Prince of Wales pistol grip fitted beautifully to his hand. He could not help smiling in glee, it was a thing of beauty and there was no other way to describe it. He turned the gun over and there in the magic Purdey gold oval, were the letters GRK. Obviously, Mr. Knott had a middle name.

"Lovely," was all that Rupert could say, realising why such a gift might hold such influence over Knott.

They went over to the counter, and the gun was packed in a car case, along with all the accessories and cartridges. Rupert produced the licence without uttering a word. The details were checked and the assistant looked up to check the photo. He looked puzzled.

"Is this your licence sir?"

"I'm afraid not. I'm picking it up for my friend, the one who telephoned."

"I'm sorry sir, I can't do that without him being here for a first registration."

"Oh, I see." *Damn*, he thought, *I knew it*. He had no choice but to call Simions.

Ten minutes later, they appeared; Simions and another man. He walked over with his customary arrogance as though he owned the shop, but when he spoke it was with a softer tone.

"Morning to you, Masters, sorry about the confusion. Rupert here must have misunderstood my intention. Still no harm done, here is the owner of the licence."

Rupert fumed. Simions had planned it all, knowing that it would not be possible to take a new gun once they checked the licence photograph. Simions indicated his companion; a short stocky man of about forty five with mousey coloured hair parted to the side, brown shrewd eyes, lined skin and a care worn look beyond his years. He was dressed in what Rupert would call a typical Local Authority suit of grey, shiny material with pin-stripes of dark, muted colours, white shirt and red tie.

Rupert forced a smile.

"How do you do, Rupert Brett," he said, shaking hands.

The handshake was limp, the greeting pitiful and not effusive.

He only had eyes for the gun. Like a rabbit caught in the head-lights he stared the way some men ogle a beautiful woman. He had picked up the offered gun, broke it, closed it, held it to his shoulder and pointed to the ceiling. Rupert had some sympathy for how he was feeling but the look of rapture on Knott's face was incredible.

"I wanted it as a surprise for you on the day of the shoot so you could, um, borrow it," Simions interjected suavely. "Trouble is, we need to put it on your licence as it is the first issue and mine is really rather full, would you mind?" he asked plaintively as though Knott was really doing him a favour. It was beautifully done and Knott was hooked. Their eyes met, each understanding the other, no word needed to be spoken "Of course," he said magnanimously. "I should be pleased to help, especially as I will be able to try out the gun."

So the deal was done, thought Rupert. He was looking forward to seeing the events of the day's shoot to see how exactly the handover would be completed. The certificate was signed and the gun packed away in the car case. The account was signed for the sum of £18,700 for the basic gun, Rupert noticed, plus the extras that took the total up to over £25,000. *Some planning notice,* he thought, *probably as much as Knott made in a year with the VAT added on.*

The next week saw the private shoot commence on the Hertfordshire estate. A resident expert was in tow to give begin-ners a helping hand and to effectively coach the more advanced participants, of whom many were veterans of driven shoots in the shires of England. A few of those present were genuine sportsmen lured only by the draw of the countryside and the love of the sport per se. However, the majority were there to be seen to be enthusiasts, loving the act rather than action with no more simpatico for the sport in its rawest form.

Their outfits to Rupert's eyes caused great mirth, some had obviously gone to their tailor and said "dress me for shooting". To which the hapless man had obviously obliged, making them look like an extra from *Toad of Toad Hall*. Some others were obvious townies who were not prepared to change their "jumper and jeans approach" for anyone. A few got it right and it was into this category that Gavin Knott fell. This group had their own guns, handled them professionally and looked the part.

The setting was delightful; rolling countryside with the woods behind providing a dramatic backdrop. The day consisted of clay shooting in the morning from normal traps, across a small hillside. There followed realistic and difficult targets, released from behind cover to emulate birds more accurately.

At the break for lunch, they all gathered around trestle tables where food was laid out with a conspicuous absence of alcohol, which for obvious reasons was not permitted.

One of the other parties noticed Knott's gun.

"Fine looking gun you've got there Gavin. Mind if I have a look?"

"No, of course, be my guest."

The shotgun was duly handed over for inspection. He broke the gun checked it and closed the breach, admiring the balance. He then looked more closely and exclaimed.

"My God, a Purdey! No wonder the balance is superb. You must be doing alright, Gavin," he remarked pointedly.

"Ah, I was fortunate, a legacy, it was a holiday or a second hand Purdey. The wife wasn't very happy though," he joked. Rupert looked across first at Knott and then Simions, the latter had a slight grin etched into the corners of his mouth and gave Rupert a small, almost imperceptible nod. The thirty pieces of silver had been taken, Rupert thought. Planning would no longer be a gamble, of that he was certain.

The next few days were very tense for both Rupert and Simions, as predicted the initial bid had been rejected by Carpenter. They had had to increase the offer by over £250,000 for it to be accepted but it was still nowhere near the "hope value" that would be achieved if planning were to be granted for retail consent. It also gave Rupert the opportunity to get one last condition accepted; that the contract be signed within two weeks, just prior to the fully revised copy of the new Structure Plan being published.

It was a gamble, the lawyers would have to work around the clock, as Rupert had no doubt that the area would be zoned for retail in the new plan, paving the way for a full blown consent.

The next two weeks were frantic and included the letter of support from Carpenter *prior* to him seeing the planning application and the revised Structure Plan. The lawyers were for once very good, not only thorough, but pragmatic in their approach. *Whatever he is paying them,* Rupert thought, *they are worth it.* All searches and due diligence were completed in time and the contracts were exchanged one day before the plan came out and completion was one week later, allowing time for all monies to cleared.

The following day Rupert was at the council offices to see the first copy for public display of the Structure Plan. Just as he suspected, the area to the front of the industrial estate, including other frontages had been zoned as retail for future use! The reason given:

"To help build integrity and synergise the area, to alleviate traffic congestion from neighbouring town centres and to provide....blah, blah..." *Bullshit, typical Local Authority bullshit,* Rupert thought. *Well for once it is to our advantage, so what the hell.*

However he was not so prosaic at the end of the week when he received a call from Graham Carpenter of Cauldron Domestics, who, when unable to get hold of Simions, wanted to vent his spleen on someone and that someone was Rupert.

"What the hell is going on?" he demanded.

"I'm sorry, Mr Carpenter, I don't understand. What do you mean?" Rupert replied in his most vague and pompous way.

"Don't play games with me young man You know exactly what I mean. The site you paid for was zoned for Industrial, now the plan comes out and its rezoned for retail. How did he do it, eh? Bribe a planner or three? I will raise hell over this. It's corruption, that's what it is, corruption!"

"I should be very careful if I were you, Mr Carpenter. The slander laws are very actionable on such statements."

"Only, when proved false. Goodbye!" he slammed the phone down.

Rupert grinned and immediately called Simions, explaining what had happened, word for word.

"Let him say what he wants and just maintain your stance on legal action. It will go no further and what's more there is no evidence. Other than that we shall be offering Section 52 agreements to pay for road improvements, more car parking and all the usual legitimate planning stops."

"Ok, will do. But in the meantime do we press on with a formal planning application for the site.?"

"Yes and tenant demand. I want a full list of potential tenants, with expected rents and any premiums payable, also funding. Speak to Hugo Curtiss and liaise with David Shingler on both matters; he must be kept informed."

"Of course," replied Rupert.

"Good, I await to hear from you and, er, well done," he finished.

"Thank you, will do." *My God*, thought Rupert, *I've made it. Praise from Simions.*

The next few weeks proved Simions correct; rumpus in the local paper, allegation, counter allegation and finally the threat of legal action for slander, with a heavy duty writ served on Carpenter with the joint appellants being Simions and the Council. Predictably, he backed down and made a formal, begrudging apology. A formal planning application was lodged with the council's backing to approve. *It did not pay a man to fight against Simions,* thought Rupert.

CHAPTER 13

CR offices LONDON, Autumn 87

The markets were becoming ever more heated. The Big Bang in the city had gone as everyone suspected, revolutionising share dealing. More importantly to the individuals concerned, it caused City bonuses for individuals to double or even triple. More Porsches and flash yuppies were seen than ever before, the feeling of optimism could, it felt, never end. Consumerism was everything, hedonistic days of champagne, parties and the new film Wall Street. Gordon Geko, said it all with the most famous line in the film "Lunch is for wimps!" A doctrine that everyone seemed to embody; power breakfasts were becoming the norm, with the constant striving to obtain information and to run faster than the competition.

Prices for land and buildings were increasing at a rate never previously known. So much so, that it was possible to "turn on" a site or buildings, whilst only just having exchanged on the deal before completion of the purchase. Sometimes for ten or twenty percent profit!

In this atmosphere of inflation, it was easy for the unwary

to get caught out and the ruthless to exploit any loop hole they could.

In the investment department, Mike Ringham was at the sharp end and learning more than a few of the tricks. He was enjoying himself immensely and had come to love the cut and thrust of investment as the fastest moving of all the sectors.

Monday morning, after a particularly heavy weekend, Rupert and Mike were having an early morning coffee, on the pretext of meeting Mike's friend, Julian Charteris who would be arriving in the next ten minutes with a colleague.

"It's incredible," Mike exclaimed. "We're on a deal treadmill, with yields getting harder pushing the prices up and the stock keeps on walking out of the door. But what is worrying, is that some of the old rules are being eroded. I offered a deal, a forward funding, to United Assurance Society to buy a retail warehouse park which has just got planning but the developer only has an option on it; doesn't actually own it, d'yuh see?"

"Yes."

"Well, once all the information was provided, they, without referring to me, went straight to the owners direct, bid them more money than the developer and bought the contract and broke the option agreement!"

"UAS did that? Bastards. But they're a supposedly respectable fund. I bet you were Mr Popular with the agents," Rupert laughed.

"Oh don't, it was Julian. He went ape shit. But guess who the fund used to broker the deal? David Shingler. So beware," he warned. "That man has a lot of fingers in a lot of pies."

"But did you get your fee?"

"Surprisingly yes, but it took a call from Hugo Curtiss and old man Cowell himself, to make them see the light."

"So you dealing?". Mike asked the time honoured question.

"Yes, I'm dealing," the response from Rupert.

It had become the mantra of the agents in this maelstrom of deals. Rupert felt it as much as Ringo; the suits he wore were louder, confidence brasher, nothing they felt could stop them in this crazy bull market.

"Luckily no danger of that happening on our scheme. We completed last week and now it's straight into planning and tenant demand as you know, hence the meeting with Julian's colleague this morning. He won't blast it around the market will he, bearing in mind that he will have a lot of the funding information?" Rupert said alarmed.

"A man from Halbern & Beams blast something around the market, perish the thought. There are still some standards you know," he mocked in his foppish way.

"But just be a little wary, I hear his colleague from Retail Warehousing has been seen with Ricky Barston on more than one occasion and he *will* blast it around."

"Ricky Barston, that man gets everywhere. What do think? He's on a backhander to supply tenant information to get an introduction in?"

"It doesn't take much and all they need is a tenant line up, with a few rents thrown in," he finished cynically.

At that moment Julian arrived with his colleague in tow, who proved to be a man of about twenty five, medium height dressed in a grey, Spivey, double breasted suit with very wide lapels. *Like its owner*, Rupert mused to himself.

"This is Richard Lloyd, from our Retail Warehouse Department," Julian said. "Should be able to help you with your tenant demand for the new scheme."

They shook hands, sat down and ordered more coffee. Rupert studied Lloyd more closely; he had fair skin with old pock marks, sandy hair and sharp eyes.

"Where is the delightful Claire? I thought she was your retail warehouse specialist," he mocked slightly, in jest, but with an undertone that Mike did not like.

"Oh, she is signing a new tenant for the scheme and has to be at the legal meeting," he explained. "She's dealing, and at what a rate."

"Yea, I here she's been made up on the back of her latest scheme?"

They confirmed it and continued to chat about market developments and exchanged gossip. Particularly, the recent events with regard to UAS and decided it was a sign of the times.

"Well if they pull stunts like that, they can't expect agents to honour the one introduction at a time rule, and put it to more than one party," Julian concluded.

He was referring to the common practice that agents should only introduce one property to one party at a time. But as the clients became more devious, taking longer to return calls and trying to avoid paying introduction fees the need to back up an introduction with a second runner was becoming more and more pressing. Although strictly against RICS rules. But as they all knew, the clients brought it upon themselves.

After coffee, Richard Lloyd invited Rupert back to the office to go over specifications for his client's retail operation and to look at some artist's impressions of other schemes where they were represented.

They walked into the reception area of Halbern & Beams; a rather clinical affair, of sterile tiles, stainless steel furniture and white walls. *Like some Italian brothel,* Rupert mused. The lift took them to the second floor where there was an open plan area filled with padded dividers in bright, primary colours, that were becoming all the rage, sectioning off secretaries and agents into different compartments.

He walked through the notional corridors following Richard

Lloyd and gazing at the various people along the way; ever the agent trying to glean knowledge as he went and trying to read letters upside down on desks as he passed. His eyes rested on a secretary who seemed familiar for some reason. *Of course,* he thought, *"Nana Mouskouri"*. Straight black hair, black glasses and with the three gold bangles. She half turned and their eyes met. He stopped, smiled and realised that she vaguely recognised him, although she did not return the smile.

"Hi. You were at CR weren't you, in retail?"

"Uh, ya, possibly, on the temp round. Different week, different company." She shrugged her shoulders, smiled wanly, then went straight back to her computer as before. Feeling himself dismissed, Rupert carried on following Lloyd to the glass box at the end of the floor reserved for meetings.

"Why her? She looks like Nana Mouskouri to me. Now, if you want some action," he nodded, "try Tracey over there, great tits and incredible arse, never been known to refuse."

Rupert grinned good humouredly. *What 'a prick'* he thought to himself.

"Well put like that…." he left the words hanging, "but there's something about her," he nodded in the temps direction, "can't figure it out, what's her name?"

"Liz Carmichael, works for that temping agency, started about two years ago with the catchy title…. Sex….?"

"Secs in the City?" Rupert guessed.

"Yes, brilliant play on words, huh?"

"Yes, clever, but you still didn't remember it. Can't be that good."

Lloyd shrugged and proceeded to talk about plans, specifications and deals, as if to cover his embarrassment. They talked for the next half an hour, getting closer to a mutually agreeable rental for the Hertfordshire retail warehouse scheme which had been tentatively named the Golden Triangle Park, marking its significance as the premier park for the area. Provisional terms thrashed out, Rupert shook hands with Richard Lloyd, liking him no more than when they had met and wended his way through to the lift. On his way, he made sure he passed Nana Mouskouri's desk but she was not there. He got to the lift and found to his surprise that she too was on her way out and waiting by the doors.

"Ah, we'll have to stop meeting like this."

She gave him a 'oh God is that the best you can do' smile. At that moment the doors opened and they both stepped into the empty lift. The silence was embarrassing and he was desperately trying for a line.

"Ok, not the most original line under the sun," he said deciding to throw himself on her mercy, "but I keep seeing you around the West end, which I find tantalisingly frustrating."

She raised an eyebrow, amused at his embarrassment, inviting him to continue.

"Oh come on," he pleaded. "Don't make it so hard, at least say something, even if it is only 'piss off'!"

At this point she giggled. It was a lovely, mellifluous sound, which caused Rupert to smile and relax.

"Now that's better, at least I got you to laugh. So now, presuming upon the acquaintance of the last two minutes, can I ask you to dinner?"

"You sound like a character from a Georgette Heyer romance. For that alone, I'll accept," she replied mockingly and when she smiled her face changed, the beauty behind the façade shone through.

"Excellent. How about Friday? Say 7.30, I'll pick you up from wherever you live?"

"Alright, but let's meet in Town, here's my number," she produced a pen and scribbled her number on a piece of paper which she found in her handbag. "You will call?" her insecurity shining through for a brief moment.

"What after this much effort?" he mocked, "Of course."

They parted as the lift discharged them at the reception and thence out into the street. Rupert waved a farewell and proceeded to walk jauntily up toward CR's offices. *Way to go Rups*, he thought. He felt good. A rocky start but a good finish. Hopefully the number was correct.

The remaining days for that week moved slowly but the lettings for GTP (Golden Triangle Park) continued unabated, much to Claire's glee. The scheme was oversubscribed, allowing for premiums over the base rents which funders loved. It was, therefore, a potentially hot property for investors and tenants alike.

Friday night came around slowly and Rupert could not wait. He eagerly anticipated the evening ahead, all thoughts of Kate had been dismissed from his mind.

He had arranged to meet her in Covent Garden as it transpired that she was a North London girl from Hampstead, so Covent Garden seemed easy for both of them. She travelled from the Northern line down to Leicester Square and he along the Central line directly to Covent Garden itself.

They had arranged to meet at the western end of the galleried open area. Housing numerous restaurants and speciality shops it was frequently used by budding opera singers, either resting or waiting for their big break. Such was the case now. A pretty buxom blond, with a round, jolly face was singing beautifully and encouraging the early evening crowd to join her for the chorus of Carmen. A tape machine by her side and an assistant moving through the crowd for offerings and selling her duet tape, which, thought Rupert, if her live singing was anything to go by would be brilliant.

It was a beautiful, balmy evening. He had arrived ten minutes early to pick up the ambience and because he genuinely liked Covent Garden. Despite being touristy and rather passé, he loved its vibrance and found it more genuine than many other popular haunts.

He had managed to shoot home and change into a casual jacket, open necked shirt and trousers with tasselled loafers. He gazed at his reflection in the shop window front and was pleased with what he saw. Rupert became so engrossed in the singing that he forgot the time until at ten past eight, an arm smelling of Chanel No.5 snaked in front of him, complete with three gold bangles.

"Sorry I'm late," she said lightly, "the tube was hell."

Neither she nor Rupert were at all perturbed, it was all part of the game as far as they were concerned, the rules unsaid, but understood. He turned within the bangled arm to look at her and gasped; his face must have been a picture because she erupted into laughter at his facial expression.

Gone were the Nana Mouskouri glasses. Her cheek bones were consequentially, heightened and sharp but the most dramatic change was her hair; it was not straight and black but short, cropped in a funky, highlighted style that was a dance with bronze and gold which accentuated her eyes. Shocking pink lipstick adorned her lips and she had on a turquoise sheath of shot silk, which set off her slender figure to brilliant effect.

"Wow!" was all he could manage. "But the glasses, your hair..?" He left the statement hanging.

"Contacts and a wig," she laughed. "I got fed up with being chatted up by all the wide boys, so I chose to do that, I knew it would put them off. It's the first test," she chided.

"Well, I obviously passed with flying colours and thank God I did," he gushed, still taken aback by the chameleon-like transformation.

They walked through the crowded piazza with its circus

performers, throngs of tourists and theatre goers. Looking in the windows of the small boutique shops as they passed, they ambled in the direction of the opera house and a small restaurant where Rupert had booked a table. They arrived outside a glass fronted building on two levels. The upper level opened out onto a partially covered decking area, which allowed the gentle, autumn breeze to waft through, cooling the humid evening.

They were shown to their table where they were bathed in sunlight and overlooked the old Covent Garden market below; it was a delightful setting.

"This is sublime," Liz remarked. "I love Covent Garden with all its' bustle and hum. Just to sit and people watch is enough but up here away from it all and yet able to be part of it, truly lovely. Thank you."

"My pleasure. It is my favourite part of London, I think, especially as the opera house is so close. Do you like opera?"

"Oh yah, very much. Not the terribly heavy stuff but Rigoletto has to be my favourite. I could watch it again and again," she enthused.

Their drinks arrived; gin and tonic and a glass of Chardonnay, which they sipped appreciatively and carried on an easy conversation over the next ten minutes while making their choices from the menu that offered a fine eclectic mix of sea food and oriental bias for the main courses.

"I would love the Tiger prawns, but I'm not brave enough to eat them in front of a complete stranger I've only just met," she laughed.

"Oh don't worry, I'll send you the dry cleaning bill after the debris has flown everywhere."

They made their choices and settled into an easy relaxed conversation, that was at once amusing and flowing with neither of them trying too hard. They had a lot in common and the evening went well. The final course arrived and Liz flicked open a packet of Marlborough Lites, offering one to Rupert.

"I don't as rule, trying to keep off them, but tonight I think I'll join you."

He took a cigarette from the proffered packet and proceeded to light them both before handing the lighter back to Liz. They relaxed back in their seats.

"So," Liz began. "If my wig didn't put you off, why did you find me attractive?" she fished, with a self-mocking smile on her face.

"Ah, well I thought you were a secret agent stealing industrial secrets and I rather fancied becoming involved in high espionage," he finished with a grin.

For a brief moment her face clouded over with a frown but it vanished before Rupert could comment.

"So what did you call me, your name for me I mean, "M" or 007"? she laughed the moment off.

"Moneypenny? Nothing so exotic I'm afraid. Nana Mouskouri or Gold bangles."

She glanced down at her wrist and giggled.

"I think I prefer that to Nana Mouskouri."

The meal finished, Rupert paid the bill and they both sauntered down into the Piazza and the warm evening air. They walked hand in hand to the Strand. The evening finished well; he kissed her lightly on the cheek as the hailed taxi arrived.

"Thank you for a lovely evening. The meal was delicious."

"And the company?" he queried.

"Stop fishing," she chided him. "But not bad, not bad."

She grinned, then slipped into the taxi and waved goodbye. Rupert grinned to himself and waved the taxi out of sight.

CHAPTER 14

Octber of that year saw some of the worst storms in living memory. The gale force winds swept through the capital causing havoc. Roofs were pulled off houses, cars were thrown aside and trees uprooted. London had never experienced anything like it before; the fatality rate was considerable and everyone suffered. While insurance claims were high, it only served to perpetually fuel the property markets.

After the recovery, in the aftermath of the storm, renewed confidence pulled the Capital together, ever onward with inflation raging and capital values rising.

Everyone wanted to buy into a slice of the cake and own property; particularly commercial property.

MAS developments was no exception, with some extraordinarily good purchases; it seemed that Paul Simions could do no wrong. He was the new golden child who appeared to buy so well and consistently.

Rupert picked up a copy of the Estates Gazette and there in the news section was a grinning picture of Simions, with a scale model of the Golden Triangle retail park by the side of him and a comment that the scheme was three times oversubscribed by prospective tenants. It was an incredible piece of marketing, which would attract all kinds of speculative bids from funding sources; keen on acquiring the jewel of retail parks, Rupert thought.

Mike Ringham called, interrupting Rupert's thoughts.

"Rups, see your scheme's hit the big time. Simions'll be offering you a job next. You'll be leaving us poor agents behind," he mocked.

"Hah, how about you: you dealing?"

"I am indeed: three in lawyers, one to follow."

"Investment surveyors easy life," he joked.

When they finished the call he thought more about Mike's parting shot. Jump the fence? Become a principal? Would he like that? He had never considered it before. Wow that would be a powerful move, but to work for Simions? He shook his head.

The following day he received a call from David Shingler, inviting him to a meeting at his offices to discuss the Triangle scheme and associated issues.

"Shall I bring Hugo Curtiss along as well for the funding?" he queried.

"No I don't think that will be necessary, just peripheral issues really," he added quizzically. The meeting was set up for the next day and Rupert, while heeding Tom Lovich's words, failed to see how he could manipulate it to take place at CR's offices.

Rupert took the Underground over to midtown, that no-man's land between the City and the West End which housed a variety of different businesses and could possibly be called home only to Fleet Street, the hive of the press. He came off the tube at Holborn, walked north towards the offices of Shingler Cariss in accordance with the directions he had been given.

When he arrived he was surprised and shocked, for the building was entirely unprepossessing. Being neither old period as so many of the west end offices were, or smart contemporary but rather a drab, concrete affair that looked like it had been constructed in the sixties, grimy and depressing.

Rupert entered the building through glass doors to a reception area that was very perfunctory in its style and was sent to the second floor by a security guard.

The offices upstairs were a little better; very stark and lacking atmosphere, although the receptionist was pleasant enough and he was offered coffee, invited to sit and wait for Shingler who, he was told, was just finishing a telephone call. *Here we go*, he thought, *the games have started. We'll see how long he keeps me waiting*, guessing it would bet least ten minutes. Finally, the door opened fifteen minutes later and Shingler walked out.

"Sorry about that," he said, sounding as though he didn't mean a word. "Just had to finish a call to a very expensive QC. David Shingler."

Rupert responded, they shook hands and he noticed that Shingler had that annoying little habit of people who are trying always to gain the upper hand; by offering his hand palm almost down causing the recipient to be at a physical disadvantage. Rupert countered this by twisting the wrist sharply as soon as he had hold and grasping Shingler's hand as hard as he could. He was rewarded by a slight wince of pain in his face.

"Come on through to my office," he gestured with his hand to the open door.

Rupert followed him through to the comfortably furnished office, at odds with the rest of the building and décor, which was immaculately tidy. *Always be wary of a man with a tidy desk*, he thought.

Rupert studied the man before him; he was in his thirties, about six foot, of medium build, with blond hair, a good looking face, well preserved and tanned by the elements as much as a sun bed.

That explained the sailing pictures of sea going yachts on the walls and the golfing photos, thought Rupert. *The hobbies of a nouveau rich, social climber, who wanted everyone to know it. It went rather well with the gold Rolex watch and the chunky gold identity bracelet on the other wrist.* The voice when he spoke was over modulated like someone trying to be something he was not.

Shingler proceeded to sit himself behind his overlarge desk and face Rupert across the expanse of leather and wood.

"Now, down to business." There were no perfunctory niceties, no 'thank you for coming over', just straight in to business. Rupert took an instant dislike to this arrogant attitude. "We need to progress this scheme to be in a position to fund it. What is the rent role to date and the full details of the tenant line up? I just need these to see if they concur with my information," he finished.

Rupert felt disadvantaged, as Tom had warned. There was an immutable feeling of being made to feel small, no ground given to move or do other than obey. The desk was used as a useful prop to support the demand. Almost as an automaton, Rupert produced the papers from the open brief case on his lap and proceeded to present them.

"No, that won't be necessary, may I just have a look for myself?" he extended his open hand, palm upwards expecting to be obeyed. Rupert leaned forward and prepared to hand the papers over, his finger and thumb slipped together in a seemingly accidental gesture and the papers fell, scattered at his feet.

"Damn, stupidly clumsy of me."

The look on Shingler's face was one of smug superiority. He tutted and sighed. Rupert bent over, putting the open brief case on the floor in front of the desk and proceeded to collect the papers. As he did so he shuffled them dropping two sheets into the back pocket of the lid with a clever sleight of hand and then timidly passed the remaining papers across to Shingler in a humble manner. Shingler skimmed through the summaries to the core of the information and frowned, looking back and forth from one page to the next.

"There are two pages missing on rents and areas for the second phase. Where are they?" he asked crossly.

He got up from around his desk and looked on the floor in conjunction with Rupert, who was making a good show of scrabbling around in a futile search.

"They don't appear to be here I'm afraid."

"Check in your brief case again," he ordered.

"Now, see here, Shingler. This meeting was supposed to be a meeting of minds not opposing forces. I don't like your tone or your attitude; the papers are probably with Claire she will have had them when I copied the file."

Shingler was unabashed.

"Can't you call her, get them faxed over?" he retorted arrogantly. Rupert entrenched himself. He was determined not to pushed around by this little shit. He was going to be more aggressive and tell him to 'fuck off' but then realised that a mild, diffident attitude would annoy him more. It was the route he chose.

"No can do. She is out at a tenant meeting until after lunch. I'll get them sent over then and-"

"Yes," he interrupted. "But we need them now, not later."

"Why, what's the hurry?"

For an answer he just scowled and shrugged.

"Well, can't be helped," Rupert responded jauntily. "What else was on the agenda that you wanted to discuss? What about the funding?"

"It's too soon for that yet. In any case, Simions may have other ideas," he commented cryptically.

The meeting was clearly at an end, with Rupert feeling he had triumphed despite the adverse attitude that he had experienced at Shingler's hands. More worrying was the last remark. *What was he alluding to*? he thought. They shook hands with tight lipped smiles on their faces; both realising each had, in his own way, conceded points to the other. This time, Rupert noticed, the hand proffered for shaking was vertical not at an obscure angle.

As he left the office, he continued to mull over the last words uttered and considered it a veiled threat -but for what?

After the door closed, Shingler steepled his fingers, a deep frown creasing his forehead. *We shall have to do something about that arrogant little shit*, he thought to himself. *Who does he think he is?* He considered how he was to obtain the information necessary for his plans before smiling; it was not a pleasant expression. Shingler then picked up the telephone and dialled.

"Simions."

"Hello, it's me. I think we may have a small problem developing. Initially, we can obtain information by other means but Mr Brett may need sorting out. He may need dealing with more permanently later," he finished.

"That might be the case but he is producing good work, and I can't give you the information without causing suspicion. It must come from him directly. You're a big boy, work it out for yourself. We may bring him onside in due course: he is a dealer and is learning fast."

The conversation was at an end. Shingler put the telephone down and smiled nastily. *Mr Brett, you don't know who you are dealing with*, he thought to himself.

When Rupert returned to CR's offices, he found that Claire was indeed out and that her secretary had left her a note asking her to call Shingler upon her return. Rupert wrote a note to the effect that she was not to speak to Shingler under any circumstances until they had first spoken.

Later that afternoon Claire appeared at his door.

"Well, why all the Machiavellian stuff? What gives?"

"Shingler. I met with him at his offices; what an arsehole!"

Rupert proceeded to give a detailed account of the events that took place.

"What's he up to?" she mused, amazed at his attitude and also realising just how much Rupert had changed since he had been at CR. The West End dealer had now taken over.

"I don't know but I think we ought to alert Hugo to this situation, especially as it could affect the funding."

They duly went down to the investment department and once again Rupert relayed the events of the morning.

"I know exactly what he's up to," Hugo Curtiss commented presciently. "He wants to tout this around the market as a funding opportunity, cut us out and keep control of the investment. With or without Simions' permission. Do not, under any circumstances, give him this last piece of information. Stall him, give him any excuse, but stall it for at least a week."

They discussed the various aspects for the next few minutes and left to consider their delaying tactics.

Two days later, Rupert and Claire met up for coffee at the end of Grosvenor street with Claire in a foul mood.

"Why so glum?" he asked.

"Bloody secretaries. Tracey was fine yesterday, now she's called in sick and I've got a damn temp. Who to boot, is useless, well not useless but I have to explain everything twice. She asks questions at least, but oh, just when I need this letting report typed."

"It's not "Nana Mouskouri," is it?" he asked coyly.

"Ah, the elusive Nana Mouskouri. When are we going to meet her?"

"When I finally do," he replied cryptically

"What do you mean?"

"Oh, I don't know. We've had a handful of dates. All great, good conversation but I'm getting nowhere, in-"

"What, not getting your leg over you mean?" she interrupted grinning.

"No, well, yes, but not in the physical sense so much as not being able to get close to her personality. It's as though a wall comes down, just as I'm about to enter the final circle."

"Well we've all been there; on both sides of the fence but too much baggage is a real problem. You can't keep bashing your head against a brick wall, God alone knows your sensitive enough to be sympathetic to the right overtures." She smiled meaningfully. Rupert smiled across at her and met a concerned gaze of one who genuinely cared for him.

"Oh stuff it," he finished. "So it's not Liz, who is it?"

"Oh some dizzy, blond called Sophie. Same agency though; Secs in the City. Clever. I like that name, always remember it."

"Yes, though Richard Lloyd didn't, strange that."

"The guy's an idiot, always undresses you with his eyes. Uuhh, revolting." She shuddered.

"Come on, let's away to the office and see how your report is getting on."

They paid for the coffee and left, walking along Grosvenor Street, watching Christmas lights and decorations beginning to appear in windows.

"Soon be upon us again. What are you up to over the break?"

"Oh, to Gloucestershire for Christmas with the "wrinklies" this year but back for a New Year's bash with Angus at a club. And you?"

"Depends on the next forty eight hours really and how it pans out with Liz this weekend. We've got dinner this Saturday and I'm going to take your advice: make or break."

She looked across at him quizzically.

"Don't get hurt Rups," she said with compassion and put a tentative hand on his shoulder. He smiled back at her.

"I'll try not to," he replied, although his mind was elsewhere and not wanting to consider the possibility that it could go wrong. He liked the ladies, but was not a womaniser like Angus and was not inured to the pull of the heart.

When they returned to the office, Claire found, to her surprise, that given the break of a couple of hours the temp had, despite being very slow and having hardly achieved anything of substance, finally got the message and understood fully what was required. Typically, though and probably for the best, Tracey had made a recovery and had telephoned to say she would be back in the office by the end of the week.

The following day saw the final compilation of the report and Claire left the office in good spirits on Friday, safe in the knowledge that it would all be completed for the meeting at MAS's offices the following week.

She was looking forward to a good weekend; a dinner party at Mike's house with Jemma. As she walked to the tube station, she mused over the idea that it wouldn't be long before an engagement was announced. Despite looking upon Mike with an almost proprietorial concern of an elder sister, she approved of Jemma, who was no gold digger and appeared to have genuine affection for him. He for his part appeared smitten, for the first time in his life. After many romances and affairs and a trail of broken hearted Sloane Rangers falling behind him, things looked like they were falling into place for Ringo. In contrast, Claire considered her position with Angus. There were hardly any parallels; it was, as they both knew, a relationship based upon the chase, the ego, mutual satisfaction and pleasure. For all that, they both enjoyed those hollow virtues to the full and the mutual attraction was becoming much more than a passing fling.

Claire was beginning to form a much stronger attachment than she had first anticipated and her general policy of letting no one too close was being tested to the limit. A rather selfish girl, who knew her attraction to the opposite sex, she had always, with the possible exception of Rupert, been able to walk away intact and fall back upon her driving ambition and sports. She was equally at home in both male or female company, a rare attribute for one so attractive to the opposite sex and this helped her to sail gracefully through all manner of potentially tempestuous relationships.

Leaving the office some time earlier, Rupert was looking forward to the weekend with some trepidation and was only sorry that he would not be able to attend the dinner party to which he too, had been invited. Similarly, he sensed an auspicious moment of occasion but was too intent on making a success of his relationship with Liz to risk jeopardising it for an invitation to dinner, much to Mike's chagrin.

The following evening Rupert had arranged to pick Liz up at her apartment somewhere in Hampstead. She had given him the address and being used to the environs of Knightsbridge and the West End became lost and was consequently late. When he arrived, he saw a large mansion block of typical 1930s Art Deco, divided up into a large number of flats, lights blazing like the Marie Celeste. The large enclosed gardens and car parking areas were clearly lit and he pulled up in an area marked VISITORS, locked the car and approached the main entrance.

He buzzed the intercom and awaited a response.

"Yes?" a voice emerged from the intercom.

"It's Rupert, sorry I'm late."

"I'll forgive you, just this once. I'll be straight down."

The intercom buzzed and clicked into silence. So, thought Rupert, I still don't get to see her lair. Five minutes later she appeared through the glass doors.

"Wow, you look gorgeous!" he exclaimed. She was dressed in a simple but extremely elegant black dress that only the best atelier could achieve. A single string of pearls was strung around her neck, heavy eye makeup, long dark lashes and elegant hair. She twirled for him in mock elegance, smiling and striking a model pose with one leg extended.

He grinned in response and moved forward to kiss her, enveloped in a cloud of perfume that seduced his senses still further. He motioned towards his company car, a benefit that came with his recent promotion to Senior Surveyor. It was a lovely car, the VW Scirroco GTX hatch back, with clean, racey lines.

"How is the new beast going?" she asked, mocking him slightly with her head inclined on one side in an endearing manner, at the same time running her hand gently and sexily along the body work. He smiled seduced by both her smile and attitude.

"Wonderful, goes like a dream and the acceleration is incredible."

"Boys toys," she disclaimed as he opened the door for her.

They accelerated off at a pace to a smart part of Hampstead and a restaurant of her choosing, where she had reserved a table. The Chinese restaurant was a far cry from the usual run of the mill standard fare.

The décor was of stark white, with modern, black furniture and an atmosphere of frenetic activity prevailed with the waiters busily bustling around, showing off their art. The couple were shown to a corner table with a good view of the restaurant and Liz was clearly a well-recognised regular, enjoying a welcoming smile from the head waiter.

"Miss Lizzy, it is good to see you again." He bowed slightly and gestured to the seats.

"Thank you Ying, it's good to be here." She smiled.

They ordered, and the food, when it came, was excellent and beautifully presented. In a relaxed atmosphere, the couple flirted and Rupert studiously avoided referencing work or related matters which normally caused her to clam up and become tense.

Over coffee, she lit her first cigarette of the evening, having subconsciously cut down since she had known Rupert. Blowing the smoke in a gentle stream through pursed lips, she toyed with her coffee cup and smiled gently across at him, half preoccupied as though considering something, yet not giving it full attention.

"Penny for them?" he said. "No, I don't want to know. My sister always said it was the kiss of death to ask any girl that question and that I would never get the right answer anyway." He grinned winningly.

"I like your sister already and I haven't even met her yet," she laughed. "Is she in town? Don't tell me she's a surveyor too?"

"No way. She wants to be a marine biologist. Save the planet and all that. She is on her gap year at the moment out in the Florida Keys, taking samples of the lesser spotted, great crested, tiger plankton, or something, I don't know. Sounds like a euphemism for a skive to me, but there we are."

"We all need saving in one form or another," she said dreamily.

Determined not to let the conversation take on a morbid note, Rupert immediately responded flippantly.

"Ah yes, let's all hug a whale and save a tree; or is it the other way round? Anyway if I promise to do my best Flipper impersonation will you hug me later?"

"You are crazy but yes, hugging a dolphin is definitely a possibility."

They finished their coffee, Rupert paid the bill and they sauntered, relaxed, arm in arm to his car. He drove slowly to her apartment block and pulled up outside, a question mark hanging in the air between them.

"Night cap?" she said finally, breaking the unbearable tension.

"Mmmh, lovely," he said.

They left the car, moved into the glazed, communal entrance and into a blast of warm air. They entered the lift holding hands and he kissed her gently on the lips with her eyes smiling back at him warmly. The lift stopped at the third floor and they stepped out into a T-shaped landing with all the flats feeding off the communal areas. She moved forward and opened her front door to her flat, which led into a small hallway and some internal stairs that went up to the main area. It was tastefully furnished, with the style of Habitat; bright, pastel colours and bold prints on the curtains, oriental rugs were hanging from two walls and haphazardly laid on the carpets. It was a flat of contrasts, reflecting aptly, the personality of its owner. She went into the kitchen and filled the kettle.

"Coffee?" she asked.

"Please."

"What else would you like? No, not that," she chided lasciviously from under half closed lids.

"I don't know what you mean," he responded innocently. "Single Malt, if you have it."

"Smooth idea. In the cupboard above, to your left."

Rupert reached up and removed two glasses and the bottle of scotch, from which he poured two generous measures.

They left the kitchen and moved on to the living room. He sat on the sofa while she put on a Sade album; the soulful music and her beautiful voice floated intoxicatingly into the room. She lit a cigarette and blew the smoke gently from her lips. The light from the table lamps catching her profile, casting half her face in gentle shadow.

"You have to be the sexiest person ever to smoke a cigarette," he complimented.

She laughed huskily, turned to face him and he kissed her

gently. Her mouth opened in response, tongue probing gently at first and then more aggressively. They broke apart briefly.

"I'll be back in a moment," she whispered, laying the cigarette down and rising from the sofa.

She left the room and returned minutes later appearing in the door way, half backlit by the landing light. Rupert could not see her properly until she entered the room and when she did his throat went dry. She had shed the black dress and stood only in a black silk teddy and stockings, looking both demure and irresistibly provocative at the same time.

"Well?" she said.

Rupert stood and stepped in front of her, smelling her scent and cupped a hard nippled breast with his right hand whilst kissing her crushingly on the lips. She responded in kind, running her hand into his hair and forcing herself against him. He felt the heat of her body through the silk as she thrust herself forward, while rotating her hips against his groin. She virtually ripped his shirt off, while he struggled out of his other clothes and she sank to the floor kissing him all the way down his body, causing him to moan in ecstasy. Her lips played with him until finally he could stand it no longer and he too dropped to the floor. She pushed him gently, but forcefully on to his back, sat astride him and pinned his arms to the floor, kissing him hard on the mouth, moaning and becoming ever more frenetic and aggressive in her actions.

She reached down between her legs pulling open the crotch of her silk teddy and with her fingers put him in just the right position so that she slid over him, causing them both to gasp. She returned to pinning his arms and rode him hard, her face a mask of intent, almost manic, as though she were trying to exorcise herself. She became more frenzied, writhing, falling and suddenly Rupert felt it was all wrong.

"No," he cried. "Not like this, no!"

He nearly threw her off him but caught her as she fell sideways. She looked at him as if in a trance and then crumpled, sagging in his arms.

"What's wrong?" she mumbled.

"Everything," he said gently.

He scooped her up in his arms and carried her through to the bedroom, laying her gently on to the bed. They lay in each other's arms in the half light, then kissed, gently, compassionately. They made love, guiding each other like experienced lovers with pleasure and warmth, until they both climaxed together in harmony and pleasure, neither having used the other. Rupert went to stroke her face and felt that it was wet, he pulled her to him and stroked her hair. She relaxed in his arms, her breathing gradually subsiding to a gentle rhythm.

He pondered over her reaction and the events of the last few weeks, which seemed more than ever, to be a bigger mystery. His last conscious thought before he finally succumbed to sleep, was that she must have been deeply hurt in the past, but in what way shape or form was unclear.

CHAPTER 15

The New Year came and went; optimism in 1988 was still the abounding word by which everyone was living. The "chattering classes" continued to discuss over dinner party conversation how much their properties had risen in value over the last month, ever a dangerous barometer of overweening, self-confidence.

In to this maelstrom of financial volatility, the Chancellor slipped the final ingredient necessary to tip the balance into economic meltdown: he declared that from October of that year, dual tax relief on mortgages of property owned by two or more people would be abolished but all mortgages (and therefore properties) bought before the cut-off date would continue to benefit from the existing provisions. This incredible piece of legislation meant, that everyone had only months in which to benefit from what amounted to, in real terms, a continued tax benefit of 25%.

The property markets, already fuelled by the Big Bang and huge City bonuses went absolutely berserk with people trying to get on to the already highly inflated property ladder, before the tax benefit disappeared forever.

The commercial markets, always allied to the economy as a

whole, benefited from this further injection of energy and surged forward with more development being carried out and new sites sought more desperately than ever.

To the forefront, as ever, was MAS with Simions leading a charmed life in his quest for new opportunities. The Estates Gazette was always featuring a news item with his latest bid or acquisition, miraculously beating off his rivals.

Rupert continued to strengthen his relationship with him, despite misgivings on a more personal level as to the man's morals and way of doing business. Both he and Claire had succeeded in virtually completing the letting to various tenants and the scheme was about to be put out for funding by the institutions with a total cost of some twenty million pounds, representing a huge profit once funded. But not everything, even for Simions, always ran true to plan and on Tuesday morning he received a call that every agent dreads.

"It's Simions. What the bloody hell's happening to my site?" he questioned down the phone. He never actually shouted, just emphasised the menace always latently present in his voice.

"What do you mean?" Rupert queried.

"You're my agent, you should know. What am I paying you for?" he almost whispered, but sounded far more menacing for all that. "I have just been offered my own site, to see if I want to buy it."

"Whaaaat! By whom?" Rupert asked incredulously. *This could not be happening,* he thought, *what a bloody nightmare.*

"Some runner was on the phone this morning. It will be all over the West End by lunchtime. Find out who is punting it and put a stop to it, I don't need to tell you what a mockery this will make of the funding package." The line cut off abruptly.

Oh great, Rupert thought, *fan-fucking-tastic, just what we need, to lose control of it at this stage.* He telephoned Claire straight away who was just as annoyed and amazed in equal doses. The next calls were to Lovich and Hugo Curtiss in the Investment Department.

They were equally pissed off, but more sanguine; age and experience giving them the advantage, having encountered this sort of situation before. By lunchtime they had found the source of the information leak and who was offering the site for sale around the market without any instructions, just a spurious price tag and the hope of a fee. An internal meeting took place in CR's offices at midday between Rupert, Tom, Claire and Hugo Curtiss.

"Bloody Ricky Barston, it would have to be him," Simon fumed.

"But what I don't see," Rupert queried, "Is how he got sufficient information to run it around the market, rents, tenants etc."

"Simple really, a letting brochure for the site plans etc., two or three tenants who may have been in the press as taking the scheme, guess the rest of the rents, assume 25 year FRI leases and guess a price. Not difficult really," Hugo finished caustically.

"But, this covering letter of introduction has more detail than that," he said waving the copy of a round robin letter. "Look, it details too many specifics for "guestimation" alone and my money says Shingler had a hand in this."

"Shingler?" All three cried with puzzled expressions on their faces.

"But why him? What motive could he have for screwing up the deal?" Claire demanded.

"When I met with him at his offices, he was more than keen to get a full tenant line up with rents and all the information, to the extent that he was furious when I failed to give them to him." Rupert continued to relate in full what occurred at that meeting and they all remembered the sketchy details.

"At the time Hugo thought he was after the funding, but I think he's gone one stage further. He wants to sell the site through the back door, get all the letting fees AND the funding when the purchaser buys it."

"No, he would never get away with it. Simions would go absolutely ballistic."

"One, Shingler would deny it and inveigle his way in and secondly have you ever known Simions to turn down a deal when there was a huge profit involved? No, exactly. I think this was his plan and also, that he has some hold over Simions."

"Possibly his plan, yes," Tom conceded, "But I don't buy that he has some hold on him. However the rest stacks up, we have got to put the lid on this before he sells it."

Rupert remained to be convinced, he was learning all the devious tricks and knew how to think like his enemy.

The meeting ended with a little more discussion of what had occurred and they all went back to their separate offices to carry out a damage limitation exercise.

But for the rest of the day Simions was incommunicado, boding ill for Rupert and his colleagues. By the time close of business had occurred they had still not heard from him.

The call came in the next day for a meeting at MAS's offices and all four arrived at the front door on Manchester Square at the appointed hour. They were shown through to the meeting room on the first floor and not unsurprisingly, Shingler was in attendance. Curt greetings were exchanged and they got down to business straight away with Simions opening the proceedings.

"What we have here, is a cock up," he espoused. "I feel terribly exposed by all this. Not to mention foolish and, more importantly, I stand to lose a great deal of credibility."

But, they all noticed, at no time did he mention a financial loss, which in a perverse sort of way boded ill for what was to occur next. He waved down the proposed response from Rupert with a dismissive hand movement.

"It is however, irrelevant what has occurred, what is important is how I salvage my position from the ruins of this exposure."

They all noted the use of the personal pronoun and expected the worst.

"The only positive benefit I can see from this farce is that it has shown me how valuable my site is. I have been offered, albeit spuriously, approximately 3 times what I paid for it, through the dubious channels of Ricky Barston and the good offices of David Shingler here." At which point he gestured in Shingler's direction who smirked, knowingly.

"Therefore, in order to save face and secure a large profit, I have decided to accept the offer."

The words hit the CR team hard and confirmed their worst fears. They realised that they had been set up by Shingler. But all bar Rupert refused to consider that he might have forced Simions' hand in the matter.

"Well, that is all very well and good," Hugo Curtiss responded. "But where does that leave us with regard to the funding and letting fees? Claire especially, has put in a lot of work into this with agreements to lease for all the parties tied up and the whole scheme let."

"Provisionally let. Those agreements to lease will be worthless once the scheme has been sold and the new owners take over the lettings. However, in the circumstances I of course appreciate all your efforts and you will, as a whole, be looked after on some form of abortive fee structure," he offered with a magnanimous gesture of his hand.

When the euphemism of "looked after " was uttered, all four knew that they were going to be screwed. There was not a thing they could do about it, except to accept the offer in good grace or never work with Simions again. He was too powerful for that and they all knew it. The meeting came to an end, with Simions refusing, albeit obliquely, to reveal the name of the purchaser only that it was a fund.

As they left the building all their frustration was aired.

"What really pisses me off, is that smug, odious, little shit is going to get all the fees while we pick up the crumbs from his table," Rupert said aggressively.

"I know, especially all the letting fees," Claire agreed. "Is there no way we can do anything about that, Hugo?"

"Only to fight it in court in which case win or lose we'll never do any business again, or appeal to his better nature. Which also holds little appeal."

"Do you know the best thing we can do?" Tom asked sagacious as ever. "And don't shout me down before you hear me out. I think," he continued, "that the best thing we can do is to find him a new deal and quickly; while the gentle discussions over fees are still open to debate."

"What?" Claire said. "But why, when the little shit has shafted us?"

"No, no speak your mind, Claire," Tom retorted sarcastically, to which he received a horrible face in return. "Well, if we are agreed that we are not going to sue him, and the reason for that is 'cause we want to do more business, then let's do just that and get on his good side which may help the fee settlement, however much as it goes against the grain. Business is business," he remarked pragmatically.

"*My father taught me, keep your friends close and your enemies closer.*"

The line from the Godfather, brought forth a laugh from them all and dissolved the tension.

"Ok, I'll find him another site," Rupert said bitterly.

"No, *we* will find him another site and this time, *we* will make sure we control it." Tom finished for him.

The following days saw Rupert sorting areas that he proposed to canvass with a view to finding a site. South of the river was becoming one of the main hotspots for occupiers and it was them who drove the market.

Rupert's experience from canvassing was telling. One of the many skills he had acquired now stood him in good stead. After two weeks of hard work, he found a site and more importantly someone who would sell. The bad news was it was let to a tenant: Moorcroft Industries. Amongst other things, they specialised in supplying oil rigs and drilling equipment all around the world. In these inflationary times, their business was booming as the price of crude rose considerably. They occupied a site on the corner of Castle Road and River Street with extensive frontage, close to a traffic lit junction in just about the most perfect location for that part of London. Following a letter of approach to the MD, Rupert received a call in response.

"Mr. Brett?" asked the deep voice, "it is Michaels here from Moorcroft Industries. You wrote to me concerning our property on Castle Street."

"Ah, yes. Thank you for coming back to me. Is this something that might, as a principle, be of interest to you?"

"Well from the tone of your letter, it would seem to imply that you are only interested in the freehold. If that is the case we will not be able to help you, as we are only leaseholders here."

"Oh, well yes, really that is the case I'm afraid. But,…umm,…." Rupert hesitated, carefully feigning slight ingenuousness. "Do you know who the freeholders are by any chance? I don't want to put you to any trouble of course."

"Yes, I do actually, you see we have only a matter of months to go on our lease and we are in negotiations with them at the moment for renewal."

Rupert held his breath waiting for the information about to be given which would save him time, trouble and money.

"It is United Assurance Society, do you know them, or would you like the address?"

Rupert feigned ignorance, took the address and finished the call, thanking Michaels for his help. *UAS! Of all the funds they would be perfect to 'steal' the site from, without them realising. They appeared sharp in all outwardly looking deals, but notoriously lax when it came to seeing the bigger picture within their own portfolio; like a few other funds*, he thought cynically.

He weighed his next action carefully. Approach the fund direct or go to Halpern and Beams, who would almost certainly have all the information as they acted for them on the professional work. He phoned the Honeymonster and explained the situation to him. He grunted in his usual way but as ever ready to help, particularly with a bit of clandestine work, rather than the usual boring lease reading. Half an hour later he called with the information. It was more than Rupert could have hoped for, he had chapter and verse on the lease, with all the terms, including the rent etc. More particularly, their Development Department were not involved and were unlikely to be so.

"So," he finished, "you owe me a serious lunch for all this. Let's put something in the diary now."

It was done and Rupert was more than happy to oblige. Better than sharing any fees he thought. His next call was to Mike Ringham.

"Ringo, hi. It's Rupert. How are we doing? Got the date set for the wedding yet?"

The dinner party he had missed was indeed to announce the engagement to Jemma, Mike had finally understood, but still been rather sad that his friend could not have been present.

"Ya, on good form actually. We think it will be Autumn this year, so keep it free. Now, cut all the nonsense, whenever you're that nice to me, it usually means you want something. Come on don't give me all the flannel."

"So harsh, so harsh. I don't know what you mean, I only have your goodwill at heart."

"Right, so what do you want?" he continued.

"Ok, UAS, you remember that conversation we had some time back just before we met with Richard Lloyd? Yea, well I need a contact there; someone who will deal with the Industrial fund. Do we know anyone?"

"Well, actually we do. We are buying something off them at the moment and they are on the lunch list for this week. Why?"

Regularly distributed amongst the surveyors, the lunch list was always the most up to date information on current target clients CR wanted a special relationship with. Rupert rummaged in his tray before pulling the list out and scanning through the list of names until he came to Clive Roberts of UAS.

"Well, I have the potential makings of a deal."

"Do tell." Mike was interested, all lethargy leaving him. So Rupert proceeded to relay the whole story, right up to the details of the lease terms.

"Well, sounds as though it has potential but make sure you get your full fees this time," he responded sarcastically.

"For those kind words, I thank you," Rupert responded. "But listen can we make an approach, sound him out and see if he will sell. We need to get this off the market, without anyone else realising the development potential of the site.

The lunch was on Thursday of that week and Mike ensured that he would be sat next to Clive Roberts; a short, pugnacious man, with a bad taste in suits, slightly greasy hair and a 'chip on the shoulder' attitude.

"We are, umm, looking for short leased properties at the moment," Mike murmured. "A specific client can get tax breaks from short leases and accordingly will pay top dollar."

"What sector and where?" he responded curtly, as he stuffed his perspiring face with pudding, social niceties not being top of his priority.

"Well, for this particular client, we would be looking primarily at industrial, got anything that might suit?" he asked languidly, as though this was all a bore and the last thing on his mind. Like many people, Roberts made the mistake of taking him for an upper class twat, ready for the shearing. His response was exactly what Mike had wanted.

"Yea, we've got some industrial tat in souf' east London, problems with a lease renewal, months left on the lease and a stubborn tenant. If that might do you," he said sprawling back on his chair, after rinsing his mouth with a gulp of wine, "I could let you have some info."

"Might well be the ticket, where is it exactly?"

"Oh, corner of Castle Street and River Street, shabby stuff. But if you're man wants some short leased crap, it would be ideal but it will cost."

Roberts grinned unpleasantly. *Not a nice experience,* Mike thought, however he had him.

"Sounds like a reasonable scheme. Send the information across and we'll run it passed our man, see what he says." Mike sounded as nonchalant as ever, no one would ever guess he had just what he wanted.

The following days were a bore for Rupert. He knew that it could not be hurried or Roberts would become suspicious. The following Tuesday, Roberts faxed the information across to Mike Ringham: it was just as they had hoped. The next call was to Simions and a meeting was arranged for the next day. Rupert and Mike attended the meeting which was deliberately set for their offices in order to gain more control and to stop Shingler being present for any spurious reason that Simions may have invented. The pleasantries over with, Simions as ever cut straight to the chase.

"Well, what have you got for me?"

"A deal," Rupert said. " A deal as good, if not better, than

Golden Triangle." He used the analogy deliberately to inspire guilt and goodwill simultaneously.

"Really, well tell me more and I'll be the judge of that."

Rupert explained the whole story up to the point of receiving all the information from Roberts, including the price they had been quoted, which seemed high, even given the circumstances. Simions considered all that had been said looked again at the site plan from the OS sheet, studied the lease details and his face became totally unreadable to the other two surveyors. He ran his hand through his grey mane in a reflex gesture, the only give away of the tension in his body.

"I like it. Run some numbers, get me tenant demand for the area-"

"Already done and its superb; a *who's who* of DIY anchors and all the subsidiary retailers."

Unused to being interrupted, Simions visibly fought to keep himself calm and not respond aggressively.

"Well done," he said quietly. "And I'd also like details of the planning for the area, zoning etc." Rupert, having learned his lesson, quietly handed over a planning brief.

"It's all in there and it looks positive. From the initial chat we've had with the planners, they would be more than delighted to see the site turned into sparkly, retail sheds. Well, as far as any planners are concerned, they are delighted," he added as a caveat. They continued to discuss one or two more aspects of the site and the possibility of getting vacant possession came up for discussion.

"I need a copy of the existing lease. Also what action has been taken with regard to serving notices on the tenant to quit. I do not need to tell you how important this is and who, may I ask, is acting for Moorcroft?"

"Halpern & Beams, their Professional Department, no involvement from the agency boys at all and it should stay like that."

"Good. Right I'll look at all the information. If it stacks up, we will make an offer subject only to contract, no planning, no vacant possession, just get control of the site asap. Please ask UAS, if and when we make an offer, not to take any more steps on the termination of the lease, we don't want the waters muddied." They all smiled and Simions prepared to leave.

"Oh, one final matter," Rupert contrived to make it sound like an afterthought.

"Shingler. If he is to be involved at a later stage, is there some way we can avoid a repetition of the problems that occurred last time?"

Simions considered Rupert and responded in kind; "You have my assurance that this will not be sold without instruction and that you will be involved in the sale of the investment or if not, I will pay you a fee. You may draw up a letter to that effect. Now I wish to hear no more about it." The subject was clearly closed and the meeting ended.

After he left Mike turned to Rupert.

"You do believe in living dangerously, I'll say that for you," he commented.

"It had to be said and he knows it's a good deal. Besides, it was fun." He slapped Mike on the shoulders and laughed softly. The cockiness and confidence of a deal maker were manifesting themselves in the 'new Rupert'.

They went to their offices, Mike to work on an offer and Rupert to do more research.

Rupert reflected that whatever else his faults might be, lack of speed was not one of them. Once Simions made up his mind he sped into action with alacrity, much faster than any cumbersome fund, who would prevaricate, go through numerous board approvals and after wasting everyone's time, decide not to buy on some spurious excuse. *Maybe*, Rupert thought, *maybe I could work for him: it would certainly be exciting.*

The full documentation came through from UAS and as luck would have it, despite having opened negotiations on the lease renewal, no formal notices had been served as it was slightly ahead of the timescale set out in the lease. In fact, surprisingly the tenant had instigated the discussions, not the Landlord, probably in an effort to come to some less than formal arrangement, without involving the courts. The legal system for lease renewals was a nightmare and conflict to be avoided at all costs. Simions called Rupert upon receipt of the information.

"I have the package of information. I will read it in the next hour or so and come back as soon as I can. From what I have seen so far this has got to be put under offer as soon as possible. There are so many ways it could leak into the market and I do not want to be bidding against all and sundry. One more thing, I see that Moorcroft are listed, can you get me a full company search, creditors etc.?"

"I have already asked our Research Department for the information," he lied making a note to do it after the call. "Should be with me tomorrow at the latest."

"Good. Sooner if possible. Speak to you later."

The line went dead. *Never one to waste words, is our Simions*, he thought shaking his head and smiling to himself. *Now, why does Simions want a company search if he wants them out*, he wondered.

Rupert would have the answer to his question if he had heard the following telephone conversation between Simions and Shingler.

"The boy Brett has done it again. He's found a great site. He has a talent for it I'll give him that."

"What? Where?" Shingler asked. "Why wasn't I in on it?"

"He's getting wise. Don't worry we'll split it as usual, stop being greedy. If I cut him out this time, he won't offer us another deal. And, as I say, he's getting good. I might have to poach him. Put Pauline on notice we might need someone in Halpern and

Beams soon. I take it she is still connected with the head of Personnel?"

"Thick as thieves," Shingler responded. "Well and why wouldn't she be with a retainer from Secs and the City? Money talks, chap, money talks."

"Indeed. Right, I'll let you know when we have more information." He curtly finished the call.

Rupert telephoned research and spoke to the one of the girls; a pretty thing called Jessica. He flirted with her for about two minutes and then begged a favour. She flirted back and demanded a drink after work in payment, which Rupert had no intention of keeping and would cry off later. He thought suddenly of Liz and had an urge to speak with her. He called Secs in the City, the West End branch just off Oxford Street.

"Liz, no, she has not been in today but we have an assignment for her towards the end of the week so if you speak to her, ask her to get in touch will you? Smaashing, take care."

The girl finished in her professional sing song voice. *Why, does everyone say "take care" when the last thing in the world they really care about is the person they say it to? It ranks up there with "have a nice day, you'all!"* he thought. *So where is Liz then?* he wondered.

Mike had continued to pursue Clive Roberts at UAS in order to try and obtain a firm figure at which they felt a deal could be struck. So far the response had been only that he needed to be higher than "book value." As fortune would have it, an acquaintance from university worked in the Valuation Department, and with a bit of luck would provide the information. Mike telephoned praying that he would help and his prayers were answered. A languid voice answered the telephone.

"Charlton."

"Morning Chaz, its Mike Ringham here, how the devil?"

"Ringo. Extraordinarily well thanks and yu'self, how de dodee?"

Mike grinned to himself at the patrician tones and insouciant manner; a great façade hiding an agile, if rather boring, brain. After the initial pleasantries, Mike turned the conversation to valuations, with the claim that he was buying something and needed some information on value.

"Shouldn't really of course, but if you give me the figure you're at and I nod at the appropriate moment. How's that sound?"

"Brilliant. I'm at the £2.75m mark. Are we on the right lines?" he queried.

"Have to sharpen your pencil a bit old boy, we're north of there."

"What? It's a fag end of the lease. I thought values were supposed to go down at this point not up," he cried.

"Ah we've had orders to push up the performance as they are lagging behind at the moment, totally independently of course," he said cynically.

"Ok, £3m?"

"I would of thought that that sort of figure may help you somewhat more," he said.

"Chaz, you're a star."

"It has been said, it has been said. Now, how about lunch?"

They put a lunch in the diary and Mike thought he would drag Rupert and Claire along to alleviate the boredom. He went along to Rupert's room to discuss what he had discovered. It had been decided that he would continue to progress the investment purchase per se, partly to share in the fees and more importantly, that it would keep the illusion that they were only looking at it as an investment, without exposing the massive redevelopment potential. Rupert telephoned Simions for instructions and was pleased to find him in a benign mood and open to persuasion on the level of offer.

The offer was put forward at just under £3m, subject to contract only with no other conditions and was, as expected, summarily rejected. The offer was duly increased to £3.1m, enough to tip the balance and cause UAS to agree to sell.

They were all euphoric at the acceptance of the offer, none less so than Rupert, who was determined not to have it sold from under him this time. The lawyers were instructed to prepare a contract as soon as possible, every moment that the deal was unsigned presented an opportunity for the deal to "leak" into the market. One week passed and the lawyers were ready for exchange, it had all been carried out in record time, only five working days! Again, Rupert thought how good it would be to be in charge and work at this frenetic pace.

Mike received a call from the lawyers to say that contracts were exchanged on the Friday morning, much to everyone's relief. Rupert was called by Simions just before lunch. He answered after two rings.

"Rupert?"

"Yes, heard the good news?"

"Deal done I hear? Good, now the real work starts. On Monday we start to turn the screw and find a way to get this tenant off the site. Have you found at Halpern & Beams who is dealing with the lease renewal?"

"Yes, a chap called uh, Steve Jackson, head of their review team. He has just been formerly instructed that he is to liaise with us on the matter."

"Also, I need to know his secretary's name, just for completeness."

"Secretary? Sure, I'll find out for you," he finished feeling puzzled.

"Do that, please. Have a good weekend, speak on Monday."

"You too." As he put the telephone down, Rupert thought that Simions must be having a funny turn; asking for a secretary's name and wishing him a good weekend.

CHAPTER 16

The spring of that year, after the terrible storms, had been brilliant with high April temperatures and bright sunshine causing most Londoners to vacate the city early on the first of many weekends away from the smog and bustle. Claire was no exception. She and Angus continued with their intense relationship and as Friday came, the weekend was discussed after a rowdy Friday lunchtime session in *The Guinea*.

"So we haven't made any plans for this week end yet," she stated

"No. Haven't got that far yet except that we have a boy's night with some of my Scottish friends down on Saturday before they fly out for skiing on the Sunday afternoon," he answered.

"Really, you didn't mention it earlier." She looked at him, studying his face carefully.

"Sure I did, last week; you were probably too wrapped up in this new deal to take any notice," he replied glibly. Claire's career was flying and in the short time she had been there, she was now making deals in her own right non-retained.

"I'm sure I would have remembered. Never mind, come around for dinner at my place tonight, I will treat you." She smiled winningly at him. Their relationship had lasted a few months now and although at times tempestuous, it was, Claire was sure, turning into something more than a casual affair, with commitment on both sides. With a typical women's intuition, she knew when to back off and not appear too clingy; giving Angus enough space while continuing to keep him entranced.

"That would be good, but we are off to the dry slope first, just so I can show them how it's done before they leave for the slopes."

Angus she knew, was a superb skier and could not resist showing off to the boys. The last time they went on the dry slope he had been asked to leave, after jumping off the lift while it was still in motion.

"What say 9.00, dinner and me in that order." She offered licentiously, giving him a beautiful smile. He responded in kind but disappointed her with his reply.

"Can we make it 9.30, that gives me time to get back," he wheedled.

"Ok, yah," she responded, hiding her disappointment. *It was nothing*, she thought afterwards, *boys will be boys!*

Later that evening she prepared dinner for him in her flat. At 9.30 she lit the candles, everything ready, wine chilled, last minute preparations ready to go and relaxed to *Everything But the Girl* playing in the background. She lay back on the sofa, sheathed in a black velvet dress with hair drawn back, accentuating her high cheekbones. She looked stunning and knew it.

For some unknown reason, Claire was nervous and unable to relax. She later flicked through the television channels unable to select anything that would hold her. This was now the second time something of this nature had occurred, the earlier event was at the beginning of their relationship and she thought nothing of it, now was a different matter. The telephone rang shrilly, breaking into her reverie. She jumped as it jarred on her consciousness.

"312-Angus?" she queried answering the telephone..

"Hi, babe. Sorry, I'm running late. Things got out of hand, I-"

"Angus, don't give me that crap. Where are you, its 9.30?"

"Calm down, I just had one too many with the lads. I'm getting a taxi now, I'll be there in half an hour, OK?"

"Oh, whatever, see you later," she responded disappointedly and put the phone down. *Oh stuff him, chauvinistic little shit,* she thought. She started to sink into a melancholy humour, then snapped out of it in a rush. *No way,* she thought *I'm twenty five, not fifty five.* She looked up at the clock, the bars in the West End would not have even begun to hum yet. On an impulse she rang a girlfriend.

"Caroline, hi its Claire. How are you?"

"Oh fab, doll, absolutely. And you?"

"Well actually, pretty pissed off and feeling like a night on the town."

"Brill. We're off to Smollensky's for about 10.30, come along. We'll see you there, ya?"

"Cass, you're a star, love to. See you in half an hour, byeeee!"

She put the telephone down, suddenly uplifted. *Sod Angus,* she thought, *he can have a curry with the boys.* She changed into something more obvious; short skirt with a slit at the side, white blouse open low, chunky jewellery, more make-up and looked approvingly at the result in the mirror. She left the flat and caught a cab to Smollensky's.

It was in full swing when she arrived at just after 10.30. She met Caroline, they embraced and kissed, genuinely pleased to see each other.

"Now tell me what the bastard has done now," she demanded. Claire told all to Caroline over the loud music and a few drinks.

"Oh he's just being a typical male thug, you'll never change him. Either ditch him or get used to it: at least he is being faithful!"

"Cass, you're such a cow! But probably right. Come on let's dance."

149

They hit the dance floor and half an hour later, re-joined to the bar. As they leant on the bar a small commotion started on the opposite side of the bar and sure enough there was Angus, with a familiar girl on his arm. It was the girl from the bar of some months ago whom he sang to.. She was certainly more than friends with Angus; draped all over him and dancing backwards onto the dance floor swaying her hips in his direction.

Claire's first instinct was to go over and slap him. Then she stopped and ducked out of sight, leaving with Caroline hot on her tail.

"Don't say I was here, alright? Not a word," she begged. "I will deal with this later."

"OK, Claire, will you be alright?" she asked putting an arm around her.

"Ya, fine, I'll get a cab," she turned on her heel. "Not a word, not a word, tell the others, please?" she pleaded.

She got home in about an hour, entered her flat, ran upstairs, flung herself on the bed and wept. She exorcised herself that night to be harder and stronger the next day.

Only one thought on her mind, vengeance!

The next day she got up and rode early in Hyde Park: the feel of a good horse putting her in a better frame of mind. She was too late to leave for polo this weekend but perhaps next weekend as the season had started again in earnest. Then a plan began to form in her mind. *Oh yes*, she thought, *just perfect.*

She returned home, showered and the telephone rang.

"Babe, I'm sorry, really I am. Couldn't get taxi for love or money. I tried to ring but it just rang out, I-"

"Stop!" she cried, steeling herself to appear natural and calm, laughing down the telephone. "Forget it. I gave up waiting for my Scottish hooligan to appear, pulled out the phone and went to bed with a good book. I must be getting old. Now, are you still on the town with the boys tonight or are they off on tour?"

He was taken aback by her calm attitude and as with all men of that type, it drew him on, which is how Claire had planned it, acting to the best of her ability.

"Aye, but Sunday would be good, are you around?"

"What to nurse your hangover? Hah. Maybe for lunch but I'm out on Sunday night with the girls. So you can take me out somewhere near Richmond Park and we can walk off the beer."

She knew he would not be able to resist the put off and, sure enough, he responded positively. She put the telephone down and clenched her hands. Looking furiously at the telephone, she said to herself; "Lying, little, shit! You wait, you Scottish git, just you wait. I'll have my revenge."

Sunday afternoon saw them walking in the pale spring sunshine through the park. The buds on the hawthorns were coming through early, daffodils finishing and the sweet, heavy, smell of freshly cut grass wafted on the air. It was so warm that they were meandering, arm in arm in just shirt sleeves and light leather jackets. Some yards away, two horses carried their riders gently through the park before disappearing into the avenue of shrubs.

"Now, that's what we should be doing," Claire remarked casually. "Except that you can't ride, can you?"

"Can't ride?" he howled as she knew he would. "I learnt to ride from the age of eight until my teens. 'Course I can ride just as well as you, not poncing around a park, but in the open countryside," he challenged.

"Ah, away the noo," she mocked. "Really, Angus, you never cease to amaze me. But would that have been in Scotland?" He nodded in the affirmative, "Well that explains it. They all ride back to front up there don't they? Not proper riding at all."

She ducked as he made a lunge for her and they ran chasing in and out of the trees, to all the world like two, carefree, lovers but Angus would have been surprised to have read her heart at that moment. She sprang the final part of the trap.

"So then 'Master of Horse'," she carried on, when he finally caught her in a laughing embrace, "come up to Gloucestershire next weekend and we can ride the polo ponies, do a bit of stick and balling and if you are good enough," she taunted, "maybe even play some practice chukkas! Providing of course they can understand you."

The last was a reference to the fact that, like most Scots, when in the company of their fellow countrymen they immediately reverted to a strong Scottish accent which lasts for days afterwards.

"Well if you talk English, what are "practice chukkas" and "stick and balling?"

"Heathen. Stick and balling is when one merely practices, passing the ball, gently hitting it and getting one's eye in. And practice chukkas are low level polo, not a full blown game only for say two chukkas of say seven minutes. It's great fun, unless of course you're frightened of falling off?" she taunted "So are we on? Come up and stay at my parent's house."

At this he span around aghast, Angus had an aversion to meeting parents.

"Um let me see this weekend I think I'm busy, I-"

"Don't worry," she interrupted. "They won't be there. Anyway, we can take two cars, so, you can escape whenever you want. The look on your face was a picture, parent aversion, classic case."

They laughed together and the date was set, next weekend was finalised.

"So a whole weekend together, what will we do all the time?" Angus asked wide eyed with innocence.

"Well, if you don't know, you're not the man I think you are," she retorted.

They finished their walk and drove back to Chelsea. Claire was delighted with how it had all gone, her revenge was in sight.

Other clandestine plans were also being put into place at the MAS offices. Shingler called into see Simions.

"Do we have good news?" he queried.

"Yes all arranged. A very bad case of spring flu about to hit H & B very soon."

"Who do we have going in? Liz?"

"Trying for her, but I think it is another girl. Liz is busy on a legitimate assignment apparently."

"Really? How odd."

The plans were hatched and Shingler left.

CHAPTER 17

Monday morning began expectantly for Rupert. Now was the chance to shine on this deal and start the pressure towards obtaining vacant possession of the site. It had been decided to avoid any face to face meetings with the MD, Mr. Michaels and to keep everything clinical and at arm's length.

Before any further action was taken however, Simions called a council of war, in order to co-ordinate matters. They met at MAS's offices later that morning.

"Right, Rupert, instruct your PSD to serve the relevant notice for termination of the lease as we are now in time to do so I believe." Rupert nodded in the affirmative.

"Unfortunately there doesn't seem to be anything to our advantage in the lease terms. Notice to be served no later than three months before termination of the lease and counter notice no later than three months thereafter."

"No 'Time of the essence clause' I suppose?"

"No and the lawyers said it was straight forward as well."

Simions continued, "Very well. Mike, carry on with the investment purchase and no press release. If questioned at all, we merely bought it as part of our plan for high yielding, short term income strategy. Some solid, meaningless, jingoistic nonsense like that." He smiled cynically. "Who knows, we might get offered more of the same product, could be interesting."

"Claire," he said turning his full charm upon her. "I would like you to, very discreetly, start putting together a list of probable tenants and the rents that they would be prepared to pay. Only in general terms, nothing too specific, understood?"

"Very much so. I know the form."

"Good. In the meantime I have been looking at the company itself. It appears in good shape financially, most of the shares are owned by family members, so no way in there. However they have some large debts to suppliers, notably Diamond Drilling Services, a small quoted company, doing rather well after the Big Bang. Maybe pressure could be brought to bear there?" he mused almost whimsically. "Yes, Rupert, could you go and look at their premises for me, just a general view, value etc."

"Certainly," he said accepting a piece of paper with the address on it.

"Right, that's it. Let's crack on and find a way to get VP!"

The meeting ended and they all left the offices. Out on the street Mike mused; "I wonder what pressure he is going to try and bring via Diamond Drills or whatever they are called?"

"Well whatever it is, it will be only just the right side of ethical, if that," Rupert retorted.

"Yes, he can be a nasty piece of work. I wouldn't want to get on the wrong side of him, that's for sure," Claire commented.

They returned to the office and Rupert went to see Chris Hughes in PSD.

"Ah, so the mountain has come to Mohamed. What's your problem this time?"

"And a lovely good morning to you too, Chris. Actually it is to give you some work. I've brought a lease with me: we need a notice serving for termination of a tenancy."

Rupert proceeded to explain the situation in full, omitting

nothing. When he finished Chris looked down at the lease, drew hard on his cigarette, blew smoke into the air and squinted in his customary manner through the blue haze.

"You have read the lease?" he asked. Rupert nodded. "Nothing special, no time of the essence?"

"No, I went through that particular clause twice, and so have the lawyers."

"So what do you need me for then, to serve the notice?"

"For two reasons; a) you're the best, and b) I need the distance so no one sees exactly what we are trying to do."

"Fine by me, I'll always take a fee. 7.5% of the rent passing?"

"Yea, I agreed that with Simions. Don't forget to send him a letter confirming the terms though, he is shifty."

"I know, I know, I taught you, remember?" He chided. Rupert pulled a face and left.

Rupert drove to the address given to him by Simions, which was located south of the river in an industrial location at the front of a 1970's estate. The estate was typical of its genre with some neat rows of uniform sheds, painted the ubiquitous, brown and yellow and lines of large, refuse cans on wheels marking the boundary of each ownership. *What the hell did he want me to look at this for?* thought Rupert. *He can't want to buy it, surely?* He drove back disgusted at the waste of a day. While stuck in a traffic jam before re-crossing the river at Tower bridge, he reached down to play with his new toy: a car phone.

The company would only pay for one if the employee was a partner or above, so he had agreed a deal, where he had installed it and all business calls would be paid for by the firm. This however was personal. He had been trying to get hold of Liz for a while. She had been at her parents for the weekend and he was keen to see her tonight. He dialled the number of her new mobile,

"Liz?"

"Morning, how are you?" The formal response indicated that she could not talk. A system they had agreed upon as she often worked for agents and property related firms, so discretion was the best policy.

"Can't talk huh?"

"That's right."

"Where are you?"

"Halpern & Beams, on Grosvenor Street."

"There again? They must have an endemic flu bug problem with their staff," he joked.

"Mmmm, something like that."

"OK, I understand. Can we meet up tonight, 7.30 at the Flask?"

"That would be good. I have to go, speak to you later." She rang off.

Whilst it was not her fault, he still found it frustrating, annoying and was almost jealous of the fact that she could not talk. She did not want to draw attention to herself, he supposed, especially as their relationship was not openly public knowledge, even amongst CR staff. *Still it was all very odd*, he concluded.

Rupert decided that by the time he had fought with the traffic, there was no point in returning to the office and so went directly to his flat to go for a run, relax and get ready for the evening ahead. He returned, entered his flat and got changed for his usual four miles route that led through some small parks. He needed to keep fit, not only for work, but more to do with the fact that he'd been a member of the TA since his teens and so it was necessary to continue with the fitness regime he had always followed. He returned from the run blown, but feeling good. He carried out some further exercises, showered and prepared for the evening.

When he arrived at her flat she was ready by the door and

clearly delighted to see him. They kissed each other and hugged as though they had been apart for weeks, not days. Their relationship had reached a breakthrough on the night they had slept together, although there were still "rooms" in her past which Rupert felt he could not enter but he was sufficiently in love with her for this not to matter.

They settled down with their drinks in a quiet corner of the pub, which was unusually busy for a Monday night.

"I don't know what happens in deepest darkest Sussex but whatever it is, it suits you. You look gorgeous." She blushed, ever so slightly, at the compliment, enhancing her fading tan.

"Well, if you're a good boy, you might be invited next time, if you faaancy a weekennd in the cunnnr'y." She laughed.

"That has to be the worst country accent I've ever heard." He rolled his eyes "But yes, that would be good, and scary. Meeting parents and things."

"Oh don't worry, they only come out of their coffins at night, just carry a crucifix, you'll be fine."

The conversation carried on in this vein for the rest of the evening, with both of them revelling in each other's company. It was only when the conversation turned to work that it became slightly tense.

"Well, actually, I am thinking of taking a full time job. The agency has put me forward for a permanent post."

"Really, but I thought you liked the freedom of temping?"

"I do, or did, but I feel like having some security. The post is for a PA, a chance to work with the business."

"What company?" he asked.

"Crispin & Howell, the quantity surveyors. They have specifically asked for me."

"Quantity surveyors?" he gasped. "My God I'm not surprised; you'll be bored out of your mind."

"Don't be like that. It's a great job and has good potential to grow with the firm. We can't all be whiz kids you know," she exclaimed.

"Sorry, I'm being an arsehole ignore me. It sounds great, it's just my natural agent's prejudice."

"I know," she said putting her hand on his knee. "All you deal junkies think about is buy, sell and *what's the angle?*"

"Well not quite *all* we think about." She read the look in his eye, smiled and finished her drink.

"Come on then lover boy, let's go."

They left arm in arm, the moment forgotten and returned to her flat where they made love and slept in each other's arms.

CHAPTER 18

The next day Rupert received a call from Chris Hughes to go up to his office for a chat; he would not be any more forthcoming on the telephone. He ran up the two flights of stairs and arrived breathing heavily.

"I don't know why you keep fit fanatics bother, a fag is much better for you, you know?" Rupert grinned.

"Come on give, have you found anything exciting?"

"Well I don't know really, depends what you call exciting," he commented being deliberately irritating and obtuse. "You said that you'd read the notice clauses and found nothing, yes?"

"Yes." Rupert felt his mouth go dry. *What had he missed?* he thought to himself, the idea of having made a howler and screwing up the deal filled him with dread.

"But what you didn't look at is the Definitions section, setting out all the minutiae, did you?"

"Oh shit, what have I missed?" he asked.

"Well, it states and I quote.'*for the avoidance of doubt all times-cales contained herein, with regard to service of notices in all clauses,* blah, blah… *will be taken to mean that time will considered to be strictly of the essence in every case……blah blah.'..*"

"Wow, so if they don't respond within the given timescale

161

to us contesting the application to terminate the lease, i.e. one month, we get vacant possession and can kick them off?"

"Well done Sherlock! Bloody agency surveyors, couldn't read a lease if their lives depended on it." he said scathingly.

"Yea, well even the lawyers didn't pick it up."

"No surprises there then."

"Chris, you're a star, wait 'till I tell Simions."

"But don't count your chickens, they will probably respond in time. Remember they have Halpern & Beams acting for them and no deals done 'til it's done."

"Yea, yea, but at least it gives us hope."

He left in a hurry, made a quick call to get an appointment with Simions and arrived at his offices within half an hour. He was shown straight up to Simons room.

"Rupert, you sounded excited on the phone. It must be good news to necessitate a visit. I have literally, twenty minutes then."

"We have been going through this lease again, or rather Chris Hughes has in PSD, and he has found a time of the essence clause that works in our favour," he finished excitedly.

"Really," Simions responded calmly. "Why didn't we find this sooner?"

Rupert shrugged and explained the whole situation. When he had finished, Simions smiled to himself and turned to look out of the window. Rupert had a déjà vu feeling but he could not place it.

"Good work. I will speak to the lawyers, give them a bollock-ing and get a definitive answer as to our position. Of course it all depends upon whether their agents spot this in time or not and respond accordingly."

"Of course," admitted Rupert. "But it still gives us a possible loophole."

"Indeed, now I must ask you to leave. Shingler will be here

anytime now and although he will be brought in if the scheme proceeds I don't want him involved at this stage."

"Yes, understood."

Rupert shook hands and left feeling slightly deflated at the response and also unnerved by the constant spectre of Shingler on the horizon. Still, at least he had guaranteed control this time. Upon returning to the office, he bumped into Claire and relayed the events to her. While she was pleased with the possibility of a loophole, she did not share his unbridled enthusiasm.

"What's up? You seem terribly preoccupied."

"Ya, well we've been here before and it's a long way from being cut and dried yet, besides I've got a lot on my mind with letting this new scheme up in the West Midlands."

"Fair enough, but it seems more than that. You sure you're alright?"

"Ya, just leave it Rup's, ok? I'm fine."

"OK, ok, but if you want to talk I'm here."

"Sorry. Yes, I know, didn't mean to be that sharp."

They left the corridor and went their separate ways. The rest of the week passed in a similar vein for Claire. The strain of appearing normal for Angus and other colleagues was getting to her and she couldn't wait for the weekend to arrive.

CHAPTER 19

When Friday finally came, she made an excuse not go the pub at lunch time and met Angus at her flat. She had to fight him off, as he had other things on his mind than just leaving for the country.

"No Angus, we've got all weekend. I want to get on the road before we hit the traffic and get all snarled up. God, you've got hands like an octopus." She then forced herself to laugh lightly.

"Mmmm, can't we just have a "quicky" before we go?" he begged, kissing her and fondling her breast. She nearly succumbed, despite herself.

"No, you sex maniac. We can spend all weekend together in bed if you want, now let's get going. Build up your passion on the journey and we'll go straight to bed when we get there."

He pulled a sulky face but finally agreed. They got into their separate cars; Claire's a Golf GTI, of which, as her first company car, she was very proud. Angus followed in his BMW 2.5i, a race would have ensued but the traffic forebade this, although both were recorded members of the Park Lane 100 club. To become a member one had to have started at one end or the other of Park Lane and reach 100 miles per hour before hitting the brakes at the other end, a particularly difficult challenge that required nerve and skill to avoid "slow" traffic.

They followed the steady line of red lights along the M4. As they got further towards Swindon, the traffic finally thinned and they turned off towards Cirencester. Claire's family home lay some ten minutes outside the town, near Edgeworth; a small hamlet with a pub, village shop and church.

It was a lovely setting; amongst rolling hills, leading down to a valley and up to Cirencester Park on the other side. The village and her parent' house were set high up on one of the many ridges that slashed through the Cotswold countryside, creating beautiful, undulating, landscapes. They arrived after navigating a series of small, country lanes, which Angus thought were never going to end. They then turned off the lane, went through open gates, across a cattle grid and along a stone driveway.

In front of them lay a large stone house in classic vernacular architecture. Constructed in an H-shape, common to Cotswold houses, it had green painted wood work and a rampant Wysteria covering most of the front. It was imposing, even in the fading light, and Angus was impressed despite being used to the large homes of his Scottish homeland. A large group of outbuildings were off to the left, including a small barn, stable block and open garaging and it was to this that his eye was drawn.

A security light had flicked on as soon as they neared the house, highlighting the cars parked in the garage. When they got out he queried; "Who do they belong to? I thought you said your parents were away?"

She laughed gently. "Don't worry. Josh will have run them to the airport, they have gone away for a long weekend to the opera in Venice. And before you ask, Josh will be off bonking his new girlfriend and couldn't give a damn about who I bring home. Now, come in and meet him, or the lights might be Mrs. Crawford; Mummy's house keeper." she pointed at a glow emanating from the house.

His nervousness temporarily abated; the last thing he had

wanted to was to come away, with no bonking and have to put up with being polite to parents. A brother would be bad enough. As Claire turned away, she grinned maliciously to herself; *part one completed,* she thought. The main light to the covered porch was switched on and as soon as the door opened slightly, a large Springer Spaniel bounded out to meet her.

"Jess!" she cried and crouched down to be licked and pawed. The dog rolled over on to his back for her tummy to be rubbed.

"Jess, meet Angus, Angus meet Jess, beautiful girl?" she said rubbing her tummy. "Where's Boot?"

At the name, a limping Jack Russell of ancient vintage wobbled into view, wagging his stump of a tail.

"Hello Boot, how are you?" She rubbed his ears and pulled them playfully. Angus foresaw a weekend of dogs, horses and AGA's ahead of him. *Thank God for bonking and no parents,* he thought. But just then his illusion was shattered. A deep, well-modulated woman's voice hailed from the house.

"Darling! Hello, what a lovely surprise."

"Mummy, what are you doing here," she said, in well-staged surprise. "I thought you were in Venice or something?"

"Oh darling, that's next weekend," she said coming over to embrace her daughter and kiss her on both cheeks. "But never mind, it's lovely to see you. Now who is this? Do introduce me."

"Mummy, this is Angus. Angus, my Mother."

She was laughing with glee on the inside. *He could not escape now,* she thought. Angus groaned inwardly, as he was presented to her mother. She was a tall, handsome woman in her fifties, slightly more rounded than Claire, with a lovely smile and twinkly, blue eyes that seemed, to Angus, to pierce right into his soul. She had on a dark, blue twin set, pearls and a tweed skirt, well fitted and not frumpy county style, good legs showed from beneath it. They shook hands.

"Pleased to meet you, Mrs. Sewell."

"And you Angus, but please call me Jane. I hope you both had a good journey? Your Father is getting logs in for the fire. We find it still gets chilly in the evenings. Now come on in, bring your bags, I'll air the beds. Angus you can go in the Yellow room; it has lovely views in the morning," she finished.

Mother and daughter walked arm in arm towards the front door. To Angus, it appeared, that Claire had taken on a new personae, one which he could neither fathom nor pierce. He had previously thought that she was a town animal; at home in that environment; but now he was seeing another side to her. One with which he was not altogether comfortable, he decided.

The door opened onto a flagstone floor with warm light spilling onto the scene from all angles. Various white painted doors opened off the hall and one of these led to the snug, which was painted a dark, warm green. Pictures adorned the walls, along with family photos and homely objet d'art. Rugs were strewn randomly on the tiled floor creating a cosy atmosphere and the log burner in the fireplace was already alight and starting to give off heat.

A door opened to the right and a slightly stooped figure appeared, carrying a log basket laden with logs. He dropped it by the fireplace and stood erect, opening his arms for an embrace from Claire.

"Darling, how lovely to see you," he enthused warmly.

"Daddy, how's you?" she asked, her familiar greeting from childhood days.

"I'm very well, mint condition," he responded.

He was a tall, lean, cadaverous man of late fifties, though still fit with dark hair streaked with grey and dressed in moleskins, check shirt and a pullover. He shook hands with Angus, introducing himself as John and they exchanged pleasantries.

"So, you've come up to see us, how lovely."

"Ah, well, I got the dates wrong," she said looking

embarrassedly at Angus who smiled. "I thought you were going away this weekend, not next, although it is great to see you both."

Her Father smiled ruefully and looked hard at his daughter, never one to be taken in. He knew that they would be in for an interesting weekend. Drinks were poured and the conversation turned to London and work, with the latest deal of Rupert's coming to the fore of the conversation.

"He should pull it off if he can get the planning," she explained.

"Yea and pigs might fly! It is such a long shot; although with Simion's dirty tricks brigade on side, he might do it," Angus said scornfully.

"Oooh. Sounds like sour grapes to me," she retorted "But what do you mean dirty tricks?"

"Well he has a certain reputation for getting things done, no matter what the cost.

We'll see," he finished cryptically.

"It all sounds as though you are both talking a foreign language to me," her father joked. Claire laughed and explained some of the more esoteric points and the evening continued in good humour until they went to retire to bed.

"I've put Angus in the Yellow Room," her mother said, a perfect smile in place. "It's all aired. Anything you want, just shout, Angus. Good night."

The good nights were said and both Claire and Angus went upstairs together. When alone, on the landing of the first floor Angus turned to her and said

"Can I sneak down later? This cannot be for real, sleeping apart?"

"Look, I'm really sorry but there is nothing we can do and no, you can't come down later, this stairs creak like a trumpet voluntary, you'll wake the whole house. Come on just one weekend, you'll have fun tomorrow and they'll probably go out on Saturday; we'll have the house to ourselves."

Angus pouted and sulked, retiring ungracefully, giving Claire a perfunctory kiss goodnight. As Claire turned and opened her door she made an excuse to return downstairs for a glass of water. When she entered the kitchen her parents were tidying up.

"Now young lady," her father said, grinning and shaking his head with mock severity. "What is all this about?"

"I knew I couldn't fool you, Daddy. But I was hoping you would both play along." She proceeded to outline her scheme, giving her reasons and the angst she felt.

"Mmm, you're playing with fire with that one. I wouldn't trust him further than I could throw him!" he commented sagaciously.

She kissed both her parents goodnight and returned to her room with a glass of water.

The following morning was bright and warm; with spring sunshine banishing the nights chill from the air. Even Angus was in good spirits; tucking into bacon and eggs at breakfast.

"I feel really good this morning; no hangover and ready to face these polo ponies," he said assuredly.

"Good, we'll finish breakfast, walk the dogs and get there for the second string, about 10.30."

"What's a string?" he queried.

"Oh, It's just the name used for each group of horses as the grooms exercise them," she explained.

Some twenty minutes later they prepared to leave.

"We'll go in your car. It will be fun turning up in a smart BMW for a change."

They packed the car with all the gear and left to travel about a mile along the lane, pulling up where Claire indicated in front of a large pair of wooden gates, so high that it was impossible to see over. A painted sign bore the legend *Edgeworth Polo Club*.

She got out, opened the gates wide and beckoned Angus through, closing the gates quickly behind him. The enclosed yard was bordered on two sides by rows of stables, with various equine heads protruding from the open, upper doors. To the right stood a large, Cotswold stone house, opening out via a back door to the parking area. Angus got out of the car and was immediately assailed by the smell of horse; creosote, shavings and sweaty leather. Claire breathed it in like a drug.

"So, this is where you hide away to."

She smiled, "Yes, isn't it wonderful?" she said breathing deeply. Again, Angus noticed that she was becoming a different person to that which he knew in London.

Looking around he saw that the yard was a hive of activity; grooms were leading horses, washing them, tacking up or grooming. Hails of greetings were directed in Claire's direction.

"Is there anyone English here or are they all colonials?"

She grinned. "I know. I think JohnP deliberately recruits them from all over the world, except England."

At that point a tall figure appeared, walking over with a horseman's rolling gait. He was slim with grey blue eyes, greying hair and a knowing smile.

"Morning JohnP, how are you?" Claire greeted. He smiled with genuine warmth, kissed her and was introduced to Angus.

"How you doing?" he asked Australian twang overlaying an English accent.

"Well, thought I'd come up and see how it was done polo style." JohnP assessed humans in the way he did horses, with an innate intuition that was rarely wrong. *Here*, he thought, *we have a maverick and a wrong u'n*. He didn't say anything or give anything away by his manner but it was there for those to see who knew him.

"Good. We can always do with people to help exercise and I gather that you're playing chukkas later?" he queried, his voice rising slightly like most people that had spent too long in the antipodes or in the company of their countrymen.

"Yes, if that's ok."

"Fine, fine, I'll see you later," he said smiling and walked off to correct a groom who was clipping a horse.

"Man of few words," Angus commented. Claire agreed.

"But what he does say usually matters."

Angus was beginning to feel more out of place with each introduction and was therefore pleased to be finally mounted with a further horse in each hand, heading out to the exercise track. The track lay some three hundred yards away from the buildings and comprised of a sanded, oval exercise run, around which strings of horses were already walking.

"How do you feel?" Claire asked enjoying his obvious discomfort at having an additional horse in each hand.

"Fine, just fine. But I didn't realise I would be leading two as well."

"Well, you said you could ride, didn't you?" At which she increased the pace to a trot and moved off onto the track, into a gap between two of the existing strings. Angus followed. After ten minutes he was told that he now had to canter with the two horses in tow for a further twenty minutes. He was aghast.

"What! For 20 minutes, you must be joking."

"What's the matter, scared or too tired?" she mocked, laughing at him gaily as she seemed to glide effortlessly forward into a canter.

He responded by kicking up hard into a canter but unused to the sharpness of a polo pony was unbalanced by the fast change of pace. He managed one lap with the pony, egged on by his increased movement in the saddle and its companions, who were virtually out of control. This caused Angus to grab the pommel in order to try and regain his balance. At this point every groom's nightmare happened; the outside horse he was leading stopped dead. Instinctive reaction took over and Angus tried to hang on to the lead rope and his own horse simultaneously. Something had to give; and it was him. He sailed backwards out of the saddle, appearing for an instant to hover in mid-air before finally measuring his length in the hard sand. He hit the ground with a woof, as all the air was expelled from his body and narrowly missed being trodden on by the oncoming horses. He moaned, rolled over and tried to stand.

"You ok?" called Claire sailing round, trying not laugh along with the other grooms who considered this an occupational hazard, one which usually called for a case of beer to be bought by the unlucky individual.

"No, I fucking well am not!" he called.

"Get off the track," he was told. He stuck up a V-sign and moved off, limping and without his horses, all of whom were caught expertly by the grooms who added them to their strings and continued four up as though nothing had happened.

"That'll cost you a case of beer," Claire laughed as she passed. "I can't stop, see you back at the yard." And she carried on cantering around the track. Angus was furious when Claire finally appeared, happy, smiling and chatting to one of her fellow gallopers.

"How are you darling?" she cooed.

"How do you think? You might have stopped, for fucks sake."

"I know, it hurts doesn't it? But the ego probably came off worst, I should think," she answered calmly, refusing to be drawn into a quarrel.

"Oh, ha bloody ha. Look at the grazing I've got here," he said raising his shirt to show friction burns.

"I'll be with you in a minute."

She un-tacked the horses and talked to Angus as she showered them with one of the hosepipes and scrapped the water off each horse.

"Ok, ok, I couldn't stop, you know why. Now let's forget it. Besides, you did look funny. Well, a game next, you on for that?" she asked innocently.

"No, I'm not, can't we go?"

"What you must be joking. This is what I came for," she said ambiguously.

At that point, a Porsche 911 Targa, purred into the yard, with the top down and music playing. The engine stopped and out stepped a suave, classically, good looking man in his forties. Obviously south American from his swept back hair, tanned olive skin, open necked polo shirt and the handmade loafers. He saw Claire and smiled.

"Bello!" she rushed across and was swept up in his arms as he planted a kiss on her lips. She responded in kind and they talked in fast Spanish for two minutes.

Finally, he partly released her, keeping a proprietorial arm around her. She turned to face a furious Angus.

"What the hell's this?" he demanded.

"What, not jealous are we? Well if you are you can go, as you wanted to," she responded cattily. "Besides, Juan and I are having dinner tonight after he's given me some lessons."

"You fucking bitch! I ought to smack his face in as well."

She smiled wickedly. "Oh, I wouldn't do that. He's an expert in some sort of Brazilian martial art, very nasty."

"OK, Martini. I know when I'm not wanted."

"Martini?" she questioned.

"Yea, anytime, anyplace, anywhere,…." he sang, a smug grin on his face. She was not to be drawn.

"Well if you want comfort, I suggest you head back to the arms of Suzzane or whatever she's called, I'm sure she'll keep you warm. And next time don't even try to cross me Angus, you lying, little shit."

He made as if to protest, then it hit him.

"You planned the whole thing, didn't you? How long have you known?"

"Long enough to start seeing Juan," she lied. "And he's much better looking than you, Angus."

He fumed, stormed off to his car and made to drive away.

"My parents will have your bags ready for you. Drive safely," she said with a smile.

As he left in a cloud of dust Juan turned to her and said; "You do wind them up, my pretty girl. Now, tell me all about it, the full story, and I can stop pretending to be the great Latin lover."

So she explained completely, rather than just the brief explanation she had given him on the telephone and he finally understood her feelings, having been a good friend of her family for many years.

"Now tell me more about your work. I need to set up an offshore fund for my family trust, away from the Brazilian tax authorities, and the UK market may well suit."

They talked at length about all aspects of her work and the markets. Juan was interested and wanted to explore the opportunities further.

"But," Claire said. "First there is a game of polo to play."

CHAPTER 20

As Rupert walked down the corridor to his office he considered, not for the first time, the way in which his Castle Street deal was progressing. He had changed over the last eighteen months and he would be the first to admit it. The keen eagerness of youth had disappeared, to be replaced by a resilience to "get the deal done" at all costs. A shell of hardness had enveloped him, inuring him to the world he was inhabiting. He had become tougher mentally, which reflected in both his work life and his personality outside the office. His family had noticed the gradual change which to them seemed much more obvious; on his rare visits home to Warwickshire.

In this world of reverie, he almost bumped into Claire as she came from the opposite direction.

"Ooops! Nearly got you. How are you doing? Good weekend?"

"Ah, actually yes, in a funny sort of way. Listen do you fancy a coffee? I need a break and we can discuss Castle Street."

"Ya, absolutely. Let me just get some papers and I'll be with you."

They walked along Grosvenor street to the usual coffee bar on the corner. Upon entering they nodded to various other agents and property people, who made up most of its clientele at that time in the morning. Conversations hushed over coffee, deals being made or broken, information being exchanged. Not for the first time did Rupert consider the value of having eyes and ears all over the place, sucking up information, being party to all that was being said. *Maybe a waitress in each coffee bar in the main area of the West End would be a good idea,* he mused to himself. They got a coffee and settled down in the corner where they could not be overheard.

"So, tell me all. You look like the cat that got the cream and a rather malicious cat, at that."

"Well, I had a rather cathartic experience at the weekend. I lured Angus away and hit him where it hurts- in his ego, before finally finishing with him," she added gleefully.

"What? Oh, do tell," he begged, grinning from ear to ear.

So she did. The full story, from catching him cheating, to finally upbraiding him with Juan. The whole story appealed, especially the bit where Angus was pulled from his horse. He was secretly pleased for ulterior motives, about which he kept quiet, despite his relationship with Liz, which was going well, if slightly mysteriously at times.

"So you just left him? Stuck in deepest, darkest, Gloucestershire? Oh classic, absolutely perfect."

"I must admit I liked it. Every single minute, from the moment he arrived and saw my parents, to when he stormed off having met Juan. Who, incidentally might want to start an investment company of his own. So, back young, free and single again," she sighed.

"You won't be that for long doll. Once they know you are on the market, half the surveyors in the west end will be around."

She leant across and gave him a kiss on the cheek. "Rup's, you're great for my ego. Do you know that?"

He grinned appreciatively.

"Now, on to work; I've lined up all the tenants I can without being too specific, which we cannot do until we know we can get VP. Agreed?" said Claire.

"Yes and we still haven't had a counter notice back from their agents. They have only got two more weeks to go and that's it. Bang!" He slapped his palm into his fist, at which various occupants of the coffee bar looked around.

"Easy, tiger you'll have the market thinking you've pulled off another coup."

He grinned proudly.

"That will do no harm at all. I did, in fact, find another site today, following my canvassing. Looks promising, great deal."

"Deal junkie!" she accused.

"Hah, hark whose talking."

They both laughed, fully aware that beneath the banter the reality was that they had become "Thatcher's Children", out for the kill in a raw, commercial, avaristic world.

CHAPTER 21

Rupert, over the next few days, was on tenterhooks and was called to a meeting at MAS's offices to discuss how the deal was progressing. The date for the counter notice was imminent. The discussions did not go as planned, due to the presence of Shingler; who again, had been brought into play as the deal climaxed. Simions was in an ebullient mood, very optimistic about the outcome of the chances to obtain vacant possession. Rupert objected that even if the notice was not served in time they could still raise an objection that the clause in the lease was inequitably harsh and apply to the courts.

He dismissed it out of hand. "Don't worry. The accounts for the company made very interesting reading; they are not as strong as they would have us believe. If anything, they should be moving to more efficient premises anyway. So who cares, we are just hurrying them along. They should be thanking us!" he laughed harshly.

Rupert left the meeting, as ever troubled by the presence of Shingler. While now able to hold his own with the man and never to be trapped as before by him, he was unable to fathom the direct relationship between him and Simions. *Why*, he wondered, *did he always get brought in? The relationship had to be strong, fine.*

But there would be an extra cost to Simions as he always paid two lots of fees on letting. There was always the danger of leakage, as with the last deal. There must be some strong link with the past that bound them together, if only I could find that link, it would release us both.

He turned his thoughts to the week ahead and thought of Liz, who, he decided was becoming a large part of his life. He missed her greatly when they were apart. Despite his feelings of guilt where Claire was concerned, (who he knew would never consider his suit) Liz's magical, elusive quality intrigued and entranced him, as no other woman before. They were good together; she was great company and they shared the same sense of humour, not to mention that she was great in bed and completely uninhibited, a big plus as far as Rupert was concerned. On impulse, he called her when he returned to the office and for once she could talk, openly flirting with him over the telephone.

"Tomorrow evening sounds good, if you're not too tired of course. You looked rather shattered after the last weekend," she teased.

"Can anyone hear you?"

"They just think I'm talking to my squash partner!" she giggled.

"OK, lover, Thursday. I'll pick you up at 8 ish but you'd better be lively."

"Mmmh, but it wasn't me who fell asleep after the second "game", was it?" she teased.

"You'll pay for that remark!"

"Promises, promises! See you Thursday, bye."

The line went dead. Rupert grinned to himself. The eagerness of the chase now over, it was a high. Still in its first throes of excitement, familiar to all experienced lovers, their relationship was at the point where they could not keep their hands off each other.

The next morning he caught the tube in and was trying to do the Telegraph crossword and caught up in concentration as he tried to decipher an anagram by doodling the letters in the blank space provided.

His mind absently scanned the business news snippets in the column above. *"Diamond Life"-mystery off shore bid.* The article carried on to say that an esoteric, off-shore company called MISSION MACHINES had bought a substantial holding in Diamond Drilling Services.

His mind sprang into focus; Diamond Drilling Services were the company he was looking at for Simions. Simions! *Hah, anagrams*, he thought, *an anagram of Simions is: MISSION. Oh, beautiful*, he reflected, *but would the man not have to declare an interest under stock market rules? No, probably not if it was offshore and to prove who the directors were, might be very difficult to trace. Very clever, no doubt there would now be some financial pressure brought to bear to induce Moorcroft Industries to vacate their site.*

Suddenly it seemed as though the gamble of getting the site for development was a real possibility. He considered the moral position for a moment. But he decided it was not strictly blackmail, just business. Rupert was concentrating hard for the rest of the day both on that and his new deal. However, the day was soon to turn into a nightmare for him, all because of a whim.

The previous day he had dropped his car in for a service at the garage the company used north of Oxford Street. And so now, he decided to walk as there were no cabs available. He walked across Oxford Street into Duke Street, with a view to cutting across Manchester Square to the garage near Portman Street car park. He turned left into the square and as he did so, he thought he might call into MAS's offices on spec to congratulate Simions on his strategy.

Looking ahead, just around the central park to the front of their offices, he was at first delighted, then horrified to see Liz. The sight of her was a pleasurable surprise; he still couldn't get used to her wearing a wig and glasses as her "disguise". What was not pleasant, however, was that she was deep in conversation with Simions! He nearly shouted across to them but something held him back. It was their attitude; familiar, almost intimate, facing each other making eye contact like old friends or, dare he think it, lovers? He changed his position and placed himself so that he was hard to see, whilst still being able to observe them.

They walked slowly around the square heading for the eastern side and Hinde Street, which in turn led to Boswells. He watched them enter the pub together and something struck a chord in his memory. It was as the sunlight, for a brief moment hit the back of Simion's shoulders, highlighting his steel grey hair. Of course, he was the man in Boswells Rupert had seen Liz talking to all those months ago. At the time he hadn't seen the man's face, and was too preoccupied with fitting in with the CR crew but he knew something about Simions was familiar, ever since he'd turned his back to the light in his office, at their first meeting. So, that was it, he was her lover, and had been all this time. Suddenly the hesitation and unexplained absences became clear.

He followed discreetly, bought a drink and thanked God Boswells had its high-walled booth arrangement. At this early hour the pub was not busy and it was possible to catch most of their conversation.

"...I don't want to do this anymore. I'm too close to Rupert now, it just won't work. He will begin to suspect. I want to finish it now."

The response was lost and she said something else, then; "Thank you anyway. But it had to end sometime and now seems right."

Rupert was furious, he nearly burst in on them then and there but he held back. Realising the conversation was at an end, he left his drink unfinished and walked quickly through the side door. Gulping the fresh air in as he walked along the pavement, he thought he was going to have a heart attack. He was livid with rage. *All the lies and deceit, how could she? So what if she wanted to end it now, very big of her, the bitch!*

He walked, needing to calm down and think. Without conscious pause for thought he headed in the direction of the garage. His mind was a whirlwind of emotion. *I cannot believe it*, he thought for the thousandth time. *Why, oh why?* At no point did he feel he had done anything to deserve it, what caused it. *Why start a relationship in the first place?* He could not fathom it. It hurt all the more because, privately, he admitted to himself that he was in love with her, desperately so and that made it worse.

The journey from the garage to her flat was slow by necessity because of the rush hour traffic and as he approached the block of flats, he saw that lights were on in the windows on the second floor. Obviously, the journey by tube had been quicker. He parked his car with great, precise care, taking his time, wanting the conflict and yet not wanting to end the relationship, despite everything.

He walked across to the front door and pressed the intercom to be let in. As he pushed the door open, it was caught by a woman who had appeared silently behind him. She mouthed her thanks, showing a slightly chipped tooth in her smile. Rupert smiled wanly back and proceeded to the lift, pressing the button for the second floor. The woman headed for the stairs.

Before he could even think about what he was going to say, the lift opened its doors and Rupert was pressing the buzzer on Liz's front door. It opened almost immediately and Liz appeared smiling. Rupert thought she looked slightly stressed but none the less lovely. She came forward, kissed him and although he responded in kind, she sensed that something was wrong.

"Come in, you look upset, what's wrong?" she asked, frowning.

He moved forward and up the small flight of stairs to the landing, where he continued the conversation.

"Well, that depends, really."

She tensed. "On what?" The old Liz returned as the tension in him became palpably apparent.

"One's point of view," he continued pompously. "You see, to my way of thinking loyalty is the key; business, pleasure or love. I value it highly and expect it from others."

"Rupert, what the hell are you talking about? Stop being so damn pompous and obtuse and tell me what this is all about. You're obviously upset, so just tell me." In a way, it was as though she had not spoken, except that he picked up on the insult of pomposity.

"Pompous? Well at least it is a genuine emotion! At least I don't have secret assignations; secret relationships and other lovers."

"Rupert, will you talk sense? Come and have a drink and calm down." She led the way into the kitchen, opened a cupboard and produced a bottle of scotch and two tumblers. She poured two good sized measures and offered one to Rupert who downed it in one go.

"Now tell me what you mean."

"I saw you with Simions! Simions of all people. He's old enough to be your Father!"

Her facial expression changed from puzzled, to hurt anger.

"You bastard, how dare you?! Have you been spying on me?"

"Spying? No, I merely came across you and your lover when I was on my way to see my client. I couldn't believe what I saw and so I followed you to the pub where I heard everything."

He relayed all that he had heard from behind the booth.

"You've been seeing him for weeks, even before we got

together, haven't you? It's so fucking awful, words just fail me! I loved you, do you know that? You've just thrown it in my face!"

"Oh I see and that is your conclusion is it. Judge, jury and sentence! No other possible explanation. Well I loved you too." She was shouting now. "I let you in to my life where no one had been for a long time, for what? For this!" She parted her arms in exasperation and disgust, emphasising her point.

"I heard your conversation. You can't deny it. You're just his part time whore!"

"You bastard, you absolute bastard! Get out!" she shouted "Get out now!"

"With pleasure." He turned on his heel and made his way down the stairs, ducking hurriedly as a missile, in the form of a vase just, missed his head and exploded against the wall. One of the flying fragments caught him just behind the ear, cutting him slightly. He raised his hand to find blood and reached for the door lock hurriedly.

"You bitch!" he fumed and left hurriedly, slamming the door behind him. He stormed along the corridor, turned left into the lobby area and took the stairs, two at a time. He did not see the figure of the woman, for whom he held the door, moving quietly along the corridor from the opposite end of the building. She watched him go, a wry smile on her lips and proceeded towards Liz's flat.

Rupert got into his car, revved the engine and flew out of the car park, wheels skidding, entering the traffic without looking and earning himself an angry rebuke from the horns of other drivers. He ignored them and sped off, thoroughly upset.

Half an hour later as he was entering his flat, a telephone call was made to a house in Stanmore.

"Double five one?"

A woman's voice responded; "It's done."

"When?"

A slight pause.

"Half an hour ago."

"Any problems?"

"No, it went smoothly. She had even just had a row with her boyfriend. It will be perfect," she chuckled.

"He didn't see you?" the concerned voice asked.

She answered decisively: "Do me a favour, of course not."

"Good, thank you for calling. We will settle up as usual."

The line at the other end went dead and Shingler put the telephone down.

CHAPTER 22

The day started badly for Rupert. He had a bad hangover, his mouth felt dry; somebody had left pigeon shit in there he reflected, probably from when he collapsed on the sofa last night and cried himself to sleep after his final glass of whiskey. *Never again,* he thought, *never again;* as the two tablets fizzed very loudly in the glass of water in front of him. He waited until they had dissolved, then gulped the contents in two mouthfuls. Uuugh, it tasted awful.

"Mmmh you look good," commented Tina sarcastically as she entered the room. "Good night?"

"No, bloody awful actually."

"Ah, burning the candle at both ends, and in the week. You boys. I don't know how you do it!" she smiled warmly, in sympathy, and walked over to her desk.

The morning proceeded in this vein until late afternoon, when, just as Rupert was starting to feel slightly better, things became unimaginably worse.

He received a call from Matthews, the company secretary querying his car and registration number, which he verified.

"Why what's the problem?" he asked weakly "not another speeding ticket?"

"I don't think so, not unless they send Detective Inspectors around to investigate speeding fines."

"What do you mean?"

"Well there is a Detective Inspector Fleming on his way to see the driver of your vehicle and he will be here in about 10 minutes, so I should buck up. You haven't done anything we should know about have you?"

"No, absolutely not!"

"Good. Well let me know will you?"

He put the telephone down and Rupert felt that cold feeling that any law abiding citizen gets when the police are involved. He did not have to wait long. Reception called about fifteen minutes later with two police officers asking to see him. He made his way down to reception with a feeling of trepidation. *What*, he wondered *had he done?* He thought of all the border line cases of illegality. Should he have reported bribing a planning officer? Was there more than just the threat of menace when Cauldron MD backed off the court case?

He walked into reception and was indicated the two men reclining on the sofas. They got up together and Rupert would have known straight away that they were policemen. It was that indefinable air; *they had a certain manner and cynical way of look-ing at one,* he decided. They were two completely different people to look at yet they both looked the same. Standing, the taller of the two walked forward with no offer to shake hands. *A bad sign*, Rupert decided.

The Inspector's voice was clipped and hard. "Mr Brett?"

Rupert nodded in acknowledgement.

"I am DI Fleming, this-" he indicated over his shoulder, "is DS Brooke." They flipped open warrant cards and then snapped them shut.

"Good afternoon, how may I help you?" Rupert continued, sounding more confident than he felt.

"Is there somewhere we can talk, Mr Brett? Somewhere a little more private."

The insinuation in the voice that they would need privacy, was another turn of the screw to intimidate, to make the recipient more uncomfortable. It was obviously a well-practised technique. Rupert offered them towards one of the meeting room doors and leading from reception, walked in, switched on the lights, offered them coffee, which they both refused and sat down.

He studied them again, trying to gain some clue as to what this was all about. He saw the cold eyes of the Detective Inspector looking back at him from a gaunt, lined face that had seen too much and trusted nothing. His hair was prematurely flecked with grey from over work and long, stressful hours.

The Detective Sergeant was stocky and square with broad shoulders hinting at great power beneath the grey jacket which did not match his trousers. An ex-policeman friend of his had once told Rupert that CID always had mismatched jackets and trousers as, while they originally matched when new, after various scuffles, or scaling fences, walls, chasing villains etc. they had to buy new pairs of trousers which did not match the remaining item of clothing.

"So, is one of you going to tell me what all this is about?"

"Yes. Do you know an Elizabeth Carmichael?"

"Liz, yes. She is my girlfriend. Why? Has something happened to her?" he asked, concern evident in his voice.

"Why should something have happened to her?" asked DS Brooke, managing to make the question sound like a sneer.

"Well, by the evidence that you're here asking questions about her. Look here, this is all starting to get a little tiresome, if something has happened to Liz please tell me what it is or get to the point." He had reached the end of his tether, police or no police.

DI Fleming looked at Rupert, as if reassessing him, as most people did after about five minutes in his company.

"We were called this morning to check on a flat belonging to Miss Carmichael as one of her neighbours was concerned. You see, she had arranged to look after said neighbour's cat as she was going on holiday but Miss Carmichael didn't call round this morning as per their arrangement. Subsequent to this, the neighbour also heard a disturbance the night before and was, understandably, rather worried.

"We telephoned but there was no answer. In the end, we had to break the door down and guess what we found?" Rupert at this point started to feel weak, he didn't know what was coming next but an awful feeling of dread was beginning to consume him. "We found her dead, Mr Brett."

"Dead, how? Why? Where?" The words were torn from him in a high-pitched squeak. Shock was apparent on his face and tears welled in his eyes as the full implication of what had been said hit him. The DI decided that he was either a good actor or it was genuine.

"Where were you last night, Mr Brett?"

He did not answer immediately. "At her flat, but why, I mean, what does that mean? I wasn't there when she died. How did she die?" He stumbled over the last words, reality hitting him that he would not see her again, made worse by their final, acrimonious parting. He would never forgive himself.

"We are not sure how she died exactly but we think it may be drugs related."

"Drugs? But that's ridiculous! She never took drugs."

They ignored his statement. "How well did you know Miss Carmichael?"

"We had been seeing each other for a few months."

"Were you intimate?"

"What! What do you mean, did we sleep together? Yes, we did and at no time did I see any needle marks."

"Who said anything about needles?" It was the DS again, being clever.

"I naturally assumed as it was drugs that it would involve a needle. Isn't that how you take drugs?"

"Not necessarily. They could be administered orally."

Rupert shook his head in disbelief. The DI changed tack.

"What time did you leave the flat?"

"Just after 7.00, I think. I don't know exactly. I came straight from picking up my car from the garage."

"Where was that?"

"Just off Manchester Square, it is the main garage the firm uses."

For some reason, which Rupert could not rationalise, he did not mention the surprise events of the meeting with Simions or the overheard conversation in the pub.

"So, straight from there to her flat?" the question was left hanging in the air unsaid.

"Yes. We had a date for that evening. I arrived to pick her up, we were going out to dinner."

"And, you arrived, then what?" The question was framed in such a way that Rupert suspected that they knew more than was being said and decided to come clean.

"We had a row. After we argued I left the flat and drove home. I probably got there about 8. 8.30."

"What did you argue about?" It was the DS again. Rupert explained in general terms this time including the events that occurred in Manchester Square and finishing with him leaving the flat.

"That is the whole story, with nothing omitted" he finished.

"So now you say another person was involved and you were

jealous? Why did you not mention this before? You didn't force her in any way?" DS Brooke sneered again.

"What! Are you crazy?" his face hardened in anger and grief at the insinuation. "I didn't tell you because I didn't think it was relevant, now it appears it may be. But, no, I did not force her. Why, was there a sexual assault? And for the last time, I did not know that she took drugs and still find it incredible. How were they taken if there was no injection?"

"We are asking the questions, Mr Brett. Now who was this other man she saw? What is his name and how do you know him?"

Rupert answered the specifics naming Paul Simions and his connection with him.

"So let me get this straight. This Mr Simions is your client, with sway over you. You see him having an affair with your girlfriend, you get mad, rush to her flat in a rage and are the last person to see her alive: is that correct?"

The silence was shattering. Rupert went red and gasped.

"No, it was not like that. We rowed, I left her alive and well, just upset. This is a nightmare," he wailed, aghast at what was befalling him.

"Did you try and contact Miss Carmichael again by telephone after you had left her flat, Mr Brett?"

"No, I didn't"

"Why not?"

"Because, as I told you; we argued and it was effectively over between us. At least it seemed that way at the time." He gazed into the middle distance, his mind wandering, tears reappeared in his eyes.

"Would you mind explaining that cut on your neck, Mr Brett?

He flinched as he touched the newly healed scab on his neck. "Yes, Liz," he paused at saying her name. "We had a blazing row. She threw a vase at me in temper as I was leaving and-"

"And you just took it? No retaliation? Just left peacefully saying "thank you very much"?" DS Brooke asked sarcastically.

"Yes. I was nearly out the door. What do you think, that I ran back up and strangled her?"

"Who said she was strangled?" came the retort.

Despite the shock, the surveyor took over, Rupert's wits his greatest asset: "Precisely: you said it was drugs related. If it was, do you think I go around armed with syringes ready to kill every person I have a row with?" he shouted in near hysteria, tears in his eyes. "I didn't have anything to do with her death," he finished vehemently.

The two detectives exchanged a glance and DS Brooke closed his notebook.

"We will have some more questions for you in due course, Mr. Brett, so please stay available," concluded DI Fleming. They got up. Rupert rose with them, his mind in turmoil. "Right, that is all for now. Thank you, Mr Brett." They made to leave. "Oh just one more thing, can we have some of your details please; address, phone number." These were duly noted and they left leaving Rupert with his thoughts.

Out on the street they walked along the pavement heading for Manchester Square.

"Well, what do you think?" Brooke asked his colleague.

"I don't know. The grief was genuine but they had a row, could be one last fling.   He was really shocked, not a twitch or anything, just tears and grief."

"Yes, but were they tears of guilt at something that had gone too far?" DS Brooke queried cynically.

"I think you were a bit hard on him mind with that sex comment."

He shrugged. "Well it got a response. Anyway we'll see what

the autopsy says, I asked for a priority so we should have it tomorrow. He is still the best suspect we have and the last person to see her alive. Where to now, this mysterious Mr Simions?"

"Yes, let's pay him a call whilst everything is still up in the air. I get the feeling that Mr Brett will not be tipping him off," Fleming smirked.

They arrived at MAS's offices on Manchester Square and announced themselves at the ground floor reception. One of the stunning blond secretaries telephoned up to Simions. The two detectives noticed the pause in the conversation despite being able to only hear one side of it.

The receiver replaced, the receptionist beamed at the two men who were completely immune: "Mr Simions is on the telephone but will be with you as soon as he can."

The detectives nodded, exchanging glances. They judged their lives by a series of rules. One of them was that those who delayed seeing them were guilty of something. Ten minutes later they were instructed to go up to Simions' office. DI Flemming and DS Brooke left the lift on the top floor. As they were shown into Simions' office by yet another gorgeous blonde, Brookes eyed the movement of the her skirt. *Wow*, he thought, *what I could do with that*! Simions watched this bye-play, smiling to himself as he made a pretence of finishing a call, assessing before being assessed. He calmly finished his call, "Yes, yes, of course, will do and please have the papers sent around by this afternoon. Goodbye."

Anyone who knew him well would know he was lying; he was rarely that polite and hardly ever said goodbye.

He rose from his chair smoothly, smiling, very urbane, every inch the captain of industry, extending his hand as he came around the desk.

"Gentlemen, good morning, Peter Simions, but I expect you know that already as you've come to see me," he joked charmingly.

They shook hands. "DI Fleming and this-" he said, turning, "is Detective Sergeant Brooke. Thank you for agreeing to see us."

"Please sit down, tea, coffee?"

"Already been asked and I understand they are on the way," he replied affably.

"Good, good. Now what can I do for you?" hands expansive, open gesture, perfectly calm.

Oh he's good, Fleming thought, *he's very good and if I hadn't been briefed by Rupert Brett first, I'd almost be completely taken in.*

"Yes, we are making enquiries about a young woman who we believe you may know."

He smiled benignly, but his opaque, lupine eyes did not. "Oh dear, you will have to be more specific. I employ a number of young ladies, as you can see, both here in and in others offices I run. What is the young woman's name?" he asked gently.

DI Fleming grinned gently at this suave show. "Miss Elizabeth Carmichael."

Simions adopted a puzzled expression seeming to theatrically search his memory.

"Elizabeth Carmichael? Oh, you mean 'Liz', well of course, if that is who you mean: tall girl very pretty, but hides it well behind glasses?"

Fleming nodded in ascent. "So how do you know her?"

"As I said, I employ a number of people, she temped for me through an agency." He shrugged as though it explained it all.

"So you didn't see her outside office hours?"

Simions continued as benignly as ever. "No not in the normal course of events. I admit that I bumped into her leaving the office yesterday evening. I asked her for a drink which she accepted (forgive an old man for his predilections, Detective Inspector) and we parted after a drink or two." He smiled, it was not a nice expression.

"Where did you go afterwards?"

"I must say Detective Inspector, this conversation is taking on a rather distasteful tone, but I will humour you. I went to my club, The Carlton, where I had dinner with two business associates, whose names I am happy to provide and the name of the club secretary whom I spoke with just before leaving at around 10.30. Then I went home to my house, my chauffeur drove, and my housekeeper provided me with a night cap upon my return. Now what is this all about, Detective Inspector? I think it is only right that you now answer my question, don't you?" he interrogated.

DI Fleming did not blink or show any emotion, he merely thrust straight ahead with the brutal statement, alert to any emotional tick on Simion's behalf; "Elizabeth Carmichael is dead and you were the last person who knew her to see her alive," he lied.

Simions went through a very creditable pantomime of incredulity, shock and finally outrage. "And what, you think because I had a drink with the woman, that I had something to do with her death? That is absurd!" he stated.

But he did not do the one thing that all innocent people do and that is ask *how* she died. It was noted by the two policemen before the rather predictable next utterance from Simions.

"Well if this the tone and direction that this conversation is taking," he continued in plaintive outrage. "I think I had better have my lawyer present before we continue this discussion any further." He reached for the telephone on his desk and began to dial a number.

Calmly and considerately, DI Fleming commented; "I don't think that will be necessary. We have asked enough questions for now."

Simions replaced the receiver. Looking up in a way which suggested he had won a point. They turned to leave, Simions rose and began walking them to the door, which he opened for them.

"That won't be necessary, sir. We can find our own way out."

"On the contrary," he objected. "I believe it will."

They went down in the lift and at reception, as they were signing out, he spoke to his receptionists; "If either of these gentlemen arrive again, the first thing you do is call Andrew Davis, my solicitor, and do not admit them any further until he arrives. Is that clear?" The two women smiled and accepted the order as though it were an everyday occurrence. They looked haughtily at the two policemen who just smiled in mockery at the thinly veiled threat. They had heard it all before.

"Thank you for your help, Mr Simions. We will be in touch for more questions, rest assured, with or without your lawyer." Fleming retorted, with pleasure ill-concealed in his voice. He finished with a curt nod and the two men left. Simions' lips thinned in anger as he span around and returned to the lift.

As the policemen reached the street, Brooke grinned. "Well that was fun. I want to put that bastard away. He may not have been there or done the dead directly but he has some connection there, much more than he let on."

"Agreed. The question is what and how does it tie in to Rupert Brett? I wonder if it is all as straightforward as Mr Brett is making out, or are they colluding somehow and sending us on a tangent? We need more information. I need the autopsy result ASAP and look into the background of Brett, Simions and Miss Carmichael. We are missing something and I want to know what it is."

Brooke nodded.

The two detectives would have been very interested to hear the conversation taking place between Shingler and Simions at that moment. After he had explained the events to David Shingler who was both furious and worried.

"What? You know this is the first time we have ever had any victim or indeed connection with Secs and the City? We need to do something about this and Mr Brett appears to be the problem. We need to dissuade him," he finished menacingly.

"We do but not in the way you mean. I intend to bring him into the fold. The police will see it as an alliance between us and he will be marked and lose credibility. The market will hear about this and they will not like it. He will be tainted; there is nothing so sorry, as a tainted, friendless agent. Mark my words."

Shingler was not convinced and although he agreed in principle he had other ideas which he put in place once his conversation with Simions had ended. It was on such actions that the game can change and this was to prove the case.

Back in the office Rupert was in shock, walking as if an automaton out into reception.

"You alright Rupert? You look as if you've seen a ghost!" the receptionist commented. Rupert did not reply but turned and rushed out into the toilet where he threw up. He staggered upstairs and called Claire, asking to see her straight away. They met in the street and headed along Grosvenor Street towards Hyde Park. He blurted everything out, finally stopping to sit on a bench in the park where he cried, sobbing on her shoulder. She comforted him, rocking gently, saying nothing, her mind a whirl. Finally she commented; "Rups, they can't think you did it. How could they? It was drugs related."

"No, but they think I am involved even if indirectly. No smoke without fire etc. Also if this gets into the market, which I bet it will, I will be ostracised, you see if I'm not. It will spread from reception, you know what gossips they are. I don't even think Matthews will be discreet."

"No, they will stand by you: you know you are well thought

of and have built a great reputation to boot. You're a dealer! Everyone loves that."

But Claire was to be proved wrong as by late afternoon the rumours were spreading; anything from an unfortunate suicide, to Rupert being a mad axe murderer. It then spread to other firms and he found by the next day some of his calls were not being returned. No one wanted to be associated with a loser and the brutal reality was; you were only as good as your next deal.

The next twenty four hours were a nightmare for Rupert. He had explained the events to the company secretary who, while sympathetic, was also keen to avoid any scandal attaching to the firm; particularly as the police enquiry, from the way in which Rupert described it, was not entirely without doubt as to Rupert's culpability in some way. Accordingly, he offered to let Rupert have time off, more with a view to distancing him from the firm, than any benevolent ideals.

Rupert however was not keen at all and the thought of sulking at home in his flat or the park, with more time to think, did not appeal at all. The weekend loomed ahead, a weekend for which they had had great plans. He still could not believe it had all happened: first the deceit, then the row, followed by her death. It was like something from a terrible nightmare which he could not escape.

He tried to concentrate on his work, looking at the numbers again for the Castle Road project, which in turn brought him back to Simions. *I wonder if he knows*, he thought. *What would be his reaction? Grief, horror, surprise at the least?* In a moment of impetuous spite, wanting to lash out at something for the terrible thing that had happened, he arranged a meeting for that morning on a spurious excuse. He was told that Simions could spare him a few minutes, late morning. He grasped the opportunity and entered the offices just before 12.30.

He was shown up to Simions' office. Suave as ever, he stood there once again with the sunlight silhouetting his shoulders, bringing back awful memories. He moved away from the light and Rupert could see he was in one of his customary beautiful, handmade, navy blue suits; immaculately groomed as ever. The aftershave reached Rupert slightly ahead of the extended hand.

"Rupert, good to see you." He was unusually full of bonhomie and polite.

Something was wrong, he decided.

"Morning Paul, how are you?"

"Very well, but rather better than you look," he said commenting upon the ashen face and the blue circles around the eyes.

"Yes, I have had some bad news."

"Oh no, tell me." *What was it with all the tea and sympathy all of a sudden?* Rupert thought. He raised his head, finding eye contact difficult but persevered with studying Simions' face for any tell-tale emotion.

"My, umm, my girlfriend was found dead yesterday, in her flat."

"Rupert, my dear boy, I am so sorry. But what are you doing at work? You should be taking some time off. Go home, the deal will be alright."

"No. I can't bare it at home. Just thinking about Liz, it all comes back." Tears welled in his eyes. "You might have even known her. Liz Carmichael, she temped, you see? Did a lot of work for property people, they seemed to ask for her," he trailed off, part acting, partly genuinely upset. Simions' face appeared to consider the name for a moment, searching his memory.

It was then that Simions realised it would have been Rupert who had seen them together and on a hunch played a card held close to his chest. "But what a terrible coincidence, thoughtless of me. You see she worked for me yesterday and indeed has done so before. We had a drink together after work, at Boswells as a matter of fact, over the road." At which he nodded with his head. "She then left, said she had a date to go on. I had no idea it was you. But the police were here as well, asking questions as I had employed her. Look, I think you should go and get some rest."

He ignored the offered advice. "What, she worked for you yesterday? But I thought she was at Halpern and Beams?"

"Oh, she popped over afterwards to pick up some information, to look at some work she was going to do for me next week," he responded suavely.

Oh brilliant, Rupert thought, *quite the consummate actor, changing everything, gently moving the subject away.* He decided to change tack too, switching to property.

"Yes, I think I will. Oh a master stroke by the way.," he added ambiguously.

"What?" He looked more alarmed than ever before.

"The anagram of your name. I saw it in the paper buying out Diamond Drilling Services. Surely, it was you. Good idea to put some leverage on them.

For a brief, fleeting moment, anger, relief and frustration fought to gain supremacy on Simions' face. Finally, denial won; with a bland, puzzled expression he fixed Rupert with his gaze.

"I'm sorry, I don't know what you mean. I have been looking into it but as yet am just relying upon non service of notice. In any case, you should not concern yourself with my affairs. Now Rupert, I really think you should be getting some rest."

The meeting was clearly at an end. *There was no point*, he reflected, *in pushing it further, enough ambiguities had already been alluded to.* He would bide his time.

He walked out of the office door and could not help but mull over the events of the past few minutes. *The lying little shit!* Not a flicker of emotion other than hiding behind his concern for

Rupert. Something else was niggling at him, something that was said or not said, which he felt was important. *Of course, why didn't he ask "how". He didn't ask how she died, surely everyone asks that?* It is always the first question on everyone's lips.

He resolved to check upon the details of the Mission company who had just taken over Diamond Drilling Services.

Once Rupert had left the room, Simions turned to look out of the window, gazing into space. He was not pleased at all with the way things were progressing. He turned abruptly and made a call.

"It's me. Yes, just left. No I am not pleased. He is putting too much together, even called me out on the Diamond Drilling deal. No, it's too risky, I don't like that idea. Mmm, possibly, alright. Try it, if not we may have to approach it from a more benign angle."

The call ended and he replaced the receiver. He returned to the window, deep in thought. *What*, he wondered, *was the date for counter submission?* He checked the file and made another call to the recruitment consultant. They answered and confirmed that a certain secretary would be available on the dates requested.

He then made a second call to Shingler confirming the date and action to be taken.

However, when Rupert returned to the office, the Mission company was the last thing on his mind. The police had returned and were waiting for him. They had been there for about half an hour when he walked into reception. With a manner less courteous than before, they asked for a meeting room where they could talk again. As soon as the door closed behind them, the receptionist was on the internal phone, and minutes later the news was flying around the building: Rupert Brett was being questioned again.

The two detectives settled down in the chairs and began asking questions. Rupert confirmed his story as before.

DS Brooke was just as aggressive as before. With the preamble over, they started the same line of questioning again.

"And at no time did this "argument" take on a physical aspect at all?"

"No. Absolutely not. We had a lover's row and we shouted at each other. It was heated, yes, but no physical contact at all. She asked me to leave, which I did, straight away. In a strop, I virtually ran from the place."

"When did she throw the vase at you?"

"Just as I was going down the stairs. Luckily I saw it and ducked just in time."

"Well that's strange you see because we have found traces of blood on a fragment of the vase and it matches that of the lock. Did she cut you with it?"

Instinctively he reached up behind his ear and felt the small scab.

"Well yes, she caught me with a fragment, but it was just a scratch, as I said before."

"And you maintain that you your reaction to being hit by a vase was to leave. Did you return to hurt her?" DS Brooke sneered.

"No. Look, I was upset, I wanted to leave quickly. Why all these questions, I thought it was suicide, drugs related? This sounds as though you are blaming me for her death."

"It looked like suicide," answered DI Fleming. "Drugs, in fact heroin was the cause of death, ultimately, but prior to that-" he checked his notes. "From the preliminary autopsy report, she suffered strange bruising around her face and on her upper arms, as though she had been grabbed and held. So we checked again on the contents of the body. She had had a lot of whisky, more than you stated and much of it was not in the blood stream, just lying in her stomach. But we also found a tiny quantity of a rare drug, which we are currently trying to identify. It seems to have the same qualities as laughing gas used by dentists, only in liquid form. Fast acting, dilutes with alcohol, very hard to trace."

"What are you saying?" Rupert asked, horror written on his face.

"We have reason to believe that she was murdered. Or certainly forced to take her own life."

"And you think I did it? This is insane!"

"Well actually, it was an injection, between her toes." DI Fleming waited for reaction to the news. Rupert's brain worked quickly.

"Ah, hence the question about being intimate. Well, curiously enough, I don't go around checking for puncture marks in between my girlfriends' toes. Which is why I didn't know that she took drugs." He paused, shaking his head in disbelief I still can't believe it. "What sort of drug was it?"

"We don't know yet, we will have to wait for the full autopsy report. DS Brookes continued, "Well, look at it this way. You had access, the door wasn't forced. You had a motive; anger, jealousy or both, and you probably felt you could get away with it."

"I had nothing to do with this. I left Liz alive and well. I think I had better call a lawyer before you make any more ludicrous suggestions."

"There is no need for that at this stage. We have not cautioned you, nor do we intend to press any charges but we will need to speak to you again as we progress our enquiries. So please be prepared to make yourself available."

"Well, if you pursue this line of enquiry, I can tell you that I do not intend to speak to you again unless I have my lawyer present. Now do you understand?" he finished aggressively. They exchanged glances, a mutual understanding passing between them unsaid. They got up to leave.

"We will be in touch, Mr Brett."

As Rupert sat despairingly in the meeting room reluctant to leave, the door opened and Sheen appeared. He was an odd, dichotomous mixture of disciplinarian, mentor and, as in this case, a friendly face. Rupert looked up at the intrusion.

Sheen gently offered: "Rupert, I have heard what is going on. I know it must be difficult for you and I just wanted to say if you need a friend or anyone to talk to about it, well, then please let me know." He attempted humour to lighten the mood, "An old rent review surveyor can often put a different slant on things..."

Rupert smiled at the refrain. "Thank you. It is much appreciated but I don't really know what anyone can do at the moment. Police are making more enquiries and are not charging me or anyone else. It is all a bit in limbo," he finished pathetically.

Sheen nodded, smiled and left, the master of knowing when to push and when to leave it.

Once out on the street the two detectives compared mental notes.

"What do you think?"

"I don't know. It looks easy enough, a moment of rage, brought on by being struck by the vase, added to the fact that he was already angry with jealousy. Then he would drug her, but..."

"But what?"

"Something doesn't feel right. For example, if it is a liquid form of biometrophoxil, where did he get it? It was clearly not premeditated. You don't go armed with a bottle of the stuff to have a row with your girlfriend, do you? No, something's not right. I want a full house to house done on the whole block and the houses opposite. There is something we are missing, I just feel it."

"A full house to house, it will take ages!" Brooke complained.

"I want it done, ok?"

"Alright, but in the meantime we keep the pressure on sunnyboy, here?" he said jerking his thumb over his shoulder.

"Possibly, but let's leave it for two days. One thing I will admit to, is that it is not all as clear cut as it seems. Somewhere, unwittingly or not, he is tied up in this. What we do know is it's drug related and suspicious. See if Miss Carmichael had any form, will you?" DS Brooke nodded in affirmation.

CHAPTER 23

The weekend began with a series of telephone calls, drinking to forget and condolences from friends. Claire came around more than once to see how he was, together with Mike and Jemma. None of them could believe it; it all seemed so unreal. Although Mike's attitude was somewhat distant. Rupert caught him looking slightly askance at him occasionally. *If Mike doubted him*, he reasoned, *what chance had he with convincing the police?* He had already felt the cold draft of the market: phone calls not retuned, a reluctance to be seen with him, cancellation of a lunch. *Was he being tarred with the dubious reputation of Simions?* he wondered.

Saturday passed and he resolved to go into the West End and see a film; something with mindless action to take his mind off things. He went to the Bodyguard in Leicester Square, having been a great fan of Witney Houston for some time. Driving in, he parked his car in the multi storey with spaces reserved for CR employees and got a cab for the last half mile.

Although ultimately a happy ending, it still depressed him that the sister died in the film and he wandered back in a fairly morose state. He walked into the car park and to the far end where the CR reserved bays were located. As he passed a pillar he caught a movement from the corner of his eye. He turned to see a man approaching from some twenty feet away having almost appeared from nowhere. His manner was positive, almost swaggeringly confident, and purposeful. Rupert was alert but also partly mesmerised by the appearance. Sensing that this was a threat, he experienced what is known to fighters everywhere: adrenalin seize. His limbs would not obey him.

As the man got closer his dark features showed scar tissue above the nose and around the hard eyes. He had a large bulk to his shoulders, moving easily beneath his open leather jacket. At 6ft 2" he seemed to tower over Rupert but when he was within two feet of him, he spoke and the spell was broken.

"I want a word wiv' you," he demanded, his voice a deep gravely East End full of unfinished vowels. "You've been poking around where you shouldn't. It's not healthy you know."

With this, his hand moved out to grab Rupert, the other clenching aggressively, posture perfectly balanced for a blow. The move was fast and practised, having used his words to distract Rupert and close the distance between them. He was supremely confident, having been told that the victim was just some wussy office worker.

In his time with the TA, one of the courses Rupert had attended was Unarmed Combat. The instructor came down from Hereford twice a year to reassess them all and sharpen their skills. At the beginning of the first course, they had all imagined that they would be fighting like Bruce Lee despite only attending one session and were swiftly disillusioned. The instructor had said that martial arts take a long time to learn and perfect, far too long for the battlefield. Instead he had taught them dirty fighting, how to deal with the first punch and do as much damage as possible in the first few seconds. It still needed practice but this was something they all did regularly and now it came into play.

The words of the instructor came back to him again and

again. *"Whatever happens, throw something forward, whatever it is, just throw something forward!"*

This he did, as the arm came forward to grab him, Rupert threw his right arm straight forward, fingers extended, aiming generally for the eyes. The other man was fast, even though surprised and tried to avoid the fingers, jerking his head back. Rupert lashed his arm down grabbing the others sleeve more by luck than judgement. Following the movement, the assailant was caught slightly off balance and turned his head to avoid a blow, exposing his ear. Rupert struck him as hard as he could over the exposed ear with the flat of his hand, driven by fear and adrenalin.

There was a satisfying "pop". The ear drum had been burst and the result was spectacular. Deprived of his balance the thug span around and for good measure Rupert launched a lucky kick, which caught him on the knee cap. He howled with anger and pain but unable to stand, he crashed to the floor sideways. Rupert, realising how lucky he had been so far, ran for his car, flicked the lock system, jumped in and turned the key praying it would start first time. He pumped the accelerator. *Wrong thing to do,* he thought in panic and tried again. It caught on the second try and he sent it, wheels spinning on the shiny concrete, flying forward towards the exit of the car park, desperate to get out, knowing that ultimately he would come off second best, despite the burst eardrum of his assailant.

As if to confirm the thought, Rupert saw the large figure lurch from a supporting pillar towards the path of his car. His brain screamed at him not to stop for anything. He thrust his foot hard on the accelerator and at the last minute the man lunged out of the way. He was too late, getting a glancing blow to the hip by the wing of the car which made an ominous cracking sound. His hip bone had been fractured and he span in terrible agony. Although a broken gladiator, he still tried to rise and follow the car, every movement causing sharp lances of agony through his body. He finally crashed to the floor, face twisted in hatred and pain and grasping at thin air with his free hand. Rupert did not stop. He accelerated for the barrier, screeched to a halt, pressed the button and shot out of the car park as soon as the barrier would permit, narrowly missing an oncoming car in the street. He was breathing hard, shaking with the adrenalin and the narrow escape. His mouth felt dry and he was sweating on his forehead. *Nothing*, he thought, *can prepare you for the real thing, no amount of practice.* One thing was for sure, the next time he met the instructor from Hereford he was going to buy him a big drink! Feeling flustered, Rupert drove in the vague direction of home.

Why? he thought. *What was it? A mugging?* The words before the attack were, he assumed, irrelevant, just said to throw him off balance. Or were they? Surely there could be no connection between speaking to Simions and the attack. He had been blatant in his allusion to Simions' activities, certainly, but would that warrant such drastic action? His brain raced along, considering all the possibilities but there were still parts of the puzzle that were not yet apparent. He drove past Paddington Green police station and on impulse turned the car off the main road and parked in one of the side streets. He was still badly shaken and considered his actions for a moment, sitting still, listening to the tick of hot metal as the car cooled down, his mind in turmoil.

He opened the car door, got out and stood up, feeling unsteady as the cool night air hit him. He resolved to report the assault and walked to the police station.

The doors opened to the reception area, security glass everywhere, buzzers sounding as the doors clicked open and closed. The pitch of cross annoyed voices with shouted commands from behind the glass and turned heads as he entered the area before the desk.

The night had not yet begun to get busy it would seem as there were only two people waiting, seated in chairs looking scruffy, the worse for drink and one with a black eye, swelling a nice purple colour as he sat there. Rupert avoided his gaze having had enough trouble for one night.

He walked to the main desk. Behind it was a lady sergeant, blond hair taken back in a bun, dark attractive eyes that were hard and knowing; they had seen too much and become world weary and tired. Rupert reflected that he would like to see her smile, as it would, he was sure, transform her face to how it was before she joined the force.

She was tall, meeting him with level eye contact, not aggressive but strong. Already she was assessing him, putting him in a box for consideration. Not *that different to any other receptionist*, he decided.

"Yes, sir, may I help?"

"I hope so. I have just been attacked in a car park. I managed to escape but there was an accident. I think I winged the man who was trying to attack me. Can I talk to someone about it?" he finished shakily, realising that his voice did not sound like his own.

She took out a form, asked for his name and address, looked at him intently again as only policemen can and asked him to take a seat. He turned to go and then a thought occurred to him.

"I don't suppose Detective Inspector Fleming is on duty, is he?"

"I will ask, Mr Brett. Do you know him?"

"Well, in a manner of speaking. He is investigating the death of, er, of my girlfriend." His face clouded with pain at the thought but he realised he had said the wrong thing and how it sounded but it was too late now. The sergeant looked at him again quizzically, with the hardened expression returning to her face.

"Right, I'll be back in a minute."

Me and my big mouth, he thought! *When will I learn? 'Just investigating the death of my girlfriend.' It gets worse.*

He sat down and waited, avoiding the eye of the other two opposite him. He jumped as the electronic locks shot open and two constables left through the glass doors, preparing for a night shift. They looked in Rupert's direction and committed his face to memory. It would be all that was necessary for a total recall at any future time. Five minutes passed by and the door went again. Standing there was DI Fleming.

"Well, well, Mr Brett, this is a surprise. Would you like to come this way?" He motioned with his hand through the bullet proof, glass door towards the corridor beyond.

"Thank you."

They walked down the corridor to a door marked Interview Room and a sliding "occupied" sign on the door. DI Fleming indicated the table and chairs, offering him a seat. The room was stark, lit by a single harsh fluorescent light and smelled of disinfectant and polish. They were followed into the room by a uniformed constable who stood quietly at the back wall.

They sat down on opposite sides of the table. Rupert was relieved to see that DS Brooke was not present. *Small mercies,* he thought.

"So, what can we do for you? I understand that you've been attacked and run someone over." He raised his eyebrows at the last statement, as if only mildly surprised at such an occurrence.

"Yes, but not quite as bad as you just made it sound." Rupert proceeded to tell the events of that evening, plainly leaving nothing out, whilst the DI made some notes and asked some questions of clarification on certain points. Otherwise he let Rupert talk.

"Now, you feel that this was more than just an ordinary mugging, because of the words used by your assailant?" Fleming asked once Rupert had finished.

"Yes, I do."

"What exactly, did he say again?"

Rupert repeated the words, exactly as he remembered them.

"Mmh. Can you think of anyone you might of upset, who would wish you to back off? Maybe related to the death of Miss Carmichael perhaps?" he questioned cynically.

Rupert considered for a moment and decided to tell all that he knew.

"I think that it may be linked to the death of my girlfriend." Fleming frowned and started to pay more attention. "You see, on Friday afternoon, I went to see Paul Simions on some spurious excuse-"

"This is the man whom you were supposedly jealous of, your client? Is that correct?" he fished.

"Yes. He, Simions, mentioned that the police had been to see him. In the course of the conversation, I let Liz's name drop and asked if he knew her through work. He denied it initially and then remembered that he did and that he had been for a drink with her earlier in the evening. Didn't even blink, cold blooded bastard. I knew that he had met her, I saw them together as I told you and DS Brooke."

"Go on. Anything else?" he encouraged.

"He just said that he had met her for a drink after she came around to go over some work for next week. But then I caught him out as he said she had worked for him this week, whereas I knew she was at Halpern & Beams. So I know he is hiding something.

"Well, I wanted to rock his boat. I made an ambiguous comment which could have been taken for anything but when I made the comment, his face changed, he looked...he looked alarmed. Yes, for a split second he actually looked alarmed as though it followed on from our previous conversation. Well, I was alluding to something else entirely." He proceeded to explain his thoughts on the takeover. Fleming stopped him once or twice when he slipped into jargon, but basically understood the gist of the whole deal.

"So you think that he interpreted your comment to relate to the death of Miss Carmichael? It still doesn't stand you in a very good light, Mr Brett. This could have been a falling out of thieves. What was this agency Miss Carmichael worked for again?"

"Secs and the City," said Rupert

It was quiet for a few seconds.

"Look, would I really have come here now offering all this if that was the case?"

Fleming gave him a cynical look.

"Also, the deal I was talking about seemed to get him pretty upset as well, or more particularly the fact that I'd found out about his little takeover scam."

The DI considered the information carefully weighing up whether to divulge more information to Rupert. His mind finally made up, he carried on.

"After we left you on Friday, we continued with our enquiries at the block of flats where Miss Carmichael lived. It has taken a long time but we think we may have something more to go on."

"Really, what?" he asked excitedly.

"Well, no matter where you go, there is a nosy neighbour. Whatever you may think, there's always someone, somewhere that sees something. Particularly somewhere as busy as a Mansion Block and when you've been seen to scream out of the car park at speed."

Rupert looked abashed.

"An old lady who lives on the ground floor notes nearly everybody who leaves and enters the place. People like her make our lives easier, it has to be said. On the night in question, she spotted a woman leaving the place, about half an hour after you.

Now because of the series of bays, protruding along the front of the block, it was possible for her to see this woman leave and walk across the car park to the road and out of sight. As far as we are aware, no one in the block had such a visitor, so until we find out who she is and what she was doing there, we would like to question her."

"What did she look like?"

He referred to his notes, flicking the pages of the notebook open.

"5'3" to 5'5", late twenties maybe early thirties, wearing a smart suit, dark hair, carrying a large hand bag, and gloves."

"When I entered the block that night, I held the door open for a woman. I didn't think anything of it at the time, I had other things on my mind." His face clouded at this point as he recalled the events of that evening.

"And you mention this now. Very convenient now I have given you the description. You see, look at it from my point of view. Every time I give you something you have conveniently 'remembered' something else."

"Well here is something you didn't mention. But one thing did stick in my mind. Did this woman have a slight scar on her cheek and a cracked, chipped front tooth?"

All languor left the DI. "You sure about this?" he was suddenly very serious.

"Absolutely. Why?"

The DI ignored the question. "What did the man who attacked you tonight look like again? Describe him carefully."

Rupert thought back and described the man as though it were thirty seconds ago.

"Right, I am going to get a mug shot book. I'll get someone to take a statement of tonight's events and we will put it on record."

He left the room quickly and five minutes later another officer arrived to take Rupert's statement. The DI returned after they had finished with a book of photographs. He opened it at a given page and turned the album the correct way up for Rupert to see properly.

Rupert looked down at the photographs on the page, then stabbed his finger out at the main frontal photograph on the right hand page.

"That's him!"

"You're sure?"

"Definitely, he will stay in my mind forever."

"And it was him you took out before you ran him over?"

"Yes, I got lucky, he will have a burst eardrum or I miss my guess. Why are you looking at me like that."

"Well, he happens to be one of the hardest men I know. He is used as an enforcer when people don't pay up, and is generally a nasty piece of work. You were either very lucky or there is more to you than meets the eye."

Rupert looked again at the photograph and felt cold about what might have happened.

"One bit of good news is that I doubt very much if he'll be pressing charges. Not his style and he would have too many questions to answer. Now look at these photos for me," he said, producing another album. Once again Rupert scanned the page and picked out a picture of the woman he thought he remembered from the flats.

"I'm pretty sure that's her but I only saw her for a few seconds."

"I think you are right. That," he said dramatically, "is his sister."

"What?"

"Her name is Maria Rico and his, Claudio Rico. She specialises in murder and professional hits. You are moving in some pretty exclusive circles, Mr Brett!"

Rupert could not believe his ears. *What is going on?* he thought, *what the hell is going on?* The DI went on to explain that they had

had nothing on the pair of them for many years, not since the petty crime of their youth. They were only suspected of various murders and extortion, none of which could be proved. He went over Rupert's statement and asked for a few more details about the events. Finally that he said that would be calling Rupert on Monday to talk to him further.

The interview was at an end, Rupert rose to go.

"One final thing, just be a little bit careful for the rest of the weekend. Stay with friends, don't go anywhere by yourself and here is my card. Any problems or if you think of anything else, call me."

Rupert wished him goodnight and was shown out of the building and out onto the street. *What a night*, he thought to himself, *and what a nightmare.* The journey home passed uneventfully; no cars followed him, no large thugs were waiting on his doorstep, everything was quiet. He checked the street, looked beneath the stairwell to the basement flat, nothing. Too many spy movies, he told himself.

After Rupert left the station, DI Fleming was very thoughtful. He scribbled some more notes on his pad and muttered to himself, "We might just get you this time, we might at that." He picked up the telephone and called DS Brooke. He relayed the evenings events to his colleague who responded with his usual cynicism.

"What? Do you think that he is still tied up in it? Could be a falling out amongst thieves. Even white collar crime can turn nasty."

"I don't know, something is still not quite right. Somewhere it is all connected and we are still missing some pieces of the puzzle. Did you find anything?"

"Well, yes actually, I just thought it could wait until Monday and-"

"Go on," he interrupted.

Brooke sighed. "Well it seems that Miss Carmichael had a record for drugs and not just taking them, but dealing as well."

"She was a naughty girl then, not quite the innocent we thought. Anything else?"

"Yes actually, quite curious. There is a note on the file that if she is apprehended or has any dealings with us, Detective Superintendent Webster is to be contacted immediately."

"Webster?" Fleming exclaimed. "Bloody hell this gets more interesting by the minute."

"You know him?"

"I do and this is going to be a very interesting conversation. Listen, as soon as you get the full autopsy report back let me know."

"Will do."

He put the phone down and dialled another number, which was answered by a switchboard operator.

"Detective Superintendent Webster, please." In less than a minute the line was connected.. "Paul, Steve Flemming, how are you?"

Rank no object, they had known each other since cadet school.

"Steve. Well, long time no speak, how are you?" They caught up for a couple of minutes then Fleming cut to the chase.

"I think I've just got something for you; note on a file to contact you." He continued to relay the events, starting with the murder. He was interrupted sharply.

"What! What did you say her name was?"

"Elizabeth Carmichael, Flat 6,-"

Then Webster finished the address for him and there was silence between both men.

"So she is dead." It was a statement not a question. Silence again. "Tell me everything again, from the beginning," he demanded.

CHAPTER 24

The rest of the weekend passed uneventfully for Rupert. He called Claire, who invited him over for Sunday lunch at her flat where they were joined by Mike and Jemma. The conversation revolved around the events of the last twenty four hours. Everyone was aghast at the attack but Mike was still sceptical as to Rupert's theory of Simion's involvement and continued with his rather reserved demeanour.

"I still can't believe that someone in his position would order such an attack and more importantly what would he stand to gain from it?"

"Just because one is a developer, it does not give one exclusive rights to saint hood," he stated defensively, getting pissed off with Mike's holier than thou attitude. "In fact, quite the contrary. My experience is that the higher one gets and quickly, the more likely you are to find skeletons in the cupboard. I mean look at his methods: bribing planning officers, putting pressure on owners, using offshore companies to lever factory closures. What more could you ask?"

"Just an average day in a property developer's life, I should say," joked Claire trying to lighten the atmosphere.

"Ya, well precisely, I rest my case. But I keep feeling that there is something missing, something tied in with Liz's death. It is staring me in the face, I'm sure, but I can't see it at the moment."

"I still think you are reading too much into it. It would be ludicrous to implicate Simions."

Rupert was too exhausted to argue and for a quiet life conceded the point. The lunch broke up late, everyone leaving at about five o'clock. The goodbyes said, Rupert lingered on the doorstep of Claire's flat.

"You can stay, you know."

"I know and it's really kind but I need some time and...." his voice tailed off not sure how to continue. The kindness of the offer also held promise, it was unmistakeable but he needed to be alone, of that he was certain. She hugged him, kissed him on the cheek and said, "Anytime, you know I mean it. Just call, OK? And ignore Mike, he gets a bit prissy sometimes, you know that."

"I do and I really appreciate it. Night."

Rupert walked the short distance to his flat, confused and at the same time glad of the support given by Claire and more than a little hurt by Mike. He felt terribly guilty, all of a sudden. A girl he had loved, by his own admission, was dead. Her body barely cold and he was already thinking about other women.

Was he really that shallow? But he then considered that she had been two timing him with another man. They had had a blazing row before they finished and it would have been all over anyway. Wouldn't it? His mind turned the facts over for the thousandth time in his head. When he reached home, he again made the provisional checks on the outside of his flat before entering, all rather self-consciously and to no avail; no one was hiding in wait for him. He went in, poured himself a drink and fell asleep in a chair, mentally exhausted.

Early Monday morning, a call came through to him in his office from reception.

"It is Detective Superintendent Webster for you." The

inflection in the voice was almost that of mockery, judgemental and unkind.

"Thank you." The call was transferred. "Hello, yes, good morning. How can I help?" Webster introduced himself and asked if they could meet somewhere other than the office. Would he, for example, be able to come to the police station where he worked? Rupert confirmed he would, was given the address and half an hour later called at a rather nondescript building in Westminster.

He buzzed the intercom system, announced himself and was let in. The reception area was austere but unlike a police station; plain painted walls divided into two colours by a dado rail and a reception desk which was manned by, Rupert assumed, a civilian receptionist in her early thirties. She gazed up at him with an unsmiling, cordial "good morning" and asked him to go on up the stairs to the first floor. The stairs were carpeted and he made no sound as he ascended to the next level.

He was met on the landing by a plainclothes officer and shown into a comfy office with a large desk graced by a computer humming away, two telephones and a table lamp. The walls were lined with book shelves. The original Georgian fireplace was still there but had been converted to a gas fire. It was not, to Rupert's eyes, a typical policeman's office.

A second door opened to the right of the office and D/Supt. Webster walked in. He smiled frostily at Rupert before introducing himself.

"Detective Superintendent Webster. Thank you for coming across so promptly. Sit down, please." He gestured to a chair fronting the desk.

"Thank you."

Rupert studied Webster, and saw a man of just under six foot with a round head and deep set, sharp eyes of indifferent colour. One would, he reflected, be hard put to describe exactly the hue, but they were however hard and shrewd. The jowls were becoming slightly chubby as he was approaching middle age. His skin had a polish, a soft sheen of good living and too many lunches. His suit, unlike those of his colleagues, was well made and the trousers matched the jacket. Rupert smiled to himself.

"I will come straight to the point," he said in a crisp, well enunciated voice, more typical of a politician than a policeman. "I have been appraised of your situation by DI Fleming who, given the circumstances, has passed this case over to me; particularly as I knew the victim." The DS studied Rupert's face for a reaction and was not disappointed.

"You knew Liz. How?"

He ignored the direct question and began obtusely by way of explanation.

"I will go back to the beginning. Some time ago the Home Office found that a certain type of crime was falling between two stools, so to speak. For example, fraud and murder, drugs and tax evasion. This sort of thing, the details are not important. However what is important, is that in an effort to combat this hybrid crime, they decided to set up a number of special units, of which mine is one. We specialise in the London area and more specifically, we are tackling the combination of fraud and murder. We are called in when the usual police units find that the lines of demarcation are crossed. This is one of those instances."

"But how does all this involve Liz?" Again he ignored the question.

"Did you ever get close to Liz? Meet her family, for example?"

"No, I could never get really close to her, something I couldn't touch, somehow."

He snorted, almost to himself. "Huh, it does not surprise me in the slightest. About two years ago we had been looking into illegal money laundering, connected to property and this coincided with a drug problem. The two were, it was thought, somehow linked and then we were called in when a third element was introduced: fraud. The drug squad had been looking closely at a number of clubs; one was Maxine's just off Sloane Square. Do you know it?"

"Yes, I've been there a couple of times. I had heard that the drugs scene was quite big, quite a few of my friends go there, mainly the girls." He shrugged dismissively, seeing a pattern begin to emerge.

"It is a big hang out for the "Sloane Rangers"; they have lots of money to spend, easy access, it is a perfect combination for the dealers. But we have never been able to prove anything, mainly small arrests. However, it is also a one way ticket from soft to hard drugs such as heroin. One of those victims was Liz. She was main lining, got caught more than once and started dealing."

Rupert shook his head in disbelief. Webster raised his hand to silence him. "Oh, only in a small way, but it was enough to cause her serious problems and she was an addict. We gave her a choice: get cleaned up, we would drop the charges and she would start feeding us information. Or she would be charged. She chose to get out of the drugs scene and help us, simple."

"But I still don't see how this links in with commercial property?"

"Let me ask you something. What is the most important commodity to you in your world?"

Rupert thought for barely a second and shrugged. "Information of course, preferably early and exclusive."

"Precisely. It is the same with us and now the two are linked. Your Mr Simions is getting early information on his deals, using the proceeds to transfer the money to hard currency without paying taxes and using drug addicts to act as couriers as well as others to participate in the scam."

"But how is he getting the early information?"

"He is using such an obvious route that it is brilliantly simple. Who has access to all the information? Who is never questioned or noticed? Who can come and go as they please with no culpability?" He paused letting the answer hang in the air for dramatic effect: "The temporary secretary. How many times have you heard *'Oh she's just the temp.'* Completely ignored in the corner; supplying information and having a part in all the letters etc.

"From the information Miss Carmichael fed us, we know he has a manager from each branch of 'Secs in the City' working for him. We are trying to find the true ownership base of the agency but it is tied up in a complicated trust, although we will get there eventually. Most of them are in his pocket; he pays cash to put a particular girl in to temp. The girl goes in to a given situation and either passes on the information or manipulates the letters. It is simple and very effective. He has a whole network of temps all over the place, all specialising in commercial property, as far as we know."

Rupert was astounded. "Incredible. But how does he get them into position in the first place?"

"As far as we can ascertain, he finds out who is the permanent placement. That person is approached to say, go sick for a couple of days for a cash payment. The agency is phoned for a replacement. Simions' girl is put in place, information is leaked or used to advantage, no one suspects. It costs Simons a few grand and what does he make? Well you tell me, millions. But the beauty is that everyone is paid in cash and it is completely untraceable. Somehow, and this is the bit we do not yet know, he gets the money from legitimate property deals, converts it into cash for payments to branch managers, temps and the permanent staff etc.

"If one considers the amounts involved, it is to the order of tens or hundreds of thousands of pounds. Small fry in terms of the profits involved, but difficult to disguise in terms of cash.

"Now Miss Carmichael, was getting very close to this, too close in fact, which is why we think she was killed and I'm afraid to say ..." and here he hesitated, looking pained, "because of her involvement with you."

It fell like a bombshell on Rupert. Suddenly the words in the pub he overheard between Simions and Liz made awful sense. She wasn't having an affair. She was finishing their business relationship, saying she couldn't spy for him anymore. *Oh God no,* he thought, *oh please God, no.*

It all started to make sense; the way the deals had been exposed on the investment sale, when Claire's secretary had gone ill mysteriously two days before the release of information to the market and Liz's permanent attitude of secrecy, her strange, unexplained disappearances. It all fell into place for him. At their last meeting he blamed her, accused her, insulted her. Then she died horribly, all because of him. He stared at Webster in horror.

"I'm sorry to have to tell you, but you had to know." He looked and sounded compassionate, genuinely sorry for Rupert's plight. He continued, "We also believe that an earlier suicide by Simions' former partner wasn't in fact suicide. Are you familiar with the story?"

"What?.. Oh yes, vaguely." He stumbled back to reality. "Didn't he commit suicide off the Bristol suspension bridge, or something?"

"Supposedly yes. But other accounts told of a woman walking her dog just afterward and before. A car parked at one end of the bridge, which was never traced. His car parked, rather too perfectly near the spot. He was a tall man, yet the seat was forward in a position close to the wheel. The sort of position a short man, or woman, uses. Some of the bruising found on his body may or may not have been consistent with his fall and hitting the water. All circumstantial evidence but put together, leads us to believe that he was murdered and it was made to look like suicide."

He paused, letting the information sink in.

"Just like Liz," Rupert muttered. "So you believe me, about

me not having murdered her or being responsible for her death?"

"Yes, just like Liz. I am very sorry. And I do believe you, although again a good deal of circumstantial evidence has been placed (deliberately or not) to make it look as though you were involved more directly than you were." He hesitated, like an actor playing the part and using the pause for effect and at just the right moment he continued, "But, there is a way you can help us and help put Simions away."

"How?"

"Well, we think that the attack on you was related. A frightener, if you like. Ill-advised and not Mr Simions usual style but…" again he paused, letting the sentence hang in the air before continuing. "I think when he reflects on all this, (if indeed it was Simions and not someone associated with him) he will reconsider and try to get you onside by offering you a job. Not unusual in your line of work anyway, is it?" he asked.

"No, in fact he has hinted at it already. Before…before Liz died. He has been impressed, so he said, with my performance. Thought I would make a good developer."

"Good. We want you to take it," he commented decisively. "He will want to keep you close and we want you on the inside to try and find out how he is laundering the money and get any evidence you can.

"Now, you can tell me all you can. Right from the beginning, leaving nothing out. Any bit of information you may have; however seemingly insignificant may help add to the information that Liz had already put together."

Rupert proceeded to relay everything that had happened from his first meeting with Simions, including the bribing of the planning officer and his suspicions about David Shingler. Webster pricked up his ears at the name. It seemed that Shingler was a potential suspect and possibly the man behind the hiring of the muscle who attacked Rupert.

As he related the facts, other minor points fell into place: like the reason that Liz was out of place for a Sloane in Hampstead; she was keeping away from her previous friends and haunts. It all suddenly became understandable.

Webster concluded the discussion: "So, what we are really looking for is the link to the money laundering, that will be the key to convicting him. The rest is just circumstantial; yes there are bribes, corrupt managers, but in reality, so what? It is just not enough and all we would do is net the small fry and lose the big fish. So you must, at all costs, not show your true feelings and knuckle under, act like you never have before."

Rupert was irritated. "Look, he hasn't even offered me a job yet. It might not work out at all but if it does, I will do all I can; if only for Liz's memory and to get revenge on Simions and Shingler."

Rupert was angry and upset at the turn of events and felt that he had heard all that he could take for the moment. His mind was going over incidents of the past few months, analysing every aspect of his relationship with Liz; his work and all facets of his conversations with Simions, looking at them in a new context.

Webster asked him not to speak with anyone else about what he had been told, it was imperative that no one else should be party to the information. Not the least of which, as it might endanger Rupert's life. The thought chilled him to the bone. He had never really considered before what he was getting into. The attack could happen again with more violent and successful results. What also concerned him was that he was in effect being black balled by the market, who were less than keen to do business with a potential murderer or one who was mixed up in it. He finally left the interview with instructions on how he might contact Webster again and what he should be looking for.

When he left the building, he stopped and called into the nearest coffee bar unable to think straight. It was all too much for him. He was between thoughts of guilt, fear and revenge. He hated Simions for what he had done and wondered how much complicity Shingler had in all this or was he just a corrupt agent, bending the rules?

In his office, Webster thought for a moment and made a call to DI Fleming.

"No, I don't think he's guilty. He was straight and completely shocked at what I told him. What worries me is how he will survive, if indeed he does. He is strung pretty tight now. To work side by side with the man who murdered his girlfriend will need exceptional courage and skill. We'll see.

"I think you may be surprised, there is a lot of steel in that boy. He is stronger than you think."

"I hope for his sake, that you are right," said Fleming.

The next two weeks were a blur for Rupert. He carried on at work, pursuing deals and more particularly the Castle Road scheme but it was getting harder. He was not getting calls returned. Whispers and rumours swirled around; the market was against him.

The time for the counter notice to be served was looming and everyone on the Cowell Rubens' team was very tense. No further indication had been given that they were aware at Halpern & Beams that time was of the essence and if they missed the response time all could be lost for their client. The last day of the month arrived and no counter response had been received by CR or MAS Investments. Everyone was jubilant, although Simions, when Rupert called him, was not at all surprised.

"Well, I think that they probably failed to spot the clause and that is the end of the legal position. We can now apply to get VP and planning"

"I thought they would spot it. They must have been over the lease with a fine tooth comb, great news, but very strange," he commented disingenuously.

"I wouldn't speculate upon it too much, if I were you. Just accept it and be grateful." The last was said almost as a threat, menace returning to the evenness of the voice.

Rupert recoiled at the implied threat then resumed his passive role.

"No, I think it's excellent. Can't wait for the look on their faces when they realise," he finished enthusiastically.

"No, neither can I but I feel they might still put up some legal argument, we'll see. But it is a successful conclusion. A great deal, which we'll win. Rupert I need to see you, about another matter, more personal and to your advantage. When can we meet up?"

"What about later today, say 3.00 this afternoon?"

CHAPTER 25

The meeting took place as planned. In accordance with Rupert's suspicions, the offer of a job was put forward but the underlying feeling was that it was for no other reason than to get him on side and out of the dangerous position of 'whistleblower'. The practice of poaching agents to client side was normal but to be offered it at this stage in his career, to such a level, was exceptional. The calm with which he accepted the offer, was taken as a sign of egotistical arrogance by Simions who assumed everyone was as driven as him and therefore it only helped to confirm that he had made a good choice.

The monetary side of the offer was incredible: twice his current salary, working with one of the most successful emerging property companies in the market. *What*, he thought, *could be easier to accept?* But all the time his heart was cold with anger; thinking of the deceit and murder committed by the man before him.

He left Simions' office not committed, instead promising to consider the offer carefully, knowing full well that he had to accept in order to feed Webster information. His first call when he returned to the office, after having a quiet moment, was to call Webster.

"Yes, the position has been offered to me. Good terms too." He went on to outline the salary, company car and other profit share benefits. Webster commented that crime was obviously paying well these days and he considered changing sides. *The first sign of a wry sense of humour,* Rupert thought and continued with the details.

"You'll take it of course?" he urged, more of a statement than a question.

"Yes. I will leave it for a decent period, accept and work my notice period."

"Good. Then we can start working together. I look forward to it." The line went dead and Rupert reflected that the powerful all had the same arrogance irrelevant of whether they were on the side of right or wrong.

On the other side of Grosvenor Street, in Halpern & Beams, those on the side of right were definitely not having a good day. The partner in charge of rent reviews, Steve Jackson was trying to explain to an exasperated client how he had failed to serve the requisite notice within the time scale.

"Look, it's impossible that it did not arrive on time. I signed my post two days before the due date. It was to go registered post, guaranteed to arrive and be signed for the following day. I distinctly remember handing it to my secretary, or rather the temp as my regular secretary was taken sick last week, which is why I was especially particular as to the date of posting. Anyway the temp was very efficient."

"In all but this matter," the client interjected.

What he did not know, was that the temp had deliberately post-dated the date on the letter by two days, held it back quietly and it was not delivered for a further two days behind the designated timescale. She reflected on her work with Secs in the

City and how easy it had been to make an extra £1,000 on top of her agency fee. It was surprising just how many times a boss did not check the individual date on their letters and just assumed all his post would be correctly dated as shown on the first letter. She smiled to herself. So simple and they were all so predictable.

Pauline from Secs in The City subsequently telephoned Shingler, who confirmed all had gone well and the timescale had not been met.

"Yes, well done. Usual payment," he replied curtly, never one to waste words.

"Yes, perfect. I'll book the flight for two weeks' time; will that do?

"Yes, I'll make the arrangements. Goodbye."

The line went dead and she smiled. *Ahhh*, she thought, *another warm summer holiday.*

CHAPTER 26

The following week saw an interesting exchange between Simions and Michaels, the MD of Moorcroft Industries. After finding that time was of the essence and that the timescale was not adhered to, he had applied to the courts for a hearing that the clause was unreasonable. A case with some grounds and throwing himself upon the mercy of the courts offered a possible solution to his problem, especially as he had nothing to lose and the strategy would buy him more time.

Michaels had, however, received a communication to the effect that his main suppliers and creditors, Diamond Drilling Services, were calling in their debts and making other financial demands. He was being squeezed and he knew it. More frustrating still, he could not get to the bottom of who was squeezing him. He did however have a pretty good idea.

He called Simions directly in the hope that matters could be resolved amicably, as any major break in production would ruin the company and destroy all chances of keeping the site or recovering. The conversation began amicably enough but deteriorated when Simions alluded to the possible financial problems.

"Now how the hell would you know about that?"

"In the financial world, Mr Michaels, there are very few secrets, and listed companies are not one of them."

"Don't patronise me, Mr Simions. I am well aware of how the stock market rumours work."

"Yes, I am sure you are," he replied. "However I might be in a position to alleviate your problems. I have, shall we say, some influence in this particular matter which may be of some help to you."

"What are you saying? That if I agree to drop all court proceedings you can get Diamond Drilling to call off their dogs, is that it?"

"Well, rather crudely put, but in a nut shell, I suppose so."

"You bastard!"

He answered rather coldly, "Business is business, it is a simple as that."

"How did you swing it? Mmmh, how? How did you influence the late service of the counter notice?"

"I have absolutely no idea what you are talking about. Now do we have a deal? If I can help you, will you, in turn, vacate your site?"

There was a long pause at the other end of the line.

"As you said, business is business. So be it. But we want full compensation. We will need to agree terms but as a principal we have a deal. Get your secretary to call mine and arrange some dates to thrash this out with the lawyers. Goodbye."

Michaels had the satisfaction of putting the telephone down first, a small victory. He was furious but knew he was beaten.

Some weeks later the deal was signed. Rupert was there at the signing, this time in the livery of MAS, not Cowell Rubens, having left CR some few days earlier. The transition had been difficult. Particularly in view of his previously vociferous, decrying of Simions' morals and business methods. There was also a large percentage of CR personnel and others outside the firm who harboured thoughts that Rupert was not exactly clean when it came to the death of his girlfriend. Rupert could not tell anyone of his part in the plan; one word in the wrong quarter, one temporary secretary listening in on a conversation could report back and get him killed, of that he was under no illusion.

Notwithstanding his ulterior motives, even his friends in the office, Mike included, treated him with a cold shoulder. The transition from agent to principle had been very interesting and not all a hardship. The perceived glamour of being on the client side of the fence was not all it had been cracked up to be and if it was not for his mission, he decided it would have been quite tedious. Not the excitement that he had previously imagined. However seeing how it all worked from the view of a client had caused a steep increase in his learning curve and one that would stand him in good stead but he had not forgotten the real reason for his presence there and continued to search for any information that might be relevant. This took him often, on spurious excuses, to Simions' office which was never locked and gave him the opportunity to look through whatever papers were to hand.

Normally this produced nothing but on this Tuesday morning, when Simions was unexpectedly late in, he took the chance to sneak another look. Ever watchful, he walked upstairs and closed the door to, as far as he dare, in order to gain as much time as possible if someone caught him unawares. His heart raced on these occasions, ever fearful of being discovered and the consequences hung over him like the sword of Damocles.

He had just finished a frustratingly careful search of all the papers and desk contents that were accessible which revealed nothing, when a sharp noise behind caused Rupert to jump and spin around. His heart thudded but to his relief it was no more than a fax machine on silent mode, accepting an incoming message. He turned to walk away perspiring from fear, then turned back to the fax on an off chance. He read the first page upside down as it came out of the machine, being careful not to touch it. Shingler, the fax was from Shingler!

It was just a single sheet and with large, loopy handwriting crossing the page and the message read:

Paul,

Cargo due on board to Rome Thursday and should arrive at Viterbo midday. Deal to be signed on sale of Casa Romero the day after. I hope this is alright, he has your power of attorney for the sale. The proceeds will be distributed in the usual way. I've found a new *notaio*, more amenable if you know what I mean.

I will speak to you once the deal is done.

David.

Yes, he cried to himself silently. He carefully re-read the text again and decided to copy it. There was no copier in the room, so he re-fed it through the fax machine on 'copy'. Out it came and he replaced the original in the receipt tray as before. He ran from the room grabbing his "excuse file" as he left. Rupert took two deep breaths, calmed his features and pretended to be engrossed in his file so much, that he nearly ignored Simions as he came up the stairs.

"Oh, morning Paul, how are you?"

"Don't ask, the traffic was crap. What are you up here for?"

"Oh, just getting this file." He flashed it briefly and went to move on down the stairs.

"Stay a moment will you, I need a word about the Castle Road deal."

Rupert nervously went back into the room with Simions, trying at all costs to avert his eyes from the fax in the corner. Simions proceeded to sit down and go over one or two points of the scheme but in the course of the discussion his eyes wandered to the fax machine. Simions stopped mid-sentence, rose and walked quickly to the machine. Rupert's eyes followed him, whilst he concentrated on securing a puzzled expression on his face. Simions snatched up the fax, read it and looked directly at Rupert. He felt as though those eyes seared into his soul.

"Have you seen this?" he demanded.

Rupert rose as if to come and read it, feigning innocence. "No, why, is it important?"

He held out his hand as if to be given the paper. The ruse worked.

"No. Never mind." He strode back over to his desk and placed the paper in a file where it could not be read.

"Now, where were we? Oh yes." He continued with the other details and finally dismissed Rupert as if he were at school leaving the headmaster's study. Rupert closed the door upon his exit from the room heaving a sigh of relief. He left the landing quickly, running down the stairs two at a time and shot into his office. He was desperate to call Webster but too frightened of being overheard.

At lunchtime, he went to a phone box, got through on the private number and explained everything, reading the fax sheet word for word over the telephone.

"So what do you think?" he finished finally.

"I think I need to talk to my opposite number in Rome. Where is this Viterbo place, do you know?"

"I do actually, it is the state capital for Lazio."

"Lazio? I thought that was a football team?"

"It is but also a major City to the north of the province. But what I don't see is how he is laundering the money there, or indeed getting it there in the first place."

"Neither do I, but it confirms one thing, Shingler is involved and we now know where to look. I have been doing some checking on our friend, Shingler. He was at school near 'little Italy' and probably knows Claudio Rico, your assailant. I am willing to bet that Rico is the courier boarding the plane. It is starting to all fall into place. Well done, Rupert, well done. I will be in touch."

Rupert considered what Webster had said and the new Italian connection; how did it all fit in? He needed more information on the buying process in Italy. He was convinced that was where the answers lay.

Of course, he snapped his fingers, thinking of the first day of Sheen's introductions around the building: Howard Bruman from the Offices Department at CR. He has bought a place there and he speaks Italian. He called Howard, who as always was keen on lunch, did not mind that Rupert was a *mad axe murderer* and coincidently they arranged to meet at an Italian restaurant just off Berkeley Square.

Howard turned up on time and they settled down into familiar territory, catching up on old times. Rupert steered the conversation towards holidays and Italy and said a friend was looking to buy a villa out there for letting-out, what was the best way to go about it?

"Tricky really. You definitely need a good *notaio*, one who is bi-lingual." He went on to outline the process of buying and selling.

"But what about taxes, do you have stamp duty?"

"Ah well, there is the beauty of it d'you see." He smiled conspiratorially. "In Italy the government levy a tax for both sellers and purchasers, so the Italians feel that it is their bounden duty to avoid these taxes and both parties have a vested interest in doing so. Consequently, they have all joined forces together. For a sale of property to take place a *notaio* must be used; he is a quasi-official of the government and in turn oversees the proceedings. He registers for example the price of the deal and sees that all the monies are paid accordingly, and that the price and taxes are registered with the central register."

"Sorry, I'm being thick, I still don't get it Howard."

He smiled: "Well, the *notaio* appreciates the position of the parties and is in no more of a hurry for them to pay any more tax than they should, so he settles the price at the lesser level in the state lists, like our rating lists for rateable value. The main difference being that these have not been updated for years. So the true price is anything up to thirty or forty percent more than declared.

"What, so you could buy a property for £1m and show only £500,000 thousand for tax purposes!"

"Exactly, dear boy."

"And the *notaio* condones this?"

"It's Italy." He shrugged.

"But how does the money get to the other party?"

"It is all in cash."

"What, you mean someone turns up with a suitcase full of Lira notes to the tune of half a million quid? Incredible. And the *notaio* goes along with this?"

"He too, is paid in cash. He often gives a discount in his fees for just such a service. Do you know what every respectable Italian dreads? That one day there might be a universal currency and all Lira notes must be handed in. Do you also know that Italy has the highest currency production of any European country because no one uses the banks, it is all under the mattress. The Italians have an innate distrust of banks; they think they are all corrupt," he finished smirking with a wink, raising his wine glass.

"So if I understand this correctly, it would be very easy for anyone to "lose" a substantial amount of money on a property deal and launder the money. All done legitimately under the nose of the *notaio*."

"Precisely, which is why Italy has the highest tax band in Europe because no one pays more than they can get away with. It is also why they have no legitimate house price guide as to rises or falls in the market. It would be irrelevant as no one records the correct price. Now don't tell me your friend wants to launder money?"

"What? Oh no, no, it's just that I find it all so incredible. No wonder the Mafia are so strong in such an atmosphere of corruption."

"It is just accepted as the norm. Now, another drink dear boy." He poured another glass of wine for them both as Rupert's brain did mental somersaults, it was all falling into place. The rest of the meal was spent comparing notes on things Italian and some final questions were answered by Howard. Lunch ended and Rupert thanked Howard for his time and information.

"Anytime dear boy, anytime and if you want the name of a good *notaio*, let me know."

"Thank you, I will, good bye."

So, he thought, *the next bit of the jigsaw is in place, all we need now is the who and where*. Rupert relayed this information to Webster who had been checking on the movements of Rico. The hitman had booked a flight to Rome and by linking back through the computer records, the time and place coincided.

"What we need is someone out there to follow him," Webster mused. "I can find out which hotel he is staying at," he thought out loud, "and-"

"Listen. I'll go, get me the information while I'm in transit and I'll call you from the airport." Rupert surprised Webster both as to his bravery and circumstance.

"But what about Simions?"

"I'll tell him I've been offered a late flight to a friend's villa in Spain, anywhere that is hot and not Italian. Look, I'll see if I can swing it, ok? I'll call you back later this afternoon."

Rupert hung up and went back to the office as quickly as possible, more excited than ever. Surprisingly, Simions was amenable to the idea and told him to take the chance offered. Rupert called Webster and it was all set up.

By the time he telephoned from Heathrow airport, Rupert had the name of the hotel Rico was staying at and the name of a local policeman, Webster's opposite number who would help him in Viterbo.

CHAPTER 27

Despite having been good weather when he left England, the heat hit him like a wall as he disembarked from the aeroplane. It was a different sort of heat, he reflected; dry, almost sweet, leaving a perceptible taste in one's mouth. He savoured it, as is often the case with familiar, but irregular, pleasurable experiences. He walked across the airport apron, passed through customs and out to the car hire centre.

The bright sunlight hurt his eyes as it bounced up from the concrete. In shirt sleeves, he sauntered across the access roads, glad of the canopy cover overhead. He hired a car from the airport, a small Fiat 1500, and drove out onto the GRA, the Roman equivalent of the M25, only much more dangerous. The Roman drivers all drove with a panache and zeal suitably descriptive of their Latin temperament; flying in and out of the traffic lines, judging their distances to the merest inch as they changed lanes, horns blaring.

Rupert headed to the northern side of the ring road and nearly missed the turn off for the SS Aurelia, the oldest Motorway in Italy, and was sent on his way to the discordant fanfare of tooting horns. *Well*, he thought, *if you can't beat them, join them!* He headed north on the SS Aurelia and turned off just before

Tarquinia, heading east, across country, to the Lazio capital of Viterbo.

The guide books he had read described it as the finest medieval town in Italy, with a fully preserved historical centre and still bounded by the original city walls. He arrived some two hours later, having stopped off for coffee on the way in the small town of Vetralla.

As he approached Viterbo it at first appeared like any other large Italian city: industrial sprawl, long, straight roads, shabby peripheral shops and run down areas. But as one entered the inner ring road, passing under the huge arches still guarding the ingress, to the inner sanctum; a more historic and better kept area evolved. The guide books were correct: most the walls were intact and had been integrated well into modern life, something the Italians did very well. The crazy, one way system caused him much trial and tribulation at first; driving the same route three times before finding his way.

He finally found his hotel; a discreet, renaissance building just outside the *Centro Storico*. He parked in the car park to the front and walked in to the reception. He wondered to himself, not for the first time, why all Italian hotels smelled the same; a savoury, sweet smell, mixed with garlic and floral polish. Wherever he went in Italy, it was always the same, whatever size or quality of the hotel.

He booked in and found it irritating when he spoke in, albeit bad Italian, that the concierge replied in English. *Still,* he supposed, *better than France where they pretended not to understand one at all!* The room he was allotted was comfortable and ornate, inkeeping with the general style of the hotel. He unpacked, called Webster to say he had arrived safely and confirmed the address of the bi-lingual *notaio's* in Viterbo, of which there were only two. There was no hurry; no one would be working now as it was lunchtime.

Rupert was not hungry and dozed in his room, relaxing on the balcony outside his bedroom, absorbing the sights and sounds. He looked at his watch: 2.30. He changed into a linen suit, Panama hat and sunglasses and headed out into the stark sunlight, making his way towards the main legal centre where the *notaio's* offices were. *The beauty of this "detective work",* he thought, *is that he could check regularly with the street map and look the perfect tourist without being conspicuous.*

He wandered down the street in the direction of the *Centro Storico*, and headed for the main street which led, according to his map, to the legal area of the city. The street, mainly cobbled, was like many of the larger towns in Italy with small shops insinuated into the existing structures that had narrow front-ages and looked either very frumpy or rather tacky. There were a few designer shops but no multiples. *The surveyor never takes a rest,* he chuckled to himself. Only the ubiquitous Benneton and McDonalds gave evidence of any form of shop multiples in Italy. Only England, that "nation of shop keepers" could boast the best shopping in the world. Here it was old fashioned and boring. Quaint though, for a few touristy days, but to live here permanently would be very dull indeed, he decided.

He moved through the crowds of tourists, blending incon-spicuously with the other holiday makers and visitors to the city. He found his way to the legal district, noted the various offices of the *notaios* from the list provided by Webster's Italian coun-terpart, Commisariate Davida Capullacci. He worked his way back to the name of the hotel where Rico was booked in to stay. As Rico was not due in until tomorrow's flight, Rupert had time to kill and he spent it relaxing, wandering the streets and visiting the local churches, an old central villa and museums. He tried to contact Capullacci at the police station but he had difficulty making his wishes known and was assured (he thought) that the detective would be in the office the following day.

There was, he considered, nothing to fear at this point, but his mind was constantly on the job ahead which was fraught with difficulties and danger.

Over dinner in a quiet back street *trattoria*, he reflected on how much had happened in the last six months. Despite the awful events of Liz's death; the move to become a client, not an agent, had been incredibly profitable and a great experience. Not that this had blunted his want of revenge. That was as strong as ever. It was just amazing how it had all worked out, especially considering his initial fear of leaving the agency background and the warm feeling of having a big team around him. Other agents had started to return his calls again: even Mike.

He realised how he had grown in the last 12 months and now it had led him to this - playing amateur detective, tracking his girlfriend's killers. He was becoming maudlin under the influence of the strong, local red wine. Looking down at the bottle to judge, he was surprised to see that it was empty. He grinned to himself in a mirthless parody of a smile, accepted the offer of a grappa from the waiter and ordered a double espresso to finish.

He paid the bill and walked unsteadily back to his hotel. As he entered, he did not see the figure opposite, stop short of the corner, light a cigarette and speak softly into a radio device held in his left hand.

The following morning was, as before, bright, sunny and warm. The temperature was already starting to hit the 80's and the man in Rupert's head with the ice pick and sledgehammer was causing him great pain.

"Damn, the grappa!" he thought to himself. "It always does this to me, but I never learn."

He shuffled out onto the terrace for breakfast, sat down, drained a pitcher of iced water and ordered a large cappuccino to follow. He blinked behind his sunglasses against the glare. Two cups of coffee and a brioche later, he was beginning to feel human again and decided he had better make a move before Rico booked into his hotel and left. He looked at his watch; it was 10.30. Rico's flight would have landed an hour ago.

He walked through the town, following the route he had rehearsed the day before and found the hotel. Rupert looked around, found a newsagent who sold English papers and settled himself in front of a small café which afforded a good, but secluded view of the hotel main entrance. Coffee ordered, he settled himself down to watch and wait. Rupert had been there over an hour and was beginning to think that he had missed Rico or something was wrong when a car pulled up outside and decanted Rico who stretched and looked around, scanning each direction. Finally happy with his environment, Rico entered the hotel with a suitcase and a bag in each hand. Rupert's heart leapt; part elation and part fear.

Rico looked, to all the world, just as indomitable as the last time they had met. Rupert hunched further behind his newspaper and turned his head to avoid eye contact, despite using the sunglasses as a disguise. He found himself sweating more profusely than ever and not just because of the heat, it was the cold, sweat of fear.

His mouth felt dry and the "fight or flight" mechanism in his body produced massive amounts of adrenalin, causing his limbs to feel heavy and his head light. He asked himself, not for the first time, if he was doing the right thing, and why he had volunteered for this job. Then he thought of Liz and the reasons came flooding back to him. Reassured, he pretended to read his paper and kept an eye upon the front of the hotel.

Time slid by slowly until, finally, Rico made an appearance. He left the hotel building and paused, studying the streets on either side of the hotel, wary as cat.

The medieval city was swathed in deep shadows, cast by the midday light which bounced, harshly off the shiny, cobbled streets. The sun was warm for spring, even in Italy. The tourists were starting to head for the cloistered piazza of the *Centro Storico*, with its many bars and cafes; thronging the pedestrianised streets with thin trains of people.

Rico reaffirmed his grip on the brief case he carried and walked cautiously down the street, constantly stopping to ostensibly study a shop window. In reality he was marking his backtracks, trying to spot any potential tail who may have been trying to follow him.

Rupert passed him twice, having no choice (for fear of being caught) in a constant game of cat and mouse. He was fortunate in that he looked the way he did, dressed as he was the previous day: the perfect tourist.

It made the job of following the figure two hundred yards ahead, all the easier. What could be more natural he thought, than a tourist meandering along the streets; looking into windows, up and down side streets, in search of the elusive "off the beaten track restaurant". The main street split; turning up hill to the left and Rico veered off in this direction, occasionally looking back or stopping at a shop window to glance over his shoulder.

Satisfied, he moved off at a slower pace, as the incline took its toll. There was no doubt, Rico was heading for the legal quarter, Rupert thought, *but where?*

He was moving smoothly through the crowds and keeping track, until Rico made the fast switch, moving across the still quite busy street: always dangerous for anyone following to cross a street Rupert reflected, it exposed their position. He took off his Panama, as if to mop his brow and proceeded to follow into the narrow side street. He went twenty yards, when a large arm reached around his neck. A huge hand covered his face; dragging him into a dark, covered alcove at the bottom of some steps, leading to part of the old castellated walls. Reaction kicked in and he struggled, trying to stamp down on the man's instep. But he seemed to be held in the grip of bear and was dragged inexorably further backwards.

"*Silenzio!*" a voice hissed. "Stop!"

He struggled harder and was rewarded for his pains by a hard blow to the stomach, which knocked all the air from him, causing him to double over. The second figure, who delivered the blow, emerged from the gloom and proceeded, with his colleague, to manhandle the Englishman up the steps to the old ramparts. They again emerged into the sunlight, overlooking the street.

"We mean you no harm signor" the second man said in heavily accented English and produced an identification card with his picture on it. "But you must be quiet and watch." he continued.

The Englishman nodded in acceptance and uttered "Si"; they let go their hold and he relaxed.

"*Qui, qui, subito*" They pointed to where a mature bougainvillea climbed above the waist high wall on a large, faded trellis and effectively screened part of the ramparts from the street, allowing any watcher to see, but not be seen. His two abductors placed the Englishman behind the natural screen and proceeded to carry on a lively discussion in full view of the street in fast, excited, Italian.

As Rupert watched, a large, typical Italian figure appeared in the street below: dark, oiled hair almost to his shoulders in a "mullett", sunglasses, padded leather jacket, white t-shirt and jeans. He had entered the side street at speed, as though following somebody and was at a loss to find that the street was almost empty and did not contain his prey. He looked back and forward and finally upward at the two arguing Italians. He spoke in rapid Italian, demanding to know if they had seen an Englishman dressed in a pale suit, with a hat; that he was friend of his, whom he had lost. They shook their heads and shrugged in that expansive Italian way that says a thousand words. The predator checked the bottom of the steps, smacked the wall with palm of his hand in frustration and sped off up the street.

When all was clear they stopped arguing and walked over to the Englishman.

"You are very fortunate, Signor, that man is an enforcer, whatever game you are playing, it is a dangerous one, also one you are not very good at."

"I think you had better come with us, for your own protection." He continued and proceeded to offer the Englishman his hand, "I am sorry I hit you so hard, but it was the only way to make you shut up quickly, no....feelings hard... yes?" He finished grinning.

"No no, you're right," Rupert replied grinning ruefully whilst shaking both the policemen's hands, thinking: how many more breaks can I get? It had been a long dangerous journey to this point and he was already on the edge.

In that moment his mind drifted back in a blur over the last three years. A journey travelled through his career of deceit, bribery, corruption, murder and more importantly, the murder of one he had loved. Was it really only three years ago that set him on the trail of a criminal conspiracy, where his very life was in danger?

CHAPTER 28

The two police officers who had waylaid Rupert and saved him, introduced themselves, showing their identification cards. They suggested that they all leave, return to the police station and meet up with their boss, Cappulacci. Rupert was aghast at the turn of events.

"How did you know and what happens to Rico? I must find out which *notaio* he uses, we must follow him," he protested.

"*Con calma signor, piano, piano,*" said one of the men, placating him.

"But, he will get away," he cried.

"Signor, it will be ok, we have the place covered," Sergeant Bardinelli explained. "There is a, how do you say, *cordone?*"

"Cordon?" Rupert hazarded a guess.

"Yes, a cordon. All will be recorded and he will be left to be trailed. Come, all will be explained."

The expansive gesture was plain; it was not an invitation but a polite order.

The police station was a sterile, unfriendly looking building, located on the outskirts of the city, surrounded by high steel fencing. As they approached, the steel gates slid back, the motor humming as the well-oiled wheels rolled. Electric cameras followed their movements. Once through, the gates closed quickly behind them and the blue and white Alpha pulled forward to the parking area, halting with a dramatic screech of brakes. The cameras followed them in through the front doors, which slid crisply shut as soon as they had entered. A second pair of doors opened as the first shut. Security was tight; it was standard practice in a *Caribinieri* station. Guards with semi-automatic weapons watched Rupert's progress with hard, unemotional eyes.

He was finally shown into the inspector's office and was surprised. He had been expecting a typical Italian: short, broad and smooth. Instead he found an unusually tall man of about six foot four with rugged looks, curly hair, striking blue eyes and an engaging, crooked smile. A hand the size of a ham grasped his in an excruciating grip. It was, Rupert decided, not intentional, just that he did not realise his own strength.

He said in heavily accented, but good, English, "Please, sit down. I am Commisariate Davida Cappulacci. How are you?"

Rupert responded affably but despite the pleasantries, he realised that the Inspector was nobody's fool and his eyes carried a piercing discernment which seemed to probe into him. Rupert proceeded to describe the events of the last few hours since his arrival and was alarmed to learn that he had been followed from the time he arrived in Viterbo. The inspector shrugged.

"But it is normal in Italy. If a scam is going down, everybody takes precautions. You merely got caught up in the security measures," he finished with a grin. "Unfortunate for you."

"Yes, thank God your men were on hand to bale me out."

The inspector went on to explain the extent of the surveillance operation that had been carried out for the last few months as a result of working in conjunction with Webster.

"But now, thanks to you, we can put the final piece together as we now know their aim: to launder money from Italy to the international market and ultimately fund drugs rings, here and in *Inghleterra*. The scheme is virtually fool proof and has been adapted perfectly to our," he hesitated, a grin on his face as he sought the correct words, "unusual system of property taxation."

"I am still slightly at a loss to fully understand how exactly it works in practical terms," Rupert declared.

"Well, we have been tracking through the *Polizia Finanzia* the movements of Signor Rico and associated companies including a *Signor* Simonisi?" he raised his voice as if the name held a question.

"Simonisi? But that will be Simions, it has to be," he exclaimed.

"So, Webster agrees. However, it will be difficult to prove everything without someone confessing or," he hesitated, "some coercion."

He went on. "The story started some three years ago," About the time of the suicide, Rupert remembered, "when Simonisi was bequeathed a large villa by his grandmother. He has since sold and resold countless properties; each time increasing the value or managing to buy two and shelve the proceeds to an off shore company in *Sardengia;* the equivalent of your Jersey accounts," he deferred to Rupert and continued.

"The proceeds were then reinvested by either a company or individually; the usual tax evasion loopholes exploited to "release" the cash and transferred to the UK mainland. But the problem we have had until now is timing. We have always been aware, how do you say, after the act? Rupert nodded.

"Just so. This time we can track him and if we are lucky, catch him with the cash, follow the route and "persuade" him to reveal everything. *Justo*?" he queried.

"I understand, but if all this is falling into place, how do I fit in and why did Webster want me here if you have it all under control?"

His eyes twinkled as though relishing the next statement. "Well, you have served a purpose already, they think you are the only tail and-"

"You mean I was set up as bait?" Rupert exclaimed.

"Bait? What is bait?"

"A trap."

"Ah yes, I am afraid so. They were aware of you all the time but don't worry, we were watching over you." Rupert went suddenly cold, so Rico and his thugs were just waiting for him. Whilst Rupert had been playing James Bond, thinking he was so clever, they had known all along. He visibly cringed, thinking of what may have been. This was for real. The Seventh cavalry may not have arrived like in the films, he could be dead, or worse tortured by some homicidal Mafiosa thug. It was all getting out of hand.

"So, if I have played my part, what more is there for me to do?"

"Ah, but the game, it is not finished. We now need to assure Rico and, more importantly, his contacts in *Inghleterra*, that you are the only opposition acting independently, all alone and unofficially. Do you see?"

Rupert saw only too clearly.

"If we went in now we would lose the proof. Whereas, if you continue your detective work, he will suspect no official action. So tomorrow, you will follow my instructions and be wherever I say when we tell you. Ok?"

The choices were limited. Rupert nodded in acquiescence, the danger suddenly very apparent.

"Just remember, we will be watching at all times. Everything will be ok."

The words sounded hollow, like a father reassuring a child, just before diving off the top board. Rupert was aware of a dry feeling in his mouth and the raw fear beginning to tie knots in his stomach. He tried to shrug it away.

"Don't worry, ok? We will be there," Said Capallacci with a grin, again a twinkle of the eyes and a genuine expression of sympathy.

CHAPTER 29

The following morning it all seemed like a bad dream to Rupert who lay in bed, blinking, awaiting the call that would set his nerves jangling and send him on towards an uncertain future. He considered the events of the last few hours and the duplicity of Webster. When he returned to England, policeman or not, he would tell the little shit what he thought of him, having been set up like that. He finally relinquished the comfort of his bed, showered, dressed and packed his bag in anticipation of an early departure. He went down to breakfast, ever awaiting the call to drop everything and travel. He sat on the far side of the busy dining room, absentmindedly considering his other guests.

The sound of cutlery clashing together echoed around the room, accompanying the chatter of mostly English and American voices discussing their plans for the day or last night's adventures. The waiters were busy, occupied by the ever demanding Americans. Rupert was considering whether to have a third brioche, washed down with yet another cappuccino, when a waiter came across.

"Signor, telephone for you at the main desk, *prego*."

He gestured with his arm. Rupert anxiously muttered his

thanks and rose to take the call. What he missed, was the almost imperceptible nod between two waiters, a mutual understanding passing between them. The closer of the two, passed quickly out of the dining room, following Rupert to the reception area. The concierge on reception indicated the telephone on the front desk and smiled, moving a discreet distance away. As Rupert picked up the receiver and placed it to his ear he heard a quiet click, which he assumed was the call being put through. Capallacci told him that Rico had made the pick-up, the *notaio* had been identified and was being watched. Rupert was to make his way to the airport as soon as possible. He was instructed that he must attend terminal B for international departures and put himself in a position where he would be seen by Rico.

"Seen by Rico?" he whispered down the telephone. "Why?"

"Calm down, Rupert. You will be watched and protected at all times, do not worry. OK?"

The last word was stressed and drawn out, in the way that Italians do with the unfamiliar expression.

"But why?" he continued.

"Because we need a *catalitica*. Someone to force him to panic. To let him know that you are right on his tail. He will then act quickly and carelessly, hopefully," he added. "So leave now and get to the airport as quick as you can, we will be waiting. Don't make it too obvious that you are intending Rico to see you and," he hesitated, "don't be too close when you do. *Va bene?*"

Rupert's stomach took on the now familiar feeling, as fear gripped him. The images of the assault in the car park in England flashed back before him. It wasn't so much the attack, it was the enraged animal he saw snarling in defiance, that made Rupert shudder involuntarily. The memories were not good and would be with him for a long time to come.

"Ok," he said at last. "I am on my way."

He replaced the receiver and rubbed a dry hand across his

forehead. It came away damp with sweat. He collected his thoughts and went forward to the concierge, paid the bill and hurried out to his car. He fought his way determinedly out of the Viterbo centre and onto the ring road leading to the SS Aurelia. The journey sped by, with thoughts flying through his head, crashing like a thousand symbols in an orchestra. When he arrived at the airport approach it was almost a shock that he had reached his destination so soon; he had no recollection of the journey.

He parked the car, returned all the documentation to the hire centre and entered the main terminal building. It was very busy. The atmosphere, as always, was tense and exciting. The presence of so many people on edge, expectant and hopeful never failed to excite Rupert. He loved airports and always had. The thought of so many others acting out their own drama, took his mind momentarily off the task ahead. He relaxed, collected himself mentally and sought the location of the correct check-in desk for departures to London. He found it at the far end of the line; British Airways, desk 9.

With his passport checked and ticket issued, he folded everything away, smiled and turned to go. As he turned, he just about managed to avoid the passenger behind him. Their eyes met and a sense of dread began to rise up in Rupert.

A horrible smile crept across Rico's face. No surprise, just a smile of cruel satisfaction. The fear on Rupert's face was palpable. He shuddered involuntarily and made to move off quickly but not before Rico grabbed him by the arm.

"You'll get yours, you little shit! I owe you," he muttered quietly in Rupert's ear, the voice filled with menace. "Ciao." Rico released Rupert's arm and the moment was gone. Hurrying away as quick as he could, Rupert found his breath was coming in short gasps. Fear had nestled itself deep in his stomach, adrenalin surged around his system and his legs felt like lead.

Calm down, he told himself, *it's done. You've seen him, he's seen you and you're in one piece.* His breathing calmed as he walked slowly past the group of offices for the Carabinieri, debating whether to report it or not. *No, keep calm, Cappallacci's men were sure to be around somewhere.* As if on cue, a smartly, but conservatively dressed, man approached him from the group of offices to his left. About thirty years old, the man wore a suit and tie had a world weary, confident air of authority about him.

"Signor Brett?"

Rupert nodded. "Yes," he replied tentatively.

The man smiled benignly. "Sergeant Scibilia. The Commisariate sent me. He has been watching the events from there." He gesticulated towards a large window with a mirror film across it. "Please, come this way."

Rupert, suddenly very relieved, followed the sergeant, who hesitated once before finally opening the door to the offices, checking around to ensure no one was paying them too much attention.

"We cannot be too careful signor," he nodded conspiratorially.

Rupert smiled back, glad of the tight protection they were placing around him. The door opened inwards and upon the sergeant's invitation Rupert stepped into the lit room, empty but for a filing cabinet, two chairs and a door on the far side. The door closed quickly behind him and Rupert sensed all was not well just before his world exploded in pain.

A shocking, numbing jab to his kidneys was delivered by the unseen man behind the door. He had struck with his fingers extended, bent at the middle knuckle, palm uppermost just between the lower ribs. The pain to Rupert was indescribable. His back arched away from the blow like a scalded cat and he instinctively sucked in air, causing more pain.

The "sergeant" appeared at his right side and delivered a round elbow strike to his sternum. All the breath left him as it felt like knives stabbed inside his chest. He wanted to cry out but no words would come. A small part of his brain thought in an abstract way, the way the body does in moments of extreme stress, that it was not like in the films; one couldn't ride the punch and beat the bad guys. It was his last conscious thought before he passed out.

As he collapsed to the floor, the second man kicked him hard in the ribs, resulting in a sickening crack. He raised his foot for a second kick and the "sergeant" stopped him.

"Our orders are to deliver him in good condition," he said in fast Italian.

The other shrugged. "Rico wants-"

"Forget what Rico wants," the first interrupted, "Rico is nothing, just a small cog, don't listen to him or it will be you who gets hurt. We need Signor Brett in a condition to talk, we need to know how much they know."

The other man scowled and relented.

They lifted Rupert with hands under his arms and legs, manhandling him through the doorway on the far side of the room. This exited on to the pavement adjacent to the departures doorway, furthest away from the terminal. A dark, blue Lancia saloon was waiting its powerful three litre engine burbling away. Both doors on this side of the car were open.

The driver looked around surreptitiously before beckoning them forward towards the Lancia. They changed position and half carried, half walked the slumped figure of Rupert between them and folded him into the car. Slamming the door shut, the "sergeant" walked around to the other rear door, got in and straightened him up. It was all done in a matter of seconds and no one appeared to take any notice.

The front passenger door closed before the driver pulled away, only to find himself waiting impatiently for a break in the traffic. Not wishing to draw attention to himself, he carefully slid the car neatly into a small gap in the traffic. A horn sounded, gestures were exchanged and the Lancia sped off as soon as a gap in front extended sufficiently to accelerate.

The boundaries of the airport were approaching as the three lanes merged with the car park traffic. The driver checked his rear view mirror and felt relieved when he saw it was all clear. Rupert groggily lolled his head from side to side with the movement of the car as it sped through roundabouts leaving the airport and heading out on to the GRA. Now they were away from the confines of the airport, the "sergeant" urged for more speed.

They continued heading north on the SS Aurelia and pulled off after 25 km, causing a blast of horns from the last minute manoeuvre. The side road led to the Port town of Civitavecchia; a major hub for the western sea traffic, as well as the main route to the island of Sardinia. They drove steadily along the front, past the old turreted fort and down to the docks.

A large derrick swooped down like a *Corvo* mandible, plucking containers for the waiting hold of containers ships. The whole dock area was a hive of activity, making it the perfect place to keep a low profile

The Lancia pulled to a halt amongst a pile of containers being readied for loading. The only other arrival was a lone motorcycle that cruised along the front dodging derrick legs and containers in an absurd game of slalom. The sexy burble of the BMW 850 reverberated off the containers as it past. It had been half an hour since the abduction of Rupert Brett, who was now bound and semi-comatose in the back seat of the Lancia.

The 'sergeant' left the car to talk to one of the dockers and a container was subsequently opened with a view to loading the car and Rupert inside. Returning to the car, he saw Rupert gaining consciousness.

"Signor Brett, so glad to have you back with us." He smirked. Rupert gradually became aware of his surroundings, twisting in horror as he saw that he was about to be loaded into a container. "Don' worry it is only a short trip to *Sardengia*, just two hours and then you will be out again. You will get plenty of air, no problem. We do not want you dead, yet."

The threat invoking more horror in Rupert. He knew that once on the island, he would never be seen again. Having holidayed there a few years ago, he recalled the rats nest of hills, hideaways and inaccessible mountains where a body or captive could easily be hidden.

He mumbled incoherently through smashed lips.

His reward was a smack around the head from the 'sergeant' next to him. Anger and fear at the attack seethed within him. He went with the blow, forwards then jerked his head back straight into the face of the of the 'sergeant' leaning towards him. It was a great blow, the hard back of his skull smashing the nose and upper lips into the teeth, blood spewing out.

"*Fica!*" he screamed.

Rupert took the opportunity even though he knew he would not get far but he had to try. *If only to attract attention*, he thought. He jacked his legs outwards, his cracked ribs screaming at him, and kicked the 'sergeant' in the stomach as he jerked upright. Rupert lurched forward, impeded by his bound hands, and began running away from the sea front, shouting for help as he went.

As he ran, he made the mistake of looking behind and seeing the *sergeant* scrambling to his feet and pulling a Berretta from inside his jacket. The distance was forty yards. *Getting towards top range for a hand gun*, he thought before, with hands still tied, unbalanced, he tripped on the rough concrete. As he went crashing awkwardly to the floor, he heard the report of a 9mm cartridge and the roar of a motorcycle exhaust.

The 'sergeant' half turned at the sound to face the oncoming BMW. The motorbike did not hesitate and there was a sickening crunch as tyre and handlebars connected with human frailty. The 'sergeant', caught in the upper leg and ribs, bent in two and he was tossed sideways into the air, the automatic leaving his hand. He slammed into the concrete motionless.

Without warning sirens pierced the air and two blue, unmarked Alfa Romeo 75 Evoluzione's converged from the entrance of the docks, coming to a screeching hold by the side of the Lancia. The driver and one of the remaining guards raised their hands as the police, including Cappallacci, flew from the car, guns pointed at the three men.

The third guard was braver, he raised the stock of his Beretta MP12, snapping off a quick burst before being hit by a wave of bullets fired by the police. His lifeless body jerked spasmodically on the way to the ground.

In a matter of moments the police rounded their cars and rammed the barrels of the guns hard against the necks of the two remaining men. They shouted fast, staccato demands for them to place their hands where they could be seen and the dazed men complied slowly.

Rupert lay still on the concrete, mesmerised by what was happening around him but also from the amount of pain coursing through his body. His chest hurt when he breathed, he could feel the bruising around his cracked ribs. His head pounded and his eyesight swam. He tried to move himself into a sitting position but the pain made it impossible.

"Ahhh!" he cried resisting, thrashing his tied arms out.

"Rupert, it's ok," Capallacci assured him, kneeling down to untie Rupert's hands. "It's ok, *calma, con calma*," he said gently. Rupert focused briefly on the concerned face, his own contorted in pain before mercifully passing out again.

CHAPTER 30

The dim light became brighter and turned into a blazing orb in the centre of the room. His eyes focused slowly as the room finally stopped spinning. The anaesthetic in his blood stream was still having an effect and the drip attached to his arm periodically pumped quantities of morphine into his system.

The last thoughts he could recall were of the crash to the floor, extreme pain and then nothing. He gradually became aware of what was around him and he realised, with the clinical smell of disinfectant, that he was in a hospital bed with a nurse peering over him. She was very pretty, in a very Italian way; large, almond shaped, brown eyes smiling kindly at him.

"Signor Rupert?"

He refocused on her face and stammered, "Wherrr,...where am I?"

"In hospital. You are quite safe now signor Brett. Don't worry. There is a guard at the door and I will now go and fetch the doctor. Be calm."

She patted him gently, picked up the telephone and spoke quickly into the hand piece, nodding her head and saying, "Si, si."

She replaced the receiver and smiled at Rupert.

"The doctor, he is on his way, don't worry, just rest." She smiled reassuringly and left the room. Minutes later a man appeared in a white coat with a stethoscope around his neck. He walked briskly into the room with a no nonsense manner familiar to all doctors. Rupert smiled despite himself at the precursory inspection and the taciturn attitude.

"Signor, you are a lucky man," he avowed, eyes crinkling into a smile, pulling his nicotine-stained moustache upwards and taking years off his age despite greying hair and thick glasses. But the eyes were kindly behind the lenses as he continued, "however you have some concussion, two broken ribs and a cracked sternum. But you are young, you will be fine. In a week, maybe 10 days you can be moved and go back to England," he finished with a dismissive shrug, as though the thought of returning to England was an extraordinary thing when one could live in Italy for longer.

"But in the meantime you must rest and take time to recover. Now, I will give you some more morphine, sleep and we will see how you are when you wake up." Rupert felt himself drifting into a deep, chemical induced sleep as the drug hit his blood stream. Dreams started to invade his sleep but even these nightmares faded as he dropped into a deeper state of unconsciousness.

CHAPTER 31

LONDON

Two days later, a completely different conversation was taking place some fifteen hundred miles away in London.

"Yes, it was in the local paper, la Republica, and made a small news item on the radio. Roughly it says...*an English tourist was hurt in a police chase and later died of his injuries in hospital...* so no need to worry. It also says that he was in a coma and never recovered consciousness. Rico assures me that all is well and that he was not followed, either before or since. The *notaio* has made the payment, it is in the offshore account and all is well. Relax."

"So you say, but it is me who carries the connection. It will be me who has to contend with police knocking at my door, me who has to answer the questions and who yet again has the attention drawn to him," he shouted.

"Just stay calm, nothing can be proved. Rico won't talk, you've nothing to worry about. He will be safely tucked up in Sardinia now telling us all he knows. Then-"

"Fine but look here-"

"No Paul," he sternly interrupted, harsh tones entering his

voice. "We've been here before remember? Don't make me remind you. And remember it was both of us who ordered the hit on Liz Carmichael and me who arranged the 'suicide'." The threat lay thickly in the air, more menacing than a raised voice. Simions was silent, his thoughts turning back to the events to which Shingler alluded.

He snarled back, totally out of character, like a cornered animal, "Fine, but I won't go down alone, just remember that," he said and slammed down the receiver.

He stared across the office, a bead of sweat appeared on his brow and he realised that he was hyperventilating. He held out his hand, palm down and looked at the perceptible shake which he struggled to control. He swore harshly in Italian. *Strange,* he thought, *after all these years, it was still the language he cursed in, that actually meant something when he used the words.*

It had been how long? He counted four days since the incident at the airport. *Soon,* he supposed, *they would come soon.* The *notaio* had signed off the deal, the Italian authorities would be an age registering the deal and the Italian police would never follow it up, they would stick with the supposed mafia connection in Italy, so it was just the English police. On instinct he rang down to his secretary to check for calls, she affirmed that there were none, but that twice a caller had rung asking if he was in the building, leaving no name. Alarmed he rang off, pacing the room, collecting his thoughts, working out a strategy, suddenly feeling calm in the eye of the storm. He felt his usually clear mind take hold. Raising his hand holding it palm down, there was not a movement, not even a tremor.

"Let the game commence," he murmured in defiance.

It was a day later that the police were announced. They had of course known of his movements, the calls were just to soften him up, put his nerves on edge and had, to a certain degree, succeeded. DI Fleming and DS Brooke were again shown up to his offices.

"Well we just wanted to ask you a few questions, to clear up a few loose ends that we have over one of your employees. Or perhaps I should say former employees."

"Oh yes, poor Rupert, I assume? So sad, we were all really upset when we heard," he faded away, frowned and looked down in a stricken manner.

"Yes, strange coincidence really, first his girlfriend and now him. It would seem to be rather unlucky knowing you, Mr Simions." The tone changed throughout the sentence, became harder, more aggressive.

"I beg your pardon? Detective Inspector... Fleming, what on earth do you mean by that last statement?" The fluster was part reality, partly put on for show. "I do not like the tone that this conversation is taking. I do not like the insinuation in that last statement Inspector."

"Well sir, we rather suspect that the death of Miss Carmichael and the incident with Rupert Brett are linked and you know more about this than you're letting on." Again he finished abruptly without any further explanation.

"Wait. Miss Carmichael's death occurred months ago in London; Rupert died in Italy and you think they are connected? You are clearly delusional DI Fleming and this conversation is at an end," he finished dogmatically. "Gentlemen if you want to carry on this conversation any further you had better wait until my solicitor is present. I resent these games and the implications. In the meantime if you are dealing with the poor chap's murder I would suggest, as a pair of detectives, you go off and do just that: detect!"

The staring contest continued for a few seconds; it was Simions who first looked away. However, the two detectives knew that they had no concrete evidence with which to charge him and moved to leave. Once they left the building the air exploded out of DS Brooke.

"He's fucking guilty as hell. But we can't do anything. Rico's held in Italy accused of paltry currency charges, money laundering at best and he is not talking. Him," he jerked his thumb backwards, "is guilty of all that and murder, corruption, bribery, you name it and we can't touch him."

DI Fleming shook his head in disgust. "I know, I know. But what can we do except keep the pressure on and hope that something breaks. I am going to speak with Webster again now we've seen Simions."

It had now been two weeks since the injuries that Rupert had sustained and he was healing fast, as all young people do. However, whilst the physical side of the healing process proceeded in leaps and bounds, the mental strain and trauma of the past few months was proving more visible and taking longer to repair.

His face had a hollow cheeked look as he ascended the austere staircase to the now familiar office occupied by DS Webster. His eyes were ringed by blue circles and dark smudges. His tan of the past week was beginning to fade; leaving a pale pallor beneath of a wan, sickly colour. His ribs ached slightly with the exertion of climbing the stairs but it was a good sign; they were healing. He finally reached the landing and walked through into the outer office, occupied by the same efficient looking secretary. She smiled weakly and motioned for him to sit, before announcing through the telephone that he had arrived.

Minutes passed before the far door opened to produce the figure of DS Webster. Ebullient, smiling and yet managing to produce a sympathetic expression of a man torn between having achieved what he wanted but yet needing to conserve his position as a figure in authority who cared. His right arm was extended to be shaken and he adopted an open posture of embrace and care.

"Rupert, so good to see you up and about. How are you?"

The false bonhomie didn't fool him for a moment but he played the game smiled wanly and shook Webster's hand.

"Yea, yea, pretty shitty. But being kidnapped, along with cracked ribs and sternum will do that to a man," he finished sarcastically.

"Rupert, I am dreadfully sorry that you were hurt. You were supposed to be looked after and we did all we could." His eyes hardened for a moment, then he relaxed by an effort of will. He motioned that Rupert should proceed through to his office and he obediently did so but for different reasons.

The door closed and Rupert let rip with all the pent up emotion of the last weeks roaring forth.

"You bastard! You knew you were setting me up, you knew that I would be followed. I was your stalking horse and you let me walk right into the trap. What? Did you need to get me beaten up to get the conviction? Is that it? Well fuck you, Webster! I came here to say that and whatever else you invited me here for can stay unsaid. The answer is no!" he turned and made for the door.

The bland response cut through: "I understand how you must feel but it is not entirely true. Yes I did-"

"You understand?" he interrupted. "I doubt that very much. How could you? I'm fed up with being lied to, now I'm leaving."

"You realise that Liz's killer is still at large and you are the only man who can put him away?"

Rupert paused slightly, hesitating, then forcefully proceeded towards the door.

"I don't give a shit," he retorted.

"Just one more meeting, no violence, I guarantee it."

"Oh, like last time," he exclaimed sarcastically.

"Just five minutes and then you can walk out, OK?"

Rupert relented with a sigh and returned to take a seat. He left twenty minutes later and the answer was still 'no'.

After he left, Webster called Fleming. "He still won't get involved. Despite Capallacci getting Rico to talk, without further proof here, we can't get Shingler or Simions. We need more conclusive evidence. Brett feels let down by us and Capallacci. He is no fool and knows he was used to spring a trap."

Rupert went home and brooded until the early evening. He had still not seen any of his friends and had only spoken to his parents on the phone. His door bell buzzed on the intercom.

"Rup's! It's me, Claire. Let me in," she demanded.

The vision presented to Claire was not good. She stormed up the stairs of his flat and was aghast at the state of Rupert. "We thought you were dead, you little shit, dead! Why didn't you let us know?"

She hugged him at which he winced protesting loudly. "Ow!"

"Oh I'm so sorry. What's the matter?" Claire ordered giving him no time to respond as emotional as she was. "Sit down, let me get you a drink. Your parent's phoned me and said you were alive, but not well. No one knows your alive. Rup's, tell me," she shook him gently by the shoulders.

So he did, everything from the moment he left, to when he got back to England two days ago. Claire sat in studied silence, listening and only wincing or exclaiming in parts, saying nothing. When he finished she hugged him very gently, rubbing his hair affectionately.

"So what are you going to do?" she asked. "I must say I don't like the sound of this DS Webster's scheme. Too many loose ends and you will end up the patsy."

"I don't know. I really don't. I am mightily pissed off but fed up with being everyone else's fall guy. All the time I have been playing catch up, following, or responding I should say, to everyone else's actions. Now I feel I need to take the initiative."

"Good man. I thought you had given up the fight there for a minute."

"Not a chance," he retorted.

"But listen, up until now you have been fighting on their terms, all of them (police as well) and by that I mean in the best sense. But it has always been with a physical end. What you need to do is to take the fight to them." She waved off Rupert's proposed objection.

"Not physically; from what you've said of Rico you'd come off a pretty poor second any way. No, I mean use you're intelligence. Hell, you were, when an agent, one of the best in the West End and you came from nothing to doing £350k a year *non-retained*. Bugger me, Rupert, that takes some doing and you didn't get it handed to you on a plate. Use your cunning and street wise ability. You're always telling me you have a virtual photographic memory for facts, numbers and deals. Well, think back and use that to your advantage, not theirs."

It was as though a light suddenly clicked on in his brain. Claire had shown him the way and opened a door he was about to step through. They talked it through over a supper of pasta, making lists of people and events that had occurred over the months before Liz's death and afterwards. As they followed through, a plan was beginning to occur to Rupert and if he was right, it could bring down the whole house of cards.

"Ok, first we need to contact Liz's parents and see if they have the notebook she wrote everything in. I really am not looking forward to that, at all."

"What will you do, telephone them?"

"Yes. I know the area that they live in West Sussex, some-where near a small town called Midhurst,"

"Really?"

"Yes, why do you know it?

"Of course, it is the polo capital of the UK. All the pony club championships were, and still are, held there. I know it quite well. In fact everyone knows everyone there. If she was horsey and a Sloane I bet I can find someone who knows the family."

She went off to get her *Filofax* and started to make a number of calls. Half an hour later she was there.

"Bingo," she exclaimed. "Here we are." She passed over a number and address. "She used to be a member of the Pony Club and this girl Louise," she pointed at the Filofax, "knew her quite well and still keeps in contact with the parents. Apparently they are still very cut up about Liz's death, so tread lightly."

"Understood."

The call was not easy and Rupert was afraid at one point they would put the phone down on him. But he gently persevered and they agreed to help by looking for the black notebook he had seen her reading to Simions from all that time ago in Boswells. As Claire said: an elephantine memory. Apparently the police had returned it as it was in shorthand and seemed to be just a secretary's notebook. They promised to post it as soon as they found it. Rupert came off the phone visibly shaken.

"That was horrible. I never want to have to do that again."

She rubbed his shoulder affectionately. "Rup's, I have to go. I have a report to draft out before tomorrow and it is a mare. I left early to see you when I heard the news."

"No, you go. You have done more than enough: thank you," he said sincerely. "Keep it all quiet please, the fewer people who know the better."

"Of course. Night." She pecked him on the cheek and left, her perfume lingering around him as a constant reminder of her presence. *Thank you, Claire,* he thought, *thank you.*

CHAPTER 32

Three days later the package arrived containing the notebook. He called Claire, using the agreed pseudonym of '*Steven Smith*'; not the most original.

"The package has arrived. Just one small problem: can you read shorthand?"

"Just one of my many talents," she crowed.

They agreed to meet up after she left work and finalise their plans. She arrived at his flat and began poring over the notebook. By itself the notes meant little, but taken in context and with the inside knowledge they already had it was dynamite. They hatched a plan and agreed to meet up at a little wine bar off Maddox street; out of the way and perfect for their needs.

Two days later, Claire was sat at a table with her secretary Tracey, who had gone off sick when the details of the Golden Triangle scheme had been leaked.

"The point is this Tracey," Claire snarled "I know you took money to pull a 'sickey' for two days; that in itself was not too bad, we all do it. But what you didn't realise is that we lost massive amounts of fees on that deal and it is all down to you."

Tracey responded petulantly, "I don't see how. Two days sick, so what?"

"Fine have it your way. I know Secs in the City called you, it's on the records." she bluffed. "I also know you were paid by them in cash. What you do not know is that Simions of MAS owns the agency. You thought it was just Pauline didn't you? Well that is how you lost us money."

"But," she started to bluff, "…what are you going to do?"

"Well you have two choices: do as I say or I go to Personnel and get you fired," she finished aggressively.

"What? No. Ok, what do I have to do? I will help but who is we?"

At that point Rupert turned around from the table behind: "Well me actually."

"What! You're dead! The papers said…" she blurted out, seeing a ghost.

"Shouldn't believe everything you read in the papers Tracey," he chided. The conversation went downhill for Tracey from there. She agreed to help and sign what they wanted. After she left, the two co-conspirators smiled, chinked glasses and Rupert commented. "Well that went well."

"Right, stage three," Claire confirmed.

That afternoon she called Secs in the City using a false name and asked if she could come in to apply for temping work, claiming she was fed up working at CR and wanted more freedom. Using herself as the reference made her a senior PA and she was interviewed by Pauline Wood herself. Claire fed in that she was hard up for cash and if any high paid PA jobs came up she would be glad of the money.

"I can invoice as self-employed, if that helps?" she said For a moment, she thought she had overplayed her hand but the sharp, hard eyes of Pauline Wood latched on to this.

"Really?" she queried. "And you're a property secretary I see?" She ran an expert be-ringed finger down the page of the fake CV. "Can you work at short notice?" Claire nodded. "Good. Well we work a lot within the property world and for rush jobs we get paid bonuses which we are able to pass on as cash. If you know what I mean?" she smiled and it reminded Claire of a hyena; it was not pleasant.

"I'll do anything for cash," Claire enthused. The hard eyes appraised her again.

"Well, sometimes we get asked to do a little bit extra. It can be-"

Claire interrupted. "I won't sleep with someone, I'm not that desperate!" all mock outrage, deliberately misinterpreting her meaning.

The hyena laughed showing very white teeth, the double chin moved.

"No my dear, nothing like that," she assured her. "Just sometimes we like a bit extra done or copied..."

Claire pretended to finally catch on, "Oh yea no probs. Anything like that."

And so it was left, the trap baited and the waiting began.

That evening, Rupert and Claire held a council of war.

"So, it went well then?" he queried.

"Yes, she seemed to snap me up. I thought I'd overplayed my hand at first but the revolting creature was delighted that she had another convert to the cause.

So now we wait. When do you think we should go to Webster? We are going to need help from him soon to pull it all together aren't we? Especially where Shingler is concerned."

"I don't know that we will. You told me to use my cunning. Well, I have and I want them to turn on each other. I have the value of surprise: they don't know I'm alive. But for every day that passes that risk becomes greater, then I will really put the cat amongst the pigeons."

"I thought we said no risky physical stuff?" she asked worriedly.

"Don't worry, there is one thing Simions won't do and that's start a fight, more's the pity. I'd just like one chance to smack him in the face!" he finished aggressively.

A week later Claire was called at her home number. It was Pauline Wood.

"Louise, it's Pauline Wood from Secs in the City. How are you?" The call progressed and she was asked to come in to temp at, of all places, Halpern & Beams in three days' time. The placement was in the Investment Department and she was to collect information on a scheme and a portfolio that was to be released for sale in two weeks' time. She accepted eagerly and put the phone down. She immediately phoned Rupert to explain everything.

"So what are you going to do?"

"I know Richard Saunders, head of investment there really well. I am going to see him tomorrow. Explain what I've heard and keep it as quiet as possible. We can then hopefully spring a trap because I am going to have a bad accident and won't be able to work there," she prophesied.

"Humm. We need her caught in the act. We also need the complicity of the Personnel Department."

"Don't worry I reckon they are up to their ears in it," Claire confirmed.

"OK, good luck."

Claire phoned in 'sick with a badly sprained ankle' saying she couldn't make the temp appointment. Pauline Wood was not best pleased giving very little sympathy for her supposed state.

"Just one more thing Louise; we like to keep this quiet and the bosses don't like this being bandied about. Do we understand each other?"

"Oh course, I want more work and as soon as this bloody

ankle gets better I'll be back. Don't you worry., she reassured her, ignoring the threat.

"Good. See that you do." Pauline rang off.

But Claire checked the day before and indeed an another temp from the agency had been placed. Richard Saunders had been more than willing to go along with Claire's plan. The hapless temp had been caught sending a fax of the details (which had been incorrectly completed) straight to David Shingler's office. Shingler would be none the wiser.

The temp signed a statement admitting everything, in return for being let off with a warning and no prosecution.

The next day, Rupert went to see an expectant Webster. He was again shown up to the Spartan office, the reception slightly warmer.

"Rupert, how very good to see you again and looking better, I am pleased to see."

Rupert acknowledged the compliment and told him what he had done and why he was there.

"That was a very dangerous and stupid thing you both did. You're playing with fire, in more ways than one."

"It's not that dangerous," he retorted. Anyway, it is Shingler that does that sort of thing, not Simions."

"Yes, but who do you think agrees and orders it?" and at that moment the final piece of how to crack this fell into place for Rupert.

"Agreed. Now you wanted my help and I'm giving it. If you agree, all within police procedure etc., I would like you to apply pressure to Pauline Wood directly."

Rupert went on to outline his plan.

The next day the police interviewed a very aggressive Pauline Wood, whose bluster and denials changed with written statements from various Personnel departments; Tracey and the hapless temp from H & B. She called for her lawyer and ensured that he in turn spoke to Shingler. At the same time Rupert was having a Lazarine moment with Paul Simions. Rather than being introduced at reception, he used his knowledge of Simions habits to 'ambush' him after lunch as he was walking from his car to the office steps. It was, to Rupert, a moment to savour. He was looking well and had clearly not yet been given the bad news by Shingler as to what had just occurred at the offices of Secs in the City.

He approached all hale and hearty, "Paul. How the devil? I was just on my way to see you now." All smiles, extending his hand to shake with Simions.

"Rupert! By all that's... you're alive. But I thought you, they said..." he finished completely nonplussed. Rupert laughed at him, filled with new found confidence: Simions was no longer the bogey man.

"Do you know, that is probably the first time that I have ever seen you lost for words."

"Well, yes well. But why didn't you call and let me know you were alright? I was trying to get hold of your parents to see when your funeral was," he finished lamely.

"Ah well, I was in hospital and then," at which point he looked around furtively "I was interviewed by the police and was not allowed contact with anyone especially you or David Shingler." Rupert was delighted at the effect the words had upon Simions' face. It fell, all fear and wariness exposed in a fleeting instant before being replaced by a mask.

"I think we had better step inside," offering the way with his hand.

The response of the receptionists was just as spectacular.

They passed on after two minutes of short explanation, Simions clearly impatient to learn everything. Whilst waiting for the lift one of them called: "Before you go up sir, David is on the line, says it's urgent. He has tried your car phone but the driver said you had just left."

"Tell him I will call in a few minutes and that Rupert is back and with me at the moment," he finished pointedly. "I am sure he will be delighted."

Upon entering his office he continued, "Now, tell me all about it from the beginning. I really am so pleased to see you," he adhered to his disingenuous self. So Rupert did, slanting the narrative his way and finishing with the premise that the police thought he was somehow involved and that it was a falling out amongst thieves.

"I felt like a bloody criminal. They have even taken my passport and told me not to leave the country and it was me that was beaten up. I don't get it."

"You poor chap how awful for you."

Rupert waved off the sympathy. "But listen, the real reason I came to you directly is that they think you and David are involved."

"Why?" he interrupted aggressively.

"Well, it's all to do with this chap Rico and apparently his sister is the one who may have murdered Liz. She was seen at the apartment block on the night of the murder and they think I may still be linked to it all," he continued, watching every nerve of Simions reaction. *I have him hooked*, he thought, so he ploughed on.

"You see, apparently there is a connection between the firm Secs in the City, David Shingler, this Rico and his sister. They are trying to do a deal I think and wanted me to admit some culpability. Now as you are so close to him I just wanted to warn you in case, you need to cut ties or something. The last thing you want is to be involved with corporate espionage and murder."

The old Simions was back, the lupine eyes regarded him balefully; the temperature in the room seemed to drop considerably.

"And why do you think that this concerns me?" he asked icily.

"I told you, from what the police have said to me. They think that they have found a connection between you and Shingler. Look, I have never liked the chap I know, but this is serious and I certainly don't want to get any more involved as one of your employees."

Simions responded as Rupert knew he would: with aggression.

"Rupert, I don't know who the hell you think you are, but one: you no longer work for me, your employment was terminated; secondly, it's none of your bloody business. I have nothing, repeat nothing, to do with this and just because David does a lot of work for me, it does not mean that we had anyone murdered. Liz or otherwise, is that clear?" the last was shouted. Rupert had never heard him raise his voice before.

Rupert blanched, then turned on his own temper knowing what effect it would have.

"Well fuck you! I came here to help, first call after being freed by the police and this is the response I get? Stuff you, matey. I don't know what you're involved in, but you won't get any more help from me that's for certain." His parting words as he was half way through the door shook Simions. "I intend to vindicate myself and if that involves pointing the finger elsewhere, so be it."

He stormed out slamming the door, once outside he let out his breath in a long stream and grinned to himself. "Yes! Now let's see what happens. You may not like it DS Webster but the results could be spectacular," he murmured to himself.

Back in Simions' office the phone rang again.

"Paul it's me. Where the hell have you been and how come Brett is alive?"

"To answer your points seriatim," he replied pompously, "with Mr Brett and because your man screwed up! Now shut up and listen." He narrated all that Rupert had said, finishing with the veiled threat.

Shingler was furious and clearly worried, explaining about the arrest of Pauline Wood who, he knew, would clearly talk in return for a lenient case against her. The rats were, to his eyes, clearly leaving the sinking ship but the most worrying point was that of murder.

"This all taking a bad turn. The bribing and espionage is enough, we could fight that with good lawyers but it is the association with murder that scares me shitless," he exclaimed.

"Just sit tight, it all relies upon Rico being strong enough and the link between you and his sister."

"All very well for you to say. You do not have this hanging over your head, I do. Listen, if Rico incriminates me, I will bring everyone down with me, including you. I am not doing time for manslaughter or criminal conspiracy to commit murder. You sit there in your ivory tower," he spat, "distanced from it all but where would you be without me pulling all the levers and making it happen, huh? Yea, fucking nowhere, that's where. So don't patronise me with 'sit tight'. We need to think about this carefully and make sure our case is solid. The police have asked to see me tomorrow, but I swear I am being followed already."

Simions changed tack seeking to pacify him. "David, look, you're right. We're in this together, we will find a way out. We have the best lawyers and we will fight it. As far as the police can prove, it is only a bit of 'white collar crime' and fraud. Difficult to prove in court, we'll sort it."

"Ok that's better." he conceded "I am going to tidy up in the office. Ensure all evidence has gone and no trail of any kind is left, fax memory the lot. You do the same, ok? You can be guilty by association and I don't want any association coming to the fore."

"A good point. I'll wait for the girls to go and clear everything out that may be in the slightest bit incriminating. We'll speak tomorrow but if anything else occurs just call me. We'll fight this thing."

Shingler finally mollified agreed. "Yea, talk later."

Simions turned around in his chair and looked out over the London skyline, lost in thought. *My dear David, you are quite right: you are the link in all this. Your link to me is the link to Rico, his sister and a lot of trouble. Everyone talks,* he thought, *no one is really loyal.* He made a decision, picked up the receiver and looked up a number in his address book. Thinking better of it, he made a note on a slip of paper and then left the office telling reception that he was popping out for a few minutes.

When he returned he asked if any anyone had called.

"No."

"Well just so you know, there are some strange rumours regarding Rupert and his former employment. If the police should call either in person or by telephone, I want my lawyer called directly. You have his number, understood?"

They nodded in assent and he passed on the same message to Gayle, his PA.

CHAPTER 33

After his meeting with Simions, Rupert called Claire first to tell her how it went.

"Was that wise?" she cried. "We agreed not to push him that far."

"I know but he just sat there: firstly with that smug smile on his face and then tried the aggressive 'I'm more important than you' tactic. Well stuff him! I loved rocking his world, second only to smacking him one. I did think at one point he was going to come over the table at me but as I said, a bully and a coward."

"Well, I hope you know what you're doing. Listen don't take this the wrong way but would you like to stay at my flat for a couple of days? No one knows where I live, or that I am involved. You say that Rico could come back to the UK, but more scary if his sister comes looking for you. If this goes wrong..." she left it hanging in the air.

"Do you know, I may just do that. I'll pick up some things from my flat and be around later." He rang off and looked into the mid distance. *Claire, Claire, Claire*, he thought. The next call did not go so well.

"You've done what?" shouted Webster. *Ah*, thought Rupert, *it was obviously the day for making the usually sanguine irritated, how rewarding.* He continued equanimously: "Yes, bumped into him in the street. Well as you can imagine he was surprised. Things just went from there really," he finished and waited for the reverberation. He was not disappointed.

"Rupert, we have just arranged for Rico to be set free as a stalking horse to try to trap them and you go and blow it. Bugger it! Have you also considered that they may come after you now they know you're alive?" Came the vehement response.

"Yes, well, it did occur to me and I am taking precautions. But I don't see how this changes things. It will just put them on their mettle and they might make a mistake." Webster was too apoplectic to continue he charged Rupert with keeping in touch regularly and put the phone down, furious.

The day progressed without incident. Rupert picked up spare clothes and essentials from his flat and walked the few streets over to Claire's, fighting with the early evening rush hour. She had left a key with a neighbour and he let himself in, awaiting her return from work.

Over in Mid-Town, David Shingler was working late. He was the last one in the office and no one was there to witness his ruthless clear out. He looked at his gold Rolex: 6:50. *The cleaners would be here soon,* he reflected, *and all the evidence would be gone.* He continued stripping files and reprogrammed the fax machine memory. Then just after 7.30 a noise startled him. The lift doors opened and with it the jabber of the cleaners' voices. *I am getting jumpy,* he thought, *the police won't come that quickly.*

The cleaners spread out, the din of Hoovers, chatter and large trolleys moving around the offices. Eventually there was a tentative knock at his door. A careworn face appeared, clad in a track suit, protected by a nylon apron and wearing marigold gloves. She pushed a large trolley holding a huge plastic bucket, laden with cleaning sprays and dusters into the room.

"Can I clean, sir?"

Shingler sighed irritably. Looking around the room, he was, he decided, nearly finished. He'd get in early tomorrow and do a few final bits then. All would be cleared and destroyed tonight, a good job done. He waved her in irritably taking his suit jacket from the back of his chair. The best thing was that all the drugs and the clubs was either in cash or legitimate: good job Simions didn't know what he had been up to in their joint names or there would be hell to pay. He smirked to himself.

"Yes, yes come in; all that rubbish to be cleared please." He motioned to the pile of the overflowing waste bins.

After one last glance, he left the room and headed for the lift. The ping of the doors opening drew his attention upwards, as another cleaner appeared, pushing the ubiquitous trolley and without waiting, went in front of him securing a place in the corner.

"'Fanks" she muttered.

He was treated to a strong waft of cheap, sickly, perfume emanating from the cleaner, dull bunches of hair fell from beneath a large headscarf. She leant over the apparently heavy cart, pushing in front of him so he was unable to make eye contact.

"No, no don't worry," he uttered sarcastically, "after you." She made no response and he then saw that she had wires going to her ears and a *Walkman* belted to her tracksuit waist, the tinny sound of music heard faintly. He shook his head in disgust, ignoring her and pressing his own button for the basement car park. The lift moved and started its journey to the basement, the cleaner oblivious, swaying to the rhythm of the music in her ears, tapping her feet as she fiddled with her trolley contents. The speaker called 'basement' as the lift finished its descent and the doors started to open. The cleaner turned as if to pull her cart and then he caught sight of her face. The scar, hard, brown eyes and the cracked tooth. Shingler's face registered alarm.

"Maria!"

"Simions and Claudio send their regards," she sneered. Her Marigold gloved hand came up with a plastic spray cleaner, spraying directly into his face and open mouth, the scent of bitter, sweet, almonds overpowering. He gasped as the hydrogen cyanide spray entered his blood stream, affecting the metabolism instantly. *Never as quick as in the films* Maria thought, *but quick enough.*

She had pulled down her head scarf covering her nose and mouth just prior to spraying and covering her face with another thick pad held in place by the other gloved hand. The doors sprang open. She gave one last direct spray into the face of the comatose figure already lying prostrate on the ground and stepped out into the fresh air, trailing a broom handle to stop the lift doors closing and moving on, if summoned. Maria pulled off her scarf and as a precaution inhaled deep gulps of air away from the lift.

She waited 3 minutes and returned to the lift, the doors having banged against the broom head twice, in an effort to call the lift back. She dragged Shingler out, propped him against the wall and checked his pulse. Faint if at all. For good measure she callously sprayed again, directly into his mouth, closing the lips around the nozzle. Leaving the dying man she fetched a small Ford Escort van, and opened the rear doors. Returning to Shingler, she noticed that his face had gone an ironically, pink, healthy colour. Keeping masked, she hefted him over to the van and heaved him head and shoulders first into the back. Shutting the doors she drove quietly off, leaving the lift doors wedged open.

Over in Claire's flat, Rupert was enjoying supper with her, blissfully unaware that his plans had spectacularly exceeded his expectations. Although, he had thought to himself, that in his heart of hearts, he knew Simions would take some sort of drastic steps, he was yet to realise just how drastic.

A bottle of wine later into the evening, saw Claire and Rupert lying back in each other's arms on a sofa, in a sleepy and as yet platonic embrace. The initial tension of the evening had evaporated and they had fallen into a conversation of plans for the future once all this was behind them. Not least of which was Rupert's future now he was back in the UK.

"Yes, that is a very good question. What am I going to do? I really don't want to go back to CR, although I doubt they would have me anyway: there is still a cloud hanging over me there. I don't think anyone with the possible exception of Sheen, strangely enough, thinks I am entirely innocent: '*a man shall be known by the company he keeps*', "he finished, quoting Aesop. "And that applies especially to my good 'friend' Mike Ringham."

"Oh don't be too hard on him, Rups. Jemma is really upset about it all and if Mike suddenly finds you're alive, I am sure he will be too."

"Mmm." was all he replied, stubbornly refusing to believe the best in him, having been hurt by Mike's unfaithful response to his circumstances.

Changing the subject she asked, "But do you think that you will become an agent again when it all blows over?"

"Yes, definitely. I mean being a client was fun, and everything but it's not for me. I like the cut and thrust, the thrall of agency; certainly for now anyway."

"And a bloody good agent you will make again," she encouraged slapping his chest and arching her neck to smile up at up at him. It could have been the wine, the enforced intimacy or maybe just circumstances, but he looked into her large green eyes and was again seduced. He kissed her tentatively at first but as she responded he was drawn into an aura of passion, warmth and release from the outside world.

A different sort of embrace was happening at the Carlton Club. Simions was ensconced in a wingback armchair, relaxing after a good meal with two friends and gently puffing on a cigar, a glass of brandy in the other hand. He was still smiling from an amusing story being told by one of his fellows when he looked up at the face of the waiter who had silently appeared at his side.

"A telephone call for you, sir."

Simions nodded an acknowledgement and spoke to his friends, "Please excuse me, my mother has not been well and I have been expecting news from a friend." He smiled benignly and followed the waiter. Picking up the receiver he answered: "Paul Simions here, is everything alright?"

The woman's voice at the other end of the line responded.

"Yes the first part of the *operation* went off well. But the secondary investigation showed nothing. Any ideas?"

"Well that is a relief: I am sure Mother will be fine. The secondary bit will, I think on reflection, be better left alone. Perhaps too many complications, don't you think? Best let everything heal up properly."

"Very good, as you wish. Just to let you know, I shall be away for a rest myself very soon. It has all been a bit busy here. I will let you know when I return."

"Very well. Have a good trip and I will ensure that I pay for all the care, don't worry," he confirmed.

"Good." The call was terminated.

You've either been very lucky or very clever Mr Brett, he thought on his way back to his friends. *But we will let it lie, the worst of the danger is past.* He would probably have to fight a court case, but so be it. It wouldn't be his first or his last.

Claire and Rupert had spent the night together, gently making love; exploring each other's bodies with the practice of experienced lovers. It was a mutually exciting and beneficial experience for both of them. Rupert awoke first, with a smile on his face.

A sleepy, tousled Claire rolled over to face him, her eyes half closed.

"What are you grinning at?" she demanded in mock aggression. In response he pulled her towards him kissing her.

When they broke apart he started to speak, "Last night was special and-" A finger was pressed across his lips.

"No. Not now. Don't ruin it with words. Just let it be and enjoy it. We will talk tonight: I have to get to work, some of us have to," she mocked, grabbing her dressing gown and dashing through to the bathroom. But as encouragement, she shot her head back through the doorway. "But don't run away will you? Promise?" He grinned and nodded.

After she had left, Rupert contacted Webster. The telephone was answered on the third ring.

"Webster."

"Morning. It's Rupert Brett here, how are you?"

"Rupert where the hell have you been? I've been trying to get hold of you."

"Why what's happened?"

"Shingler has disappeared; didn't return to his home last night and no sign of him. Last seen in his office by the cleaners as he was leaving. Not a sighting since. We had a man on his home and he never went there, he's just disappeared into thin air. And talking of which, where were you last night? We had your flat watched as well and I might add a good job we did: you had a visitor."

"Who?"

"Maria Rico." Webster let the name hang in the air and Rupert went cold. "Tidying up loose ends. What the hell did you say to Paul Simions? You knew this would happen didn't you? If I didn't know better I would say you orchestrated it: you set them against each other and damn nearly got yourself killed in the process. We need to talk," he continued brusquely. "You had better come in and see me." Rupert agreed to see him later and the call ended.

Rupert jabbed his fist in the air. *Yes*, he thought. *So Shingler got his. Liz you are avenged and all without any recourse to me, whatever Webster may say. Now we just wait to see how it pans out with Simions. I know he won't get a murder charge or anything like it, but just to see his smug face as he is sentenced will be enough*, Rupert considered. And as Claire said, all done using cunning and intelligence, not a blow struck in anger.

However, two hours later in Webster's office he got a severe grilling. "I did not give you information to go off on a one man revenge spree you know? Apart from the fact that you could have got yourself killed, think about your friend Claire Sewell. It would not of been beyond the ken of man to put two and two together to realise that she may have been involved. Did you consider that? You knew that whatever you said would set Shingler and Simions off didn't you?"

Rupert looked diffidently at Webster, his face a picture of composed innocence.

"I had no idea," he lied. "I told you, I bumped into him in the street, he invited me in to his office, we chatted and the whole story came out about the fraud aspect," he answered, shrugging disingenuously.

"Do you know what, I don't believe you. But I can't prove anything and for what it's worth I am glad Shingler got what was coming to him but what I am intensely irritated about is that we still haven't got anything on Maria Rico. For which, DI Fleming will also be mightily pissed off. Well, I suppose it's a result and we will nail Simions on fraud amongst other things, but we will never get a conspiracy to commit murder charge to stick."

Rupert risked a jibe.

"Do you really think you would have anyway? Do you really believe they would have ratted on each other and you would have been able to persuade a jury to convict one or both? I wonder." He looked across at Webster, his true Machiavellian self-revealed.

The piercing eyes looked back over the top of his spectacles.

"Well, we'll never know will we? But just take care 'til the trial is over, ok? Although if I know Maria Rico she will have left the country, with 'proof' that she was never here when the crimes were committed."

"Noted," he responded noncommittally. "I will take extra precautions and not stay at my flat for a while."

"Good, and keep in touch regularly." Were Webster's final words as Rupert made for the door. He nodded in assent and left. *Yes, I stupidly hadn't thought about Claire,* he realised. *We need to talk and I can't stay there indefinitely. I think back to my parents for a while, recuperate properly.*

That evening Claire and Rupert went to a little Italian restaurant around the corner from her flat. Neutral ground was better, she felt, for both of them. Rupert was more nervous about the evening than any of the other situations he had found himself in over the last months. They settled down after ordering and Rupert tentatively took Claire's hand across the table. She sensed his diffidence, which was a revelation considering how confident he was normally.

"Claire I have so much to say and yet don't know how to begin. I have so many thoughts and feelings all whirring around in my head..." he gave up, shrugging in frustration.

"Then," she responded very gently "you should just let them all come burbling out and we will understand each other better. Hell, it's not as if this is a first date and we don't know each other."

He smiled encouraged by her attitude. "Ok, this going to

sound really weird but I have really strong feelings for you, always have, ever since university and even," here he hesitated, "when I was seeing Liz. Yet, I thought I loved her. Is that strange?"

She smiled; it was a beatific sight to Rupert and he knew then that everything was going to be alright. "No it is not weird and I am certainly not going to analyse it. I think we both have debts owed to our past, otherwise we would not be here. You to Liz and me to Angus."

"Really?" he interrupted surprised.

"Hah," she mocked herself. "Yes, it was in a way my last fling with a wild side, when I wasn't sure which direction I wanted to go in: carry on down an outrageous path of meaningless affairs, work and little else; or consider being a little more stable and happier for it. I suppose what I am really saying is: it made me grow up!" she laughed humourlessly.

Rupert felt the pressure on his hand increase as she made this statement and he knew that it had taken a lot of courage.

"No, you're right. I had never really thought of it in those terms before. Thank you," he finished quietly. From there the evening went well, the barriers down, there followed a mutual exploration of feelings and a genuine affection for each other.

As they walked home in each other's arms, the tricky subject of accommodation reared its head.

"You're really welcome to stay here with me," she offered. "I mean I am not trying to be claustrophobic or pushy or anything like that but if it is dangerous to return permanently to your flat, in the short term, well..."

"Thank you. But I think that it would be a mistake for both us. I want this to last and it would be too much too soon, don't you think? I think I will go back to my parent's for as long as I can stand it: I mean I love them dearly but for weeks on end?" He winced and they both laughed.

"I know and you're probably right. Good choice. But you'd

better let me come and see you at weekends and do not take a lover!" she chided.

"Mmmh, but that does mean that we can spend tonight together first," he laughed.

Epilogue

It was six months later when the trial of Paul Simions was finished. It was the main excitement at the Old Bailey for months, with much speculation and a confirmation in the eyes of the public and the City that '*estate agents*' were all a bunch of crooks.

Rupert was called as a witness and so were various secretaries, personnel heads and surveyors; including Pauline Wood whose evidence proved crucial.

David Shingler's name came up on many occasions and of course, he was never present at the trial. A badly, decomposed body was found floating in the river Thames some weeks after his disappearance: headless and without finger tips, but the general consensus, without conclusive proof, was that it was Shingler. He was made to be the 'fall guy' and in the absence of a defence of his name, this clearly helped Simions' case.

However Simions did not have it all his own way. The jury for once, were not taken in by his suave ways and he was duly convicted on three counts of fraud amongst other crimes. The CPP would not consider anything to do with Liz Carmichael's murder: the evidence, they said, was too circumstantial. Paul Simions was sentenced to 15 years in jail. Rupert attended the sentencing and enjoyed every minute but was annoyed that Simions did not get a longer term in jail.

Two weeks after the trial ended, Mike and Jemma were getting married. The wedding was a rather grand affair, to be held at St. Georges in Hanover Square. The reception was at the Grosvenor House Hotel in Park Lane and it was all that it should have been. The right people were there in attendance in all their finery and a beautiful horse drawn carriage transported them to the reception.

Upon learning the news of Rupert's Lazarus-like return from the dead, Mike had actually gone around to his flat to apologise for his behaviour and was sad that he had doubted him at all. Rupert had accepted the apology with a good grace but he was also aware that there would, for the foreseeable future, be a shadow over their friendship.

Claire and Rupert were now very much an 'item', having been seeing each other regularly for the last few months since the fateful night at her flat. It was in the middle of a slow dance at the reception, towards the end of what had been a splendid evening, that he asked her if she would move in with him. She replied with a tighter hug and her usually parenthetical refrain: "Oh Rup's, of course. I don't know why you took so long to ask me."

ABOUT THE BOOKS

THE RUPERT BRETT 'DEAL' SERIES

A DEAL TOO FAR

Autumn, 1990. The Gulf conflict is beginning andoil fields lie in ruin creating a global crisis as American conglomerates scour the world for crude.

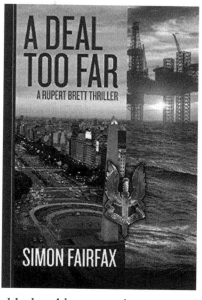

The IRA are suffering from moles within, their funding decimated as terrorism bites America and grips nations worldwide.

The British government is on red alert: rumours of a second invasion of the Falklands swirl. The UN has refused Argentina's claim to oil rights on the islands and now the fate of the land and its black gold are at stake.

In London, property surveyor Rupert Brett and TA soldier is facing his own global crisis. The international property market is imploding as fund managers tussle with a world in deep recession and Brett finds past adventures come back to haunt him when the authorities require his specific skills once more. Tasked to open a new international office in Buenos Aries by the British government, and partnered with a mysterious SAS operative named Chris Adams, Brett is thrust into a new deadly game. Time is running out an invasion is imminent.

A DEAL WITH THE DEVIL

Rupert Brett is back and it is 1995, with the property markets raging and the Sub-Prime madness just beginning.

The Irish Sea, a shipment of drugs is intercepted, the IRA lose the cocaine and their most feared enforcer, Tir Brennan, is captured.

Deauville, a wealthy French aristocrat has a terrible accident with far reaching consequences.

Bogota, the head of the old drug cartels is dead and Ballesteros is now running new routes to the US and beyond.

The events are all linked and somehow drugs are being smuggled with impunity across the globe. With a source originating in Palm Beach, US, Rupert Brett is again asked to go undercover, with SAS Sergeant Chris Adams as protection. They must find out how the drugs are being smuggled into the corporate world of property, polo and high finance. The answers run deeper than either could imagine and a dangerous former nemesis returns, throwing their lives into turmoil.

About the Author

Simon Fairfax has been a lifelong reader of thrillers, particularly the novels of Ian Fleming and Dick Francis. *No Deal's Done 'til It's Done,* his first book, was inspired by his own thirty-five-year career as a chartered surveyor, including living and working in Italy for three years.

Fairfax attended Southampton Solent University. His firsthand knowledge of multimillion-pound deals greatly influenced this story of the heroes and villains in the real estate world.

www.simonfairfax.com

A PHOT...

B

JAVA, SUMATRA
AND BALI

TONY TILFORD

Photographs by
ALAIN COMPOST

NEW
HOLLAND

Reprinted in 2003

First published in 2000 by
New Holland Publishers (UK) Ltd
London • Cape Town • Sydney • Auckland

www.newhollandpublishers.com

Garfield House, 86-88 Edgware Road, London W2 2EA, United Kingdom
80 McKenzie Street, Cape Town 8001, South Africa
14 Aquatic Drive, Frenchs Forest, NSW 2086, Australia
218 Lake Road, Northcote, Auckland, New Zealand

ISBN 1 85368 730 8

Commissioning Editor: Jo Hemmings
Editor: David Christie
Assistant Editor: Michaella Standen
Design: D & N Publishing, Hungerford, Berkshire
Cartography: Carte Blanche, Paignton, Devon

Reproduction by Modern Age Repro House Limited, Hong Kong
Printed and bound in Malaysia by Times Offset (M) Sdn Bhd

10 9 8 7 6 5 4 3 2

Front cover photograph: Banded Pitta (Alain Compost)
Title page photograph: Bali Myna (Alain Compost)

Acknowledgements

Photographs in this book were taken by Alain Compost except where other
photographers' names are indicated next to the photographs.

The author gives his special thanks to the many people who have provided
valuable assistance in the preparation of this book, in particular Dr John
Cooke, not only for checking the manuscript but for inspiration and his
memorable company in Indonesia. Without John and his wife Joyce, and not
forgetting Robert Tilford, many of the pictures would not have been possible. Likewise, Edi Swoboda, Mark Norrie, Maryke Andriani and staff of the
Bali Bird Park (Taman Burung), Singapadu, Bali, were of invaluable help in
providing facilities for photography. Hidden Worlds of Berkeley, California,
made possible access to rich birding areas far from the tourist routes. Bayu
Wirayudha, Leksmono Santoso and their colleagues from Best Tours of
Renon in Bali have been exceptionally helpful with information and advice,
not only on the birds of the region but also in travel matters. Special thanks
are due also to Mr Nyoman Bagiarta, Nyoman Witama and Yeni for the
superb hospitality and facilities provided at Puri Lumbung Cottages,
Munduk, Bali, and to the many villagers there who helped in locating birds.

Contents

Introduction

The islands of Java, Sumatra and Bali total some 613,000 square kilometres, almost 2½ times the area of the United Kingdom, and possess approximately 635 bird species. With such a rich avifauna, it is scarcely surprising that birds are widely kept there for their beauty and song. Visitors, who now reach the region in ever-increasing numbers, cannot fail to notice that almost every house has caged birds hanging from the eaves, often in large numbers. Close inspection reveals that many of the birds kept in captivity here are often the same as those to be found in pet stores around the world. This is a reflection of the fact that many birds traded on the international pet market are local species from this region.

Trapped and exported in increasingly greater numbers, natural populations of many species are severely reduced, and some have been brought to the edge of extinction in spite of protective legislation. So far, only the Javanese Lapwing has become extinct in recent times, but several other species, most notably the Bali Myna, are hovering on the brink. With fewer than 30 individuals of this striking species left in the wild in western Bali, in 1999, it is no coincidence that some 3,000 are to be found in aviaries throughout the world. The demise of the Bali Myna is well documented and is largely the result of illicit trapping, exacerbated by human disturbance and loss of habitat. The same dismal picture is repeated for many other species, including the Java Sparrow, Brahminy Kite and Black-winged Starling, all of which were, not many years ago, a common sight.

It is fortunate that the Indonesian authorities, in particular the Directorate General of Forest Protection & Nature Conservation of the Indonesian Ministry of Forestry (PHPA) in conjunction with BirdLife International's Indonesia Programme, have recognised the urgent need for protection, and vast areas have now been designated as National Parks and reserves with special protection for wildlife. Visitors should bear in mind that permits are officially required to enter many of these reserves and prior arrangements may be necessary. Even outside the reserve areas the most threatened animals are protected, at least in theory. For further information, the World Wide Web addresses given later in this book are a good place to start.

Within the space limitations of this small book it would be impossible to cover all the 635 or so bird species that have been recorded in Java, Sumatra and Bali. The selection has therefore been based upon the birds that are reasonably common throughout the region. A few less common but interesting and more spectacular species have been added, so as to reveal the enormous biological diversity to be found there and to provide an understanding of its characteristic nature.

The 236 species treated include a reasonable representation from most of the families likely to be encountered in the region. The reader will undoubtedly come across others, and these are certain to be covered in the more specialized (but unfortunately more cumbersome) books listed for further reading.

Birdwatching

For most of us, birdwatching is really putting a name to a bird, but there is so much more to be gained from more detailed study. Behaviour, life cycles and interaction with the environment are fascinating subjects which not only can give us enormous enjoyment, but can add much to our knowledge of the world around us.

Initially, however, identification must be the first priority. We should consider all the clues available and, ideally, identify not just the species but also its sex, age and race where possible. There are always many clues to go on, and by combining them all we narrow down the possibilities until our problem is solved. We all accept the value of visual clues, but tend to neglect the importance of sound until we become more experienced. For the seasoned birdwatcher, his or her tape recorder is just as important a part of the kit as are note-book, binoculars, telescope and field guide. That important call can often be identified later in the day. It is always a help to have a checklist of the species found in the area, and a good place to find this is on the World Wide Web. Try some of the addresses listed under 'Useful Web-sites' later in the book; it is amazing what information is available.

Whatever equipment you take, it should be well protected from the ravages of the weather. Rain and high humidity provide the worst conditions for cameras, binoculars and electronics. Any equipment should be kept dry and well aired and, if at all possible, stored with a bag of silica-gel desiccant to protect against fungal attack. It is always astonishing how much damage fungus can cause if inadequate precautions have been taken.

Ideally, lightweight waterproof binoculars such as the Nikon close-focusing WP/RA II range are recommended, particularly if you are going to venture into wet and humid areas, but for general use the not too expensive kind, such as the Nikon Travelite IV range, is perfectly adequate for most observation. For the more serious birder there are many other 'professional-style' binoculars to choose from, as well as spotting scopes for more distant observation. For sound recording, the Sony Mini-Disk Recording Walkman with a directional microphone gives superb reproduction, but for identification purposes many of the smaller cassette recorders are equally useful. As for cameras, they are not recommended for regular birdwatching trips, not only because of the possibly detrimental effect of the weather on equipment, but also because it is almost impossible to concentrate on both activities at once, particularly in a group.

It is fortunate that many of the good birdwatching areas are accessible by car, but there is always public transport and, except in Bali, at the end of the journey the ubiquitous motorbike-taxis known as 'ojeks'. In the field, the energy-sapping heat and humidity are perhaps the biggest drawbacks. It should be unnecessary to advise here on hygiene and the need to carry sufficient bottled water. Keeping fit and healthy is extremely important, particularly in areas where medical facilities may be poor or non-existent. Do not forget to take essential medication with you, and always be prepared for stomach upsets. Remember, 'Bali Belly' is not confined just to Bali. Insects can also be a problem at certain times, and insecticide sprays and creams could save you from some nasty bites. Suitable clothing is also essential, not only as protection against the elements but also as a disguise. Lightweight, dull-coloured clothes are really necessary. Visitors are recommended to carry a light poncho with a hood, and in lowland forests long trousers are very desirable for preventing leeches and stinging plants from making contact with your skin. Sturdy footwear is a must, although many people prefer heavy-duty sandals of the 'Teva' type, particularly in wet conditions. Lightweight canvas boots are better than leather ones, which quickly become mouldy.

How to use this book

In line with other books in this series, this one uses symbols as a guide to families and family groups to which the birds belong; a key to these symbols is shown opposite. Photographs depict the bird in its commonly seen form where possible, and variations are well described in the text. The order of the 236 species covered generally follows the Peters sequence adopted by Paul Andrews in *The Birds of Indonesia: A checklist*. Vernacular and scientific names are those used by T. Inskipp, N. Lindsey and W. Duckworth in *An Annotated Checklist of the Birds of the Oriental Region*. Other checklists exist, and the process of revision based on more recent scientific knowledge will continue. It must therefore be expected that not only will common names vary, but so too will the scientific. Ultimately, the scientific names prove more reliable.

Each species description includes a common name followed by its scientific name, and then the species' overall length from the tip of the bill to the end of the tail. The remaining description follows no particular order but provides most of the clues necessary for a fairly reliable identification. Only for a few species has any attempt been made to describe calls and song, as it is felt that written descriptions lack meaning without the experience of hearing the actual sound. Nevertheless, the value of sound must not be under-estimated. In many cases, it can be the only determining factor in successful identification. Much of the description is necessarily brief and written in a semi-technical language adopted by most bird books, but for easy understanding many of the technical terms are explained in the following glossary, and the illustration showing bird topography (*below*).

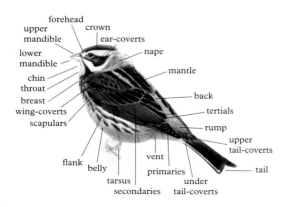

Key to corner tabs

 Petrels to pelicans

 Herons, egrets & storks

 Raptors

 Ducks & geese

 Gamebirds

 Rails & allies

 Waders

 Terns

 Pigeons & doves

 Parrots

 Cuckoos & allies

 Owls & nightjars

 Swifts

 Kingfishers & bee-eaters

 Dollarbird & hornbills

 Barbets & woodpeckers

 Broadbills & pittas

 Larks, swallows, wagtails & pipits

 Minivets

 Bulbuls

 Leafbirds

 Shrikes & shortwings

 Robins & chats

 Thrushes & babblers

 Mesias, prinias & warblers

 Flycatchers, fantails & whistlers

 Tits & nuthatches

 Flowerpeckers, sunbirds & spiderhunters

 White-eyes

 Avadavats & munias

 Sparrows & weavers

 Starlings, mynas & orioles

 Drongos & woodswallows

 Jays & crows

Glossary

axillaries Feathers of the `armpit'

canopy Unbroken layer of branches and foliage at tops of trees in forest

cere Bare fleshy or waxy protuberance at base of upper mandible, including nostrils

chin-stripe A marking around area of chin

coverts The small feathers at base of quill feathers forming main flight surfaces of wing and tail

dimorphic Occurring in two genetically determined plumage forms

echolocation Navigation by ultra-sound radar

endemic Indigenous species restricted to a particular area

eyebrow Contrasting line above eye (supercilium)

eye-stripe Contrasting line through eye

flank Side of the body

frontal shield Skin or hard unfeathered area on forehead which extends to bill

fulvous Pale brownish-yellow

Greater Sundas Borneo, Sumatra, Java and Bali, including off-shore islands

gregarious Frequently occurring in groups

gular pouch Bare, fleshy patch of skin around neck of cor-morants and hornbills

gunung Indonesian name for mountain

hackles Long, narrow and often pendulous feathers around neck

lores Area of feathers between bill and eye

mandible Upper or lower half of bill

malar In area between base of bill and side of throat

mesial Dividing down the middle

migrant Non-resident traveller

montane Relating to mountain habitats usually above 900m

necklace A line of markings around front of neck

Nusa Tenggara Area covered by the islands of Lombok, Sum-bawa, Sumba, Flores and Timor

orbital ring Unfeathered bare ring around eye

primaries The main outer flight feathers (show as longest part of folded wing)

primary forest Original natural forest

race Another name for subspecies

rackets Paddle-shaped ends to tail feathers

resident Remaining in a local area throughout year

roost Resting or sleeping place

secondaries The inner flight feathers on rear half of wing

secondary forest New forest replacing primary forest

spatulate Having thickened rounded ends

speculum Contrasting iridescent patch on a duck's wing

subspecies A population which is morphologically different from other populations of same species

Sundas Region covered by the Greater and Lesser Sundas and Sulawesi

supercilium A stripe above eye (eyebrow)

terminal At the end or tip

underparts Undersurface of body from throat to undertail-coverts

undertail-coverts Small feathers below tail covering bases of tail feathers

underwing-coverts Small underwing feathers covering bases of primaries and secondaries
upperparts Upper surface of body
vent Area around anus, including undertail-coverts
wattles Brightly coloured bare skin hanging from head or neck
wingbar A visible line of colour at tips of wing-coverts
wing-coverts Small feathers on wing covering bases of primaries and secondaries

The region

Java, Sumatra and Bali lie along the edge of the South-east Asian tectonic plate, where it rides over the Australian-Indian plate generating intense geological activity. A line of volcanoes, some still active, others dormant, forms a spine along the island chain. In Sumatra these create the Barisan mountain range, stretching the entire length of the island, and falling precipitously into the depths of the Indian Ocean in the west; in the east it drops more gently, giving rise to large swampy areas before reaching the Sunda Sea. In Java, the mountains arise in isolation from alluvial plains and, as in east Sumatra, slope gently northwards to the Sunda Sea.

At one time Bali was connected by landbridge to Java, but today it is separated by some 3km of turbulent waters, renowned for their fierce currents. Not surprisingly, the fauna and flora of Bali show close similarities to those of eastern Java. Sumatra, however, shows closer affinities with Borneo than with Java.

The fragmentation of the landmasses combined with geological and climatic activity has resulted in the formation of many habitats, which in turn support a rich diversity of wildlife. This includes many endemic species: those confined to a single region or smaller area and found nowhere else.

Java and Bali are among the most densely populated regions on earth, and the destruction of their remaining wildlife habitats is a matter of serious concern. Only on remote mountain slopes can one find significant areas of natural forest. A few patches of lowland forest survive in National Parks and Nature Reserves. Sumatra, with only a tenth of the population density, is a little better off, but the growth of the agriculture, plantation and forestry sectors are responsible for increasing forest destruction there.

The avian fauna

We might expect that these landmasses, which were at various times joined to mainland Asia, would have fairly similar flora and fauna. As the various islands were not all separated simultaneously, however, and since subsequent local climatic conditions have varied, the composition of the avian fauna differs significantly from one island to another. Perhaps the most dramatic changes have been caused more recently, by man and his destruction of the lowland forests. There are ample records dating back as far as 1657, and it is quite clear from the reports of the early 18th-century explorers who founded Indonesian ornithology that birds were far more plentiful then.

When and where to find birds

As the region lies close to the equator, the climate is hot and humid. The monsoon weather patterns of the region are characterized by wet and dry seasons, which differ little in temperature. Even so, the birds show distinct breeding cycles. During the wet season, from October to March, large numbers of wintering migrants fly down from the north, with a smaller number of Australian species appearing during the dry season.

Many waterbirds arrive at the end of the wet season, nesting in the safety of isolated trees in a flooded landscape. This is also the peak of the insect breeding season, when abundant food is available for insectivorous species to rear their young. Frugivorous species delay breeding a little longer, until the trees and bushes are bearing ripe fruit.

Good birding areas, with a rich diversity of habitats, abound throughout the region. Clearly, it is not possible to list them all in a book of this size, but, to guide the birdwatcher to some of the more productive areas, the major reserves and National Parks are described below. These are shown on the accompanying map.

Important birdwatching sites

Sumatra:

Gunung Leuser National Park
This is a huge area of rainforest and mountains with a small coastal and lowland extension. It is an ideal place to explore the birds of northern Sumatra, such as Wreathed, Black, Oriental (or Asian) Pied, Helmeted and Rhinoceros Hornbills, Great Argus, Crestless Fireback and Crested Partridge, Brown, Yellow-crowned and Gold-whiskered Barbets, White-rumped Shama and Black-and-yellow, Green and Dusky Broadbills, Crested Jay and Red-bearded Bee-eater.

Kerinci-Seblat National Park
The park includes the dominating peak of Mt Kerinci and the Kerinci valley wetlands. The best place to see Sumatran montane birds, as well as several of the endemics such as Schneider's Pitta, Bronze-tailed Peacock Pheasant and Sumatran Cochoa. Also recorded there are Salvadori's Pheasant, Silver-eared Mesia, Chestnut-capped Laughingthrush, White-throated Fantail, Sunda Bush Warbler and Golden Babbler.

Way Kambas National Park
Situated in the south-east of Sumatra, Way Kambas includes remnants of lowland rainforest and coastal and swamp forest. A large number of species have been recorded there, including White-winged Duck, Storm's Stork, Stork-billed Kingfisher, Lesser Adjutant, Crested Fireback, Crested Partridge, Great Argus, Hill Myna, Black-bellied Malkoha and Scarlet-rumped Trogon, Gould's, Sunda and Large Frogmouths, Black-thighed Falconet and Orange-breasted and Cinnamon-headed Green Pigeons.

Berbak National Park
This reserve is on the east coast and includes coastal forest and

peat swamp, as well as mangroves. It is a good area for Büttikofer's Babbler, Wallace's Hawk Eagle and Milky and Storm's Storks.

Bukit Barisan Selatan National Park

Situated at the southern tip of Sumatra, at the end of the Barisan mountain range, the park reaches from the sea to the top of Gunung Pulung and includes all forest types and some very wild areas. It is relatively unrecorded but could bring some interesting surprises. Among the rarer birds in the area are Sumatran Treepie, Helmeted Hornbill, Red-billed Partridge, Lesser Adjutant and Milky and Storm's Storks.

Java:

Ujung Kulon National Park

At the extreme west tip of Java, Ujung Kulon boasts many rare species in a great variety of habitats, from lowland rainforest and evergreen forest to coastal scrub, mangroves and open grazing areas. As many as 24 endemic or threatened species are to be found there, including Javan Coucal, White-breasted Babbler, Javan Sunbird, Javan Hawk Eagle, Blue-throated Bee-eater and Green Peafowl.

Gede/Pangrango National Park

This West Javan National Park consists mainly of luxuriant evergreen submontane forests, but with mossy elfin forest and alpine meadows at the peak of Gunung Pangrango. It is a wonderful place to see many of the Javan endemics, such as Javan Tesia, Javan Cochoa, Javan Hawk Eagle, Chestnut-bellied Partridge, Javan Scops Owl, Javan White-eye, Dusky (Horsfield's) Woodcock, Pygmy Tit, Mountain Serin, Volcano Swiftlet and the Blue-tailed Trogon.

Meru Betiri National Park

Meru Betiri covers large areas of moist primary and secondary forests, mangroves and a rather rugged coastline with some beautiful beaches. It is one of the less explored areas where new discoveries are likely to be made. Among the rarer birds recorded are Wreathed Hornbill, Banded Woodpecker, Violet Cuckoo, Pintailed Parrotfinch, Black-crested Bulbul, Grey-cheeked Green Pigeon, Black-naped Fruit Dove, Javan Owlet, Waterfall (or Giant) Swiftlet, Black-banded Barbet and Crescent-chested Babbler.

Baluran National Park

Situated at the north-east end of Java, Baluran National Park is spread around the dormant volcano of Gunung Baluran. It is one of the easier places for birdwatching, being more open and easily accessible. A good place to see Green Peafowl and Green and Red Junglefowl. White-bellied Woodpecker, Oriental Pied Hornbill, Spotted Wood Owl, Banded Pitta, Lesser Adjutant and Grey-cheeked Tit Babbler are all reported from the area.

Kebun Raya (Botanic Gardens), Bogor

Being easily accessible, Bogor's Botanic Gardens become crowded with local visitors at the weekend. A weekday visit, however, can be very fruitful in the comparative tranquillity. The enchanting

settings of Kebun Raya, covering a 1-kilometre square, have been established for around two centuries and provide some very ready opportunities to see many town and woodland birds. There is a roost of Black-crowned Night Herons, and it is difficult to miss the Black-naped Orioles, Sooty-headed Bulbuls and Oriental Magpie Robins. Other species likely to be seen are Black-naped Fruit Dove, Collared Kingfisher, Blue-eared Kingfisher, Grey-cheeked Green Pigeon, Horsfield's Babbler, Olive-backed Sunbird, Purple-throated Sunbirds, Hill Blue Flycatcher and the Yellow-throated Hanging Parrot.

Pangandaran Nature Recreation Park

Just west of Cilacap on the south coast of Central Java is the peninsula of Pangandaran, taken up by the Nature Recreation Park. Consisting mainly of dry forest, it is a good area for Green Junglefowl and Banded Pitta. Other species present are Oriental Pied Hornbill, White-rumped Shama, Scaly-crowned Babbler and Oriental Dwarf Kingfisher. To the east lie the mangroves of Segara Anakan, where many waterbirds can be seen. Among the large population of herons, egrets and terns, Lesser Adjutant and Milky Stork may be seen. Javan Coucal and Stork-billed Kingfisher have also been recorded there.

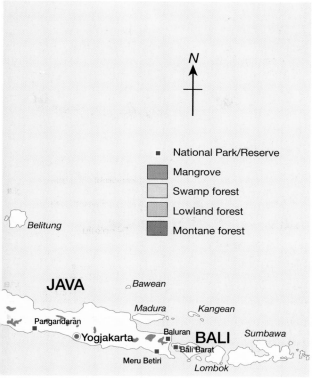

Bali:

Bali Barat National Park

Situated at the western tip of Bali, Bali Barat is a mixture of dry and moist forests with coastal scrub, savanna and mangroves. It is the only place to find the wild, endemic Bali Myna. Many other interesting species reside there, including Banded Pitta, Green Junglefowl, Pink-headed Fruit Dove, Black-backed Fruit Dove, Shiny Whistling Thrush, Sunda Bush Warbler and Lemon-bellied White-eye.

Visiting National Parks

Permits to enter national parks can be obtained at the parks' entrances. In most Indonesian national parks, facilities such as trail networks, the provision of experienced bird guides, and accommodation close to the best birding sites, are limited.

Wilson's Storm-petrel *Oceanites oceanicus* 17cm

Roger Tidman, Windrush Photos

This diminutive species characteristically flies low over the sea, making slow progress as it rises and dips, moving from side to side searching the water surface much like a butterfly. In flight, its general plumage appears blackish-brown with a paler wingbar and a very conspicuous white rump and uppertail-coverts. The tail also appears short and square, with the feet protruding behind. It is the commonest small oceanic bird likely to be encountered on the coast. It arrives in the region after breeding mainly on small islands in the southern oceans, and spends its time at sea feeding on floating organic matter and small crustaceans.

Little Grebe *Tachybaptus ruficollis* 25cm

Ray Tipper

This tiny waterbird appears as a very small dark duck swimming high in the water, repeatedly diving and remaining submerged for prolonged periods. During the breeding season, its upperparts are brown, becoming darker on the crown and nape, while the throat and the sides of the neck are chestnut. It has an obvious yellow patch at the base of the black bill. In non-breeding plumage it is greyer, the neck becoming whitish. It is a rare resident in Java, Bali and northern Sumatra, where it frequents lakes and flooded rice paddies, although its range extends from New Guinea to Europe.

White-tailed Tropicbird *Phaethon lepturus* 39cm

Tilford/Cooke, TC Nature

Adult birds are usually white, some with a yellowish tinge, and have long white tail-streamers. They are marked with black on the wing-tips and have a black bar on the upperwing. Juveniles have no tail-streamers, and their upperparts are barred black. Although resident in some parts of the region, visitors also arrive from other areas. Individuals occurring around Sumatra, and recognizable by their golden plumage, belong to the subspecies (*P. l. fulvus*) which comes from Christmas Island in the Indian Ocean. Breeding colonies have been located on Nusa Penida, Bali, and along Java's south coast.

Little Black Cormorant *Phalacrocorax sulcirostris* 60cm

A bird with fairly uniform black plumage with a purplish-green iridescence, except for mottling on the wing-coverts. In the breeding season, it acquires a small patch of white feathers behind the eye. It has a small greyish gular pouch and bare skin around the eye. The bill is grey-blue and the feet black. Mainly a bird of lakes, estuaries and fishponds, it is occasionally seen along the coast. This species' range extends from Australia up through New Guinea and westwards to the Greater Sundas, but few birds reach Sumatra. It is not a common bird, although the number present at Pulau Rambut on the north-west Javan coast might lead one to believe that it is.

David Tipling, Windrush Photos

15

Little Cormorant *Phalacrocorax niger* 56cm

Chew Yen Fook

This is the smallest of the cormorants found in the region. The plumage is generally greenish-black, with a few tiny white feathers on the neck and head. The bill is brown, with a black tip and purple near the base. After breeding, the plumage darkens and looses the white flecks, except for the chin and throat, which become white. It frequents mangroves, marshland, lakes and estuaries, often in small flocks swimming low in the water and diving for fish. A fairly common resident of the coasts and lowland waterways of Java. Those seen in Sumatra are likely to be visitors from Java.

Darter *Anhinga melanogaster* 84cm

Chew Yen Fook

Very similar to the cormorants apart from the long slender neck, small head and yellow-brown dagger-like bill. It is a mainly black bird, with white-streaked plumed coverts on the wing and back. It swims very low in the water with only its head and neck showing, so it often becomes waterlogged and has great difficulty in taking to the air. It spends a lot of time standing alone on low, exposed perches, often with its wings outstretched to dry, but it roosts communally. Darters prefer to inhabit large, clean freshwater lakes and forested rivers where they dive underwater in search of fish.

16

Australian Pelican *Pelecanus conspicillatus* 150cm

Very similar in size to the Great White Pelican *Pelecanus onocrotalus,* the Australian Pelican can be identified by its black tail and upper-wing coverts, pinkish gular pouch stretching the full length of the very large pinkish-purple bill, and lack of bare facial skin patch. The primaries and secondaries are black; legs and feet are grey-blue. It flies with a laboured wing-beat and catches fish by plunging into the water. This pelican is occasionally found singly but more usually in small flocks on estuarine sand bars. It breeds in Australia, migrating north to New Guinea and west as far as Bali and E. Java.

Grey Heron *Ardea cinerea* 100cm

A predominantly grey bird with paler underparts, the Grey Heron has a prominent black streak on the head and black flight feathers. It also has a line of black streaks down the front of its neck. Legs and bill are yellowish. It appears smaller than the Purple Heron and lacks that species' reddish-brown coloration. Found mostly in the lowlands, these herons frequent wet areas such as paddyfields, lakes, mangroves and swamps, hunting fish, frogs and crabs. This is a colonial nester, often seen in tall trees in the proximity of mangroves. Widely distributed, it is resident throughout the Old World temperate regions as well as the tropics.

Great-billed Heron *Ardea sumatrana* 115cm

The largest heron found in the region, the Great-billed Heron has a dark greyish-brown plumage and shows a small crest. Its feet are grey and the bill is grey-black. It has a repetitive 'roaring' call, as well as low-pitched croaking. It prefers a habitat of mangroves and mudflats, and also frequents the beaches and coastal reefs of small islands. It is generally solitary in its habits, and may be seen stalking along the reefs and creek edges in search of small fish. Although not common, this species is a resident throughout the Greater Sundas.

Purple Heron *Ardea purpurea* 95cm

Chew Yen Fook

Similar in height to the Grey Heron, this more elegant, slimmer bird has a less hunched stance. It is easily distinguished from other herons of its size by its dark underparts and its black-streaked russet-coloured neck and upper breast. The back and wings are greyish-purple with a scattering of long russet plumes. It has a brown bill and reddish-brown legs. Normally a more solitary species, it congregates in large colonies to nest. It is found in typical heron habitat of paddyfields, swamps, mangroves and lakes, often inland, where it feeds on small fish and amphibians.

Great Egret *Casmerodius albus* 90cm

The largest of the white egrets, with a more substantial bill and a peculiar kink midway along the neck. During the breeding period, the bill is black, the bare facial skin becomes greyish-blue and the bare thighs turn red. At other times of the year, the facial skin is dull yellow, the bill is yellowish, often tipped black, and the feet and legs are all black. It prefers mudflats, mangroves and coastal marshland, as well as rice paddies, where it is found either alone or in small groups, generally feeding on small fish and frogs. Although this species occurs throughout the Greater Sundas, nowhere is it common.

Intermediate Egret *Mesophoyx (Egretta) intermedia* 68cm

Chew Yen Fook

Also known as the Plumed Egret because of the adornments of its breeding plumage (although other egrets also develop such plumes to a greater or lesser degree when breeding). This all-white bird is in fact intermediate in size between the Great (*Casmerodius albus*) and Little Egrets (*Egretta garzetta*), but it is less common than either. It may be distinguished from the smaller Little Egret by its yellow bill, and from the larger Great Egret by its smooth, unkinked neck. In common with its relatives, it can be found in paddyfields, mangroves and swamps and on coastal mudflats.

19

Little Egret *Egretta garzetta* 60cm

Larger and slimmer than the Cattle Egret, this species has greyish-black legs and a black bill. Normally all brilliant white in plumage, in the breeding season it develops long pendulous plumes on the breast, back and nape. Its small, dirty yellow bare facial patch becomes pink during the breeding season. The Asiatic migrant race is distinguished by having yellow toes. This common heron is found mainly in mixed flocks in coastal lowlands, where it occurs in paddyfields, on riverine mudflats and sandbars and alongside small streams. It mixes freely with other herons and egrets in their breeding colonies and at nighttime roosts.

Pacific Reef Egret *Egretta sacra* 58cm

The Pacific Reef Egret possesses two colour morphs. The commoner form has a uniform grey plumage, a short crest and a very pale chin. Less common is the white form, which resembles the Cattle Egret but is considerably larger, and has a sleeker head and neck. It has relatively short greenish legs and a pale yellow bill. This species is generally confined to the coastline, where it can be seen resting on rocks and cliffs when not hunting at the water's edge. It is found more commonly on the sandy beaches and reefs of offshore islands.

Cattle Egret *Bubulcus ibis* 50cm

Commonly found in paddyfields and fresh-water swampy areas, this species is also attracted to grazing cattle, feeding on the insects they disturb. A smallish bird, it is normally white, sometimes with a faint tinge of orange on the forehead. In breeding plumage, however, it develops an orange wash over the breast, head and neck, as well as red bill, legs and lores. Its more rounded body, short neck and short, thick bill distinguish it from other egrets. It nests and roosts colonially. In Bali, a large nocturnal roost (shared with other species) in the village of Petulu is protected by the belief that the birds carry the souls of Balinese killed in the 1966 anti-Communist slaughter.

Javan Pond Heron *Ardeola speciosa* 45cm

Seen singly or in small groups, often in the company of other water-birds, as it slowly stalks its prey in muddy areas or at the waterside. This heron normally appears dark brown, streaked with light brown, with buffish-brown tail and underparts and white wings, but in breeding plumage the neck and head become golden-buff and the back black-ish. It has a black-tipped yellow bill and dull green feet. Found in both inland and coastal areas of Java and Bali, where it is fairly common on freshwater marshes and paddyfields. In south Sumatra, it is thought to be only a non-breeding visitor.

21

Little Heron *Butorides striatus* 45cm

Also known as the Mangrove Heron or Striated Heron, this little bird is a solitary hunter which will stand motionless in one position, awaiting its prey. Adults are mainly dark grey, with a very dark greenish crown and long crest feathers; they have a pale buff neck and facial markings. Juveniles have a more stocky appearance, and are brown with a streaked breast and mottled upperparts. Quite common, particularly around the coastal wetlands, this shy bird prefers to remain close to vegetation cover, but it is infrequently seen also on rocky shorelines and exposed reefs.

Black-crowned Night Heron *Nycticorax nycticorax* 60cm

Adult *Juvenile*

Adults have a distinctive plumage of black back and crown, white neck and underparts, and grey wings and tail, with two long white plumes emerging from the nape. In breeding plumage, the normally dirty yellow legs become red. Females are slightly smaller than males. Juveniles are streaked and mottled brown. By day these birds congregate to rest in tree roosts, but as evening descends they circle the roost, giving characteristic croaking calls, before leaving for freshwater feeding areas in paddyfields, swamps and mangroves and on mudflats. They often breed in large and very noisy colonies in mangroves or in trees overhanging water.

Malayan Night Heron *Gorsachius melanolophus* 50cm

As it is nocturnal and very timid, and prefers dense vegetation, particularly bamboo and reed surrounding inland marshes, this species is seldom seen except when it ventures out into open areas to feed. It is solidly built, having chestnut upperparts finely barred and speckled across the back and wings, and a pale chestnut neck and head with black trailing crest. Its underparts are white, and flecked heavily with chestnut, buff and black; the throat is white, streaked black along the median line. It has olive-green legs, and the short stubby bill is olive-brown with yellow on the lower mandible. A winter visitor to Sumatra and its islands and occasionally Java.

Yellow Bittern *Ixobrychus sinensis* 38cm

Chew Yen Fook

Rice paddies, reedbeds, swamps and beach forest are all favoured by this very quiet and secretive bird. It occasionally appears briefly in the open, only to dart back into the reeds and disappear. In flight, the adult's warm buffish-brown upperparts often appear yellow, contrasting with the black tail, flight feathers and crown, while the underparts are buff. Juveniles are duller, with brown streaking. Feet and bill are brownish-yellow. Although an uncommon resident in Sumatra, this is a common winter visitor in Java and Bali. Sadly, as it reaches the northern coasts of Java, it is caught in fairly large numbers to be fried and eaten with other shorebirds as 'Burung Goreng'.

Cinnamon Bittern *Ixobrychus cinnamomeus* 41cm

One of the smaller, more timid bitterns of the region which remains under cover while stalking its prey in grassland, freshwater swamps and rice paddies. When disturbed, it rises quickly from cover with a croaking alarm call, and flies off with slow powerful wingbeats. Adult males have fairly bright cinnamon-brown upperparts and orange-buff underparts, and are streaked black down the centre of the belly and along the upper flanks; the sides of the long neck are streaked dirty white. Females and juveniles appear darker, with a black cap, but juveniles have a more mottled appearance. Although very common, it is usually found alone.

Milky Stork *Mycteria cinerea* 90cm

This large stork normally occurs in single species groups but is occasionally found in the company of other storks and herons. It is primarily white but with black flight feathers. It has a prominent bare patch of facial skin which varies in colour from pink to red, a long decurved olive-yellow bill and greyish legs. Juvenile birds are a dirty pale brown, but with the rump white and the flight feathers black. A relatively rare species but found throughout the region, it occurs in mangroves and mudflats of West Sumatra, the northern coast of Java near Jakarta, and Brantas Delta, near Surabaya.

Woolly-necked Stork *Ciconia episcopus* 85cm

This large stork is predominantly black, but has a very 'fluffy' feathered white neck. The undertail and lower belly are also white, as are the forehead and a narrow eyebrow. It has a patch of dark grey facial skin. The feet are a dirty red, while the bill is blackish, tinged red, with a red tip. Immature birds differ from adults in having the black plumage tinged brown. Although uncommon in Bali and Java, this species can be seen feeding in paddyfields and pastureland in the company of other storks, and often roosting with them in tall trees. It is not a colonial breeder.

Storm's Stork *Ciconia stormi* 80cm

Another of the region's very rare storks, this species is similar in appearance to the Woolly-necked Stork. It has predominantly black upperparts, a black breast, white neck with black patterning at the side, and a black crown. The tail and belly are white. During the breeding season, the bright pink facial skin patch and the yellow eyering are very evident. The slightly upturned bill is reddish and the legs are pink. A good place to view this bird, which is found only in the freshwater pools in lowland forest in Sumatra and West Java, is Way Kambas in Sumatra.

25

Lesser Adjutant *Leptoptilos javanicus* 110cm

Not a pretty bird, this is a strange-looking creature. Its massive bill on a virtually bald head, and patches of bare red skin on the head, neck and upper breast, give it the appearance of being deformed and sick. The back, wings and tail are dark grey, and the underparts and upper back are white. The bill and legs are greyish. Juveniles have brownish-grey upperparts and dirty white underparts. Hunting and habitat loss are responsible for the rarity of this bird in Java and Bali, but it remains locally common in lowland areas of south Sumatra. It is a colonial nester, and often joins with other storks and raptors to soar on thermals.

Glossy Ibis *Plegadis falcinellus* 60cm

The only ibis in the region with all-dark plumage, this species has blackish-chestnut coloration with green, purple and bronze irides-cences. Immature birds are dark brown, with buff streaking on the head and neck. Usually found in small groups in paddyfields, marshland and lake fringes, where it probes the mud with its long bill. It often associates with egrets and herons, both at night-time roosts and at breeding colonies. A good place to see this bird is at its only Javan breeding colony at Pulau Dua. Although this ibis has an almost worldwide distribution, it is uncommon in the region.

26

Black-shouldered Kite *Elanus caeruleus* 30cm

At first sight, particularly in flight, this elegant little raptor might be mistaken for a gull. Its grey upperparts and white underparts, along with long black primaries and fairly squarish tail, can be confusing. Its distinguishing features are the black shoulder patches and the fact that it often hovers like a kestrel before dropping on its prey. It prefers open countryside and can be found in dry areas of sparse woodland, along woodland and plantation edges, as well as in cultivated areas. It may also be seen from the road, where it perches on exposed branches of old trees and on telephone poles. Numbers have declined in recent years.

Brahminy Kite *Haliastur indus* 45cm

This fairly common brown and white kite is mainly seen soaring on thermals, occasionally in small groups. Adult birds are deep reddish-brown with contrasting black primaries; the head and neck are white. It has dull yellow feet and a pale greenish-grey bill. In flight, long broad wings and longish tail distinguish it from the White-bellied Sea Eagle. Mainly a scavenger feeding on carrion, it occasionally takes small mammals, frogs and birds. It has a shrill mewing call. Generally associated with wetlands, coasts, rivers, lakes, mangroves and mudflats. Found throughout the region, but rare in western Java.

White-bellied Sea Eagle *Haliaeetus leucogaster* 68cm

Adult   *Juvenile*

One of the very large eagles found in the area, this species is distinguished by its magnificent white head, neck and underparts. The rest of the plumage is grey, apart from the black primaries. Immatures show buff where adults are white, the rest of the plumage being dark brown. It flies with slow, powerful wingbeats and occasional glides. It feeds on fish, which it grabs in its talons from the water surface after a swift spectacular dive. Occasionally feeds on refuse. This eagle can often be seen perched upright in trees or on cliffs. It is a fairly common resident, associated with rivers and lakes and especially wooded coasts and rocky shores.

Crested Serpent Eagle *Spilornis cheela* 54cm

A common eagle, that is often seen over woodland and forests, and often attracts attention by its loud, shrill call, *cwee-chee, chee-chee, chee-cheee*. It is dark-coloured, the upperparts being a greyish chocolate-brown and the underparts similar, but the belly and flanks are spotted with white. It also has a raised patch of white-spotted feathers on the top and back of the head, giving the appearance of a crest. In flight, the broad white tail-band and the band of white on the underwing-coverts are significant. The juveniles appear paler below and on the head. It has yellow feet and a greyish-brown bill. Frequently sits in shade high in a tree, while observing the landscape below.

Besra *Accipiter virgatus* 33cm

Ray Tipper

Males have uniform dark grey-brown upperparts with a dark greyish-brown head, and a white throat with a black mesial stripe. The breast and belly are rufous-grey, heavily streaked with black and white in the centre of the upper breast; the lower belly is barred white, leading into white undertail-coverts. The tail has a pale tip and shows three wide black bars. Females are generally browner. Sumatran birds (*A. v. vanbemmeli*) are more rufous. The bill is black and the cere grey. This quiet forest bird is confined mainly to mountain and foothill forests, where it preys on birds and reptiles. Resident and fairly widespread throughout the region, but its population is very sparse.

Black Eagle *Ictinaetus malayensis* 70cm

C. Inskipp, BirdLife International

This very dark eagle with its long wings and long tail appears huge in flight. Apart from its yellow feet, yellow cere and the grey tip on its bill, it is all black. There is slight shading on the tail feathers, giving a barred appearance. In flight, a pale area is apparent on the underwing-coverts. Immatures are generally paler, with buff streaking. This eagle feeds on mammals, birds and some carrion, and is known to raid the nests of other birds for both eggs and young. It prefers lowland and the lower hill forests, where it can be seen gliding and circling, often in pairs, over the treetops in hunting forays.

29

Javan Hawk Eagle *Spizaetus bartels* 60cm

Indonesia's national bird, this raptor is easily identified by its very obvious black crest. It has a black moustachial stripe and crown, buff throat and underparts streaked black on neck and brown on belly, and white-feathered legs, while the sides of the head and nape are a rich russet-brown, blending into dark brown upperparts. The tail is brown with black barring. Immatures lack the streaking on the throat and breast, having plain reddish-brown underparts. A rare endemic, found only in hill and mountain forests and open wooded areas in western Java, and down to the coast at Meru Betiri National Park in the east. A last stronghold is in the Gunung Halimun National Park.

Black-thighed Falconet *Microhierax fringillarius* 15cm

This minute falcon has black upperparts, but shows white spotting on the tail and secondaries. The crown is black, edged with a white patch above the bill and a white stripe behind the eye, and the sides of the face and ear-coverts are black. The chin and belly are rufous with white margins. Although primarily insectivorous, feeding on dragonflies and grasshoppers, it has also been known to attack larger prey, including small birds. It lives along edges of forests and mangroves and in open country and scrub, and is sometimes seen hunting over paddyfields. Now quite rare in Bali and Java, it has nevertheless managed to survive in reasonable numbers in the wooded lowlands of Sumatra.

Wandering Whistling-duck *Dendrocygna arcuata* 45cm

Also called the Whistling Tree-duck, this species makes a series of high-pitched whistling and twittering calls in flight. Its plumage is generally a deep chestnut-brown on the back, tail and breast, but with white undertail-coverts and rump, and a line of black-edged white feathers showing below the folded wing. The head and neck are a paler brown, and there is a dark brown elongated cap running down the back of the neck. The legs are blackish-brown and the bill black. Fairly common throughout the region on wet marshland and on freshwater lakes, where it can be seen diving for food.

Morten Strange

Lesser Whistling-duck *Dendrocygna javanica* 41cm

Very similar in appearance to the Wandering Whistling-duck, this species is slightly smaller and has no black and white feathers showing below the wing. Its back, crown and underparts are a reddish-brown, but the head and neck are buff. There is often buff streaking along the flanks. The feet are dark grey and the bill black. It calls in flight with a repetitive shrill whistling phrase. It frequently uses trees to roost and rest, and normally nests in tree holes. This is a gregarious duck, usually found in small groups in paddyfields, swamps and mangroves and on lakes. It is resident throughout the region.

31

White-winged Duck *Cairina scutulata* 75cm

Chew Yen Fook

With an estimate of only about 250 individuals worldwide, this large black and white wood duck is seriously endangered. It is a dark-coloured duck with a white head, that of the female being spotted with grey. The back is blackish with green iridescence and the underparts brown. The wing has white lesser-coverts and a greyish-blue speculum. The bill is yellow, tipped black, and the feet dirty yellow-orange. A few of these ducks are located in West Java, and the old logging area at Way Kambas in south-east Sumatra is one of the places where it still hangs on, albeit in small numbers. Here, the dense lowland swamp forest provides conditions to its liking.

Cotton Pygmy-goose *Nettapus coromandelianus* 30cm

Unlike most wildfowl, this species regularly perches in trees and normally nests in tree holes. It is a small black and white duck, the male being predominantly white, with iridescent black plumage on the crown, back, wings and tail and a black neck band. The female's plumage is more subdued, being buffish-white where males are white and brown where males are black; she has a brown eye-stripe and lacks the neck band. In flight, males show a white wing patch. This bird prefers a habitat of marshland and lakes, as well as flooded paddy fields and grassland. It occurs in south Sumatra and West Java.

Sunda Teal *Anas gibberifrons* 42cm

This small grey-brown duck is probably the commonest duck of the region, but particularly so in Java and Bali. It is easily distinguished by its unusual bulging forehead. Its sides and back are russet-brown, and it shows a blackish, iridescent blue-green wing speculum. The head and neck are pale buffish-brown, with a dark brown crown. It has grey legs and feet, and the bill is pale grey-blue, turning yellowish towards the tip. It can often be located near water at night by the female's eerie cackling call. Usually in pairs or small groups, often way inland on ponds, rivers and lakes, as well as in mangroves.

Pacific Black Duck *Anas superciliosa* 55cm

The name 'black duck' is a misnomer, for this bird's body plumage looks black only in flight when contrasted with the conspicuous white underwing plumage. It is actually dark brown, with the head striped black and white. The speculum is iridescent green and purple, the legs are yellow-brown and the bill is grey. It is a surface-feeding duck which dabbles in shallow water. A resident, confined mainly to the mountain lakes of East Java and Bali, but often found feeding on marshy areas and grassland. A favourite haunt for it in Bali is the sewage farm at Nusa Dua.

Blue-breasted Quail *Coturnix chinensis* 14cm

Although the male of this species is distinctive, females are easily confused with the Small and Barred Buttonquails that may be found in the region. The Blue-breasted Quail's yellow feet are the main recognition feature. The upperparts are dark brown with lighter streaks, the female being a little lighter than the male. Males have a distinct black and white bib pattern, with the breast, sides of the head and flanks a rich grey-blue; the belly and undertail-coverts are bright chestnut. The female's underparts are brown, streaked buff, with darker brown barring across the chest; she has a whitish throat patch and buffish eye-stripe. The newly hatched young are tiny, almost like bumble-bees.

Chestnut-bellied Partridge *Arborophila javanica* 25cm

Endemic to Java, this partridge occurs in three subspecies. Confined to the west and central parts of the island, each has a different head pattern of reddish-buff with black markings and a black collar. The breast is grey, varying through chestnut to a white vent. The flanks are chestnut, the back and tail grey-brown and barred black, and the wings brown with black barring and small white spots. The feet are red and the bill blackish. This is a bird of montane forest and is often seen in more open spaces, usually in pairs but occasionally in small groups, foraging among the undergrowth.

Crested Partridge *Rollulus roulroul* 25cm

The very distinctive male sports an ostentatious tufted, spiky red crest above a white crown patch. His overall plumage is blackish-blue with a purple sheen, appearing green towards the tail; the wings appear dark red-brown. Females lack the crest, and have green body plumage and a grey head; the wings are more chestnut. They both have red legs and bare red skin around the eye. The bill is black, but males show some red at the base. Congregates in close family groups, foraging through the littered forest floor for insects and fallen fruit. Found in the lowland and hill forests of Sumatra, but not in Java or Bali, the species also occurs in Borneo and the Malay Peninsula.

Crested Fireback *Lophura ignita* 55cm

It is extremely unfortunate that this beautiful pheasant, once common in the forests of Sumatra, Borneo and the Malay Peninsula, now occurs only sporadically. Destruction of the habitat and hunting have reduced its numbers to isolated populations in the more remote and secluded forests. Sumatran birds have a very dark blue, almost black, body with a tufty black crest and a red patch on the rump and lower back; the belly and flanks are faintly streaked with white. The extended and arched central tail

Male (above); female (below)

feathers are white. Females are brown, with white-striped underparts. These are ground-living birds which forage like chickens for fallen fruit, seeds and insects.

Red Junglefowl *Gallus gallus* male 75cm, female 46cm

Two subspecies of this wild ancestor of the domesticated fowl exist in the region: *G. g. spadiceus* in north Sumatra and *G. g. bankiva* in south Sumatra, Java and Bali. Males are recognized by their serrated red comb, face and wattles, their long bronze hackles (longer in the north Sumatran race) and their long, dark green arched tail feathers; they have a chestnut to golden mantle, and blackish-green breast and primary coverts. The females are much duller, being various shades of brown, with black streaking on the neck. The bill is buff and the legs slate-grey. Found in the more open, scrubby areas of forest edges and clearings.

Male (top); *female* (bottom)

Chew Yen Fook

Green Junglefowl *Gallus varius* male 60cm, female 42cm

Endemic to Java, Bali and Nusa Tenggara, this large blackish-green fowl is very similar to the Red Junglefowl but with an unserrated purplish comb. Males have red wattles and bare skin around the eye, a glossy green mantle and nape and iridescent green hackles, with uppertail and wing-coverts orange and yellow; the rest of the plumage is black. Females have brown upperparts sparsely mottled with buff, and buffish underparts mottled with black. This bird prefers the more open grassy areas and often associates with grazing animals, which disturb insects on which it can feed.

Great Argus *Argusianus argus* male 120cm, female 60cm

Frank Lambert

The Great Argus is one of the most spectacular of the region's pheasants. The males have extraordinarily elongated secondary and tail feathers, used in their mating display to attract females. With tail raised high and the wings spread wide, the beautiful patterning of green 'eye' marks (ocelli) is shown off to perfection. The plumage is otherwise mainly chestnut-brown, broken and patterned by spots and flecks of buff and black. The female is generally darker, has shorter wings and tail, and lacks the male's 'eye' spots. Both sexes have a short dark brown crest and bare blue skin on the head and neck.

Green Peafowl *Pavo muticus* male 210cm, female 120cm

This spectacular pheasant can be found roaming forest edges and savanna woodland by day, roosting in bare trees at night. Predominantly iridescent green, the males of this species have conspicuous ocellated tail feathers and a vertical crest on the head. Females are similar, but with shorter tail and paler underparts. During the breeding season, their mewing and loud pairing calls are very obvious and the male's striking display with tail feathers fanned is unmistakable. Once a familiar sight in open woodland, pastures and plantations, this beautiful bird has been virtually exterminated by hunting. Within the region, Java's Ujung Kulon and Baluran National Parks are the last remaining strongholds for this species, but a few local relict populations exist elsewhere.

Slaty-breasted Rail *Gallirallus striatus* 25cm

Chew Yen Fook

Not only is this a very secretive and mainly solitary bird, it is also partly nocturnal and therefore seldom seen. Distinguished from other rails in the region by its chestnut crown, it has a grey upper breast and white chin. The upperparts are brown with fine black and white barring; lower-breast and underparts are white, barred with black. The bill has a pink base and a grey tip, while the legs and feet are grey. It is a common bird of low wetland habitat such as man-groves and marshy areas, as well as paddy-fields and even drier areas of dense alang-alang grassland.

Ruddy-breasted Crake *Porzana fusca* 21cm

This crake is easily confused with three others that frequent the region: the Red-legged Crake (*Rallina fasciata*), the Slaty-legged Crake (*Rallina eurizonoides*) and the Band-bellied Crake (*Porzana paykullii*). On close observation, it is the only one with both head and breast a bright chestnut, with a white chin, and blackish-brown underparts finely barred white. Upperparts are plain russet-brown. Like the other crakes, it is a shy bird and partially noctur-nal, preferring the seclusion of paddyfields and reedy habitat and often bushland adjacent to water. A relatively common resident found throughout the region's lowlands.

38

White-browed Crake *Porzana cinerea* 27cm

This little crake can be quite noisy by day and night during the breeding season. It is easily distinguished from all other small crakes in the region by its conspicuous white head markings above and below the black eye-stripe. The tail and wings are brown, the back and crown are dark greyish-brown, and the belly, neck and throat are white, becoming greyer at the sides. It is ideally adapted to living in marshland, rice paddies and flooded vegetation, where its proportionately large long-toed feet allow it to move around on top of floating vegetation and pick out aquatic invertebrates. It is, however, very timid and will run for cover at the slightest disturbance.

Chew Yen Fook

White-breasted Waterhen *Amaurornis phoenicurus* 33cm

Chew Yen Fook

The most conspicuous and easily identified rail found in the region. Its white face, foreneck and breast, along with rufous flanks and lower belly, are well demarcated from the dark grey-green upperparts. The bill is greyish-green with a red base, and the legs and feet yellow. It is very vocal at dawn and dusk, making a cacophony of weird squawks, grunts and croaking sounds. It is a wandering feeder, frequently out in the open but never far from dense cover. Very agile, it runs over floating vegetation and clambers through bushes, searching for insects. More often seen alone, but frequently in twos and threes.

39

Common Moorhen *Gallinula chloropus* 31cm

Tilford/Cooke, TC Nature

This very adaptable aquatic bird is almost entirely dark grey to black, with a broken white stripe along its flanks. It also displays white patches under the tail, particularly when dashing for cover with its tail raised. It has a characteristic red frontal shield and bill with a yellow tip. The legs are greenish-yellow. Not only is it a good surface swimmer, it will also dive and even run over the water's surface to avoid predators. It feeds mainly on aquatic insects. It frequents freshwater pools, lakes and rivers, and is naturally 'at home' in the rice paddies of the region. Found on almost every continent worldwide, and is also a common resident of Sumatra, Java and Bali.

Purple Swamphen *Porphyrio porphyrio* 48cm

A rather clumsy-looking bird, big and brightly coloured, its large size, and blue-black plumage, offset by a substantial bright red bill and frontal shield making it easily recognized. Its under-tail-coverts are white and it habitually flicks its tail. Its long, ungainly pink legs with huge spreading claws are ideal for both trampling through and over aquatic vegetation. Although not uncommon, it is a rather quiet and secretive bird, that keeps to the edges of undisturbed reedbeds, marshland and occasionally paddyfields. It is found throughout the region.

Grey Plover *Pluvialis squatarola* 28cm

In winter plumage, this rather attractive wader has upperparts mottled grey and brown and underparts pale grey to white, with a black bill and dark grey legs. In flight, it shows a pale wingbar and rump and, below, a white underwing with a large black patch near the body. These features easily separate it from the Pacific Golden Plover, which is also slightly smaller and is shorter-billed. The Grey Plover breeds in the Arctic and is a winter visitor to the region's coastal areas. Found in small groups on tidal mudflats, where it feeds on marine invertebrates and often roosts on isolated shingle spits.

Tilford/Cooke, T C Nature

Pacific Golden Plover *Pluvialis fulva* 25cm

Chew Yen Fook

A typical plover in shape, with a robust body, thin neck and largish head with a short strong bill. When in the region it is usually in non-breeding plumage, having lost the distinctive black face and underparts it had on its breeding grounds. It can be identified by its speckled gold, brown and buff upperparts and buff breast, face and supercilium. The bill is black and the legs grey. This species breeds in north Siberia, north-east Asia and Alaska and is a winter migrant to South-east Asia and Australia, stopping off around the coasts of the Sundas. It is common on mudflats and open grassland near the coast, where it often congregates in flocks.

41

Malaysian Plover *Charadrius peronii* 15cm

Morten Strange

One of the less timid waders, this small bird is more likely to be seen alone or in small groups, and it is unusual for it to flock with other waders. Like many of the small plovers, it is black, brown and white and has a short black bill. It is significantly smaller than the Lesser Sand Plover and Greater Sand Plover (*Charadrius leschenaultii*) and it also has a narrow collar, which is black on males and brown on females. Unlike on the Kentish Plover, its narrow black eye-stripe is separate from the dark brown ear patches. It is quite common on sandy beaches, where it forages along the shoreline.

Greater Sand Plover *Charadrius leschenaultii* 23cm

B. R. Hughes, Windrush Photos

This brown, white and grey plover joins with flocks with other waders, especially the Lesser Sand Plover (*Charadrius mongolus*), on mudflats and sandy estuarine beaches, typically probing the ground for invertebrates. It is most easily separated from the smaller but otherwise similar Lesser Sand Plover by its more substantial bill; apart from the latter, all the other wintering plovers likely to be encountered in the area show a breast-band or a collar. Early arrivals, however, may show remnants of the breeding plumage and have a russet breast bar. This common winter migrant ranges from Africa and Asia through to Australia and New Zealand.

42

Whimbrel *Numenius phaeopus* 43cm

Tilford/Cooke, TC Nature

A large, long-legged wader with a fairly long neck and long decurved bill. Its plumage is heavily mottled brown, with a prominent black crown-stripe above a buff eyebrow and dark eye-stripe. In flight, it shows a white underwing, rump and lower back. Normally quiet, it will often give a trilling call when alarmed. A common visitor to the region's coastline, where it congregates with flocks of other waders on tidal mudflats and estuaries. It also occurs on coastal marshes and rough grassland. Non-breeding birds are often present throughout the year.

Bar-tailed Godwit *Limosa lapponica* 37cm

Tilford/Cooke, T C Nature

Both this species and the similar Black-tailed Godwit (*Limosa limosa*) can be present at the same time. They are largish, long-legged waders with a fairly straight and long bill. Both have greyish-brown upperparts, more heavily mottled on Bar-tailed, which also has an obviously barred tail and slightly heavier grey streaking on the whitish breast. It is generally found in areas frequented by other waders, especially tidal mudflats, estuaries, open expanses of sandy beach and saltmarsh. This fairly common winter visitor to Sumatra is not nearly so common in Java and Bali. Those seen in the region breed in north-east Asia, and are usually in their non-breeding plumage.

43

Wood Sandpiper *Tringa glareola* 20cm

This is quite a noisy species, frequently uttering its *chee-chee-chee* call. Its greyish-brown upperparts have contrasting black and white speckling, and its underparts are white, with a greyish breast; the forehead is buff, leading into a narrow eyebrow. It has long yellowish-green legs. In flight, the white rump and underwing are obvious; there is no wingbar. Breeds in north Europe and north Asia, wintering as far south as Australia. A common visitor throughout the region, seen in small groups, in wet muddy areas, not only on coastal mudflats and mangroves but also in marshland and paddyfields far inland.

Common Sandpiper *Actitis hypoleucos* 20cm

This is a very 'busy' feeder with a constant tail-bobbing action, and when disturbed it often flies a short distance and continues, seemingly unperturbed. It has brown upperparts and white underparts, with a brown patch extending down from the neck to the breast side. In flight, its white and brown barred outer tail feathers are evident, as is the white wingbar. It is most likely to be found alone, feeding on coastal mudflats and along muddy river banks, but occasionally it visits surrounding marshland and paddyfields upstream. A very common migrant from Eurasia, seen throughout the year.

Sanderling *Calidris alba* 20cm

Tilford/Cooke, T C Nature

This highly active wader can often be seen following the retreating waves as it feeds on marine invertebrates thrown up on to the beach. It usually occurs in small groups. In non-breeding plumage, it has pale grey upperparts and white underparts, with black bill and feet. A black shoulder patch helps to distinguish it from other waders. It shows black primaries and a prominent white wingbar in flight. The Sanderling breeds in the Arctic and occurs as a non-breeding migrant throughout the region, but is not common. Found almost entirely on sandy beaches.

Long-toed Stint *Calidris subminuta* 14cm

Ray Tipper

This little wader has a relatively long neck and legs compared with others of its size. In non-breeding plumage, it has heavily streaked brownish-grey upperparts, with a grey-brown crown and bold white eyebrow. The underparts are white, the breast streaked brownish-grey. In flight, the centre of the rump and tail appear black and the outer tail buff. A regular, at times numerous, passage migrant from Siberia, passing through the Greater Sundas on its way to New Guinea or Australia; juveniles occasionally stay through the summer. It usually occurs on coastal mudflats and estuaries, but frequently inland on muddy marshland and rice paddies.

45

Black-naped Tern *Sterna sumatrana* 30cm

Apart from the conspicuous black band through the eye and around the nape and its very pale grey upperparts, this small tern appears very white. In flight, its very long forked tail is obvious. The legs are black, and the black bill is tipped with yellow. Juveniles, however, have grey-brown mottled plumage over the upperparts and on the crown, with black mottling on the nape; the bill-tip is also brownish and the tail unforked. This quite common resident breeds on offshore rocky islands, and is generally seen in the company of other terns on sandy shorelines.

Bridled Tern *Sterna anaethetus* 37cm

Although resident in the area, Bridled Terns spend most of their time out at sea, being driven ashore by bad weather or by the necessity to breed and moult. They feed on small fish or floating invertebrates, taken from the surface of the sea. This is a medium-sized tern with dark grey-brown back, tail and wings, white underparts and a long forked tail. The crown, nape and eye-stripe are black, leaving a thin white forehead leading into a short white supercilium. The leading edge of the wings is white, as are the outer tail feathers. Seen ashore more during the summer months, but then only singly or in small groups.

Great Crested Tern *Sterna bergii* 45cm

This tern appears very large, and has a grey back and rump and white underparts, neck and patch above the bill. In breeding plumage, it has a black cap extending backwards to form a slight crest. During the summer, the black crown becomes heavily mottled with white, and gradually turns to white-mottled grey as winter approaches. It has a yellow bill and black feet, the bill colour distinguishing it from the very similar but slightly smaller Lesser Crested Tern. Juveniles are heavily marked with brown on the upperparts and have a dark grey tail and outer primaries. A very common tern of inland waters.

Lesser Crested Tern *Sterna bengalensis* 40cm

Steve Young

This species looks very similar to the Great Crested Tern, but is slightly smaller and has a distinctive orange bill. In breeding plumage, the black cap extends forward to meet the bill. After breeding, the forehead and forecrown become white, leaving a black crest. Juveniles appear more like non-breeding adults, but with greyish wings and mottled brown upperparts. Often associates with other terns, sometimes in large flocks. Occurs in coastal waters and often far out to sea, but is more often observed along sandy and muddy shorelines. A common winter visitor to Java and Bali, but less so to Sumatra.

Thick-billed Green Pigeon *Treron curvirostra* 27cm

This is a fairly robust pigeon with red feet and a yellow iris surrounded by a pale bluish-green eye-ring. Males have a maroon mantle and back, whereas females are green. The underparts are bright green, the flanks darker green and barred white. The neck is green, becoming greyish on the ear-coverts, with the forehead and crown grey. The two subspecies in Sumatra (*T. c. curvirostris* and *T. c. harterti*) have a substantial pale green bill with a red base, while that of *T. c. hypothapsina* from the islands of south-west Java has an olive base. A fairly common and noisy bird of lowland forest, especially among fruiting trees.

Pink-necked Green Pigeon *Treron vernans* 27cm

This small green pigeon is distinguished from similar pigeons by its grey tail with black band and pale grey tip. The male has a blue-grey head merging through pink to orange on the lower breast; the abdomen is green and yellow, and the back and wings green. The female is green, lacking the male's brighter colours, but identified by tail pattern and by its company with the distinctive male. Its calls are a 'cooing' whistle and, when feeding, a series of crow-like rasps. Common in lowland and coastal forest as well as in more open countryside, becoming even more conspicuous when trees are fruiting. Occurs from southern Burma through to the Lesser Sundas, and normally resident.

Black-naped Fruit Dove *Ptilinopus melanospila* 27cm

Tilford/Cooke, TC Nature

This species usually occurs in pairs but being very timid it is seldom seen except when it congregates in flocks at fruiting trees. It is, however, usually detected by its resonant *ow-wook-wook... ow-wook-wook* call. It has predominantly green upperparts, tail and lower breast with a yellow vent and red undertail coverts. The male has a pale grey head with a conspicuous black nape and yellow throat. Females have all green heads. Both have red feet and greenish-yellow bill. It is a locally common fruit dove of the lowland and hill forests of Java and Bali not normally found on Sumatra.

Jambu Fruit Dove *Ptilinopus jambu* 28cm

Predominantly bright green upperparts, white underparts and red face separate this from other fruit doves. The male's face is crimson, and he has a black throat patch, a bright pink tinge to the upper breast and chestnut undertail-coverts. The female has a dull purple face, her undertail-coverts are orange-brown and the upper breast bright green. The bill is pale orange and the legs crimson. A common lowland bird of Sumatra, it is rarely found beyond West Java. It prefers more open wooded areas with an abundance of fruiting trees. It occurs mainly around the coast and on small offshore islands.

Chew Yen Fook

49

Green Imperial Pigeon *Ducula aenea* 42cm

Chew Yen Fook

A large green and grey pigeon which prefers to live high in the tree-tops, where it feeds on figs and nutmeg and other small fruits, normally swallowing them whole. It is the commonest pigeon of the region's lowland rainforest, but is becoming increasingly more difficult to locate as its habitat is lost. Head, neck and underparts are soft pinkish-grey, with chestnut undertail-coverts. The upperparts are green with a bronze iridescence. It has a dull red base to the blue-grey bill, and dark red feet. This species inhabits coastal mangroves and, especially, riverine forest. It occurs from India through the Sundas to New Guinea, and is resident.

Pied Imperial Pigeon *Ducula bicolor* 40cm

Chew Yen Fook

This is a striking bird, mainly creamy to ivory-white, with black flight feathers and tip of tail; the bill and feet are blue-grey. Immatures are greyer. Found more often in mangrove and coastal forests, it sometimes congregates in substantial breeding colonies where fruiting figs are readily available. Hunting has decimated the population of this beautiful pigeon, particularly in Java and Bali. Fortunately, it still remains quite common on the offshore islands of Sumatra and elsewhere in its range, which extends from the south of Burma to New Guinea. It is a resident species, but often moves long distances between islands.

Ruddy Cuckoo Dove *Macropygia emiliana* 30cm

This species is usually treated as an Indonesian form of the Brown Cuckoo Dove (*Macropygia amboinensis*). It is much smaller than the Barred Cuckoo Dove and more of a chestnut-brown. The male's upperparts are uniform brown, with a light purplish iridescence on the neck and upper breast. The underparts are slightly paler chestnut-brown. Females are similar, but have black barring on the back and wing-coverts and slight barring on the upper breast. It prefers primary-forest edges and clearings, where it spends much of its time in search of food. Common in the hill forests of Java and Bali, with endemic forms occurring on the south Sumatran islands, although there are few records from Sumatra itself.

Little Cuckoo Dove *Macropygia ruficeps* 29cm

Morten Strange

Smaller than the other brown cuckoo doves, the Little Cuckoo Dove is separated by its buff breast and by the dark brown subterminal bar on its outer tail feathers. The upperparts also are lightly barred black and the upper breast is often heavily barred, especially on the female. Males have green and purple iridescence on the nape. They have red legs and a brown-tipped black bill. This species congregates, often in large flocks, along forest edges, feeding in grassland and ripening rice fields. It is a common bird in the hills and montane forests throughout the region.

Spotted Dove *Streptopelia chinensis* 30cm

This very familiar dove has a generally pinkish-brown plumage, with slightly darker flight feathers and dark-mottled back. On each side of the neck it has an obvious white-spotted black patch. The outer tail feathers are broadly tipped white, this being very obvious in flight. It has red feet and a black bill. It is frequently found close to human habitation, from city gardens to rural cultivation, open country and forest edges in lowland areas, where it forages on the ground. Very common throughout the Sundas, and widely kept as a cage-bird and bred in aviaries throughout the world.

Peaceful Dove *Geopelia striata* 20cm

A very common cagebird throughout Indonesia, but particularly in Java, where it holds a special significance in Javanese philosophy. Also known as the Zebra Dove for its finely barred pale brown and black plumage from neck to tail. The back of the head is pale brown, blending into a buff face, crown, neck and chin. The long tapered tail is brown and black with white-tipped outer feathers; very evident on take-off. This is a ground feeder, occurring around gardens, cultivation and open grassland and scrub. Although common in lowland south Sumatra, excessive trapping in Bali and Java has dramatically reduced its numbers.

52

Emerald Dove *Chalcophaps indica* 25cm

Chew Yen Fook

This attractive ground dove has iridescent emerald-green wing-coverts and mantle, with a dark grey lower back crossed by two conspicuous white bars. The underparts, neck and sides of the head are dark pink, and the short tail is black. Males have a white forehead, with the crown and nape tinged grey. Females are duller. The species occurs singly or in pairs, preferring the seclusion of thick forest or forest edge. Throughout its range from Australia to India it is quite common, but it is becoming rare in Java and Bali, probably as a result of habitat destruction and trapping for the pet trade.

Nicobar Pigeon *Caloenas nicobarica* 40cm

One of the more unusual pigeons, recognized by its long, iridescent purple, mane-like hackles. Apart from the short, stubby white tail, the plumage is dark green, with an iridescent sheen of gold, purple and bronze on the upperparts. The bill is black, with a conspicuous knob-shaped cere. The legs are purplish-red and the claws yellow. This is a wary bird and almost silent, making an occasional deep croaking call. Although it is a secretive ground feeder, it rests low down in trees for the greater part of the day, only becoming active at dusk. It is fairly rare, occurring mainly on the offshore islands of Java and Sumatra.

Rainbow Lorikeet *Trichoglossus haematodus* 24cm

Tilford/Cooke, TC Nature

This is a brilliant multi-coloured parrot with a very dark purplish-black head. Apart from the yellow collar, the upperparts are green. It has a red breast and underwing-coverts, and a yellow patch under the shoulder. The belly is very dark purple, and the thighs show alternate green and yellow narrow bands. The feet are grey and the bill red. It is normally seen in small, noisy, foraging parties flying low over the forest canopy. A resident species in Java, Bali and the Lesser Sundas through to Australia. Once common in Bali, it is now quite rare, having been exploited for the pet trade.

Yellow-crested Cockatoo *Cacatua sulphurea* 33cm

Tilford/Cooke, TC Nature

A fairly large, white, parrot-like bird with a lovely crest of stiff yellow feathers and yellow cheek patches. It has a black bill and dark grey feet. Its flight appears very laboured, with alternate glides and fast flapping wingbeats. It can often be seen in small groups, but usually lives in pairs, and is very noisy, with screeches, squawks and whistles in its repertoire; it has a habit of raising its crest as it calls. Also known as the Lesser Sulphur-crested Cockatoo, this bird is endemic to Sulawesi and the Lesser Sundas, with a population on Nusa Penida, Bali, and another on Mesalembu Besar in the Java Sea. Has been widely exploited by the pet trade.

Yellow-throated Hanging Parrot *Loriculus pusillus* 12cm

These very small and well camouflaged parrots are more often seen in the treetops, clambering around and hanging, often upside-down, to feed on flowers and small fruits. They fly around in small flocks, often making high-pitched shrieking calls. They are mainly leaf-green, with brighter yellow-green underparts, and are particularly difficult to observe as their colouring blends in so well with the foliage. Males have a small yellow patch on the throat. The feet and bill are orange. A fairly common endemic of Java and Bali, inhabiting lowland rainforest.

Tilford/Cooke, TC Nature

Oriental Cuckoo *Cuculus saturatus lepidus* 26cm

This very secretive species spends much of its time high in the forest canopy, and is very quiet outside the breeding season. In February and March, it is usually the resident race (*C. s. lepidus*) that can be heard giving its three-syllable *hoop, hoop-poop* call. This quite small cuckoo has a grey breast and upperparts and a dark grey tail; the underparts are buff, barred black. It has a yellow eye-ring, grey bill and dirty orange-yellow feet. There is an hepatic form of the female which has black-barred rufous upperparts and white-barred underparts, very similar to the juveniles. Apart from the resident race in the Sundas, migrant races from Eurasia occur during the winter.

Tilford/Cooke, TC Nature

Drongo Cuckoo *Surniculus lugubris* 24cm

Morten Strange

This predominantly black cuckoo has a forked tail like a drongo. Its plumage is shiny black, apart from white bands on the undertail-coverts and all-white thighs. The bill is black and the legs are grey. The plumage of the juvenile is flecked with white and the white tail-bands are wider. Although shy, this species has a loud, clear call consisting of an ascending scale of up to seven notes and less often a series of warbled notes. It occurs in the lowlands throughout the region, both as a resident and as a migrant, but its timid nature confines it mainly to forests and forest edges.

Asian Koel *Eudynamys scolopacea* 42cm

Chew Yen Fook

This bird's loud call, a shrill repeated *koel, koel, koel* …, is the origin of its name. Its other call, a loud and accelerating *kow-wow, kow-wow, kow-wow* …, can be heard by day and night, but you will be lucky if this very timid bird reveals itself. Like others of the cuckoo family, it is a brood-parasite, searching out nests of orioles, crows and drongos in which to deposit its eggs. The adult male is glossy black, with a long tail, buff bill and red eye-ring. The female is grey to golden-brown, with heavy white speckling and barring.

Male (above); female (below)

56

Red-billed Malkoha *Phaeicophaeus javanicus* 46cm

Separated from other malkohas of the region by its large size and strong red bill. The upperparts are mid-grey but tinged with a pale bluish-green iridescence. The underparts are chestnut with a grey band across the upper breast and the grey tail feathers are tipped with white. The eye is surrounded by a bare patch of blue skin and the legs are grey. Found in the lowland and lower hills of Java and Sumatra, it prefers forest edges and secondary scrub. It usually moves about in pairs or small family groups often foraging amongst alang-alang grassland. It has a 'whining' call.

Tilford/Cooke, TC Nature

Chestnut-breasted Malkoha *Phaenicophaeus curvirostris* 50cm

The tail of this malkoha is over half the bird's total length, appearing dull green above with a rufous tip and rufous on the underside. The upperparts are also dull green, with the crown and nape grey. There is a bare red patch of facial skin surrounding the eye. The Sumatran race (*P. c. erythrognathus*) has grey throat and cheeks and a black patch across the lower belly. There is also plumage variation in other island races. This locally common lowland bird is usually found among forest thickets and can often be observed perched stationary in the tops of small trees.

Morten Strange

57

Greater Coucal *Centropus sinensis* 52cm

Chew Yen Fook

Although often on the ground, this large, black, crow-like bird with chestnut-brown wings is more likely to be seen lumbering about in small trees and bushes, where it can hide in thick vegetation. The bill and feet are black. Its very eerie, far-reaching, low-pitched call starts with a series of *poop, poop, poop* sounds, increasing in tempo and then slowing again, but occasionally a series of just four deep monotonous *poop, poop, poop, poop* notes is given. It is heard more often in the morning. A resident throughout the Sundas, preferring forest edges, mangroves, grassy banks and secondary scrub.

Lesser Coucal *Centropus bengalensis* 40cm

Morten Strange

Very similar in appearance to the Greater Coucal, this species is smaller and has duller plumage, and is also more common throughout the region. Its flight is weak, consisting only of short, laboured, flapping forays low over the vegetation in search of insects. It hops when on the ground, and clambers around when in trees and bushes. Like other coucals, the plumage is black except for the chestnut back and wings; the bill and feet are also black. Found especially in the lowlands, where it frequents open grassy areas, particularly the denser alang-alang grassland and marshland.

58

Collared Scops Owl *Otus bakkamoena* 20cm

This common owl can often be seen hunting for insects and small rodents from trees and prominent perches in built-up areas of towns. The regular soft *whoop* call of the male and the *weeoo* and *plop* calls from the female are often heard alternately as a continuous duet. Identification is not simple, as the species occurs in several colour forms. It can be dull reddish-brown to grey-brown, with the upperparts mottled and blotched with buffs and black; the underparts are paler and streaked with black. It has a pale sandy 'neck collar'. Bill and feet are yellow. Found almost everywhere below 1500m and possibly the commonest owl encountered.

Tilford/Cooke, TC Nature

Barred Eagle Owl *Bubo sumatranus* 45cm

One of the larger owls to be found in the region, this magnificent bird is unfortunately rarely seen, confining itself to the lowland forests and emerging from its daytime roosting place only at dusk. Recognized by its large size, its prominent horizontal ear-tufts, and its pale grey underparts heavily barred with black. The upperparts are dark brown, flecked and barred with buff. The eyes are brown and the feet and bill yellow. It has many unusual calls, which are often thought to be attributable to mysterious demons by the local people. Its familiar call is a loud *whooa-hoo, whooa-hoo*, followed by a deep groan.

Chew Yen Fook

Buffy Fish Owl *Ketupa ketupu* 45cm

This large owl has an amusing appearance with its bright yellow eyes and its conspicuous horizontal ear-tufts. Its upperparts are brown, streaked with black and buff, and the underparts are bright rufous-buff with narrow black streaks. It has whitish eyebrows, a grey bill and yellow feet. It is a mainly nocturnal species, preferring to remain hidden among trees during the day. At night, it ventures outside the forest into parks, paddyfields and often alongside roads. It is never far from water, on which it is dependent for its fishing for frogs, fish and other aquatic life.

Spotted Wood Owl *Strix seloputo* 47cm

Being nocturnal, this bird is seldom seen, but its presence is disclosed by its low growling and resounding *hoo-hoo-hoo* calls. It is a large owl, similar in shape to the Barred Eagle Owl, but without the ear-tufts. Its facial discs are light rufous and the underparts are whitish, tinged rufous and lightly barred with dark brown. A white throat is characteristic. The upperparts are a rich chocolate-brown, marked with black-edged white spots. The bill is greenish-grey and the feet grey. Found in the lowland forests of Java, it may also be attracted to woodland close to villages and sometimes into towns.

Large-tailed Nightjar *Caprimulgus macrurus* 30cm

This quite large grey-brown nightjar spends the daytime in shady areas on the ground, concealed by its camouflaged plumage. Its activity commences at dusk when, for half an hour, either perched in a tree or on the ground, it utters its slow and repeated *choink-choink-choink* call. In flight, the broad white tips of the two outer pairs of tail feathers and the distinctive white patch covering the centres of the four outer primary wing feathers aid identification. Widespread from India to Australia, this bird is locally common throughout the region, where it prefers lowland wooded country, mangroves and forest edges.

Savanna Nightjar *Caprimulgus affinis* 22cm

One of the smallest nightjars in the region, this species has a monotonous repeated call, *jweep*, which is heard around dawn and dusk, often from birds in flight. Its fairly uniform but well-camouflaged brown plumage has a white patch on each side of the neck; the male has white outer tail feathers. It is common in dry open areas around the coastal lowlands, but is found also, somewhat surprisingly, in big cities, where it exploits the hordes of flying insects attracted by the lights and uses the large flat rooftops of buildings on which to rest. In open country it roosts on the ground by day, and is seldom seen perched elsewhere.

Glossy Swiftlet *Collocalia esculenta* 9cm

This is the smallest and commonest swiftlet in the region, identified by its glossy black upperparts and whitish belly. It also goes by the alternative name of White-bellied Swiftlet. The chin is pale grey, and in flight a small notch is apparent in the tail. Both bill and feet are black. It nests in the entrances to caves, but it does not use echo-location and the nest is inedible. Like all swifts it is insectivorous, catching aerial insects as it flies over forests and agricultural land, from the coastline to the highest peaks. It often flies over water, dipping down to drink. Widespread throughout the region.

House Swift *Apus affinis* 15cm

This medium-sized swift, also commonly known as the Little Swift, is usually seen in large groups hunting insects over open countryside. It can be recognized by its white rump and throat and slightly notched tail, unlike the similar but larger Fork-tailed Swift (*Apus pacificus*), which has a distinct fork to the tail. Otherwise it has blackish plumage, black bill and brown feet. It prefers coastal habitats up to the lower hills and is frequently found in towns and villages, where it nests under the eaves of houses; it also uses over-hanging cliff faces and cave entrances as nesting sites. It is locally common over much of the region.

Common Kingfisher *Alcedo atthis* 15cm

This is the common kingfisher seen from Eurasia all the way to New Guinea. Upperparts are a shiny bright blue-green, with paler blue uppertail-coverts and a small patch in the centre of the back. The underparts are rufous, as are the ear-coverts. There is a white stripe on the side of the neck. Feet are red and the bill black. In flight, it has a drawn-out high-pitched *tseeep, tseeep* call. Frequents lowland open country with freshwater mangroves, rivers and lakes. Uses an over-hanging branch or rock beside water as a perch from which to dive for fish. A common visitor to Sumatra, but less so to Java and Bali.

Blue-eared Kingfisher *Alcedo meninting* 15cm

This is the woodland counterpart of the Common Kingfisher, and is very similar in its behaviour, moving between waterside perches in rapid flight. It dives into water to catch fish, which it kills by bashing it on the perch before swallowing it whole head-first. The Blue-eared has a more contrasty appearance than the Common Kingfisher, its upperparts being a darker but shinier blue and its underparts a bright orange-red. The ear-coverts are blue. It frequents forest rivers, streams and lakes, and occasionally estuarine habitat, throughout the lowlands of Sumatra, Java and Bali.

Cerulean Kingfisher *Alcedo coerulescens* 14cm

Morten Strange

Also known as the Small Blue Kingfisher, this tiny species is easily identified. The upperparts are a brilliant pale greenish-blue, with the crown, wing-coverts and a neck patch barred with dark blue; it also has a pale greenish-blue band across its upper breast. The throat, lores and belly are white. In typical kingfisher fashion, it perches on prominent places above water, waiting to dive in on its prey. It is quite common on estuaries and in the coastal mangroves and marshland of Bali and Java, reaching west into southern Sumatra. A good place to see many of the kingfishers is around the numerous coastal fish-farms.

Oriental Dwarf Kingfisher *Ceyx erithacus* 14cm

Morten Strange

This brilliantly coloured little kingfisher has adapted to feeding on insect prey and lives in forests often some distance from water. It has a rapid low flight, during which it often emits a very high-pitched whistle. It hunts from a perch, and often snatches spiders from their webs while in flight. It has distinctive brilliant yellow underparts and bluish-black back and wing-coverts. The crown and tail are red, as are the bill and feet. There are usually small patches of blue in front of the eye and behind the ear-coverts. Widespread in suitable habitat throughout the region, but not common.

Stork-billed Kingfisher *Halcyon capensis* 35cm

This kingfisher, too, being the largest encountered in the region and having an enormous red bill, is easy to identify. The back, wings and tail are blue-green and the underparts pinkish-orange. The head is brown, becoming lighter around the neck. It has short red legs. It inhabits coastal mangroves and lowland rivers and marshland, as well as agricultural land, paddyfields and woodland adjacent to rivers. It feeds on fish, crabs and amphibians. Once recorded throughout the area, it is now an uncommon resident, and possibly extinct in Bali. Farming practices, pesticides and disturbance are thought to be the main reasons for its decline.

White-throated Kingfisher *Halcyon smyrnensis* 27cm

Ray Tipper

The white throat and 'bib' contrasting with the chocolate-brown head and underparts are distinguishing features for this large kingfisher. The upperparts, tail and upper surfaces of the wings are iridescent mid-blue, and there is a patch of brown on the upperwing-coverts. A noisy loud screaming call, *kee-kee-kee-kee*, emitted while perched or in flight, announces the bird's presence as it hunts over rivers and ponds and even along the coast. Found mainly in Sumatra, with a few records in West Java, this kingfisher inhabits mainly lowland open areas near to water.

Javan Kingfisher *Halcyon cyanoventris* 25cm

This dark-looking kingfisher has adapted well to a diet of insects and terrestrial prey, and is not reliant on fishing for its survival. It can often be seen on an isolated perch in open grassland, waiting for insects to come into range, although it remains near water where prey items are more abundant. It is dark brown on the head, with lighter brown collar and upper breast. The belly and hindcollar are purplish-blue, and the back and wing-coverts dark purple. Flight feathers and tail are bright blue. The white wing patches are particularly conspicuous in flight. Both bill and feet are red. Endemic to lowlands in Java and Bali.

Collared Kingfisher *Todiramphus chloris* 24cm

A very familiar kingfisher, this species is quite evident from its continual calling throughout the day. Its harsh, noisy *chue-chue-chue-chue-chue* carries over long distances and announces its presence almost everywhere except in the mountains. At first sight it is bright blue and white, but at close range the blue of the crown, back, wings and tail has a superb green iridescence. It has a beautifully clean white collar and underparts. The lores are white, and a black stripe passes through the eye and around the back of the head. It prefers open country around the coast and wherever there is water in which to fish, and must be the commonest kingfisher of the region.

Chestnut-headed Bee-eater *Merops leschenaulti* 20cm

Like all bee-eaters, this species congregates in parties which wander around searching for insect prey, which it catches in flight. These birds habitually choose exposed perches from which to survey and make their sweeping excursions to catch insects, bringing them back to the perch to break up and eat. It has a light chestnut crown, nape and mantle, a yellow throat and below this a chestnut and black band. In flight, the pale blue rump contrasts with the dark green back and tail, and the underwing appears orange. The tail is square-ended and lacks the streamers of similar species. Quite common in open wooded habitat, particularly in the lowlands.

Blue-throated Bee-eater *Merops viridis* 27cm

Although gregarious and delightfully aerobatic, this bee-eater appears a little less inclined to hawk its prey like other bee-eaters, preferring to wait around on exposed perches and making only short dashes to catch passing insects. Its distinguishing features are its blue throat and solid black eye-stripe and the male's rich brown cap and mantle. Its elongated central tail feathers are blue, as are the outer tail, vent and rump. The back, wings and breast, and the female's crown, are light green. Preferring drier terrain, such as open grassland or more open scrub and woodland, it occurs particularly in the coastal lowlands of Sumatra and West Java.

67

Dollarbird *Eurystomus orientalis* 30cm

This is the only member of the roller family to occur in the region. It is usually seen in ones and twos, hunting from exposed perches in the open country; it dives on its insect prey, either in the air or on the ground. It is frequently mobbed by other birds because of its crow-like appearance. Overall, it appears dark bluish-black with an upright stance, with a large head and solid orange-red bill. In flight, two circular light blue contrasting patches on the underwing-coverts are very evident, and these give the bird its English name. Although widespread, it is not common.

Bushy-crested Hornbill *Anorrhinus galeritus* 70cm

One of the smaller hornbills, this species is easily identified by its thick drooping crest. Its plumage is all black except for the greyish-brown upper two-thirds of the tail. The patch of bare skin on the throat is blue and that around the eye is either blue or white. The feet are black, as is the male's bill. The bill of the female is grey, although it can sometimes be whitish. This hornbill is gregarious outside of the breeding season, when noisy flocks of as many as fifteen birds can gather together to feed high in the tree canopy. It is found in the lowland forests of Sumatra.

Wreathed Hornbill *Aceros undulatus* 100cm

Apart from the whitish, often dirty yellow, tail and the male's chestnut-crowned creamy head, the remaining plumage is black. The male has a bare yellow gular pouch, that of the black-headed female being blue. Like all of the hornbills, this one relies on hollow forest trees when nesting, the male restricting the size of the entrance hole with mud while the female is incubating, and the female doing likewise after hatching until the young are ready to fledge. It is particularly fond of figs, but also takes other fruits and insects. Although common in lowland and hill forests of Sumatra, its distribution in Java and Bali is confined to a few remaining undisturbed forests.

Oriental Pied Hornbill *Anthracoceros albirostris* 75cm

Recognized by its mainly black plumage with a white lower breast, belly and flanks, this species also has white patches behind the eye and at the base of the lower mandible. The huge horn-coloured bill is surmounted by a banana-shaped casque marked with black at the front end. The tail shows variable amounts of black and white, particularly on the outer feathers. It is normally found in small parties, which give a very chicken-like *puk-puk-puk-puk* cackle; also utters a loud, raucous and cackling laugh. Inhabits edges and clearings in more remote lowland forest and secondary forest right down to the coast, throughout the Greater Sundas.

Chew Yen Fook

Rhinoceros Hornbill *Buceros rhinoceros* 110cm

Chew Yen Fook

Although not present in Bali, this hornbill gives the impression that it is more numerous than it really is. A very large bird with a loud voice, usually seen in pairs and duetting in flight, it creates a false impression of numbers. Its head, breast, wings and back are black and the lower belly a dirty white. The tail is white with a broad black band. It can be identified in flight by its all-black underwings, white belly and banded tail. The enormous yellow bill, becoming red at the base, is surmounted by an upturned casque. Found in low densities in most large pockets of hill and lowland forest in Sumatra and Java.

Great Hornbill *Buceros bicornis* 125cm

Usually travelling about in pairs, this huge hornbill feeds noisily in the high canopy. Its call can be described as a loud and harsh barking roar. The enormous yellow bill and casque, black face, its yellow-stained white neck and upper breast, and black subterminal bar on a white tail separate it from other hornbills of the region. The back, lower belly and wing-coverts are black, and a white wingbar is often stained with yellow. This uncommon species confines itself to lowland and submontane forests, ranging from India through South-east Asia and the Malay Peninsula to Sumatra.

Fire-tufted Barbet *Psilopogon pyrolophus* 26cm

As with most barbets, the main plumage is bright green. This species has a yellow band across the breast, outlined with a black line below. The rear crown and nape are red, the chin green, the ear-coverts grey and the eye-stripe and forehead black, and it has a prominent red-tipped black hairy tuft at the base of the lores. It is very fond of ripe fruit, particularly small figs, and it will sit stationary high in the trees for long periods while frequently uttering its harsh buzzing call, which is reminiscent of a cicada. Confined to the Malay Peninsula and Sumatra, where it prefers tall forest trees in the lower hills.

Lineated Barbet *Megalaima lineata* 29cm

This barbet has a green back, wings and tail, and a brown head and upper breast heavily streaked with buff. The remaining underparts are green and also streaked with buff. It has a broad orange-yellow orbital ring of bare skin. The heavy bill is pale pink, and the feet yellow. It is frequently seen in sparse, dry coastal woodlands, edges of savanna, acacia forest, orchards and cultivated areas. Not found on Sumatra, but quite a common resident in open forest, along forest edges and in clearings in the more remote areas of Java and Bali.

Red-crowned Barbet *Megalaima rafflesii* 25cm

The combination of a bright red crown, a yellow cheek patch and a blue throat is diagnostic of this medium-sized barbet. The main body plumage is bright green, and there is a small red patch below the rear of the eye which blends into black on the ear-coverts. A wide blue eyebrow separates the crown from the ear-coverts. The bill is black and the feet are grey. Juvenile birds are much duller in appearance. Like the rest of its family, it nests in holes in trees. This quite common barbet prefers the lowland forests, where it inhabits the upper canopy and is often difficult to catch sight of.

Black-banded Barbet *Megalaima javensis* 26cm

Tilford/Cooke, TC Nature

Quite large, with green body plumage and tail, this barbet has a yellow crown and a yellow spot under the eye. It also has a red throat, under which is a solid black collar which joins up to a black stripe running through the eye. The feet are pale olive-green and the bill black. As with other barbets, the feet are adapted for climbing tree trunks, having two toes pointing forward and two back. It is mainly a fruit-eater with a penchant for small ripe figs, but also eats seeds, buds and flowers. More likely to be encountered around clearings and forest edges of lowland and hill forests, this endemic of Bali and Java appears quite plentiful.

72

Blue-eared Barbet *Megalaima australis* 18cm

A small barbet, more likely to be heard than seen, but careful examination of fruiting fig trees will often lead to its being located. This species' calls are a fast repeated *tuk-trrk, tuk-trrk ...*, and a series of high-pitched whistled or trilled notes. Two races occur in the region, both having green body plumage, a black malar stripe and breast stripe, and a blue chin and crown. The Javan race has patches of yellow on the cheek and below the black breast stripe. The Sumatran race lacks the yellow but has red cheeks. This is a common barbet of forests and plantations, being found from the coast to the lower hills.

Coppersmith Barbet *Megalaima haemacephala* 15cm

A drawn-out resonant *tonk-tonk-tonk-tonk* call, reminiscent of a vibrating hammer on metal, announces this bird's presence. While frequently found in trees in open country, it also ventures into town gardens and parks. Usually solitary, but often flocks with other barbets at fruiting trees. The back, wings and tail are green, with fawn underparts streaked with black. The race found in Java and Bali (*M. h. rosea*) has a red crown, chin, throat and cheek, the Sumatran race (*M. h. delica*) having the throat, cheek and eyebrow yellow. A thin black necklace separates the red and yellow neck markings. A fairly common resident of open lowland forests throughout the range.

Laced Woodpecker *Picus vittatus* 30cm

Morten Strange

This woodpecker has green upperparts and nape, a yellow rump and a black tail. The underparts are buffish-yellow with the feathers edged in green, giving the laced appearance. Males have a red crown, this being black on females. The cheeks are blue-grey, bordered by a black eye-stripe and malar stripe, both of which are mottled with white. The black primaries are barred with white. The bill is black and the feet grey-green. Prefers coastal woodland and forest, and often found in mangroves, bamboo thickets and coconut plantations. It is locally common throughout the region, but is rare in Sumatra.

Common Flameback *Dinopium javanense* 30cm

Chew Yen Fook

Male   *Female*

Usually in pairs and noticed by their continual 'churring' contact calls, the male has a red crown extending into a crest at the rear, while the female's crown is a more flattened mass of black and white feathers. Otherwise both sexes are similar, having a golden-yellow mantle and wing-coverts, red lower back and rump, black tail and primaries, and a white face with a black eye-stripe and single solid malar stripe. The white underpart feathers are edged black, forming a scaly pattern. It is unusual in having only three toes. A quite common lowland woodpecker of secondary and open forests and mangroves, but regularly appearing around cultivation, plantations and even in gardens.

74

White-bellied Woodpecker *Dryocopus javensis* 42cm

Rather solitary, this woodpecker usually makes its presence known by its loud 'laughing' and 'barking' calls, as well as its heavy hammering on dead branches. It often calls in flight with a raucous, echoing *kiow, kiow, kiow*. It has a very conspicuous appearance, being very large, with all-black plumage apart from a white belly. Males have a red crest and cheek patches. The long pointed bill is black and the feet grey. This bird of open lowland forest is found throughout the Greater Sundas as far east as Bali, but is relatively rare in both Java and Bali.

Fulvous-breasted Woodpecker *Dendrocopos macei* 18cm

This smallish woodpecker is quite adaptable and fairly tame, making it relatively easy to observe. It spends a lot of time in the higher branches of tall trees, but can often be seen foraging lower down on tree trunks. Its back and tail are heavily barred black and white, and the underparts are buff and lightly streaked black. The male has a red crown and the female black. The side of the face and the chin are white, separated by a black malar stripe. It is a bird of open forest, which has a liking for plantations, parks and gardens. Although it is quite common in Bali and Java, there are few records from Sumatra.

Tilford/Cooke, TC Nature

75

Sunda Pygmy Woodpecker *Dendrocopos moluccensis* 13cm

Also known as the Brown-capped Woodpecker, this little bird is usually seen on its own as it works through the dead branches and bark of trees, often close to the ground, searching out insects and larvae. Its short legs have grey feet with two toes pointing forward and two backward. Its upperparts are dark brown with white barring, giving a partially spotted appearance. The underparts are whitish with black streaking. It has a rich brown crown, black malar stripe, white face patch with a greyish-brown centre, and thin red stripe behind the eye. It prefers mangroves, open woodland and coastal secondary forest.

Black-and-red Broadbill *Cymbirhynchus macrorhynchos* 23cm

This insectivorous species is identified by its black upperparts and black band across the upper breast, its white wing-stripe, dark red underparts and throat-stripe, and its large yellow and blue bill. Juveniles have a pinkish-buff belly and grey-tinged throat. It is attracted to scrubby and wooded areas and gardens in the vicinity of water, and can frequently be found alongside rivers and streams, where it hawks insects from exposed perches. Ranges from South-east Asia through the Malay Peninsula and Borneo to Sumatra, but not found in Java or Bali. In Sumatra it is common at lowland forest edges.

Banded Pitta *Pitta guajana* 22cm

A beautiful ground-living bird with a distinct plumage. Three races are present in the region, all having a black head with a long, broad yellow eyebrow and a white chin. The tail is blue and the back and wing-coverts brown. The wings are dark brown and have a thin white wingbar. The Sumatran race (*P. g. irena*) has breast and flanks barred blue and orange, a blue belly and orange nape, and more distinct wingbar. In West Java, *P. g. affinis* has breast and flanks barred black and yellow. *P. g. guajana* in East Java and Bali is also barred black and yellow, but has a blue bar on the upper breast. Inhabits mainly lowland forest and shaded dense thickets.

Hooded Pitta *Pitta sordida* 18cm

A forest-floor dweller, this bird hops around foraging for various insects among the leaf litter and rotting wood. It is a plump medium-sized pitta with long legs. Residents have a green plumage with a black head, blue-grey wing-coverts, and crimson undertail-coverts and lower belly. Migrants have a dark brown cap. The bill is black and the legs are pinkish. If disturbed, it flies close to the ground with rapid wingbeats. In flight, it reveals conspicuous rounded white patches on the wings. Not found in Bali, but resident and wintering northern populations occur in Sumatra and West Java.

Australasian Bushlark *Mirafra javanica* 14cm

This small bird occasionally perches in trees, but is more often seen walking around on the ground. It is a black-mottled russet-brown, with paler underparts and white outer tail feathers. Its short pinkish-grey legs have long claws. The brown bill is tinged yellow below. It has a weak undulating flight. Like many other larks, it has a fluttering hover-flight in which it often sings, with a high-pitched trilling, before gliding slowly back to ground. Not found in Sumatra, but fairly common in Java and Bali, particularly in open areas of short grass, paddyfield stubble and dry cultivated fields.

Barn Swallow *Hirundo rustica* 20cm

The Barn Swallow is more likely to be seen wheeling in circles and gliding with an occasional flutter high in the sky, hunting aerial insects. Depending on the weather conditions, it may come very low and be seen skimming the surface of lakes and streams. It also often perches on overhead wires and bare branches. This gregarious bird sometimes gathers in huge flocks to roost in reedbeds, tall grasses and even on city buildings. It is dark blue above, with a white breast and very long outer tail feathers. The forehead is red, and the throat red with a blue bar below. Juveniles are duller and lack the tail-streamers. A common winter visitor throughout the region, from breeding grounds in northern latitudes.

78

Pacific Swallow *Hirundo tahitica* 14cm

Similar in appearance to the Barn Swallow, but lacking the long tail-streamers and the blue bar across the upper chest. The breast appears a dirty buffish-white. It otherwise has a dark blue plumage with a chestnut-red forehead. It has brown feet and a black bill. This swallow usually forms small parties with other hirundines and swiftlets to feed over water. It neither roosts nor nests communally, preferring an isolated mud nest fixed under an overhanging ledge, bridge or roof. It is resident throughout the region.

Yellow Wagtail *Motacilla flava* 18cm

Many subspecific variations in plumage occur throughout the many races of this species, especially in winter plumage, and it is difficult to identify many individuals in the field. Of typical wagtail shape and behaviour, the species is olive-brown or olive-green on the back, with yellow underparts. The commonly occurring race, *M. f. simillima*, has a grey crown, yellow throat and white supercilium, and any variations could relate to other, more rare races. Immatures have browner upperparts and whiter underparts. A common winter visitor from Eurasia, found mainly around coastal lowlands, particularly pastureland, paddyfields and dried-up marshland.

79

Grey Wagtail *Motacilla cinerea* 19cm

Tilford/Cooke, TC Nature

A typical wagtail in shape and tail-wagging behaviour, running and skipping among the rocks and running water. Its flight is markedly undulating. It has a grey crown and mantle, with bright yellow on underparts and rump. The chin and eye-stripe are whitish and the ear-coverts greyish. The underparts of juveniles are much paler. The very long black tail is edged white. The bill is dark brown and the feet pinkish-grey. Mainly a winter migrant from northern latitudes, preferring stony river beds, streams and damp meadowland from the coast to tops of mountains.

Richard's Pipit *Anthus richardi* 18cm

Chew Yen Fook

The only pipit resident in the region. On the ground it appears as a pale, long-legged bird, often seen running around in grassland, and at other times very still in an upright posture. It is warm brown above with darker streaks, and buff below with fine streaking on the upper breast. It has a pale rump and uppertail-coverts and a prominent buff eyebrow. The flight feathers are dark brown, edged buff. In flight, the white outer feathers of the dark brown tail are very visible. Attracted to open grassland and cultivated land, dry paddyfields and roadside verges. Widespread and abundant from the coast to the mountains.

Small Minivet *Pericrocotus cinnamomeus* 15cm

David Tipling, Windrush Photos

Like other minivets, this one is rather gregarious, moving among the treetops in small groups, continually calling to each other as they search out insects and ripe fruits. The head, mantle and upper back are grey, with rump, vent and outer tail orange. The long central tail feathers are black, and the black wings have a prominent yellow-orange patch. Males have a black throat and red to orange belly; females are paler, with a whitish breast. It inhabits the more open lowland forest and also trees and copses around cultivated land, gardens and mangroves. Widespread in Java and Bali.

Scarlet Minivet *Pericrocotus flammeus* 19cm

Tilford/Cooke, TC Nature

A forest-dwelling bird which forages through the treetops in small groups. The male's head and mantle are jet-black with a blue sheen, and the underparts, rump and outer edges of the tail are red. The mainly black wing has two distinct red patches. The female has a grey crown and upperparts, with yellow to orange underparts and outer tail; the yellow underparts continue up to the chin, forehead and ear-coverts, but leaving a suggestion of a grey eye-stripe. She has two yellowish wing patches, and her rump is grey-green. Locally common throughout the region.

81

Straw-headed Bulbul *Pycnonotus zeylanicus* 28cm

Chew Yen Fook

Its clear melodious song is responsible for this species' popularity as a cagebird in Indonesia, where birds are exported from Sumatra to Java and Bali. It is one of the largest bulbuls, and can be recognized by its golden-straw-coloured crown and ear-coverts and its black moustachial stripe. The back, wings and tail are shades of greenish-brown. It also has a thin black eye-stripe, and a white chin and throat, grey breast and belly, and yellow vent, the upper breast and back having a small amount of white streaking. Once a common bird of lowland and hill forest, particularly of riverine habitat, it is now becoming scarce.

Black-headed Bulbul *Pycnonotus atriceps* 17cm

Usually alone, but also in small groups foraging with other species, this bulbul can be recognized by its mainly yellow body plumage and glossy black head and throat. The upperparts are greenish-yellow tinged brown, and the underparts are a bit brighter. The wings are black, and the tail yellow with a black subterminal bar. A rare colour form exists in which the yellow areas are replaced by a dull grey, but it has a white vent and undertail-coverts and white tip to the tail. It is more often seen at forest edges, in riverine and coastal scrub and often along roadsides, and in secondary forest. Fairly common in lowland areas of Sumatra and Java, but much less common in Bali.

Black-crested Bulbul *Pycnonotus melanicterus* 18cm

Sometimes referred to as the Ruby-throated Bulbul, the subspecies *P. m. dispar* is resident in Sumatra, Java and Bali and is distinguished by its bright red throat. It is quite a large olive-tinged yellow-green bulbul with black head and upright tufty crest. The underparts are paler, and the iris is either cream-coloured or dull red. It is relatively timid, keeping out of sight in well-foliaged tall trees in secondary forest and along forest edges as it searches for ripe fruits. It is reasonably common in both lowland and hill forests of Sumatra, but its numbers seem to decline going eastwards through Java.

Orange-spotted Bulbul *Pycnonotus bimaculatus* 20cm

Ray Tipper

This is quite a noisy bird with its harsh continual *toc-toc-toc-toroc* call, often several birds joining in a chorus as they roam the trees in search of fruit. It is brown to olive-brown above, with paler ear-coverts and two distinguishing orange spots, one around the lores and the other above the eye. The throat is black, blending into a brown upper breast that becomes off-white with brown mottling as it leads to a white belly. The vent is bright yellow. Some birds from north Sumatra have a grey belly. A common endemic, found at montane forest edges and in clearings almost to the top of the highest mountains, where it is attracted to fruiting blueberries.

83

Yellow-vented Bulbul *Pycnonotus goiavier* 20cm

Chew Yen Fook

This quite gregarious bird not only forages with other bulbuls but also roosts communally. It is frequently seen picking over fallen fruit and taking the occasional insect. It has a bright yellow vent, as its name implies, but is otherwise relatively sombre in plumage. The upperparts and tail are brown and the underparts white. The crown is dark brown and the face white, with black lores. It has pinkish-grey feet and a black bill. Common throughout the region, preferring a more open habitat and especially attracted to cultivation, plantations, gardens and parks, even in towns.

Olive-winged Bulbul *Pycnonotus plumosus* 20cm

Morten Strange

Like several other bulbuls, this one has rather dull, nondescript brownish-grey plumage with olive-coloured wings. It is greener and larger than the similar Cream-vented Bulbul. The throat is pale buff and the undertail-coverts pale brown. The ear-coverts are brown, streaked with white. It has red eyes, a black bill and brown legs. It keeps to the treetops as it forages for ripe fruit and insects, occasionally uttering a short, soft chirping song. Found through Sumatra and West and Central Java, but not in Bali, this is a resident bird of lowland woods and forest edge, as well as secondary growth and occasionally scrubland.

84

Cream-vented Bulbul *Pycnonotus simplex* 17cm

Morten Strange

Similar to but smaller than the Olive-winged Bulbul, this species is easily separated as the race found in Sumatra and Java has white eyes. The upperparts are a dull brownish-grey, the belly white and the vent cream. Both chin and throat are pale buff to white. The bill is black and the legs brown. An inhabitant of forest, it also ventures into more open countryside, secondary growth and sometimes plantations, but invariably it keeps to the treetops. In Sumatra it is fairly common in lowland primary forest, but in Java it is now restricted to the southern lowland forests.

Red-eyed Bulbul *Pycnonotus brunneus* 17cm

Chew Yen Fook

Another of the smaller bulbuls found in Sumatra but not in Bali or on the Javan mainland. It is very similar to but smaller and much browner than the Olive-winged Bulbul, and its ear-coverts are brown, lacking any white streaking. The underparts are buff, with the breast buff-brown. The red eyes of the adult are brown in juveniles, and the legs and bill are brown. These birds inhabit the higher canopy, where they forage for insects and ripe fruits. Relatively common throughout the lowland forests, with a tendency to be found more at the edges of the more scrubby secondary forest.

85

Common Iora *Aegithina tiphia* 14cm

Tilford/Cooke, TC Nature

This very secretive little leafbird requires patience if you want to get a good view of it. It habitually remains among the leaves of small trees, using its colour as a marvellous camouflage. It has olive-green to bright green upperparts, a white rump, and yellow underparts. The wings are black, with fairly distinct white and yellow edges and two very clear wingbars. There is a clear yellow eye-ring. Both bill and feet are bluish-grey. Mostly alone but often in pairs, it inhabits open woodland, secondary forest and mangroves, but can frequently be found in town gardens. Quite common in the lowlands of Sumatra, Java and Bali.

Greater Green Leafbird *Chloropsis sonnerati* 22cm

Of the seven leafbirds resident in the region, the Greater Green Leafbird is by far the largest. It is generally bright green on the back and tail, with slightly paler underparts. The male has a black throat and face with a blue malar stripe, and the shoulder of the wing is marked by a small blue spot. The female has a yellow throat edged by a blue malar stripe, with a distinctive yellow eye-ring. Juveniles are very like the female, with the blue malar stripe being very dull or non-existent. Typically found with other leafbirds in small flocks, high in dense foliage of tall trees in mangroves and primary or secondary forest.

Blue-winged Leafbird *Chloropsis cochinchinensis* 17cm

Two subspecies of this leafbird are found in the region: *C. c. icterocephala* is found in Sumatra and *C. c. nigricollis* in Java. Both have the typical colour of most leafbirds, being generally yellowish-green above and more yellow below. This species is recognized by the blue wings and edges of the tail. The male has a black patch below the eye which extends down into a yellow-bordered black throat. The Sumatran race has a yellow crown and yellow to orange nape, whereas the Javan race has a green crown and yellow upper breast. Females lack the black head and throat markings. All have a blue malar stripe, a little less evident on females. Absent from Bali.

Male (top); *female* (bottom)

Golden-fronted Leafbird *Chloropsis aurifrons* 19cm

The male is identified by the bright golden-yellow patch on the forehead and a large black throat patch extending up to the eye and across to the base of the bill. The centre of the throat is ultramarine-blue. The rest of the plumage is bright leaf-green but for a small shiny pale blue patch on the shoulder. Females are bright leaf-green all over, apart from the blue shoulder patch and a blue malar stripe. A common resident of mixed and deciduous hill forests of Sumatra. Like so many other birds with a pleasant musical song, it is trapped for the pet trade and kept as a cagebird not only in Sumatra, but in Java, Bali and worldwide.

Tilford/Cooke, TC Nature

87

Asian Fairy Bluebird *Irena puella* 25cm

Tilford/Cooke, TC Nature

Apart from the black face, neck, underparts, tail and primaries, the male's plumage is brilliant blue. Females are a duller blue with a greenish tinge, apart from their brighter blue rump. It can be distinguished from other bright blue and black birds by its larger size. More likely to be seen at fruiting fig trees, where it is often in mixed flocks with other birds. Otherwise it confines itself to foraging, usually out of sight, through the tops of tall trees of primary and secondary forest. Commonly found in the lowland forests of Sumatra, but less so in Java and not at all in Bali.

Long-tailed Shrike *Lanius shach* 25cm

The long black tail, upright stance and brown, black and white plumage make this shrike easily identifiable. It has a grey crown and nape, with chestnut mantle, back and rump; the underparts are clean white. Adults have a black mask from the forehead through the eye and across the ear-coverts. Juveniles tend to be duller, with dark grey head and nape and barring on flanks and back. Often in pairs, it roams through grassland and scrub, venturing into cultivated land and plantations up to the edge of human habitation. Quite common in open areas, frequently seen perched on bare branches scanning for aerial insects or grasshoppers. Resident in Java, Bali and Sumatra.

White-browed Shortwing *Brachypteryx montana* 15cm

Chew Yen Fook

This tiny member of the thrush family is very timid, seldom leaving the protection of undergrowth on the forest floor. However, it becomes bolder near to mountain tops where it can often be seen in the open. It usually skulks beneath bushes, feeding on invertebrates and occasionally berries. Its presence is often advertised by its high-pitched resonating alarm call. Males have dark blue plumage all over, with a conspicuous white supercilium. Females vary being all blue in Sumatra but in Java they have a blue head and nape with rufous wings, back and tail. Ranges from Nepal through to China and SE Asia to Flores.

Oriental Magpie Robin *Copsychus saularis* 20cm

Two subspecies are found in the region, *C. s. musicus* in Sumatra and West Java and *C. s. pluto* in East Java and Bali. The former has black wings and central tail, with white outer tail feathers, belly and vent, and a broad white patch across the wing-coverts. East Javan and Bali birds are all black, except for the white wing-covert patch. Females are much duller, with the black plumage replaced by grey. Juveniles have similar but mottled plumage. Common in the lowlands, with a wide choice of habitat from mangroves and forests to town gardens, although trapping for the pet trade has caused a serious decline.

White-rumped Shama *Copsychus malabaricus* 27cm

Another beautiful songster which has declined through the actions of trappers for the pet trade. This bird spends a lot of time foraging in low dense undergrowth, hopping around on the ground. The male has a very long tail, about half its total length, with dull black central feathers and white outers, which it habitually flicks on landing. Its head, neck, back and wings are black with a blue sheen, its lower underparts are deep orange, and it has a conspicuous white patch on the rump. Common in Sumatra, where it sticks to denser parts of the forest, but far less numerous in Java.

Pied Bushchat *Saxicola caprata* 13cm

Tilford/Cooke, TC Nature

Like all the chats, this bird prefers a habitat of scrubby grassland, where it perches on exposed bushes or posts to locate its insect prey. Males are all black, apart from a white rump, vent and distinctive wingbar. Females have dark brown streaked upperparts, dark brown tail, buff underparts with rufous flanks, and pale rufous-brown rump. Juveniles are spotted dark and light brown. Often sings from a prominent perch while cocking its tail. A fairly common resident of the dry open lowlands of Java and Bali, occurring sporadically in the hills; not present in Sumatra.

Sunda Whistling Thrush *Myophonus glaucinus* 25cm

Two races occur in the region. The Sumatran race (*M. g. castaneus*) is the larger, the male having a dark blue head and upper breast, with the nape and shoulders a brighter blue; the lower back, wings and tail are dark chestnut-brown, with lighter belly and undertail-coverts. The female is duller, with blue shoulders and black crown. In the smaller Javan race (*M. g. glaucinus*), the male is dark blue with blackish underparts. The plumage is more uniform than that of other whistling thrushes, lacking spangles. Both races have a blackish bill. An endemic of the Greater Sundas.

Blue Whistling Thrush *Myophonus caeruleus* 32cm

Chew Yen Fook

A largish blue-black thrush having a moderate purplish sheen and sparsely flecked and spangled white on the wing-coverts. The contrasting yellow bill is often marked with black, particularly on Sumatran birds. Legs are black. It has a high-pitched screeching alarm, *screech-chit-chit chit*, and a loud whistling song often incorporating imitations of other birds' songs. A ground feeder, taking insects, invertebrates and small fruits, it is generally found in denser lowland hill forests beside rivers and among exposed limestone rock formations. Absent from Bali and not very common in Java or Sumatra.

91

Orange-headed Thrush *Zoothera citrina* 21cm

The usual haunts of this thrush are in more secluded forest among thick undergrowth, but its high-pitched whistling alarm call betrays its presence. It has a very nice song and this, along with its attractive colouring, makes it a prime target for local bird-keepers and, more recently, the export pet trade. Its head, nape and belly are bright orange, the back grey-blue, and the tail and wings dark grey. It has a white vent and wingbar. The female has greenish-brown upperparts. Widespread from Pakistan through to the Greater Sundas, but many of those seen in Sumatra are likely migrants; in Java and Bali it is a bird of hill forest and lowland, but is not really common.

Chestnut-capped Thrush *Zoothera interpres* 16cm

Chew Yen Fook

Chestnut-capped as its name implies, this small thrush otherwise has a pied appearance. The chestnut crown extends down the nape, stopping at the slate-grey mantle and upperparts. It has two distinctive broad white wingbars. The throat and upper breast are dense black, leading into a black-spotted lower breast and flanks and white belly and vent. The bill is blackish-brown and the legs pink. It has a typical thrush diet of invertebrates, and often takes fruit and berries. Occurs in Java, but rarely in Bali and Sumatra.

Scaly Thrush *Zoothera dauma* 28cm

David Tipling, Windrush Photos

In typical thrush fashion, this species spends much of the time for-aging on the ground. It has only a quiet whistling song and just a feeble *tzeeet* alarm call. Its upperparts are brown with golden-brown and blackish scaly markings, these being bolder on the back and upperwing-coverts. The brown-scaled underparts are more whitish, with a pale chestnut wash on the upper breast and flanks. It prefers dense wooded areas and montane forest in Java and Bali, but in Sumatra is confined to the mountain woodland of the north. Found from north-east Europe west through to the Sundas and as far as Australia.

Island Thrush *Turdus poliocephalus* 20cm

Morten Strange

This is a medium-sized thrush with a dark grey head blending into dull blackish upperparts. The throat and upper breast are mid-grey, while the belly is chestnut and the vent white. The eye-ring, bill and legs are yellow. It has a pleasantly melodious song and a rather rau-cous rattling alarm call. This is a bird of the highest mountains, but it is rare in Bali. It is more common in Java, where it can usually be seen close to the volcano on Mt Tangkuban Perahu and in the mossy forests of Mt Gede. In Sumatra, the peaks of Mt Leuser are its home.

White-chested Babbler *Trichastoma rostratum* 15cm

This small jungle babbler has fairly plain coloration of dark brown upperparts and buffish-white underparts. The sides of the breast are tinged grey and the flanks are tinged brown. The bill is black and the legs pinkish. The Moustached Babbler (*Malacopteron magnirostre*) and the Sooty-capped Babbler (*Malacopteron affine*) are similar in size; it can be separated from the former by not having a black malar stripe or eye-ring, and from the latter by having a brown (not black) cap and no pale eyebrow. Absent from Bali and Java, but occurs in small groups in the damp lowland forests and mangroves of Sumatra.

Horsfield's Babbler *Malacocincla sepiarium* 14cm

Chew Yen Fook

This noisy little babbler has a monotonous and repetitive call, *pee-o-eet, pee-o-eet* ..., given particularly at dawn and dusk. Usually in pairs or small groups, it forages for insects among low vegetation. The upperparts are warm russet-brown, becoming chestnut on the rump and tail. The flanks and vent are also chestnut, while the throat and belly are white and the breast grey. It has a heavy grey and black bill. Separated from Abbott's Babbler by its darker and greyer crown. This is a locally common resident throughout the region in the dense undergrowth and low thickets of hill and submontane forests.

94

Abbott's Babbler *Malacocincla abbotti* 16cm

Chew Yen Fook

Like Horsfield's Babbler, Abbott's is small and brown and has a heavy bill. It is distinguished by being lighter and duller and having a longer tail. The upperparts are brownish-olive, with a pale chestnut rump. The underparts are buffish-white on the throat, with a pale grey-green breast, buffish-brown belly and rufous undertail-coverts. The sides of the head are buffish-brown with a pale grey supercilium. Usually found low down at forest edges and in scrub and thickets, generally singly or in small groups. Locally common in Sumatran lowland forests, with a few records for Javan islands, but absent from Bali.

Chestnut-backed Scimitar Babbler *Pomatorhinus montanus* 20cm

This bird has a striking greyish-black head with a long white eyebrow, and a longish, decurved buffish-yellow bill with black at the base. The throat and breast are white, the back, flanks and vent chestnut-brown, and the tail and wings dark brown. The feet are grey. It is frequently seen in pairs or small groups with laughingthrushes, foraging in ground litter and through low bushes but also in the lower tree canopy. The subspecies from Sumatra (*P. m. occidentalis*) is quite common in lowland and hill forest, whereas birds from West Java (*P. m. montanus*) and those in East Java and Bali (*P. m. ottolanderi*) tend to occupy higher montane forests.

Tilford/Cooke, TC Nature

Rusty-breasted Wren Babbler *Napothera rufipectus* 18cm

F Lambert

One of the more substantial ground-hugging babblers, this species prefers dense cover in both lower and upper montane forest in which to seek out its mainly insect food. It can be recognized by its generally brown-streaked appearance and its white throat. The upperparts are dark brown with light brown and black streaking, and the underparts streaked dark and light chestnut. The short tail and the primaries are dark brown. Like many of the wren babblers, it has various loud whistling calls. An endemic, found particularly in the remoter mountains of the Barisan range in Sumatra.

Striped Tit Babbler *Macronous gularis* 13cm

Morten Strange

The upperparts of this small tit babbler are all chestnut-brown, including the tail. The underparts, in particular the breast, are conspicuously streaked finely with black on an underwash of pale yellowish-green, becoming whitish at the lower belly and vent; the Javan race is more greyish below. The sides of the head are grey, sometimes tinged yellow. The bill is brown and the legs grey-blue. A common bird in lowland Sumatra, where it lives in small groups in dense thickets, especially bamboo, and secondary growth. An occasional resident in West Java, but not found in Bali.

Rufous-fronted Laughingthrush *Garrulax rufifrons* 27cm

This species is particularly noisy when roaming beneath the canopy with other birds, foraging for insects. It is a largish babbler with a long tail. The plumage is mostly a soft olive-brown but with a slight reddish tinge below. The throat is white to fawn, with a reddish chin and forehead, and the wings are chestnut. The bill is black and the feet a dirty yellow-brown. An endemic, inhabiting mainly primary mountain forests of the western half of Java. Although restricted in range, locally it does not appear uncommon.

White-crested Laughingthrush *Garrulax leucolophus* 30cm

The white head and black face-mask with a superficial erectile crest are distinguishing marks of this cocky babbler. It is an arboreal bird, found in the lower storeys of primary and secondary hill and montane forest. Forms noisy flocks with others of its kind, foraging through the foliage with occasional visits to the ground. West Sumatra is the eastern limit of the species' natural range. The Sumatran subspecies has a dark back and short crest. The chestnut-backed subspecies found elsewhere in Asia (depicted here), is a popular cagebird in Java, and escapes are often encountered.

97

White-browed Shrike Babbler *Pteruthius flaviscapis* 13cm

Chew Yen Fook

Usually seen in pairs with other species, this plump little bird appears to have a proportionately large head and thickish bill. In characteristic manner it sidles along branches in search of food. Males have a black head with a conspicuous white eyebrow, grey mantle and back, and black wings and tail, with the primaries tipped white and the tertials tinged chestnut and yellow. The underparts are whitish. Females have a grey head with less distinct eyebrow, and greyish-green upperparts. Found in the more open lower montane forests of Java and Sumatra.

Silver-eared Mesia *Leiothrix argentauris* 18cm

This brightly coloured medium-sized babbler has a deep black head enhanced by silver ear-coverts. The mantle, breast and forehead are bright red, sometimes orange-red, as are the rump, undertail and primary coverts, and the back, tail and wing-coverts are grey-green. Both bill and legs are yellow. It has a cheerful little whistled song and a range of other chattering calls. A locally common resident of montane and secondary forests, particularly fond of dense thickets but also inhabiting forest edges and more open scrub, it occurs from the Himalayas through to Sumatra. Often kept as a cagebird.

Oriental Reed Warbler *Acrocephalus orientalis* 18cm

Chew Yen Fook

This is a fairly large brown warbler with a very obvious pale buff supercilium underlined by a thin dark brown eye-stripe. Its underparts are whitish, blending into buff on the flanks, rump and upper belly, with the upper belly and the sides of the breast sparsely streaked brown. The largish bill is brown above and tinged pink below, and the legs are blue-grey. A regular winter migrant, visiting the region from its breeding grounds in eastern Asia, this species is usually found in lowland reedbeds and marshes, but frequently occurs also in rice fields and scrub close by water.

Zitting Cisticola *Cisticola juncidis* 10cm

Tilford/Cooke, TC Nature

Commonly known as the Fan-tailed Warbler, this little bird occurs from Africa and Europe through India, South-east Asia and the Sundas down to northern Australia. It is a small, rather inconspicuous brown bird, heavily streaked with dark brown and buff on its upperparts. It has white underparts and vent, with warm buff flanks, and the brown and black tail is tipped white. Its white supercilium distinguishes it from the Bright-headed Cisticola. A common grassland and reedbed bird throughout the lowlands of Sumatra, Java and Bali, and naturally attracted to the wetter habitat of rice paddies.

Bright-headed Cisticola *Cisticola exilis* 11cm

Non-breeding birds and females are very similar to the Zitting Cisticola. They differ in having a more golden head colour and in the buff supercilium being the same colour as the nape and head sides. The throat is white and the underparts buff. The dark brown tail is tipped buff. Also known as the Golden-headed Cisticola, breeding males have a golden-yellow crown and brown rump. In the lowlands of Java and Bali this is a common bird of alang-alang grassland, as well as rice paddies and reedbeds; only locally common in Sumatra. It prefers taller grass than the Zitting Cisticola.

Bar-winged Prinia *Prinia familiaris* 13cm

A noisy, versatile and gregarious little bird, often uttering its loud high-pitched 'tweeting' call as it searches for insects from ground to treetop. It is recognized by its long tail of black- and white-tipped feathers, rather drab olive-brown upperparts, and two distinctive white wingbars. The white of the throat extends down the middle of the upper belly, with the flanks pale grey and lower belly and vent pale yellow. It favours secondary growth, especially parks and gardens, mangroves, plantations and scrub. A very common endemic in the lowlands of Java and Bali, but less so in Sumatra, particularly in the north.

Yellow-bellied Prinia *Prinia flaviventris* 13cm

Chew Yen Fook

This prinia has a weak song and shy habits, with a tendency to remain hidden among long grass and reeds. Appearing as a long-tailed warbler, it has olive-brown upperparts and tail, a bright yellow belly, and a very evident white chin, throat and upper breast. The head is greyish with a reddish-orange eye-ring and a very thin, and often broken, white supercilium. The legs and feet are a dull orange, and the bill is dark brown above and pale brown below. Found on Sumatra and West Java, it occurs fairly commonly in grassland, reedbeds and thick scrub in the lowlands.

Mountain Tailorbird *Orthotomus cuculatus* 12cm

Chew Yen Fook

A gregarious and timid little bird, very difficult to observe as it moves around in small groups, foraging through the thickest vegetation. It can be identified by its bell-like tinkling call of about three or four notes, culminating in a short trill. Like most of the tailorbirds, it has olive upperparts and a high-cocked tail. Apart from the orange forehead, the head and upper breast are grey, but lighter on the throat and centre of the breast, the remaining underparts and vent being bright yellow. An inhabitant of montane forests throughout the region, more commonly found in bamboo thickets, evergreen forests and scrub.

101

Ashy Tailorbird *Orthotomus ruficeps* 11cm

A small and rather plain-coloured tailorbird with a grey-brown back and greyish underparts, becoming white on the belly. Males have a dark rufous face, crown and throat, whereas females have a white throat and a much paler rufous face and crown. This energetic little bird is frequently seen in more open lowland forests, where it forages among the treetops. It also occurs in mangroves and coastal scrubland, as well as bamboo thickets and well-vegetated gardens. Common in Sumatra, but in Java found only in the northern wetland areas, and absent from Bali.

Arctic Warbler *Phylloscopus borealis* 12cm

This small leaf warbler spends much of its time foraging through wooded areas in search of insects, often accompanying other warblers and small insectivores. It is identified by its conspicuous long yellowish-white supercilium above a blackish eye-stripe. It also has a poorly defined single white wingbar. The upperparts are dark olive and the underparts almost white, blending to olive-brown on the flanks. Similar to the smaller Yellow-browed or Inornate Warbler (*Phylloscopus inornatus*), but much duller and with less obvious wingbars. A winter visitor from northern Asia, found generally at primary and secondary lowland forest edges and mangroves.

Mountain Leaf Warbler *Phylloscopus trivirgatus* 11cm

Chew Yen Fook

Like many of the leaf warblers, this bird is not easy to see as it flits through the tree canopy, often in mixed groups, foraging for insects. It is mainly green above, with greenish-yellow underparts. Its prominent greenish-yellow median crown-stripe and supercilium are interspaced with a blackish stripe along the crown side and a black eye-stripe. The legs are grey, and the bill black above with a reddish tinge on the lower mandible. Juveniles are duller and greener below. Fairly common in the region's montane forests, keeping to the treetops and forest edges.

Asian Brown Flycatcher *Muscicapa dauurica* 12cm

Chew Yen Fook

This species of submontane forest and forest edges can frequently be found in plantations, open forest and even gardens. It hunts for aerial insects from exposed perches, often shaking its tail on arrival back at the perch. It is greyish-brown above and whitish below, becoming grey-brown on the flanks and the sides of the breast, and has a pale eye-ring. The black bill has a yellow base to the lower mandible. Almost certainly a winter migrant to the region from north-east Asia, but some may be resident in north Sumatra. Occurring throughout the lowlands of the Greater Sundas, it is particularly common on offshore islands.

103

Verditer Flycatcher *Eumyias thalassina* 16cm

Tilford/Cooke, TC Nature

This is a fairly large blue flycatcher. In typical flycatcher fashion it chooses exposed perches from which it can launch its attacks on passing aerial insects. It prefers open forest and forest edges, but is often seen perched high in the tree canopy. The male's plumage is a fairly uniform greenish-blue, with white fringing to the undertail-coverts giving a scaled appearance. The area around the lores is dark grey to black. Females look duller and greener, and juveniles are a mottled brown tinged with green. The feet and bill are black. Found in the lowlands and hills of Sumatra.

Indigo Flycatcher *Eumyias indigo* 14cm

Morten Strange

The plumage of this species is mainly a deep indigo-blue colour, especially on the upperparts and breast, the blue becoming dense blue-black on the throat and face towards the base of the bill. The forehead is tinged white, leading into a bluish-white supercilium. The belly is grey, becoming white and then buff at the vent. The legs and bill are black. Confined to dense forest, where it often mixes with other species low in the canopy and often close to the ground. It is a relatively common resident of montane and submontane forests in Java, but less so in Sumatra, and is not found in Bali.

Little Pied Flycatcher *Ficedula westermanni* 11cm

Chew Yen Fook

This species is sexually dimorphic, the male being black and white and the female brown and white. The male's upperparts are all black, apart from a white wingbar and supercilium and also white edges to the base of the outer tail feathers. The underparts are all white, and the legs and bill black. Females have brown upperparts and whitish underparts, the tail being rufous-brown. It frequently mixes with other species, feeding throughout the forest, and it has a quiet *pi-pi-pi-pi* call followed by a vibrating churring sound. Relatively common at the edges of submontane forests above 1000m.

Hill Blue Flycatcher *Cyornis banyumas* 15cm

Males have dark blue upperparts with iridescence on the forehead, eyebrow and shoulder. The chin, lores and a thin line around the eye are black, as is the bill, while the throat and breast are rufous-orange, blending into white at the lower belly and vent. The legs are dark brown. Females have brown upperparts with an off-white eye-ring, and underparts similar to the male's but paler. This is a bird of high mountain forests, favouring low undergrowth and bamboo thickets and the edges of forest glades. Ranges from Nepal through China to Borneo and Java, but it is not found in Bali or Sumatra.

105

Mangrove Blue Flycatcher *Cyornis rufigastra* 15cm

Not only are different races of the Mangrove Blue Flycatcher present in the region, other very similar species also occur which can cause confusion. Considering all factors together, it is not difficult to separate this one. It has blue upperparts and orange underparts, although the female is paler and has a whitish chin and a white loral patch. It is most likely to be confused with the Hill Blue Flycatcher (*Cyornis banyumas*), which also has a clear melodious, warbling song, but that has a pale blue forehead and blackish chin. Usually inhabits coastal forests, plantations and mangroves close to the beach.

Golden-bellied Gerygone *Gerygone sulphurea* 9cm

Chew Yen Fook

Also known as the Flyeater, this is the only Australian fairy-warbler found in the region. As a tiny but active bird, and well disguised among foliage, it is noticed more by its shrill fluty song. Its upperparts are brown-tinged grey, and its underparts bright yellow. The chin and neck are white, and it often shows a whitish loral spot. The dark grey-brown tail is tipped black, with a subterminal line of white spots. It shows a preference for open forest and bamboo and conifer thickets, as well as mangroves and even plantations, and is quite common up to around 1500m.

Black-naped Monarch *Hypothymis azurea* 16cm

When this beautiful flycatcher leaves the shade of woodland and comes into the open, its delightful azure-blue head and back are very obvious. The male's head has a short erect black crest on the hind-crown and a thin black band above and below the bill. Another narrow black band extends across the upper breast, with the grey belly paling to a white vent. The wings are grey and the tail blue-black. The bluish bill has a black tip. Females have a duller blue head and greyer breast, without any of the male's black markings. It prefers lowland and secondary forests, where it is usually common.

Pied Fantail *Rhipidura javanica* 19cm

This very active small bird is a typical fantail in its wing-drooping posture and regular flicking and fanning of the tail. The plumage is black and white, and it has a diagnostic black band across the otherwise white underparts. When the tail is fanned, the broad white tips to the feathers are very obvious. The upperparts are a dusky black, and there is a thin white eyebrow. Both bill and legs are black. It is found particularly in mangroves, open woodland and secondary growth at elevations of up to 1500m, and is often present in gardens. A common resident throughout the region.

Golden Whistler *Pachycephala pectoralis* 17cm

The male of this species has quite brilliant colouring of black, white and bright yellow. The yellow nape patch is joined by a narrow yellow band right through to the breast, belly and vent, while the head is black except for a white chin and throat, leaving a narrow black band between the throat and belly. The upperparts are olive-green and the tail is almost black. Females are much duller, having drab olive upperparts and dirty buff underparts, with the lower belly and undertail-coverts tinged yellow. Found in hill and montane forest in East Java and Bali, but absent from Sumatra.

Great Tit *Parus major ambiguus/cinereus* 13cm

Of the world's 31 subspecies of Great Tit, two are resident in the region, both very similar in appearance but quite different from those at the extremes of the species' range. Those in Sumatra, Java and Bali are relatively small, black, white and grey birds. The head and throat are black, with a black strip from throat down to vent; the ventral strip is wide on males, but on females can be very narrow and even broken. There is a large white patch on the cheek and a small white nape spot. Usually in pairs or small groups foraging for insects, particularly in mangroves and open forests, and often comes to gardens.

Velvet-fronted Nuthatch *Sitta frontalis* 12cm

Tilford/Cooke, TC Nature

A very active and attractive bird which, unlike other nuthatches in the region, is well adapted to creeping both up and down tree trunks in search of insects and spiders. It is identified by its red bill and reddish feet, dirty pinkish-white underparts and whitish throat. The upperparts are mainly violet-blue, with black-edged feathers in the tail and primaries, and the forehead is velvety-black. Usually seen in pairs but occasionally in small parties, moving erratically through the understorey branches of forests and plantations. Fairly common in lowland and hill forests in Sumatra and Java.

Blue Nuthatch *Sitta azurea* 13cm

Chew Yen Fook

This nuthatch typically forages along branches and tree trunks, levering off fragments of bark to get at grubs and insects. In shady forest it appears to have black upperparts, but in fact its back, wings and tail are shiny dark blue; only the crown, nape and sides of the face are black. The throat and breast are buffish-white. East Javan birds (*S. a. azurea*) have a bluish-black lower belly and vent, but these are black on West Javan and Sumatran birds (*S. a. nigriventer* and *S. a. expectata*). It has a yellow bill and grey feet. Not recorded in Bali, but in Sumatra and Java fairly common in lower mountain forests.

109

Crimson-breasted Flowerpecker *Prionochilus percussus* 10cm

Chew Yen Fook

The adult male is brilliantly coloured, with bright yellow underparts being broken only by a bright crimson breast patch. The upperparts are greyish-blue, with a bright red patch on the crown. The forehead and primaries are black and the tail is dark blue-grey. It has a white malar stripe finely underlined in black. Females are olive-green above, with only a tinge of orange on the crown, and have a yellow-tinged grey throat, a white malar stripe and a yellow belly with greyish-olive flanks; the undertail-coverts are distinctively white. A rather scarce and local bird of Sumatran and West Javan lowlands.

Yellow-vented Flowerpecker *Dicaeum chrysorrheum* 9cm

Chew Yen Fook

With its diagnostic plain bright yellow or orange undertail-coverts and its black-streaked white remaining underparts, this bird is unmistakable. Juveniles are duller, having only a pale yellow vent and greyish underparts with less obvious darker grey streaking. It has a repeated contact call, *tzit-tzit-tzit*, uttered especially in flight. This little flowerpecker seeks out its diet of insects and small fruits in open forest and secondary growth, occasionally venturing into gardens. It is found throughout the region's lowlands, but nowhere is it common.

Orange-bellied Flowerpecker *Dicaeum trigonostigma* 9cm

This tiny little bird frequents the tops of small trees, searching out small insects as well as small ripe fruits. It is very active, flitting among the forest canopy, garden trees and mangroves throughout the lowlands of the region. The orange belly, vent, rump and lower back, and the blue-grey head, wings and tail are diagnostic of the male. The female is pale olive-grey with a grey throat, becoming yellowish on the belly, the rump being dirty orange. The bill is black and the legs grey. Juveniles look like very dull females lacking yellow or orange.

Plain Flowerpecker *Dicaeum concolor* 8cm

Chew Yen Fook

Very small and rather drab compared with the males of other flowerpeckers, this bird is easily confused with females and juveniles of similar species and so may be overlooked. Both sexes have olive-green upperparts and greyish-olive underparts, becoming whitish-yellow along the centre of the belly up to the throat. Yellowish-white pectoral tufts are occasionally visible. It has a black bill, finer than that of many other flowerpeckers, and dark grey-blue legs. It inhabits hill forest and secondary growth, as well as plantations and cultivated areas, and is attracted to mistletoe. Found throughout the region.

111

Scarlet-backed Flowerpecker *Dicaeum cruentatum* 9cm

Males show scarlet-red on the crown, back and rump, and black on the sides of the face and neck as well as on the wings and tail. The underparts are greyish, with a wide pale buff band down the centre of the belly and on the throat. Females are olive-brown with paler throat and belly, have a scarlet rump and upper-tail-coverts, and lack the reddish-washed crown and mantle of the Scarlet-headed Flowerpecker (*Dicaeum trochileum*). A fairly common resident of Sumatran lowland and submontane forests, scrub, plantations and gardens, even in cities, it is also attracted to mistletoe.

Brown-throated Sunbird *Anthreptes malacensis* 13cm

Chew Yen Fook

Of the region's 12 different sunbirds, only Brown-throated and Olive-backed occur in Bali. They are the most common, found throughout the region, and are usually seen in open plantations, gardens, coastal scrub and mangroves. Identified by their bright coloration and long curved bill, they usually hover in front of flowers in search of nectar. The male Brown-throated has a yellow breast, belly and vent, and a brown throat often fringed with dark purple. The face and chin are olive and the upperparts are iridescent olive-green, blending into a dark bluish head with a green sheen. The female is olive-green above and yellowish below.

Ruby-cheeked Sunbird *Anthreptes singalensis* 10cm

Morten Strange

Although this small sunbird is brightly coloured, its iridescence when in the shade is not often visible and males even appear blackish. In bright light, however, the male's iridescent dark green upperparts and crown are brilliant and the ear-coverts reveal a deep red. The throat is orange-brown, blending into a yellow belly. Females (depicted here) are duller, with olive-green upperparts and pale orange and yellow underparts. The bill and legs are black, the legs often with a greenish tinge. This bird of forest edge and sparse woodland occurs alone and in pairs, often in the company of other species.

White-flanked Sunbird *Aethopyga eximia* 13cm

This colourful sunbird is aptly named after the cluster of soft white feathers on its flanks. Apart from the rather drab olive and black wings, longish blue-green tail and olive underparts, the male has a bright yellow rump and red throat and upper breast, the last crossed by a bluish-green necklace-like band, and his crown is iridescent purple. Except for the white flanks, the shorter-tailed female is dull olive, a little lighter on the throat and vent. This species is endemic to Java, where it is resident in mountain forests at forest edges and alpine scrub, and is particularly fond of flowering trees.

113

Copper-throated Sunbird *Nectarinia calcostetha* 13cm

Chew Yen Fook

Males dark, even appearing blackish. Upperparts have green iridescence and the breast and malar stripe purple. The throat and upper breast show a dark coppery-coloured gleam, while the flanks are yellow and the tail bluish-black. Separated from the smaller Purple-throated Sunbird by lacking the red breast but having yellow flanks. Females have a greyish head, dark olive-green to brown upperparts and black tail; their undertail-coverts and throat are pale grey, blending into a greenish-yellow breast. A mostly lowland resident in Java and Sumatra, found in coastal scrub, woodland and mangroves.

Olive-backed Sunbird *Nectarinia jugularis* 10cm

Chew Yen Fook

A very active and often noisy little bird, either flitting between flowers or hovering to extract nectar. It also feeds partly on insects and pollen. Quite small, with a long, curved black bill, it has olive-green upperparts with darker wings and black tail. The underparts are bright yellow, with white showing below the tail. Breeding males have a black chin and upper breast with a purple iridescence. The nest, a wonderfully woven structure of fine grasses and hair-like materials, is suspended precariously from the end of a branch or among foliage. It is found throughout the region, particularly in lowland areas.

114

Temminck's Sunbird *Aethopyga temminckii* male 13cm, female 10cm

Also known as the Scarlet Sunbird, this bright red sunbird has a relatively long and slightly notched red tail. Its upperparts, throat and breast are crimson-red, apart from the iridescent purple eyebrow which extends around the nape and the malar stripe. The uppertail coverts are also purple adjacent to a bright yellow rump patch. It has greyish-white underparts. Females are smaller with a shorter reddishbrown tail. They are dark olive-green above, with greyish head, wings tinged brown, and paler and yellowish below. It is an occasional bird of the more open montane forests of Sumatra and Borneo.

Chew Yen Fook

Javan Sunbird *Aethopyga mystacalis* 12cm

Now considered a separate species endemic to Java, this little sunbird, along with Temminck's Sunbird (*Aethopyga temminckii*), was previously considered to be a subspecies of the Crimson Sunbird (*Aethopyga siparaja*). It also goes by the name of Violet-tailed Sunbird. The male has a bright crimson head, breast and back, yellow rump, and long iridescent purple tail. The crown and malar stripe are also purplish, the wings olive-green and the underparts whitish. The female, very much smaller and with only a short tail, is dull olive-grey. It inhabits forests and forest edges, usually in pairs, and is particularly attracted to mistletoe flowers.

Little Spiderhunter *Arachnothera longirostra* 15cm

An inconspicuous little olive and yellow bird with a long, curved bill which is black above and grey below. The upperparts are drab olive-green and the underparts brilliant yellow. It can be separated from all similar species by its whitish throat. It inhabits gardens, plantations and logged forests, where it can often be seen moving rapidly across open areas as it searches for nectar, in particular from the flowers of banana and ginger. Common throughout the region, especially in lowland and hill forests, and in some areas way into the mountains.

Long-billed Spiderhunter *Arachnothera robusta* 21cm

Chew Yen Fook

This very long-billed and largish spiderhunter is normally a solitary bird, even to the extent of driving away all other spiderhunters that encroach on its territory. It has a habit of perching high on exposed branches and uttering its repeated and uninteresting call, *chew-lewt, chew-lewt*. In flight, it gives a simple *chit-chit* call. Its upperparts are olive and its underparts yellow, with the breast and throat streaked with olive-green. Separated from the Spectacled Spiderhunter (*Arachnothera flavigaster*) and the Yellow-eared Spiderhunter by lacking yellow ear patches or eye-rings. A resident of the lower hill forests of Java and Sumatra.

Yellow-eared Spiderhunter *Arachnothera chrysogenys* 17cm

The Yellow-eared is another sombrely plumaged spiderhunter which has olive-green upperparts and is olive-grey below, with moderate streaking on the breast. The vent is yellow. It has a largish yellow cheek patch and narrow and often incomplete eye-ring. It is not found in Bali, but in Sumatra it may be confused with the Spectacled Spiderhunter (*Arachnothera flavigaster*), which is, however, a more robust bird with a shorter bill and broad yellow eye-ring. It is usually found in lowland forest, along forest edges and in gardens.

Grey-breasted Spiderhunter *Arachnothera affinis* 17cm

Chew Yen Fook

More likely to be encountered around banana thickets and high in the tops of flowering trees, this species' most significant feature is the long, decurved bill. Its plumage is fairly dull, being olive-green above, with fine black streaking on the crown, and olive-tinged grey below with rather obscure black streaks. Tail and wings tend to be blacker. The subspecies in Java and Bali (*A. a. affinis*) has a pale yellow front edge to the wing and a yellow tinge to the breast. Sumatran birds (*A. a. concolor*) have a duller, more washed-out appearance. A common resident of coastal and lowland woodland and thickets of the region.

Oriental White-eye *Zosterops palpebrosus* 11cm

Tilford/Cooke, TC Nature

An active bird with upperparts bright olive-green, and a bright yellow throat merging into a greyish abdomen and undertail-coverts; wings and tail are darker. It has a ring of bright white feathering around the eye contrasting with darker face sides, and sometimes a yellowish forehead. The lores are black, bill dark brown and feet grey. Often in large flocks with other small birds, roaming the canopy. Ranges throughout the Sundas, inhabiting forest edges and mangroves; common in lowlands and hills up to about 1500m. A popular cagebird in Indonesia.

Mountain White-eye *Zosterops montanus* 11cm

Tilford/Cooke, TC Nature

More likely to be observed in noisy parties as it forages for insects through the treetops. Similar in size to other small white-eyes, this darker species resembles the Black-capped White-eye (*Zosterops atricapilla*) in Sumatra, but without the black on the head. Its upperparts are olive-green, with slightly darker wings and tail. The underparts are buffish-grey, becoming brownish on the flanks and yellow on the vent. The throat is also yellow. A very common bird of the region's lower mountains, preferring open forest and forest edge as well as plantations and copses in agricultural land. It is seldom found in the lowlands.

118

Javan White-eye *Zosterops flavus* 10cm

Smaller and paler than most other white-eyes, this species has fairly uniform bright olive-yellow upperparts and plain bright yellow underparts. Legs and bill are black, and it has a brown iris. It should not be confused with the slightly larger Lemon-bellied White-eye, which is a little duller and has a black loral spot. More a bird of coastal scrub and thickets, as well as mangroves, it is found in small flocks with other white-eyes, feeding on insects and nectar. A fairly rare endemic of Java's north-east coast, but more common in south Borneo.

Red Avadavat *Amandava amandava* 10cm

Tilford/Cooke, TC Nature

For most of the year males and females look alike but, as the breeding season approaches, sexually dimorphic plumage becomes very apparent. Females have greyish-brown upperparts and greyer sides to the head, with greyish-buff underparts and blackish wings and tail. The rump and bill are bright red. Breeding males become crimson-red on the back and breast, with small white spots on breast sides and flanks and also on the rump. The feet are pinkish-grey. Although still fairly common in East Java and Bali, trapping has reduced its numbers drastically in West Java and it is thought extinct in Sumatra.

119

Pin-tailed Parrotfinch *Erythrura prasina* 15cm

Tilford/Cooke, TC Nature

This pretty finch often mixes with large flocks of munias, raiding rice crops as they become ripe. The upperparts are green, the rump and tail red, and the lower belly and vent brownish-buff. The male has elongated central tail feathers, a red patch in the centre of the belly, and blue throat, cheeks and forehead. The female's head is greenish. A bird of scrubland and thicket, particularly bamboo, adjacent to cultivated land and rice paddies. Resident in Java and Sumatra but not in Bali, it was once very common but is now confined mainly to the lowlands.

Javan Munia *Lonchura leucogastroides* 11cm

Chew Yen Fook

This munia has dark chestnut-brown upperparts, tail and vent, black chin, throat and sides of face, and a white belly. It should not be confused with the White-bellied Munia (*Lonchura leucogastra*), which has fine pale streaking on the upperparts, brown flanks and a yellowish-brown tail. Normally a grassland bird, it is attracted to the easy pickings of cultivated land and especially rice paddies at harvest time. At other times it congregates in small groups, noisily foraging through grassland. An endemic to the region and particularly common in Java and Bali; in Sumatra, it is found mainly in the east.

Scaly-breasted Munia *Lonchura punctulata* 11cm

Tilford/Cooke, TC Nature

Familiar to the cagebird enthusiast as the Spicebird or Nutmeg Mannikin, this species is easily identified by the scaly appearance of its breast and flanks, the white feathers being edged with brown. The upperparts and throat are brown. Like other munias, it is often regarded as a pest to the farmer, raiding paddyfields and cultivated crops, but it also inhabits secondary scrub, gardens and open grassland. A very common munia, found from the coast up to the lower mountain slopes, and regularly exploited as a cagebird. Its range covers India through to Sulawesi.

White-headed Munia *Lonchura maja* 11cm

Tilford/Cooke, TC Nature

The White-headed Munia is very much like other munias, gathering outside the breeding season in mixed flocks to exploit seeding grasses and especially the rice harvest. It is quite small, with the head, nape and throat completely white. The remainder of the plumage is chestnut-brown, apart from a small area of black on the undertail-coverts. The bill and feet are pale bluish-grey. It prefers open grassland, as well as swamps, reedbeds and rice paddies, and is fairly common throughout the region. It is often kept and exported as a cagebird.

121

Java Sparrow *Padda oryzivora* 16cm

Adults are largely grey, with a black head and throat, large white cheek patches, a black tail and white undertail-coverts, and a heavy pink or red bill. Juveniles are brownish-grey, with a buff or brown breast. It is usually found in small groups feeding on rice and seeding grasses, and in other low vegetation, mangroves and scrub. Seen in cities, towns and villages, but far less commonly than in the past. A endemic of Java and Bali, it has been widely introduced over much of South-east Asia. This once common bird has declined alarmingly in recent years, probably due to agricultural practices and the demands of the pet trade.

Tilford/Cooke, TC Nature

Eurasian Tree Sparrow *Passer montanus* 14cm

This is perhaps the commonest of all resident species throughout the region. It has a chestnut crown, black throat, sides of face and ear patch, pale buff underparts, brown back and wings mottled with black and white, and two pale wingbars. It is commonly seen feeding on the ground, and in large flocks raiding seeding crops. It is found particularly in open habitats with scrub and low vegetation, from the coast to mountain villages. It is well distributed, particularly in the lowlands, and has colonized almost all areas, from cities to forest clearings. Its range extends from Europe eastwards to Australia.

Tilford/Cooke, TC Nature

Streaked Weaver *Ploceus manyar* 14cm

Breeding males of this colonial species have a black head with golden-yellow cap, dark brown upperparts with russet-brown feather edges giving a streaked appearance, and white underparts with black streaking on the breast. Females and non-breeding males have a black-streaked brown head and buff eyebrow and chin. Large nesting colonies are established in isolated trees near good feeding areas, the polygamous males leaving the females alone to weave their elaborate suspended nests. After breeding they form large roaming flocks, stopping off at seeding grassland and often around rice paddies. They occur locally around reedbeds, rice paddies and swampy grasslands in the lowlands of Java and Bali.

Morten Strange

Baya Weaver *Ploceus philippinus* 15cm

In breeding plumage, the male has a bright yellow crown and nape and black cheeks and throat, the upperparts being streaked and mottled dark and light brown and the underparts buff. Females have the crown streaked and mottled brown, a whitish chin, a buff eyebrow, and light brown cheeks and upper breast. This master nest-builder suspends its tightly woven grass nest from the leaf of a palm tree or convenient branch, the tunnel entrance below the globular nest body ensuring protection from rain and predators. Numerous nests are concentrated on isolated trees. Found mainly in open areas of the lowlands and hills of Sumatra and West Java, it has become rather scarce in East Java and Bali.

Morten Strange

Asian Glossy Starling *Aplonis panayensis* 20cm

Adults are all-black and can be separated from the Short-tailed Starling by being larger and having a green iridescence. Juveniles have black-streaked whitish underparts, with upperparts streaked black and brown. Both have dark red eyes. Feeds mainly on soft ripe fruits hanging on the trees, but also takes insects, rarely visiting the ground. Often congregates in big noisy flocks to roost and also nests colonially. A common lowland bird of open areas near forest and secondary vegetation and coastal scrub, but also attracted to coconut plantations and cultivated areas and gardens, frequently in towns and cities. It is found throughout the region.

Tilford/Cooke, TC Nature

Asian Pied Starling *Sturnus contra* 24cm

Tilford/Cooke, TC Nature

This bird's gregarious nature is evident in its communal night-time roosting habits and its daytime feeding behaviour, when small flocks probe and search the ground for insects and other invertebrates. Like many starlings, it is noisy and utters the typical squawks and whistles of its family. The upperparts are mainly black, tinged brown. It has a white wingbar, with forehead, cheeks, belly, vent and rump also white. Bare orange skin around the eye, yellow feet and white-tipped orange bill give the bird a colourful appearance. Common in Java, Bali and south Sumatra, especially in more open and cultivated lowland country.

Black-winged Starling *Sturnus melanopterus* 23cm

This striking starling is all white, apart from black wings and tail and a yellow patch of bare skin around the eye. The tail is tipped white and there is a white wingbar. Three subspecies occur which differ in the amount of black in the plumage, birds in the west of the region becoming much lighter and having black only on flight feathers and tail. It lives in pairs or small groups and is attracted to short grassland and even mown lawns. Endemic to Java, Bali and Lombok, but often seen as a cagebird throughout the region.

Tilford/Cooke, TC Nature

It is in fact a protected species, and is now thought to be declining in number. However, it may still be found in the open lowlands, and can be seen in some towns and gardens in East Java and Bali.

Bali Myna *Leucopsar rothschildi* 25cm

This beautiful myna is endemic to Bali. Its distinctive plumage is entirely white, apart from black wing-tips and the tip of the tail. It has a long white crest, and a patch of sky-blue skin around the eye. It prefers the drier lowlands of West Bali. This is one of the world's most threatened species, with very few birds now surviving in the wild. The destruction of habitat and collecting for the pet trade are the main causes of its decline, but efforts are being made worldwide to secure its future by increasing the protection it receives and by establishing a captive-breeding and release programme.

Hill Myna *Gracula religiosa* 30cm

Another species under great pressure from habitat loss and trapping for the pet trade, this bird is particularly in demand for its ability to mimic, as well as for its own enormous repertoire of whistles and calls. It is black overall, with orange wattles both behind and below the eye, and has a white wingbar. It has yellow feet and an orange bill. Although it occasionally congregates in small flocks, it is more likely to be seen in pairs in tall trees. Once a common bird of lowland forest edge, it has become rare in Bali and Java but remains in reasonable numbers in Sumatra.

Black-naped Oriole *Oriolus chinensis* 26cm

The male is a brilliant yellow, with a distinct black stripe passing through the eye and across the nape. The flight feathers and tail are black, edged yellow. The female is much duller. Juveniles show olive where adults show black, and they have black-streaked whitish underparts. Keeps to the tree canopy while foraging for insects and soft fruit. A fairly common bird throughout the region's lowlands and hills, favouring secondary and open forest, parks and gardens, mangroves and coastal scrub. Widely kept as a cagebird throughout the region for its melodious fluting calls and brilliant colouring.

126

Black-and-crimson Oriole *Oriolus cruentus* 22cm

Chew Yen Fook

This is a bird of the treetops, rarely seen on the ground. It often occurs in pairs, but frequently alone, as it forages for insects and ripened fruit. It has a cat-like mewing call. Easily identified as a medium-sized oriole, the males having all-black plumage apart from the crimson-red upper belly and a small crimson patch on the primary coverts. It has a distinctive pale blue-grey bill and blue-black legs. Females are all black, with the breast tinged chestnut and streaked with grey on the belly. Found mainly in the hill forests of Sumatra, but less so in Java and not at all in Bali.

Black Drongo *Dicrurus macrocercus* 28cm

Unlike most other drongos, this one favours open country and often associates with cattle, which disturb insect prey. It is frequently seen in open scrub, cultivated land and rice paddies, where it perches rather conspicuously on fencing, isolated branches and telephone wires alongside roads. It has dull black plumage, with a long, deeply forked tail with outer feathers which tend to turn outwards at the tips. Juveniles show pale grey barring on the underparts. A common resident of Java and Bali, but the few birds found in Sumatra are thought to be migrants.

127

Ashy Drongo *Dicrurus leucophaeus* 29cm

Chew Yen Fook

Usually observed in pairs waiting on exposed branches to swoop on large passing insects, this drongo has the typical long, forked tail and upright stance. Its plumage is light blue-grey, with a tuft of black feathers at the base of the upper mandible. There are five subspecies within the region, all differing slightly in their grey coloration. Mimics other birds, and has mewing-type calls as well as a loud song. A common bird of open woodland and forest edge and clearings, resident throughout the region's hills and mountains.

Lesser Racket-tailed Drongo *Dicrurus remifer* 26cm

This spectacular drongo, fairly big and glossy black, has a square-ended tail with extended outer tail-streamers which are about 50cm long. Each streamer consists of a feather shaft which terminates with an elongated oval web around 10cm long. A substantial tuft of short black feathers covers the base of the upper mandible, creating a long-headed appearance. It is smaller than the Greater Racket-tailed Drongo (*Dicrurus paradiseus*), has no frontal crest, and has no fork in the tail. Inhabits dense montane forest and secondary forest, especially along the edges, in Sumatra and West Java.

128

Spangled Drongo *Dicrurus hottentottus* 32cm

Two aspects of this drongo's plumage are rather unusual. It has a peculiarly fork-shaped tail, which has the outer feathers spread outwards and upwards almost into a lyre-shape. It also has an extraordinary crest of long hair-like feathers from the front of the crown, hence its alternative name of Hair-crested Drongo, but this feature varies among races. The general plumage is glossy black with an iridescent spangling, particularly on crown and upper breast. In East Java and Bali it is common in open areas of lowland and submontane forests. In Sumatra it is replaced by the Sumatran Drongo. It hawks insects from a low perch.

Chew Yen Fook

Greater Racket-tailed Drongo *Dicrurus paradiseus* 30cm plus 35cm tail rackets

A large drongo with a forked tail, and with beautifully extended outer tail feathers terminating in rackets on the outer edge of the feather shafts, the rackets twisted in a short spiral. Its forked tail easily separates it from the Lesser Racket-tailed Drongo. The plumage is a glossy black, and adults often display a short frontal crest on the crown. The bill and legs are black. It is usually found in pairs, often hawking for insects in glades in swamp, primary and also secondary forests and in mangroves. It remains a common bird of the lowland forests of Sumatra, but it is becoming rarer in Java and Bali through habitat loss.

Chew Yen Fook

White-breasted Woodswallow *Artamus leucorynchus* 18cm

This is the only resident woodswallow in the region. It shows similarities to the true swallows in its stance and its gliding flight, but it can easily be distinguished by its more stocky appearance, broad triangular-shaped wings and squarish unforked tail. Its quite heavy bill is grey, and the entire upperparts except for the white rump are dark slate-grey. The underparts are white. This species feeds on insects, which it catches in flight. Quite a common bird of open spaces, particularly in the lowlands and hills. Frequently seen on posts and wires.

Tilford/Cooke, TC Nature

Crested Jay *Platylophus galericulatus* 28cm

This is a relatively inconspicuous bird until it starts to call, when its rather harsh and rattling sounds soon reveal its presence. Its plumage is very dark grey to black, apart from a broad white neck patch. It is easily distinguished by its tall, flat, upright crest. Its bill is black and the legs dark grey. It is frequently observed in small, very noisy groups foraging through trees and bushes in search of large insects. Found in lowland forest in Java and Sumatra, but not in Bali.

130

Racket-tailed Treepie *Crypsirina temia* 35cm including 18cm tail

This member of the crow family has a uniformly blackish plumage with a greenish-bronze sheen. It has black feet, a strong black bill and blue eyes. It differs from all similar birds in the region in having a long tail with spatulate ends to the central feathers. Usually seen alone or in pairs, it inhabits lowland and hill forests and plantations, often occurring in secondary growth and the more cultivated areas, as well as scrubland and gardens. It is resident in both Java and Bali, where its numbers are diminishing owing to habitat destruction and collecting for the pet trade.

Large-billed Crow *Corvus macrorhynchos* 48cm

Chew Yen Fook

By far the largest crow of the region. Usually in pairs or small flocks, scavenging where it can, it is nevertheless a wily creature and keeps its distance from man. It is distinguished by its large size and very heavy bill. It is black all over with blue and green iridescence. The area of the forehead appears rather small compared with the size of the bill. In flight, its broad wings with spread primaries are beaten slowly and it often calls a harsh *kaar* as it goes. Fairly common in open country, around villages and at all altitudes.

131

Further reading

Howard, R. and A.A. Moore. *Complete Checklist of the Birds of the World*. 2nd edition. Oxford University Press, Oxford, 1991

Inskipp, T., N. Lindsey and W. Duckworth. *An Annotated Checklist of the Birds of the Oriental Region*. Oriental Bird Club, Sandy, England, 1996

Jepson, P. and R. Ounstead. *Birding Indonesia – A Birdwatcher's Guide to the World's Largest Archipelago*. Periplus Editions, 1997

King, B., M. Woodcock and E.C. Dickinson. *A Field Guide to the Birds of South-East Asia*. HarperCollins, London, 1975

MacKinnon, J. and K. Phillipps. *A Field Guide to the Birds of Borneo, Sumatra, Java and Bali*. Oxford University Press, Oxford, England, 1993

Mason, V. and F. Jarvis. *Birds of Bali*. Periplus Editions, 1989

Sibley, C.G. and B.L. Monroe, Jr. *Distribution and Taxonomy of Birds of the World*. Yale University Press, New Haven and London, 1990

Steffee, N.D. *Field Checklist of the Birds of Java and Bali*. Russ Mason's Natural History Tours, Kissimmee, Florida, 1981

White, T. *A Field Guide to the Bird Songs of South-east Asia*. National Sound Archive, London, 1984 (tape and notes)

Whitten, A.J., D. Sengli, A. Jazanul and H. Nazarudin. *The Ecology of Sumatra*. Yogyakarta Gadja Mada University Press, 1987

Whitten, T. Roehayat Emon Soeriaatmadja and Suraya A. Afiff. *Ecology of Indonesia Series Vol. II. The Ecology of Java and Bali*. Periplus Editions, 1996

Voous, K.H. The Breeding Seasons of Birds in Indonesia. *Ibis* **92** (1950): 279–287

Useful Web-sites

Tony Tilford: http://www.paston.co.uk/users/presto/
John Cooke: http://www.foothill.net/~arachne/
Indonesian Nature Conservation Database:
     http://www.bart.nl/~edcolijn/
Directorate General of Forest Protection & Nature Conservation of the Indonesian Ministry of Forestry – PHPA:
     http://www2.bonet.co.id/dephut/dephut.htm
Birdlife International Indonesia Programme:
     http://www.kt.rim.or.jp/~birdinfo/indonesia/index.html
Nikon Binoculars:
     http://www.nikon.co.jp/main/eng/products/binocular.htm

Index

133

135

136